The Pur␖

By
Ted L. Williams

The Purple Mirage

Ted Williams

Published by Ted Williams, 2024.

THE PURPLE MIRAGE

First edition. October 1, 2024.

Copyright © 2024 Ted Williams.

ISBN: 979-8227575180

Written by Ted Williams.

Also by Ted Williams

The Purple Mirage

Table of Contents

This book is dedicated to life itself, and all people that's living. And the colors that we see around us in the world, with many colors we love in the *Mirage. (Like Purple:)*

The
Purple
Mirage

The Family Tree

Genesis

It was Saturday morning, around 4:15 a.m. as the *Davia* in Ms. Jacqueline Myers stepped into the door from one of her amazing rendezvous. Into the mists from one of her ghetto parties she tends to every Saturday night at 12 midnight, as the boss of the household. Derek Osiris. Which, he rather be called, Daddy-D. Because of his inconspicuous woman of nature, begins to play bolt rows as the queen, and the father of all three daughters. That was biological he's as a good man, and father. Jacqueline and Daddy-D were together for ten years in the cycle of confusion and uncertainty, between heaven or hell unbalanced lovers. They always fought to the death. Wondering who had the power. And, who wore the pants around the kingdom home in Villa Rica Georgia. Jacqueline normally wins the fight confrontational with Daddy-D. And Daddy-D knows it. Since they started dating in 1982, during the good-ole days, when the dating game was cool and unique. And. Years later. They had three daughters. Which was, Kimberly Sonora, and Stacy in the mix through heaven of hell. Derek wanted a boy through the blood line of the woman he loves, and respects highly as the general. But. Couldn't control his household as the man. But Jacqueline wouldn't aloud it in her soul as the black woman. After her first child with Derek in 1984, when Kimberly came into this world as the first baby girl. Then... Six months later. Jacqueline was pregnant with a boy. That made Derek so happy as a black man. To bring a boy into this world. Now. Derek consciously was ready to teach his son. When he finally arrives outta Jacqueline's body in 24 weeks in counting.

Derek was ready to train his boy, from evil to good. But not the worst, too bad. Between *God and the Devil.* And. The rules of civilization tradition in the world.

The implement in Derek's mind for the boy in the future to come was seal. As his boy grows up to a strong man. And organize for his wife and kids in the blood line. Derek had the whole plan laid out for his son. And the final request for his boy.

To be a philosopher king in his kingdom. With plenty of discipline through his destination, as the battle scars comes mentally between the man, and woman, occasionally in vain to darkness. As Derek's mind manifests in time. Wondering if Jacqueline A. Myers will have the baby through faxes. If the prophecy doesn't be fulfilled and achieved in her reality. As she sees it through the future, as a vindictive black woman. Revenge was coming so sweetly towards Derek Osiris' plan. In her two months period, carrying his baby into her stomach organs. As Derek was clueless. That his black woman was going to destroy his baby in due time in the making. Ms. Jacqueline Myers was-a-little thick, black woman that had. Lots of plots, and dangerous motive for Derek Osiris man hood to come. For a 5.9 woman that weighs 180 pounds of weight. For the past three weeks. She's been drinking milk with Vodka. With a little bit of sugar into the mix. Just to spice things up during the pregnancy of destruction. Jacqueline drinks warm milk with Vodka, that tastes so good in her tummy every night. Until, one night. She planned her spontaneous brainstorm method on Derek when he came home to meditate himself real hard through his stress box outta random. By starting some mess with him on the funny tip. Just to test the mental. Or fuck with him when he's tried and sad. "Where you been, Negro?" "I know you're being fucking." Knowing in her mind. He hasn't done so. Ms. Myers knew. He was going along with the thick into his mind as a man, that she's been planning all day with baby Kimberly in her arms. As the vibe builds up, between the un-bounce black couple.

She slaps Derek in the face for talking back at her like a child. That was disrespecting the motherhood, of all mothers in the black woman culture. Jacqueline told Derek. "You know your place as a weak man.

"You, stupid bitch!" "You can't put your foot down for nothing in this household nigga." "Respect my house."

You do what I'd tell you to do Mr. The humbleness inside of the man, was trying to be cool within the body from Derek Osiris. The rage became like Ryu from Street Fighter, ready to flame up on Jacqueline's personally within the G.O.G. Derek's manhood didn't allow him to be disrespected like that by her. Even doe. It wasn't going to work consciously without a messy fight on her behalf as a woman. But... If it continues. A bloody war will be committed through her. And she will, definitely... kill the legacy, of... Derek Osiris, of what he stands for. "She didn't give-a-damn, if she turns religious for the higher power of God. "It wasn't going down like that in her world." (*Never!!!*) As Jacqueline did the knowledge. "Your, not going to have this type of power over this bitch!" I'm the king... and queen in this Mothafucker!! "All women rule, Derek." So. *"Don't-you-ever- forget-it."* The rage was pumping outta Jacqueline soul towards Derek. As his mind gotten frustrated real hard within. More and more, Derek wanted to grab his pistol, to shoot Jacqueline, directly in the head. The ideal prevented him from doing so. He left to cool off from outside towards the car inside. While drinking his fine bourbon, that set the mood right for him-and-his moment of truth.Derek the ass kicker, was drinking the pain away from the crazy Jacqueline, like his mother. AKA. Girlfriend, and wifey status. Derek decided to share his night inside the car. To avoid the evil monster, of Jacqueline Myers, ridiculous renting voice of a program. Over, and over again. She kept punching her stomach, about ten times.

Until she had a miscarriage in vain. When the blood arrived so, heavenly through the belly, all the way down from the legs to the ankles. Like a blood bath in the kitchen, while baby Kimberly watches and plays on the floor.

Thinking it's fun with the word, mom-mom out her mouth. An hour later sitting on the floor, holding her daughter in her arms, while Kimberly cries to death around 1:15 in the morning.

That's when Derek walks in, and realizes Jacqueline had a miscarriage sitting at the kitchen table. Slipping on her Vodka and milk without Derek realizing all this time. She was adding Vodka into her milk for two months straight behind his back. Jacqueline was laughing in Derek's face. And told him. "I killed your baby on purpose bitch!" While hurting inside the soul within the man. Cussing his ass out. And throwing milk in his face. Telling him. She's been putting Vodka inside her milk throughout the pregnancy. Derek drops down on bolt knees. And cries like a little baby. Leaning on the edge of the wooden table. After pushing Derek on the table like a weak bitch. And. Slowly walks off, saying. "I'd didn't want to have your boy anyway nigga." So... "Suck-it-up." As she walks away happy in the face, carrying Kimberly in her arms.

And... Derek Osiris... never been the same ever since. That's why. While sleeping in bed. Hearing his black woman come home, around 4:25 a.m. on the scene. Derek Osiris name was deleted from his pedigree, ever since. Jacqueline purposely. And. Intentionally, to punch her way outta the miscarriage to kill the baby. So. Another male want be created, to be a strong **KING** in the future, through Jacqueline's blood line as a woman. That's why, in her prophecy. She's glad she had three girls throughout the anatomy. So, the girls can rule over the boys. As they grow older as women.

That's why Jacqueline Myers had the miscarriage, to stop all male babies from growing up to be ruling kings. When the year 2021 hits soon. As Jacqueline made that premonition towards Derek Osiris in his face, six years ago. When she killed the baby with punches, on a beautiful Sunday afternoon. As the smelly Easter Anniversary, through the elements of life. Daddy-D, rise like the phoenix out the bed at 1:20 P.M.

Hearing whipping and screaming in the girl's bedroom. With the knowledge of Daddy-D knowing what time it was. As the whipping through the blood line shredders. At the age of 37 for Daddy-D, as life continues in the household.

The whipping, and the yelling was making Daddy-D blood pressure goes up immediately to have his chest hurting from the impact of her devastating voice. To make any man go crazy through human life. That's why Daddy-D takes high blood-pressure pills every day when he comes from work each night; just frustrated each time at work. With all different men, wondering why? Their wives are-not respecting, and. Supporting their loving men to death. After coming outta the bedroom from daddy. Hearing the girls getting the beat-down from mommy, about the girl's schoolwork. That needs to be turned in on Monday. After the pain and suffering, and blood. The girls came out when the homework was completed from the vicious mommy. With a smile on her face. "Good job, girls." Their happiness, and laughter was glad to see daddy this morning with tight great hugs into life. After working two jobs for his discombobulated, *blood witch of a date.* That doesn't respect how hard he works to provide for his queen, and three daughters he loves dearly. But, getting abused by their vindictive mother, once a day through hard abuse from their mommy, when she was seven years old from her pedigree **BLOOD LINE**. For not spelling the right vocabulary to being perfect for the new world to come as a date-process during protocol, that's govern by AI. As the girl's showed daddy much love and support. Mother Myers was feeling angry. And displease from the disconnection she was receiving, that. Jacqueline hasn't felt from her little girls for years. A little jealousy was creeping in, through her feminine behavior. If she had depression in the mind. With purity of old ago, as an old program disesteeming. During that moment of daddy time with the girls. Mother Myers needed a fix of yummy warm milk. With great Vodka inside the black coffee mug.

Revelation

As a hard mother's conquest, of educating the girls with knowledge. As Jacqueline sits and meditates on one pacific daughter. Which is? Kimberly Myers. That's catching on pretty-quickly, as the oldest breed to come, and control the next *family tree in her daughter's eyes.* As Jacqueline knows from daughter Kimberly... The fine specimen into the future. And Jacqueline can feel it from the bottom of her heart, forever, until her dying days in hell into the ground.

As four years came to pass, in the year 1996, in the new era. The girls were getting older. And the parents were getting much older in time and reality. That's how life works when old father time. And. Old mother time catches up with you in age. Can't live forever, as life continues in the future and on. As time went on, two years later, in 1999 before the Millennium hit. With the miscalculation of computer shutdown. The girls have gotten much older, and smarter at certain levels in time. Kimberly was 19 years of age. Sonora turned 15 years old. And. Stacy just turned 15 two weeks ago. Mother Myers, no longer had to beat her favorite daughter, Kimberly no more. Because. She has gotten the whole concept of prefect learning, and education from her mother's beatings. To get her to adjust to the socialization movement, to be somebody. And-so. The beating submission has worked. In the superior level of Jacqueline Myers favor as the ruler *God*. The other two daughters, that need more beating, are from Mother Myers back hand, and the thick extension cord, from the black culture ritual. That's been passed down for many generations in the blood line family. Even. Mother Myers.

Had audacity to train Kimberly to be a beater in Jacqueline's bidding to octane Sonora, and Stacy to be perfect like Kimberly Myers in the educational system of subjugation. It would be many occasions, where.

Sonora and Kimberly would fight about doing her math, or. Social Studies activities throughout the night, while Mother Myers would drink her milk with Vodka. Just laughing and watching TV and other mess. During that time, Stacy was crying in her bedroom with a bruise on the jaw, bleeding out the mouth suffering. "Can't wait to be grown and leave for good. Stacy said. Stacy heard Sonora crying from upstairs. Until she came out of her room, from the step rail. And watch Sonora get punched in the stomach from Kimberly. While her mother watches her do-it and laugh. And, Sonora gotten so angry, that. She told her sister. "I hate you bitch!!" And slapped the glass outta her mother's hand with her fix. Just splatted all on the floor. And then, told her mother. "I hate you to." With vicious words that were powerful and direct. That's when. Mother Myers had enough of Sonora's filthy mouth as a teenager girl. And gave her two hard slaps at the mouth, with a kick to the stomach as well. During the time Jacqueline was setting Sonora up for another round. Daddy-D walked in. And said... "What the fuck is going on here!?" "What the hell, are you doing

Jacqueline?" Sonora ran to daddy. After Jacqueline let her hurt daughter go so quickly. Sonora yelled towards daddy three times with tears in her dark mind and mist. After hugging Sonora so tightly with love. The question was asked? While Kimberly begins to shiver into goosebumps about, what daddy is about to say in anger, and hostility during the moment. Sonora told daddy. Kimberly punched me in my stomach, outta anger about my schoolwork. When Daddy-D turned around at **his** older daughter. He went berserk on Kimberly. By grabbing her with full-force on her white button, long-sleeve shirt.

And pushed her to the floor. "Take-your-ass upstairs, before I whip your ass." And take Sonora with you too! "You-bear-not touch her either!" With the finger pointed towards Kimberly's face.

Kimberly grabbed Sonora by the hand. And ran upstairs, as soon as possible, with stumps emotionally in fear. "How, dare you!" "Do my daughter like that, mothafucka!!!"

As spit was coming outta her mouth towards Daddy-D face and chin. And neck to neck like a man. "I'm-am tired of you beating on Sonora and Stacy, like-their-are boys, are something!" "They're not boys Jacqueline!!" "There are girls." "Not, punching bags at the gym." "What's wrong with you?" "I had enough, of your bullshit over the years." "I-really-have!" "It's too bad!" "You have our oldest daughter train in your crazy method, over this education, you want them to have. "I'd don't mind, if you show them, that. Education is very important in life. But. "The way you are doing it." It's ridiculous!! Daddy-D said. "Now, you-have Kimberly in your perception." Forcing Sonora, and Stacy in your tactics as you Jacqueline. "That shit needs to stop." And...! It needs to stop right now woman." "Or, else what!!" Jacqueline said. "If, you don't stop your crazy-ass shenanigans." "You are going to force me to beat you." "Like you did our daughters Jacqueline." Enough, is enough woman! "It ends tonight!" Yeah-right-bitch!! You-aren't going to do shit nigga! But stand-there and take this verbal abuse like a man. "Your-talking-about." "You're-goanna put your foot down." "What foot!!" "The only foot, that you're going to put down." Is my ass! Mothafucka!! "You-aren't going to do nothing." But! "Take this ass whooping from me bitch." "Now." "Shut the fuck up!" while I go up here and continue where I left off at. "Before your ass came." The act of being deception lies in Derek's heart. From Jacqueline. His black woman, that was talking to him like that. The rage got beside himself. And pull both legs. While walking the third step.

And landed on her shoulder real hard, unconsciously for five minutes. As he walked outdoors for some airtime to cool off for a little bit on the wooden steps, with a bottle of Brandy. While Kimberly was helping Stacy patiently with her homework. Sonora saw her mother stab her daddy in the back, several times back-to-back, with hate in her. Because he stood up like a black man in front of her, with his chest up high. And. Sonora just, watch and scream ten times in her room.

While Kimberly, and Stacy cried over their dead daddy on his back, and. Told the girls. I... love... you. As Kimberly, and Stacy hug their daddy. While he passes away into another life. As Jacqueline sits on the porch, mentally crippled forever with the sorrow of Sonora Myers' eyes. As they weep for daddy in peace. But, one day in time. Will seek vengeance on her mother in the future. Seven years later, in 2006 in a new era of life. The funeral was hard on Sonora back then. And the other sisters as well. When the night of the murder took place, seven years ago. During a terrible last. In the report. It reveals. Daddy committed suicide on his on attempt from depression. That's what Kimberly told the police back then. Just, to protect her mother from going to prison. But Sonora didn't like it, not one bit in her sorrowful heart. But. She kept it within her consciousness for one purpose. And one purpose only. To seek revenge forever. After everything was set and done for the future. The three sisters went on with their lives, as grown women. While Mother Myers sits in the house, remembering the bad memories of chaos, and temptation from love. Until, one night. When Sonora made a visit, to see her mother for the last time, before she leaves forever, and embedded with a kiss on her forehead. And, with her favorite. A glass of warm milk, and Vodka for the final fix to end the sage for good. While Mother Myers sits in the dark, with a death kiss from her daughter Sonora. And her other daughter, Kimberly Myers gone to college with her life.

And Stacy Myers gratefully does and living her life, while Sonora cruises in her white, 1989 Chevrolet Celebrity. Listing to the rap group, Goodie Mob. With the song. Greeny Green, with all the windows down bumpin' like crazy. Leaving the place where she was rise from. Looking at an old family picture. That was her mother. Jacqueline Myers, and her loving father. Daddy-D. With her two sisters

as little girls, back in 1987 when life was so good. And now...
Sonora, is finally free forever.

Chapter 1

It was a beautiful sunny day around the Riverdale area by Garden Walk, by the Aldi store on the sidewalk right down the steep hill. Sonora Myers was coming from the upper Riverdale Rd, coming from work around 5 p.m. on the dot feeling lovely on some Absolut Vodka in her pure body. Sonora always carries a pint, as a stash inside the cubby hole ready to slip, and ride through the long distance from Bankhead. In a rhythm she's been doing for years on the road as an alcoholic. Caution is the key to be very careful during these days in 2010 as a woman. Sonora indefinitely needs to be very careful through the dangerous streets as a female behind the wheel from destruction. She already has a DUI record from two years ago from reckless driving. It's like, every time Sonora has a flashback in the back of her mind. It would be a drunken type of mentality in her situation, and beyond. That remembers that DUI like it was yesterday, every time she thinks about her life, time after time and on.

When Sonora witnessed the last DUI years back with a colleague from a job she was kicked-it with, years ago since she's been working. The friends back in the days between her and David were lovers at one point back then. Sonora always thought about David every now and then, in her tipsy world when she's feeling good, and wonderful as a black woman within her joy ride home in her destination at piece.

When Sonora finally passed QT and Church's Chicken facility on the edge from the Vodka. She decided to pull over towards the low budget convenience store on the right-hand side into the traffic so quickly rushing flying through the traffic light. Trying to beat the green light like a damn fool into the street.

As Sonora Myers enters the BP station, coming in with the music up loud with the windows down having fun and laughing out loud. After getting out the fabulous ride that she loves so dearly in front of the convenience store on Riverdale Rd, by the traffic from destruction.

After she walks inside the BP store so sweet and innocent with her dark shades on her pretty face she has. Draco Dawn walks up towards the parking lot with all brown on his whole flesh with an old black book bag on his slim back. Draco just came from Highway 85 from Walmart center, buying some more brand-new black boots for his distance walking as the Peacemaker and Don. As a day walker coming from highway 85 on a good stroll. Draco doesn't to mush respect the modern times that has occurred through history civilization throughout his pedigree. In the pass, he had three vehicles through his lifetime coming up as a young black man, in the military fighting the Government War. During his military background as a skillful Combat Cadet in the Jungle. Draco begins learning a lot from the world, once he gotten out of the Army during his 10 years in the military world.

Once Draco finally came outta the military world of combat warfare. That's when he realized, that's how the civilization was going to be like, when you meet your destination in the graveyard forever. Draco is a very intelligent black man with knowledge of self with lots of experience as a dark-skinned day walker that walks the universe in piece. Once Draco Dawn approaches the convenience store like he normally does when he comes from Garden Walk from Highway 85 to his walking destination.

That's when he noticed a familiar picture in his eyes of a Lexus vehicle that he sees every time he walks up into the parking lot BP store market on foot. As he stands in front of the convenience store like a military security guy on standby, by zorbing people. Sonora *AKA Stoney* was standing in line with five people in front of her purchasing drinks and food, and lottery tickets as well.

She wanted to burst open the Monster drink immediately with thirst in her dehydrated soul as soon as possible at will. Because, she still had the major urge to drink again, after sipping on the road with that Absolut coming from downtown traffic from Buckhead. Normally she would have the nerve to open a drink while she is waiting in line so patiently and calm into her tipsy mode. But instead: she waits in line like the rest of the customers, so smooth and collect. After Sonora got through paying a $ 1.99 for the Monster drink with her debit Visa card to the cashier. The two black guys, that was in the right was looking at Sonora from the back, while smiling and playing scratch-off from the Lottery station to win the big prize of the century.

Sonora knew they were looking at her with their anxious eyes as a predator as weak men in history. "Just look at those two Negros, watching my juicy ass." If I was a gaud mammal in the free world. The power I got!! I can play the hell-out those two Negroes in a heartbeat with my amazing woman skills, as the Goddess.

That's how Sonora was thinking as a stubborn evil woman that's crazy inside her bad heart, as she walks out with confidence towards her Lexus. As she was getting inside her fabulous Lexus to drive off so smoothly with style, to go home for the evening and party again like she normally does on the weekend. Sonora Myers always been the party type female, that parties to the end, until she passes out with a major blackout into a serious coma, like she's dying eternity. Draco watches Sonora jump into her car and drive like a damn-fool from the gas pump as the Ghost Rider with flames coming from the back of her gray Lexus. Draco kelp telling himself, that. "Look how stupid this woman looks when she does stunts like that on the road, driving reckless like an idiot." When Sonora finally pulled off from the BP convenience store with the music all-up through the atmosphere around Garden Walk. The only thing Draco could do was, just shake his head back and forth. Saying to himself. "What a damn shame." "The way she is driving is like." She's going to kill herself one day out there in the dangerous streets with another drivers.

Chapter 2

It was going on 6:30 p.m. on schedule for Sonora on the road, passing her apartment complex on high mode, just singing to herself with the song *The Humpty Dance* by Digital Underground. Sonora didn't want to go home at this unparticular time around 6:50 p.m. 10 minutes till 7 on her iPhone five. The way Sonora was feeling now coming-up-towards the traffic light on red by the Raceway convenience store. Sonora decided to head towards the bar right next to the BP gas station, so she could drink some more and meet guys inside the place and mingle just a little bit. Knowing her: she's planning to have them buy her lots of drinks on her behalf at the bar joint. When Sonora finally arrives at the bar plaza with 2 cars sitting in the parking lot looking like a ghost town from Halloween. David decided to give her a call on the DL, as Sonora begins to park the vehicle away from the tinted bar from a distant to answer her iPhone. "What's up David." "Nothing much baby?" David said. What's up with you Sonora? I'm just sitting, chilling in my ride in front of this bar, that I came to about 2 minutes ago. You up-there by yourself Sonora? That's why I was asking you. What were your plans when you left, after you dropped me off at the Five Point train station? You just left Sonora. That wasn't the plan for me to go to the bar David.

It wasn't!! So. Stop tripping. After David said, yeah-right to Sonora ears and laugh. "Damn Sonora!"

"You way out there in Riverdale, in the deep parts of the city that no one fucks wit." Especially, the police laws that deal with supremacy. But. You should have brought me along the ride Sonora. You know, I'd be-wanted to chill with you for a while Sonora.

You are my road dog, when it comes down to partying like it's 1999 out there in the crowded clubs in the summertime. Yeah. "I know what you mean boo." We do be partying like we don't give-a-damn- inside the clubs, don't we. We do be partying. David said. But. Spite of it all. "We just don't give a damn!" "Hell, yeah nigga." "You know how we do it out there in the streets, baby." Sonora said. Yeah, I know-it girl. David said. So, while you are inside that unknow place you be manifesting. What type of scheme are you plotting tonight, Ms. Sonora Myers? You know me baby boy. "I'd be gettin'-them-nigga inside the bars and clubs with my reputation. Girl, you need to stop doing those guys like that in the clubs. "You know, karma is a bitch Sonora." I quite sure you heard that term before black sister. Yes, I know Negro. My sisters keep telling me all the time when I go to visit them from time to time. Especially my oldest sister Kimberly. She bugs me to death, when she tells me that in my face, about men that I screw around in the clubs. She says, I need to stop playing with these guys' feelings, so emotionally in the clubs at night. "I'm tired of Kimberly lecturing me about the same old bullshit about, what I do with my men in the street. Messing around is my thing! That's that!! Well... You know your sister is right Sonora. "I don't care what she says, what I do out there." That's my business!! "Okay, I hear you." David said. But you know how your sister is about you and me hanging out in those clubs like that. She doesn't even like me hanging out with you on some occasion, as we are clubbing. Your sister doesn't like me like that since I met her from you. Now. Your other sister Stacy. She's cool with me when we talk to one other on the funny tip, just laughing and joking to one another. Yeah, Stacy and I are the same age. But. Kimberly is the oldest.

Sonora said. As, for as Stacy my blood sister for six months apart within one another. She's cooler than my middle sister than Kimberly. "Kimberly just be on that bullshit!"

As I talk to her in a normal conversation as a blood sister. "Sometimes I just hate her guests, every time she lectures me in my freaking brain, constantly. That's why, when, me and Stacy has a very good connection when we hang out together doing our shopping thing. After David got through conferring Sonora's hatred heart towards her sister Kimberly, repeatedly, to calm her down that very instant, just to calm down Sonora. Don't get to rouse up about the situation about your sister, okay. It's not that serious homegirl. "Yes, I know that. David." "But she gets on my damn nerve with the bull clap she is talking about." But. I'm-ma-com-down for right now. "This situation is working my damn nerves, you-know." Well. Don't even worry about it, okay. Don't waste your time stressing on your sister like that. Just go inside the bar you are at and have a good time with yourself, Sonora. I wish I'd was there with you Sonora. Yeah. She spoke. I wish you were here with me as well. I need my sidekick drinking buddy in my corner. That would be more exciting, David. Yeah. I know-it boss. I want to be there as well Sonora. Just make sure you drink one for me while you are doing your thing black sister. Okay! Black brother. After they said their peace to one another and hung up with love. It was going on 8 o'clock on Sonora cell phone, when her face was glued to the iPhone screen when she was looking down, not paying attention at all. The way Sonora was getting out the vehicle, just stumbling and staggering all over the place in the parking lot. She didn't need no more to drink at this point. If someone had observed her in eye rang. They would say. Enough is enough young lady. After all that stumbling, she was doing, before she got inside the bar. Sonora Myers needed to take herself home immediately. Because she must work tomorrow morning around 8 a.m. as a supervisor. Because she knows it's very important to be there on time at UPS. But.

Usually, sometimes she doesn't care at all when she's in this drunk mode. As Sonora walks in like, she needs an old lady cane to support her balance to walk straight.

There were only four people inside the dim bar as she approached the customer at the bar. After sitting down on the black stool with her black shades on looking really cool like. A smooth lite voice just hovers over her ears on the sneaky tip with surprise. "Oh shit, you scared me." I'm sorry sweetheart. I didn't mean to scare you. That's okay! Sonora said. "How are you tonight?" As he replies towards Sonora Myers. I'm good boo: how are you? I'm good my lady. I'm just up here chilling, that's all. I have been up here since noon, baby. I see. Sonora said. I can see it in your red eyes.

While Sonora was getting excited with her legs crossed in front of the light-skinned gentleman in her mind. It was time for her to begin her plots and mind games towards this young man she sees. And Sonora was ready for him to spend some money on her tonight and have fun. What are you drinking pretty lady? I'd will take a Brandy on the rocks for right now. When the bartender finally came from the back and began to serve them. The light-skinned stocky dude wanted to say some more smooth stuff towards Sonora at that exact very moment, as he watches the whole-body frame as a black brother.

Chapter 3

As the beautiful nighttime into the bright moon was surrounding the whole city of Riverdale around 9 p.m. approximately. The light-skinned gentleman was still paying for many rounds for Sonora Myers for one hour into the max. After those many rounds. You would think he would be tap for tonight, as long as he's been there. "Sonora didn't give-a-damn how much he was spending on drinks, as the rounds kelp coming tremendously while they conversated through the night." Sonora was already on her 5th Brandy on the rocks, laughing at George on the side of his face. I have been meaning to ask you pretty lady. What's your name Ms. lady? My name is sweet baby girl, sweetie. "Sweet baby girl, ha." George said. "I like the sound of that baby."

George was admiring the lovely name she had given him right off her mind. That's how slick Sonora stubbornness was becoming with men she meets inside the club. During the mind games that she was playing with George. Her mind was just laughing mentally into the background until she took her shades off by her Brandy mixture during the reality. The reason why Sonora was laughing so hard, that. She knew what the hell she was doing with George situation. George kelp looking at Sonora real-weird within.

"What the hell is this woman laughing at" Is she that drunk from the inside, or what? That's what he was trying to figure out with her. Even doe: he didn't give a damn about what she got going on. After Sonora was laughing so much into the situation.

George started to laugh along with Sonora, as well during the drinking and having fun together. George was already on his fourth pitcher around 9:45 p.m. behind schedule for work in the morning. They both were drunk like crazy. Around 10 minutes till 10 p.m. on the clock. The bar doesn't close till 2 a.m., through Monday through Sunday straight through.

Sonora and George were so drunk. Even the bartender would say. "That's enough from you two." Now, get outta here." As the bartender's voice penetrated.

The time was decent around 10 o'clock on Sonora's iPhone when she was staring at it, when George was looking directly at Sonora real sexy like. Is everything okay over there, sweet baby girl? Yes. Everything is fine George. George just wanted to call her, sweet baby girl once more. Until she said. Not sweet baby girl sweetie! Because, in his mind he thought the whole name was too long for him to say. After saying sweet baby girl one more time in her ears. What time are you leaving sweet girl? When George said that towards Sonora out the blue. Sonora looked at him like he lost his damn-mind or something. "Why in the hell would he ask me, what time is am leaving the bar? "I know this Negro isn't trying to get him some tonight?" If he is! He can forget it! He just doesn't know it yet. While George was staring Sonora down from head to toe with his desperate eyes.

Sonora was telling herself that. I'm just using this Negro for tonight only. Nothing else: if I ever see this fool again soon down the line. I'm just going to use this Negro for his company and drinks, and conversation for the plot. "This dude is a damn fool." That's why woman like us. Always rule the world. Like my favorite singer Beyonce.

"I just love when she talks her shit into her songs that she does." So. That's what I'm doing to with George punk ass, while he's buying me these many rounds for my soul!

I will have him buy drinks until he's dead-broke and empty, with no existence in his brown wallet. And that's how I'm rollin' when it comes down to clubbing with men.

Sonora evil ways were very strict around men she meets around clubs and bars, and other places. Especially, when she has her road-dog David with her through this amazing adventure they both go through as leeches. David, her right-hand man, that she known for only two years at UPS. Doesn't treat women how Sonora treats men in her world with no respect as the Alpha. David Dill tries to give the women lots of respect, when it comes down to conversating with them on a regular basis in certain situations. David is at one end of the club. And Sonora is on the other side of the club as well. The time was 10:42 p.m. when Sonora Myers checked her iPhone for the 11th time since she had been in the bar. And she's already on her 8th Brandy on the rocks with many rounds straight through the night with George credit. George knew Sonora was halfway drunk sitting on the skinny bench, just rocking back and forth with her nice-looking booty with her blue jeans on real tight. Sonora knew she was over the limit with herself indefinitely, around 10:55 p.m. during the night hour. George was watching Sonora closely with his red crimson eyes into lust, just ready for anything to go down between him and her at will. Bob the bartender was watching the whole scene as he stares at both of their crazy-drunken asses with stupidity. Bob wanted to tell Sonora and George it's time for you two to leave at this very moment, as soon as possible. He didn't like the whole picture that he was seeing around 11 p.m. on his gold skinny watch. Bob has been at this establishment for years. He seen so many people leave this bar. And, Riverdale police will pull them over, in less than 10 minutes. Bob doesn't want anything to happen to either one of them, when they finally leave and hit the dangerous streets of Riverdale. After Bob had enough of watching George and Sonora drinking their self-half to death at the bar.

He decided to leave the scene immediately to go into the back to do something else. As George was stuttering towards Sonora behalf around her ears spitting on her Brandy on the rocks. George still kelp asking her, can I come home with you tonight sweet lady? The voice in George told her about five times in the row, as he was so drunk. Sonora started to get fed up with his stupid ass, just all in her face. Her frustration was building up so fast, that. "She wanted to slap-the living shit outta him, just for saying that-crap." The way George was looking at Sonora in between her eyes. George wanted to grab her face and kiss her right on her red lipstick that was looking very tasty, with that pretty smile into the flash. She was wondering, why this crazy looking man was watching her like that? In his mind. He already thinks he's going to get some at midnight. Within the man! In Sonora's mind. "I don't think so!" Even if I decided to give up the flush. "I can really dominate his wallet without mercy in the blink of an eye." That's how I would do his stupid ass if I had to. That's my instinct as a black woman. To plot and own a bunch of negroes in clubs and fabulous establishments.

Chapter 4

The music was lovely coming from the hollow club on Highway 85 on Riverdale RD around 11:10 p.m. on a creepy night, when more people started to come in to have fun.

After Sonora gave her speech into her mind about the male species. With the quote: I don't give no man no respect at all in this strange universe that I live in. George was waiting for Bob to return, so he could get another round for him and Sonora for the 12th time in a row for more party time and drinks as he was feeling so good and great. George decided to leave and go towards the music jukebox to play some get down type funk-groove into his ears. George felt like singing and dancing through his soul for some rhythm within. After he moonwalked himself where the buttons were. He began flipping through the CD collection to find something decent for the inside atmosphere for Sonora and him to move to for this beautiful occasion. After 5 minutes of going through the jukebox collection; George finally selected a song, party all the time by Eddie Murphy, just sounding so good out the jukebox speakers like a surround throughout the club. Once that song came on.

George was ready to dance his ass off into the middle of the floor, as more people started to inter the 6043-club scene to party. As the mixed couple walks in to have fun as well. George just kelp dancing and dancing around the whole floor having a very pleasant time showing off in front of Sonora and throwing kisses at the same time. "He really likes you, don't he." Bob said. Something like that. But... he's not my type. And he's really getting on my nerves right now. And George wants to go home with me when we leave here also. Oh... so, he wants to have a little fun time with you tonight, ha? Petty much, yeah. Sonora said. Every woman he sees coming inside this place. He gets gullible suddenly. "Damn!!!" Sonora said. He's always been like that since I have known him for two years. Yeah. As the mind was surprised by Sonora. George is a weakling when it comes down to women inside the poison. So. I can easily take his money if I want. You-sure-can! Bob said. What's the plan for you and George darling? "What's your name again?" Bob said. You can just call me Stoney. But. To answer your question. "We will not be doing anything together tonight." It's not going down like that Mr. Bob. I'm just going to use him to buy me drinks, that's all. I see you catch on quick Stoney. Even doe, Stoney wasn't her real name. This is the first time I have ever seen you here before. Yeah Bob. I was just strolling through the city when I got off from work earlier today to free my mind just a bit, because. I really wasn't trying to go home just yet. I always did travel like this when I get off from work for some reason. So, you pretty much do this every night when you get off from work, ha? "You-damn-right." Seven days a week Bob. Wow! You really like to party, don't you? Bob said. That's right Bob. That's my model. Like George says. Party all the time! As Bob and

Sonora continued their conversation with one another. One of Sonora's guy friends was giving her a quick call to chat for a bit. After four rings on Sonora iPhone while talking to Bob on the side.

Sonora looked at her screen to see who was calling around 11:30 p.m. until, 30 minutes to midnight into the morning. "Oh my God!" It's my boo Rico. I haven't heard from him in two weeks. "Where the hell he been at?" He can't call a bitch! Sonora immediately called Rico back to hear from his deep Barry White voice that she loves so passionate in the unique form. Sonora Myers always admires his voice when they occasionally go out to fancy restaurants during the weekends.

When she was distracted from Bob Stewart, looking at George acting like a crazy fool on the floor. It was 5 miss calls in a row, by socializing with Bob in a hollow way. She had to call her baby right back at that very instant. What's up girl? How are you? I'm doing just fine boo. "How are you doing?" Said Sonora. It's been a while since I heard from you Rico. Yeah, I know Sonora. I've been busy on the road you know. You know how my occupation is like as a truck driver. Always busy boo! Said Rico. Yes, I know *Negro*. I only see you every three weeks, or so. Well. Don't worry about it. I'm on vacation all this week. So, that way we can spend all the time we need. How does that sound Stoney? That sounds good to me boo. You're the one with all that cheddar, big money! As the greed kicks in within the *devil* in Sonora. After laughing so hard from Rico DL on the phone. "Stoney, you are a funny woman, you know that." While Sonora was quiet and laughing to herself in her devious ways as usual.

Rico DL thinks *Sonora aka Stoney* is a good girl for him towards the future as a beautiful bride as a partner. But little does Rico know. He's on the list of being manipulated as well as the other fellas she plays during the present of life. Sonora Myers doesn't love Rico DL. Like Rico loves Sonora in a deep connection type attraction. Rico loves Sonora so deeply to death in his peaceful heart, every time they spend time with each other in a different type of environment together. I hear music in the background baby. "Where you at?" I'm at this bar called 6043 or something like that.

It's a small little join over here in Riverdale where I'd stay up the road. It's not a bad little spot where I'm at baby. Maybe when we get together sometime this week. We can chill out and have a few drinks for makeup time. "What do you think about that boo?" Yeah, that sounds good Stoney. And then, we can have some good makeup sex as well; when I touch base with you when I'd get there. Said Rico. That sounds wonderful boo. I'll be waiting for your love when you arrive here in Atlanta. What time are you supposed to arrive here in Georgia Rico?

It should be around 2:30 p.m. at Delta Airport, if you want to pick me up on the way. I don't get off until 5 o'clock at the UPS distribution plant.

Chapter 5

While the spooky vibe surrounds the 12 o'clock midnight around the 6043-club bar into the city of Riverdale Georgia. The sweat conversation was going well between Rico and Sonora into untrue love on Sonora's end of the journey. The beauty and deep divine of the smooth voice of Rico's tone was giving Sonora a wet feeling in lust towards his words and breath through the signal into the phone along with her sexy body from hearing a love song from outta the blue, while sitting and listening to fine Rico. George was throwing kisses towards Sonora, as he kept dancing around with a 360 spin to make him really dizzy from the cranium on down, while feeling the alcohol excursion through his skinny body. As Sonora watches George with a fake sexual desire into his red drunken eyes, as the imagination renders. George was liking the seduction ways coming from Sonora eyes, to where she's telling him to come here and kiss me now as a mind game type tactic. It was like. George was beginning to feel lust over Sonora's power as she kept looking at him so deeply, like she wanted to take the feeling to the next level for both him and her lust making. While Rico and Sonora were still having their romantic conversation with one another so quietly. George was still being an ass hole from a distant still dancing like a fool. Do you need another round, Ms. Myers? Said Bob. After shaking her head, as a-sign language of saying yes towards Bob Stewart. So, you saying, you-want-be-getting off around 5 o'clock Sonora? Yeah! Somewhere around that time boo. I must do a lot of paperwork in the office. So, when I'm done reserving the whole warehouse, and watching the conveyor line. Sometimes it will be around five or six when I'm done.

"Damn Sonora!" You have that much work to do? "Hell, yeah Rico." A lot!! Okay. Well... don't worry about it, baby. I don't want to rush the situation on my account, okay. We don't want that type of pressure on you Sonora. "That's alright Rico." I can get off a little early to come pick you up when you get to the airport. I can get someone to cover me when I get off early tomorrow around 1:45 p.m. for an emergency. Precise! I want to leave early for you anyway my boo. We been busy on Tuesday real hard with those heavy-ass-boxes, coming down the conveyor fast. "Are you sure baby." With the concern on Rico's face. I don't want you to get in any type of trouble at your job tomorrow. It-really-isn't a big deal Sonora. I can chill out with one of my home boys, out there in College Park somewhere in the hood. I have a partner of mine I need to holler at anyway. I can chill out there until you get off baby. You don't have to do that Rico. "I got you! Sonora was eager to see Rico DL for tomorrow's loving date for both lovers. Sonora was so ready to see her baby. Until, it became so ridiculous, how her friend was taunting his love into the bliss of missing him daily. But. Even doe, the love wasn't there for poor Rico in Sonora's eyes like it supposed to be in the future. "But if you look at it." That's the way Sonora wants it to be for her life from this point on. The time 12:15 a.m. was coming around the time zone at a speeding light on the phones and watches on everybody's devices. After George just got through listening to the jukebox after two songs he likes. Sonora decided to pour some sleepy powder into his pitcher of beer on the slick side, to put her men's that she meets to sleep, after clubbing with them constantly. After slipping the powder so smoothly. Bob couldn't catch what she was doing in the mix of things. When George finally came back for Sonora's love and affection to quench his thirst. Bob asks George. Do you want another round? Or are you done for the night? No!! "I'm not done yet Bob." I need to finish where I started from. And bring me another round please. I'm almost done with the third pitcher.

Bob Stewart was saying to his mind, that. George doesn't need any more to drink towards this midnight hour. Are you sure you can handle another pitcher George? You are looking wasted, right about now George. Bob already knows how George gets wasted around 12:20 a.m. when it gets crowded with people. While Bob was telling George, will you be okay with one more round for the road. Sonora was laughing in the background, while talking to Rico on the love tip about tomorrow's hot date. What's so funny Stoney? I'm just laughing at this dude named Bob hair style. It looks very funny to me when I look at him. He's a chubby white dude with a long ponytail in the back with a bald spot from the forehead on back to his hair line. "He has a long ponytail, ha Stoney?" "Hell yeah!" It's all the way down to his back. "He's needs to cut that shit off!" He looks stupid! Sonora said. "I'd don't know why some men where their shit like that?" They must realize. They must cut it off and leave it bald headed. "As she speaks her shit!" You know how us men are about our hair baby. We don't want to cut it off, no matter if we do have a big bald spot in the middle of our head. We love our hair! We just like y'all women, when y'all love your hair the same way. But, in a different way Rico said. So. I can understand how he feels about his hair. Bob didn't want to give it up just yet. He might just cut it off one day in the future. But he's not going to cut it off no time soon baby. I feel what you are saying about different men cutting their hair, when yeah started to receive, when y'all get older in age. You don't have to worry about that Rico baby. You are good for right now. "You are still young just like me boo." Don't worry. Once Rico heard all that from his so-called girlfriend on the cell phone running her mouth. He said, yeah right, about five times slowly to himself in his mind with a smile that was hidden and disguised behind the face. Sonora just didn't know it through her iPhone, as she watches George ignorant ass with her red eyes, as he does the same thing in his vision reality.

Chapter 6

The whole 6043-club bar was jammed pack with different cultures in the mix, during the music playing inside the jukebox old machine. After Sonora and Rico DL said their love and peace to one another on the phone. George was still in Sonora's face when she finally got off her iPhone with Rico her love of pretending that she does. Sonora was seeing the difference that George was making with his strange demeanor upon himself, as he was trying to hold himself together on the bar. Sonora already done pore some sleepy powder inside his drink while he was dancing like a crazy freak on the dance floor at the 6043-club. As Sonora sits back and watch George slip away with his arm leaning on the bar rail scratching his elbow like a turntable at a party just mixing. Ms. Myers couldn't wait until he reacted to the white powder into rhythm form, while intoxicated in his stands position looking weird. Bob looks at the two like they are about to tongue kiss one another in the mouth with passion and dignity in the morning. So, Sonora decided to tell George. Let's go-ahead and have this quickie right quick, since it been on your mind while we are chilling. "What about-it George?" Do you want some of this loving or what? "I know you been fiending for this brown sugar right here baby." What 'cha going to do George nigga...?!" What's up!

Sonora asks. When George heard that from Sonora Myers mouth. His tongue was hanging down like a thirsty puppy in the dirty street.

After Bob heard the message that Sonora told George on the DL and shook his head slowly and left. Before Bob left and went towards the back for the third time. Bob was just laughing at the whole scheme that was happening up front with Sonora and George sexual, of what's about to go down with each other. Sonora and George were strolling towards the restroom to have some awesome fun for 10 minutes in the club scene. Sonora already knew it wasn't coming down like that from her magnificent bargain as the devil. George doesn't know he's going to be played psychologically and tricked at the same time while walking in the She-Devil's pit. While the kissing was delivered inside the shall with the door closed into darkness. The restroom was safely locked, so now one can't enter the nasty chamber facility with no interruption whatsoever. George was loving the kisses that Sonora was delivering on his light skinned neck with full of hickeys, just everywhere. As the sex play was so deep in motion between George and Sonora inside the shall while Sonora was laughing at George leaning against the fragile gray wall to support his drunk balance. Sonora can tell he was getting very weary when she was kissing him from head to toe like a soft female, like a first-time verge during this experience affair. By Sonora deriving all kinds of kisses and laughing at George, when he finally passed out so quickly against the gray wall leaning. She grabbed his black short-sleeved shirt from the chest up like a mean bodyguard, ready to toss him out of the club like George wasn't anything at all. After scatting him up from his tight shirt with her bare hands outta nowhere. George just easily falls towards the hard floor with his legs wide open like a plastic play-doll looking silly and crazy at the same time. As Sonora leans back against the shall wall restroom, just laughing in George face while he's in sleep mode on the dirty hard floor. The whole outcome was getting weird and crazy on Sonora end, as she continued to laugh out loud to herself like she was on cocaine or something like a dead nigga.

If George wasn't knocked out on the other end of the wall. He would think she was out her damn mind or something in that nature. Her whole world was so crazy, that. She wanted to take all George clothes off and embarrass him throughout the whole club scene while naked and expose and worthless in her red eyes. So, she took it in consideration by doing so, in her crazy sick mind, with a devilish smile look. During the 10 minutes of stripping him down to head to toe, with his white Fruit-of-balloons still on his skinny little body. Sonora decided to take his drawers off as well, as his other clothes that she had folded up by her foot to throw away in the garage. Sonora couldn't believe George the queasy was still knocked out from the powder she gave him an hour ago, before they came into the nasty restroom to play. Sonora balled her fist and punched George in the private area to see it he would wake up from the powder she had given him earlier, after one and two punches from the growing. She still didn't get the reaction from George whatsoever, by punching his hairy penis two more times for the final test. After she got through torturing George with her fist into his body so aggressively and walked away. Sonora left George in peace, after she carved her initial into his penis with a small razor that she had in her mouth that was rusty the whole time she was inside the 6340-club, while socializing with George and Bob at the same time. It was clever how she carved the initial SM on the top of George penis head in small letters on the side of it. She thought it was very fascinating and cool on her behalf with her own design, when she walked away with the razor stuck inside her mouth while breeding under her tongue and saliva, by passing the bar standing without Bob reality in sight. Sonora begins to rush quickly with George clothes, all folded up and neat under her armpits with Inferno while she's outdoors at 3 a.m. in the morning as the music flows through Highway 85 from the club.

Chapter 7

As the beautiful morning came around 7:20 a.m. on Draco electrical clock, before the alarm went off at 7:30 so he can get up for his daily studies for 4 hours for this exciting morning from good rest. Draco always studies 7 days a week, from Monday through Sunday to get knowledge of self from his, mind, body, and soul. And spirituality as a 5 percenter of Allah. Draco loves dealing with the mathematics of life. When it comes down to dealing with certain people in this universe. Draco finally gotten himself out of bed for this Tuesday morning routine for today. Before Draco could do 65 pushups for the early morning rise. He was trying to wrap his leg up with a white bandana around his sore knee, from all the hiking that he was doing as a day walker, walking from Valley Hill Rd. to Garden Walk by the Aldi store to enjoy the journey into the sunshine traffic. Draco had to run some hot water inside his bathtub to soak his left knee before wrapping for today's adventure after his lesson and studies. The News was important as his conscious needed to catch up on the weather and fatalities, and everything else in life that's program within the body. After he checks his water level and temperature, once it was warm enough for his dark skin body. He took his 165-pound body and soaked it, as he leaned back and listened to Channel 2 News for some information, while the body was marinating in peace, and prosperity with consciousness. The New reporter was reporting a new robbery outburst in Fulton County area toward a local convenience store last night mayhem. It was two young teens aged 15 and 16 who were gunned down. As soon as they came out of the store with the bag of money.

They started running when the cops pulled up immediately, when they spotted them running out with the cash, after the cops said freeze towards the individual. And then, the reporter said. The young teen didn't honor the freeze protocol when the cops told them to pause immediately. One of the teenage decided to pull out his gun and fire at one of the police officers without thinking.

While the 16-year-old teenager was shooting his gun towards the black and white officers, before they gotten out of their vehicle. And then. The male reporter also said. When the teenager was firing towards the police officers about ten times in hard mode. The officers were trying to tell the young teens to stop firing their weapons during the protocol on site. After pleading over and, over again with the young teens about their shooting towards the officers. That's when the officers decided to gun down the two teens immediately at will. And by the officers gunning down the two young teens in that awful way during the protocol on duty. That's when the reporter said. It was a devastating loss for the two teens that fired first, directly at the two cops. After the male reporter was reminiscing about the incident just happened a while ago. All Draco Dawn could do was, shake his poor head inside the nice warm bath, that he was marinating on his dark skin body for cleanness. As Draco praised Allah for another day waking up this morning with both hands in front of him, praising the **G.O.D**. He finally washes and purified the body by soaking his left knee that was hurting when he got up for the day. The day's mission was to read, study and manifest to Allah in prayer before he starts his daily walk for today. Once he marinated his body into the warm water of purification through the arm leg, leg arm around the knee joints for relaxation. He ate him a bowl of delicious Noodles for the pure body into his appetite. Draco Dawn always kept a case of Ramen Noodles inside his cabin for emergency purposes only during the weeks of feasting.

Draco normally gets about seven cases of Ramen Noodles, when he goes to Food Depot to rack up on food on a normal basis for every 4 weeks. That's all he eats in his man cave, three-bedroom home that he owns forever, when it's time for him to perish for his final resting place to Allah. Draco ate him a green apple, and two fresh oranges with a glass of cranberry juice for the body before leaving the home where he prospers the soul. If you enter his cool refrigerator to find some type of good meat for a nice, delicious sandwich to eat on. Well, you can forget it! As a guest. He doesn't like any type of meat inside his body at all floating through his system in the mix to make him sick into the stomach when he inhales and smells the flesh inside. By him being a good vegetarian and staying away from the prison for 13 years straight. The sunshine was coming in very deeply and hot at the temperature of 93 degrees around the Clayton County area with no rain for today. While sitting on his small deck, with less space around his backyard with some nice green grass to feel proud from his brown wooden fence. That would match his yellow and brown house that he has owned for 10 years and forever. As the reality continues to say. Every noon around 12:30 p.m. before he begins his journey walking. He always walks his neighbor's dog every day for 30 minutes around the cul-de-sac, and to the Southern Regional Medical Center across the street around the parking lot for exercise and back. *Most people would say!* Why would he walk his dog like that around the hospital 5 times around different vehicles repeatedly for? As fuck-up conscience relate to the disagreeable vibe wave in Draco.

After fighting and challenging himself across the street with all that heavy traffic going back and forth, running with the gray and white Yorkie. Ms. Pemberton was waiting on Draco to return with her beloved precious, little Nookie to feed him and caress him with gentle love for the evening.

Chapter 8

Once Draco conversated and dropped off little Nookie to Ms. Pemberton and give her a happy day hug for love peace and happiness. He went back to his brown wooden deck to relax a little bit more before he left out into the world as the day walker into the streets. His brown Dickie uniform was already laid out on his comfortable bed on the edge, with a stern crease from shirt to pants just ironed before he left. After drinking his cranberry juice on the rocks in his clear glass. The time was going on 1:14 p.m. on his black watch; as he prepares his self for that journey walk around the Riverdale perimeter to site see and watch how people operate and maintain, by listening how they talk and communicate with other individual by sparring minds, in this day in age. Other people don't have time to monitor other people's minds during conversation while they walk and talk and travel through the world of A.I. Draco Dawn was looking very crispy clean with his brown Dickie suit to ware outdoors for the public to see as he walks to Southlake Mall with his black boots, and black hat for the next mission. He has a vehicle hidden inside his garage for emergency purposes only, if need it. Especially, if it's storming bad for him to walk his different route around the whole Riverdale district he loves. Draco doesn't have to walk if he doesn't want to in his own decision. Draco chose to walk-that-walk on foot as he pleased. He says it's good for the body, soul, and the mind. As far as exercise purpose during the walk. It helps strengthen the heart around the chest area for good breathing tactic.

Draco was looking in the clean mirror to make sure his beard and Mohawk were intact before leaving the house in good condition and oily around the face. The clean debonair of Draco Dawn looked magnificent in his brown Dickie suit, as he was confronting the outside into the fresh air atmosphere. As walking on the sidewalk concrete feeling the sunshine breeze on his thick arms. He found a $50 bill on the sidewalk, crossing the river on his right-hand side as the breeze was pushing the money away towards the convenience store that he needed to go in. Once Draco picked up the money for a good luck charm and stashed it into his pocket like a direct deposit. Draco felt like he just got paid when he found that $50 dollar bill on the concrete five minutes ago. Quickly Draco rushes towards the store to get him something cold to drink for his warm temperature from the sun high-rise. Draco walks inside, as the crowd watches him enter the store like he was a Hip-Hop rapper on tour. The vibe was very strong when the eyes were staring at him so deeply and strangely. Draco knew the vibe was going to be heavy on him once he entered the convenience store with a unique appearance. Some people don't understand the physical force of power, by dealing with the entity form into the vibe of the human soul. When he went into the left side of the aisle to dodge the eyes and faces from three men and woman with 3 kids standing in line. Immediately Draco grabbed 2 Rip-it energy drinks for the long walk to enjoy himself in peace as a drifter with his wooden staff. Once he popped the cool drink that was inside his hand, with a smooth feeling. The Rip-it was so energized flowing inside his warm body when the substance began to hit him when Draco reach the Checkers burger joint with the half of can. Draco loves drinking a nice cold energy drink when he walks his 3 to 4 miles distance as a day walker. Draco couldn't believe how thick the traffic was at the time of 2 p.m. exactly.

The scorch from the sun was hitting hard around this time, as he was standing and watching while the traffic flies by. Draco Dawn was waiting patiently to cross the busy street to safely get on the other side of the pavement towards Red Lobster. While Draco was crossing the street on Tara Boulevard, during the clearing of the traffic for 10 seconds. An old school 79 Cutlass just flew by with the music turned up real loud, saying. "Get the fuck out the way, mothafucka!" The man said. When Draco heard that unnecessary nonsense from the man inside the car cussing. Draco Dawn just ignored the stupid black male that was inside the beat-up old vehicle yelling. The only thing that Draco did was. Just brush the situation off with his right hand while crossing the street near the parking lot plaza area. Silly stuff like that doesn't fade Draco mental state of mind. As more people go crazy with certain drivers in this world through evil. While Draco was on his second energy drink, walking through the unbusy plaza area sightseeing. Five Clayton County police officers' rushes through plaza for a major bust on a white Chevrolet Impala, and a lime-green Cutlass with shiny silver rims just spinning all around the surface. While many cops were making their outrageous bust on two black males' arena. Draco just stood there with an unpleasant look on his face with concern towards the two black males getting arrested. The clouds were hovering around the Buckhead area at the UPS distribution ready to rain into hell on dry ground concrete forever. After Sonora came back from her one-hour break from Burger King with a full belly inside. Sonora Myers was still drunk from last night's escapade inside the 6043-booking club birthday party during the midnight. The way Sonora was feeling. She almost called out for work on a cloudy Tuesday with a major hangover into her cranium that was pounding on her so hard. It was already going on 10 minutes to 2 p.m. on her cell phone, while she was still in her car relaxing. She has one hour to go before leaving for the day and getting her handsome man from the airport around 2:30 p.m. as schedule.

Rico DL send Sonora a quick reminder through a text that. Is the pickup still on for today? Sonora didn't get the text, because she was taking a quick little nap, while her seat was leaning back for some shut eye time. After Sonora woke up from her sleep-sleep time for five minutes all-of-a-sudden. My baby just texted me just a while ago. I'm surprised I didn't hear that from my phone earlier. She said. After receiving that wonderful text from Rico DL, with a sweet smile. She gotten out the vehicle jumping with joy during her handover from last night party time with George crazy ass. When Sonora finally entered the building around 1:05 p.m. laughing to herself consciously. David Dill came from behind Sonora and scared her half to death, out of her pink panties. Boy! -_ You scared! "Ah, girl." "I know, I didn't scare you like that." Just stop playing! David said. "I'm not playing." "You scared the living daylight out of me nigga." "You need to stop your shit man." You always doing bullshit like that to me all the damn time, you punk!! Ah girl! "I'm just fucking with you." "Stop trippin', stupid girl." Fuck-you, David!! After hearing that from Sonora Myers, towards David Dills conscious. David just smiled and blushed it off immediately and kept the conversation going towards Sonora pretty face like he didn't have no care in the world. What happened to you last night at the club girl? I did the usual like I normally do David. "Play them damn fools like always nigga." You crazy girl! David had to give Sonora some good dap on that funny compliment she delivered. What's up with you David? Aren't you support to be on the line Mr.? How come you're on this side, anyway? She asks. You need to get back on the other side of your town Negro. And... That's an order! Damn Sonora! You sure-are being very demanding all-of-a-sudden. "Negro please." "I'm just fucking with you." "Stop trippin'." As Sonora tries to be funny towards David Dills. You funny Sonora! Really funny! I'm just playing with your mind baby boy.

Sonora said. In her crazy mind. Sonora wanted to indulge in the conversation like hot fudge as quickly as possible, as she had her head turned to the right side of the office. I know you want to continue this conversation that we are having here. But. I have some paperwork I need to complete before I leave today at two. "What the hell." After receiving a wonderful loving-sweet text from her baby Rico DL on the smooth tip. Sonora decided to return the favor by texting him back with her beautiful word that she does best. Just before she could bring those beautiful words back to her lover boy DL Sonora had to read that wonderful text again for her excited heart and soul to relax in the cool AC with the temperature at 68 degrees. While reading the text that said. "Hey, Sonora my love." I was just wondering, that. Is the plan still on for this evening for you and I'd girl? But. If-it-is. I will be landing in 30 minutes or so, on the plane Sonora. I'm here to let you know. I love you baby. And I miss you so much, Sonora my love. I can't wait to see your pretty face once again, around 2 p.m. on the dot. We are going to have lots of fun with each other tonight sweet Sonora. Your man is going to take you out to a nice fancy restaurant, just the two of us my love. And. By the way: I have a beautiful surprise for you as well, lovely girl. You are going to love this when you see it in person, my beautiful brown chocolate. I can't wait to make beautiful love to you tonight, Ms. Myers. "I can't wait beautiful." The text became deeper and deeper through its passion into Sonora's heart, that. She almost shed some tears inside her eyes; after saying damn three times with her legs crossed, shaking sexually, and, emotionally in vain *in the Goddess*. Sonora texted back by saying. I love you too boo. See you at 2 Rico my love.

Chapter 9

The rush hour was beginning to dawn on Sonora Myers behalf, as she was racing against time in her pretty Lexus going 88 miles per hour with the windows down screaming her lungs to death, like her throat was bleeding from the inside and out the mouth. The way she was flying through the expressway heading towards the Downtown city area. You would think a State Patrol would have seen her driving like a damn fool in her pretty style. Sonora was driving so fast that. She didn't have time to call Rico DL through her Speed Demon capability as a furious driver. The time was going on 1:56 p.m. on her stereo system, rushing hard to pick up her baby Rico DL, right at 2 p.m. during her destination for the rescue. Rico wasn't going to touch base around 2:28 p.m. at the airport before 2:30 hits on schedule at Delta. Sonora just didn't have any clue that Rico was landing 5 minutes till his normal destination that he planned for the day. Sonora Myers was still heading towards her mission to get her baby Rico by passing through other vehicles left and right, throwing her middle figure up at other drivers, by saying fuck-you through the window cussing and fussing at will. The way Sonora was driving through the light traffic insane and wide open. She didn't give a damn about nobody on the expressway passing Cleveland Avenue exit laughing to herself in vain. Sonora was 10 minutes away from the airport by passing Hapeville where the old Ford plant used to be in the perimeter. Once Sonora came around the loop to pass Swift Port Cargo to get to the entrance to the airport for her arrival. That's when Sonora finally arrived, by coming up the loop hill slowly and calmly.

The traffic was ridiculously jam packed. At least 40 vehicles at a time. The magnificent sunset was leaving the area around the airport slowly, as the clouds creepily creep up in a sneaky flow into the atmosphere chemical reaction. After slugging trying to get through the heavy traffic by the curb towards the sidewalk where Rico DL needs to be picked up where the saddle buses are parked. The arrival of the time was 2:15 when Sonora was looking crazy into her face with concern while looking through the crowd for Mr. DL. Sonora became puzzled while looking for Rico with her head sticking outta the vehicle while the door was wide open with her dark shades on. Sonora continued to look dazed on the sidewalk standing next to her Lexus looking for Rico to come on from the crowd of fifty, in between the front entrance where you travel in and out the airport doorway. As the mind of Sonora was still searching for Mr. DL through the crowd, while Rico was getting off the Delta flight during the plane delay of scheduling. By getting off the plane and almost stumbled on the last step, trying to rush with his two large luggage with wheels to get to his precious Sonora. Rico wanted to text Sonora during the mix while jogging with his luggage through the amazing crowd of people. Sonora Myers was getting frustrated by walking towards the crowd slowly when she was typing on her phone. "Where are you baby?"

Through a text to Rico. Sonora immediately turned her back to text Rico again for one more attempt, before she could type one letter on the phone. Rico DL was calling her from the background into the crowd before she got inside her car for the second time during the traffic. As soon as Sonora got herself seated for a little. She looked to her right, and seen Rico was yelling and waving towards Sonora Myers with a big smile at her beauty. When Sonora heard Rico was calling her from the background into the crowd. She was so glad to see her baby Rico DL come from the crowded people at the time during 2:55 p.m. on schedule. Even doe. He was 30 minutes late on his long flight from California. "What took you so long baby?"

She said. For some reason: they were having terminal problems into the air, in between the gray clouds, as the Pilots were flying through the blind. Damn!! That sounds dangerous. Good thing y'all didn't crash coming from the air with those many people on flight baby. I can't see you dying like that Rico. "I'd just can't baby." When Rico heard those sorrow words coming from Sonora mouth outta nowhere while they were hugging and kissing each other to death. Not knowing enviable was lurking upon the souls of their bodies.

Chapter 10

The time became 3:15 p.m. when Sonora and Rico left the crowded airport, with all that crazy traffic that was going on around the Atlanta Delta. "What the hell is going on with this crazy-ass traffic today baby?" Sonora said. I-know-right! As Rico DL spoke loudly; and shook his head back towards the airport with a big smile. How was work today baby? Work was okay today, Rico. I was kind of sluggish today at my desk doing paperwork with a hangover. "Damn Sonora!" You really got busy at that club you were at last night, huh? Yeah... I guess you can say that. I was partying like my life was depending on it, Rico. "Damn, Sonora!" "You were drinking like that?" Hell, yeah baby!! I was drinking like crazy, Rico darling. Wow! He said. I told you about drinking like that Sonora. That's not good baby. You keep drinking like that. You're going to end up catching a big DUI or something. Or. You are going to end up dead somewhere, Sonora. You are scaring me Rico with that statement. "I don't mean to be baby." But. I'm telling you for your own good Sonora. You're doing too much with your drinking Sonora. Sonora was thinking. "I don't feel like hearing this bullshit from Rico."

Chapter 11

The beautiful nighttime was looking shiny as ever, like a Hollywood Walk of fame, as the city lights were bright through the Downtown area. The time was 8:20 p.m. close to eight-thirty through the Peach Street area around the Chicken and Waffle restaurant. The restaurant was very crowded at this unparticular time on a Monday night when it comes down to eating Chicken and Waffle around the table with different energy surroundings through the inside. What do you think about the Chicken and Waffle baby? She said. "It's not bad baby." "Not bad at all Sonora." It's really cozy up in here, I see. You must've been here before? Rico asks. Me and my girlfriend came in here one-night last month, when we came from the club in the Downtown city. We had a wonderful time that night, me, and her. Knowing you. You probably turned up that very night. As Rico put it. You know me baby. "I don't be bullshitin' when it comes down drinking in clubs. The only thing Rico could do was. Just shake his little head towards Sonora wild night out that time. Sonora Myers was just eating her Chicken and Waffle and reminiscing about her and her girlfriend's night extravaganza they had at the club, and the Chicken and Waffle back then. We had a ball that night baby. I know you did baby girl. I know how you work sometimes. Why do you have to say it like that Rico. You make it sound like I'm a bad influence towards my friends or something. Rico wanted to say yeah outside his dark box immediately to Sonora. He didn't want her to be upset with him inside the restaurant while they were eating and talking at the same time. My private feel real weird in between my legs right about now. It feels like you bit me or something down there. Rico said.

I can't believe you would do me like that Sonora. You must really miss me, ha? The only thing that Sonora could do was. Shake her 360 conscious towards her baby and laugh within. Sonora was smiling inside her soul like a sneaky red devil when she heard Rico through his consciousness on the right side of her little ear with her golden earrings on, listening to her beautiful music in her mind. After Rico had to step into the restroom to use number 2 for a couple of minutes while Sonora was eating her delicious plate. David decided to give Sonora a friendly call at that very moment waiting for Rico to come back from the restroom round back. The voice was like! "What's up girl." "What the hell do you want?" Damn Sonora!! "It's like that!" No boy! "I'm just fucking with you, that's all." What's going on with you, Sonora? On my date with my baby. Your baby! David said. Who is your baby Sonora? Don't worry about that *Negro*. It's my prerogative around here buddy. That's okay, it's all good. Said David. You don't have to tell me Ms. Sonora Myers. After trying to be funny around the whole situation. He wanted to ask her when she was going back to the bar again in his little silly mind. David loves going out with his road dog Sonora into the nighttime lounge on the weekend. That brings him life when he's with her as a wonderful teammate around her circle. And Sonora just doesn't know it yet mentally. After passing each other during good conversation into the ten-minute zone. Sonora had to tell David. I must talk to you later, sometime tomorrow at work, brother-man. My baby is coming back, okay! I will talk to you later.

When she hung up within an instinct in David's face so quickly and fast, like it wasn't nothing. Rico DL was arriving back towards the table with his baby Sonora in a heartbeat for her. That's how much he loves her to death and beyond. When Rico DL came with a big smile, while sitting down eating his fabulous Chicken and Waffle good dish.

Chapter 12

The nighttime was already here when Draco Dawn came out of the South Lake Mall, to make his way home for the night as the day walker. Draco Dawn just got through buying him some more Dickies for his collection in the closet. That's all-Draco wears in his famous Dickie world, when he goes out in public with unique fashion. Draco was glad he had brought him two pairs of Dickie outfits as he laughed with joy walking back home. Draco Dawn told himself, that. When he reached the distance by the Red Lobster inside the plaza. He was going inside the Jr. Cricket to have a few rounds at the bar for an hour or so to observe people and laugh. Draco loves coming to the Jr. Cricket with laughs and looking at people and tripping around the bar. What would you like, Mr. Dawn? Give me the usual Tom. While Tom was preparing Draco's pitcher of beer for the first round. The energy was very deep, while Draco was waiting for his tasty cool beer within. A thick black woman in a white sophisticated tight dress, just sitting five seats down where Draco were sitting. In the mix. Draco was drinking his cool beverage on the smooth tip like he normally does as the *G.O.D.* Draco was watching the black woman in the corner of his eyes as she continued to watch him on the sneaky trip. Didn't want to impose into the situation, as far as approaching the woman in the white dress drinking, while other people were coming inside Jr. Cricket to feast their love with food. Before Draco could turn around and look at this gorgeous woman again. A smooth suave looking-type dude stepped-up towards the black woman with a casual wear as a black man. As the young man kicks game towards his pray with a whisper inside her ear like he's kissing her on the down low. Draco was laughing towards the young man within his self from the inside talking to Tom about his day.

The time was 10:30 p.m. on the dot when the smooth gentleman was still socializing with the beautiful thigh woman that he was trying to capture in his arms. Draco knew he wasn't-not going to gravitate by not getting that woman in the white dress at the bar. The young dude and the thigh woman were still talking and drinking with one another when things were heating up with each other into the faze. But the woman was still looking at Draco Dawn from the corner of her eyes, as she was talking to the young man on the right side of her, trying to fit in swiftly towards the thick woman. Tom was telling Draco, as he was preparing his second round of Miller Highlight for Mr. Dawn. I see the young woman down towards the end is still staring at you Mr. Dawn. The only thing that Draco could do was. Just shake his head and laugh at the woman with the thick white dress on. How long will you be staying tonight, Mr. Dawn? Not too long Tom. It's already getting too late as it is coming towards midnight here. The time was 11:05 p.m. on Draco's watch, approximately on schedule as he expected. It was time for him to exit immediately, so he could get home before it began to rain as it sprinkled on the concrete ground. Leaving so soon my friend? Tom said. Yeah... it's time for me to retreat before the rain catches up with me on my journey back home. You have time, Mr. Dawn. They say the rain is supposed to hit around midnight some time. After giving Tom some power dap on the knuckles for peace out during the mix. Draco had to walk pass the thick woman, as well as the young gentleman that was lurking with energy, while Draco goes out the front door as the drizzle hits Draco on top of his forehead so smoothly with love. While leaving the building unexpected with curiosity in her eyes, wondering what's the significant in Draco's outlook from a man. It was like his vibe was very attractive into her eyes as a wonderful woman, during the conversation with the young gentleman she was talking to. When Draco drifted away into the cool wind into the atmosphere as the day walker.

The young woman decided to leave the young man all-by his lonesome self into the hollow entity. As Draco was heading towards the mean street highway, going directly to the Southern Regional near his house. The black woman from the Jr. Cricket in all white, was seeing Draco about to cross the street, and decided to blow her horn directly at him immediately. During as the deeply rain was coming down so vaguely and hard on Draco when the woman was rolling down her window to conversate with Mr. Dawn in the parking lot night. The sweaty voice said. How are you baby? As she stares him into his handsome eyes, as a suspicious surprise outta nowhere. Before Draco could say anything out the ordinary. The rain was coming down even harder than before, when she decided to invite him into her vehicle for a safe reason out the rain. The conversation was beginning to get interesting from bolt anatomies as adults during this magic moment. Once they shook each other's hands with a self-conscious debonair, so softy around the beauty as Dominic felt the present from his soul and spirit within. Her gravity, and passion loved the way Draco hands were feeling, after shaking each other hands in a seven-second range during the connection of love. What is your name Ms. love.

You can call me Dominic.

How are you doing Dominic?

I'm doing just fine tonight. I didn't catch your name. She said. Draco Dawn is the name, sweetheart. I'd never seen you up here before Draco. I just come up here occasionally, every blue moon, or so. "Or really." As the voice of Dominic was surprised.

I come up here every Wednesday to chill and mingle with myself sometimes too. That's the only time you come up here Dominic. Just on Wednesday's? No! Sometimes I come on the weekends, every now and then. That's good. Draco said. Last time when I saw you.

You were in the same seat that you were sitting in when I was watching you all night. When Draco said really towards Dominic so softly in the passenger seat so cool. He didn't think she would be that direct, so comely towards him like that out the blue. He was so crammed by her loving tone when Dominic was coming outta her box so well from the raining night around the surface.

Chapter 13

As the beautiful murky night was going so smoothly with Draco and Dominic in the mix, driving through Tara Boulevard busy street, along with the conversation that they were having amongst the reality during the ride to his humble home in Riverdale.

The rain was coming down much faster and harder as the clouds thickened up into the black atmosphere skies above. The time was 11:35 p.m. before 12 hits midnight around the time zone. How was your conversation with your so-called friend at the bar, while you were watching me on the other side of where you were? He was alright. The conversation wasn't that appealing to me baby. I came off better talking to you, Mr. Draco. Oh really!! Said Draco. Did you walk all the way up here in the rain Mr. Draco? Yeah, you can say that, Dominic. It wasn't raining when I was walking earlier to the mall during the noon time when the sun was out. I love walking through the week from Monday through Friday. Sometimes Saturday every now and then. So... you walk like this all the time, ha? With confusion in Dominic's consciousness. That's right! Five days a week. Draco said. That's why I call myself the day walker, because. I love to walk that long distance and miles for energy. I hate to walk, I really do. Dominic said. It's like... I don't have enough energy for that type of exercise for my size. She said. When you do that type of mind method consciously. It's like your soul is free from the world you are civilized to for years as human beings. Damn!! That's deep Mr. Draco. "That's what you think." Said Dominic. "That's right, sweetheart." I'm just giving you a little knowledge about human anatomy Dominic. You are giving me a little knowledge, ha? As Dominic's brain scan began to wonder. That's what I do sweetheart. Give you something to think about Dominic. Some of my amazing knowledge towards certain people in the world. That's good to know, coming from you. Said Dominic. Draco was very proud of the compliment that Dominic had given him at that instant moment by taking him home.

The conversation was dimming down for Draco and Dominic, as they approached his home as the *G.O.D.* into the kingdom. Wow! "This is a unique home you have Draco." Not bad... not bad at all. As Dominic was rubbing her long silky perm hairdo so comely. Draco quickly asks Dominic; does she want to come in for a little while to accommodate his company for a few minutes or so. She hesitated for a little while before answering Mr. Draco for caution reason for her sake. After 5 minutes of agreeing with herself to go inside with Draco. It was going on 12:45 a.m. around midnight hours for two strange individuals just met. Draco doesn't normally let unusual women inside his comfortable cozy place as a conscious man. That's just how he operates with different women through the universe. As Dominic was walking into his unique and eccentric home, to the humble wise man. "I love this, Mr. Draco." "I really do." Your house looks better than mine. Even doe. I just stayed in a townhouse in College Park around the way in the neighborhood. You're not that far from me sweetheart. In the back of Draco's mind. He was very puzzled from the inside of his soul and out. Draco was watching Dominic from the corner of his eyes like a lurking Eagle in the house around the living room. Not intensely. But, for safe precaution as a black man. His knowledge of self keeps him very sharp and disciplines himself for years. As they sit and chat and watch different programs on television together. Dominic was asking Draco what type of work does he do for a living out of the blue? Well... I am a retired veteran from the Army, and all-American Cadet, until death. That's that!! The God said. So, you already done pay your debt to society, ha? Dominic said. "That's right sweetheart." It's a good feeling for a lot of vets around the world that's retired from the combat life experience.

As Dominic smile and looked at Draco with so much respect in her eyes as a black woman for him. So... what do you do in your 7-day period through the week Mr. Draco? Like I told you. I do a lot of walking around the Riverdale premiere, five days straight, starting in the morning time around 10 o'clock a.m. sharp. But you have a car underneath your shred Draco. You shouldn't have to walk, you know. Well... I get what you're saying sweetheart. But... It saves me a lot of money from time to time when I don't drive somewhere in the eerie atmosphere. I just love the joy of being a day walker as an occupation within myself daily. You are serious about this walking thing, aren't you? Said Dominic. That's right sweetheart. I just do what I do

Dominic. Maybe one day, you should walk with me on my journey of freedom. "What you think?" No... I don't think so, Mr. Draco. Thank you! But no thanks. It's too much pressure on my thigh body these days, you know. As the insecurity manifests in Dominic's darkness as a woman. I hear you sweetheart. Walking helps you with your mind, body, and soul routine. That's how I'd look at-it Dominic. I had that mentality for years as a military war head when I used to walk and run at the same damn time in my boots. After shaking her head towards Draco's word play immediately. She asked him can she use his bathroom right away as much as possible. After saying yes directly to her present. Draco went into the kitchen to grab two glasses of ice water for him and her joyful time together for the night. While Dominic was inside the restroom, potting for Draco's down-fall on the sick side of things. A strange dark vehicle approaches Dawn's humble home outta nowhere on the down low. Out of curiosity during his sight in range. Draco noticed a suspicious vehicle was sitting in front of his driveway so quietly and invisible looking. By Draco being so hollow, and aware of things in his surroundings.

He pulls his black curtain just a slight bit to check out the vehicle with no lights by his mailbox on the creepy tip. The great Draco was still staring through the curtains with that one eye like a mean Pirate mode. Draco was telling himself. I'm about to get robbed during this dark scary point. Draco wasn't sure what was going on during his thinking process with the car outside. When Dominic finally came out the restroom after 25 minutes into delay time. Draco wanted to know what was going on with her consciousness when she came out. Dominic was looking very suspicious, and funny-looking through her expression as she continued to stare down into her cell phone in the Matrix.

Chapter 14

The time was 1:30 a.m. after midnight into morning time for Draco and Dominic Walker during the moment of their existence. As my mind was racing outside the atmosphere into my home. Dominic was having a deep conversation on her phone with someone out the ordinary for some strange reason. I didn't know who she was talking to on the down low on that suspense. I really didn't. I was too busy observing the mystery vehicle, that was parked outdoors for 15 minutes or so. The shit was too hard to bear into my eyes, as I started to wonder about Dominic surroundings around my house that I rule. As I continued to watch the hollow vehicle from the inside of my comfortable home I cherished. I was feeling some type of way during the process, what was going on in my place. I didn't like this dark terror that was going on at this point at random right now. I really don't! As I try to recognize the situation between her and me. That's when the strange vehicle that was parked outdoors like Batman in the dark. And, immediately she told me she had to run outside for a minute or two. Which was unusual and suspicious on her behalf. I told Dominic yeah, just to keep things real cool for myself on the couch sitting down. That's the type of wise brother I am. Cool calm and collected. While Dominic was outside into the hollow dark side. Dominic was chatting with someone so heavily with good intentions by the mailbox by the vehicle. That whole entire time. Nobody even stepped out of the car since it had been parked. "What the hell is going on here?" Why is this woman outside for? What's really going on? He said. Draco Dawn was slipping more of his cold water just to cool his DNA body down into the morning.

Once Draco was done with his refreshing cold water that he had in his hand. He decided to go into his bedroom to get his thoughts together, of what was going on with Dominic and the strange vehicle that was still parked. Dominic was headed towards the dark car after she stopped texting when a young woman, with the cool-dark-shave on with a wine cooler in her right hand. After getting out of her car and snuggled Dominic with love with a big hug. Sonora was truly glad to see Dominic Walker, after a tremendous loving hug just a little while ago. Draco was wondering who was the unusual woman that came outta the blue? What Draco didn't know was. It was the same young woman from the convenient store on Garden Walk where Sonora lives at in between. After they got through hugging one another during the contact. Draco noticed an unfamiliar face that he had seen a couple of months ago in the wind. When Draco kept looking at the unfamiliar through his visual into the window in between his black curtain. Draco didn't want Dominic or the other woman to see him peeping through the window. Which the other woman was Sonora in the mix. The time was going on 10 minutes to 1:00 on Draco's watch, while he was sitting down all patient and everything like the knowledgeable man he is. He was feeling some negative vibe going on around his household with Dominic and the other woman's name Sonora Myers. What the hell is going on with those two women on my driveway for 30 minutes? What's really going on with them? Is the question. The deep consciousness was sitting in the back of his mind for five minutes looking at them through the window. The one sister said. How have you been doing, my sister? Dominic said. I been doing alright sister girl. As Sonora applies. Me and Rico just came from our delicious, wonderful date from Downtown at the Chicken and Waffle restaurant. "Really!!" Dominic was surprised. Hell yeah! Sonora said. Tell me about this man you're being talking about Ms. thing. He's a good man and sweet inside his heart. It's almost like. He's perfect for me, my sister. "Too damn perfect."

That's not good for me. I want me a weak man to control in my relationship. Is that right. Dominic said. "You are a trip Sonora." "One of these days, A man is going to fuck you up mentally." I've been telling you that Sonora. Whatever Dominic! These niggas are not going to do shit to me. I will fight a nigga if I have too. I don't have a problem with that. You know how I get down. "I will fucken it up girl." Dominic was laughing her ass off, of what Sonora had said to her about many men. You need to stop your mess Sonora. As she continued to laugh with Sonora. As the thought wonder in Dominic. So... this new dude that you are with. Are you going to play him, like you do the rest of your men? The more I think about it sister girl. "Hell, yeah Dominic!" I'm going to play Rico to the last end, when we finally get married, with a nice house with kids and everything he has. "Damn Sonora!" It sounds like you trying to kill him and take the living soul outta his body. "You damn right, sister girl. Sonora said. "You're crazy as hell Sonora." You know that: I know, sister girl. You know how I am, Dominic. I been doing niggas for years in the game. Girl... You are a damn fool for saying shit like that. Don't hate the player, hate the game. Said Sonora. You stupid!! Dominic said. While the two black sisters were still talking to one another on Draco's driveway. Draco Dawn was still looking through his window on the sneaky tip, so Dominic and Sonora couldn't see him looking through a beautiful distance. The time was ten minutes till two in the morning for everybody on this amazing occasion. Draco Dawn wanted to step outdoors to say something to Dominic and the other chic out the ordinary. While Draco was inside the bathroom handling business. The time became 2:15 a.m. in the morning when Draco came out the bathroom feeling ten times lighter into his pure body during the situation. He decided to run outdoors to tell Dominic and Sonora to get off his property, a-sap like the new generation would say as, a slang. As soon as he stepped outdoors to burst *Goddess*, handedly, outta nowhere. They were mysteriously gone outta sight and, just vanish all-of-sudden. The mind was like! What the hell did they go!? As Draco thinks in deep thought. Draco didn't give-a-damn anyway. If they were gone. After Draco seen what time, it was. He brought himself into the house, so he could rest his tired body to sleep, like it was forever in paradise like a gate keeper for life, and eternity.

Chapter 15

While the morning funk was rising through the area around Tura Boulevard and Forest Park City district hell bound. Sonora was riding heavily throughout the cities, and ever place else around the way into the Morrow City of Clayton County. Sonora Myers was already on the high edge of things on the cautious road into the city of Lake City where cops could be surrounding around the evil premiere of Babylon. Sonora already had a pint of liquor in the back seat and front as well.

As she was riding with the window down with the music turned up like she was crazy through the dangerous city. Sonora was traveling hard in a mix of things as she entered the city of Forest Park, where the cops are very suspicion and hideous during the zone. As she was deeply drinking back-to-back with the powerful pint in her hand. She was drinking ridiculously in vain along with the R&B soul just surfacing around her ears and the whole outside rim. The music had her so hype that. Forest Park was right behind her so swift and smooth, that. Sonora didn't know the police were right behind her in her visual view. As the sound was drowning her surroundings forever. The male cop kelp following Sonora in her final devastation towards the Bank of America passing the cemetery. The police officer finally turned on his blue and red lights officially on Sonora immediately. When that happened. That made Sonora scared to death inside her pretty Lexus with the half of pint of Crown Royal in the passenger seat just linking out. Sonora didn't know what to do in this strange predicament with the police officer. She knew if she had gotten pulled over. Her life was indefinitely over from a cosmic paradox.

The whole car was smelling like, straight alcohol inside the surface and the passenger seat. Sonora Myers was trying to come up with a routine to avoid being pulled over for a DUI at this occasion. Sonora kept telling herself; she shouldn't do this, whatever sick mind she thinking about at this moment? "What the fuck is I'm going to do!" As she was hitting her stern wheel with serious impact. It was at a point; her patients were getting the best outta her behind the wheel. It was like! The craziest were coming out of her outta the ordinary. Her mind decided to snap when the pressure suddenly hit her personality. Once Sonora pulled off, by pushing accelerator so quickly. The action was going to have a major impact, with this high-speed escapade that was about to happen around Forest Park. After Sonora burn rubbed into the 3:20 a.m. morning light. The cop hit his accelerated, as well behind Sonora stupidity as a dysfunctional driver. When Sonora pulled away as a crazy driver without pulling over like a good Samaritan. The white cop face was turning real red in his whole complexion, as he chases Sonora all over town. Sonora was ducking and dodging around the police officer after she crossed the railroad tracks, passing the Funeral home on the right-hand side rushing through the red light fast. Sonora couldn't help her speeding and driving like a speed demon through the streets on Phillips Drive heading towards Forest Park High School district. About time Sonora could pass High School premises. Two police officers were already posted at the traffic light blocking the street way, so Sonora couldn't get through the next destination in her vehicle. Once Forest Park police officers were getting outta they're vehicle holding their gun hose, preparing for Sonora to get out her vehicle at this very instant. Sonora was trapped in the middle of the road, nowhere to run or hide in her rearview mirror as she stared with tears coming from her eyes. While she was in a state of shock behind the wheel.

Forest Park was coming from both directions from both ends by the school. Sonora Myers was screaming out the car when they had both hands behind her back on the sidewalk still drunk in the mix of reality.

Chapter 16

As the morning was rising around Forest Park High School at 5:03 A.M. Still hollow through the night during the atmosphere. Forest Park just took and hauled Sonora Myers to the small jail precinct around the city of *Demons.* Once they got all the information that they needed from Sonora while she was crying behind bars like a baby infant. The officer told her to quit down inside the little cell, because she was causing a lot of attention around the facility. Ma'am, you need to quit down in here, before you in up in the hole for a whole week Ms. So, you need to sit there like a nice little nigger, and keep calm, so Clayton County can arrive and pick you up, okay. While Sonora was just sitting there shaking her hand over and over crying repeatedly with her second DUI in her possession. Sonora was-just sitting on her buckle all frustrated about to pull all her hair out while she was in a deranged state of mind going crazy. It was like she couldn't take this-shit any longer in her pissed-off mind. It was getting to a point that. Sonora was beginning to scratch herself on the right cheek indefinitely, as blood was dripping down on the side of her face like water. The officer was looking at her like she was damn-crazy or something. The officer was telling himself. "It's a damn shame how she is doing herself, with so much torture inside." After ignoring

Sonora with foolishness inside her cell. He continued reading his Newspaper like he normally does when he's on duty during the week. Sonora stood up from her buckle and started grabbing the bars and started shaking them like she was a Gorilla or something. After bringing her head softly two times on the cell with no patient. The officer just laughed and kept reading.

The time was 7:30 when the officer opened the cell door to wake Sonora up immediately when Clayton County finally arrived. The officer couldn't wait for Sonora to leave for this special occasion on her behalf. Sonora couldn't believe she got herself in this dark mess for the second time with a DUI that came like a thief in the night. When the officer took Sonora out from the cell. The walk seemed like it was like the yellow brick road like The Wizard of Oz with the handcuffs real tight on her brown flush. The handcuffs were so tight, that. She started to tell the officer. "Can you please loosen the handcuffs from my fragile wrist, you stupid cop." The rage was camouflaging her personality as she was looking at the officer with a devilish look on her face. When the two cops made the exchange with Sonora Myers, and good riddance from the other officer during the hour period. Officer Hank assist Sonora Myers in the back of the police car like she was paralyzed from top to bottom with her street clothes smelling like straight alcohol. As the black police vehicle with the red Clayton County sticker headed towards his journey to Tara Boulevard. Sonora mind was racing intensity as she was looking out the police vehicle just wondering about life itself. Sonora was thinking about her baby Rico DL and everybody else that she was reminiscing during the course. Sonora thought about Rico so much, that. She started to daydream into a deep sleep into the back seat of the police car in deep motion during the ride. Her arm was feeling uncomfortable and numb with the handcuffs tight with no blood flow traveling in vain. Her whole body felt like she was about to flint from the grip of the tight sliver handcuffs that were so secure. The travel time was approximately 8:50 a.m. on a Thursday morning schedule, at this in-particular time of the morning. Sonora would be on her way to work right about now, slipping on a cold Red Bull energy substance in her hand while rowing on the expressway. She was so frustrated and sick, that. She can taste that Crown Royal in her dry and dehydrated chemistry that was reacting inside her mouth so anxiously.

Once the officer told Sonora to quit down from the back seat with anger in his voice. They were close towards the City Hall precinct like going towards Lovejoy area around the way, where the Bond companies are into the dark and the mist. Finally, the destination was over for Sonora Myers when they pulled up from the side where the walk ramp was located by site. Sonora begins to prepare herself for the worst nightmare that she ever had in bark for the second time since the first DUI back then.

The clock was 10:03, as she waited in the lobby for her name to be called for all the information that they needed to have for the data system on the computer. The lobby was heavily clouded with trifling black women that did ugly crimes as well during the conversation. While the other women were talking about their bullshit history to one another. Sonora was agitated and furious with her arms crossed looking mean as ever in her perpetual existence. She didn't want to communicate with anyone around her cipher as she sees it through her eyes. The clerk behind the booth was calling one convent at a time when she felt suicidal during duty, from massive constellation of life. The other clerks were on lunch break around 10:00 to 10:45 and some changes. The other women were already on break too late as necessary as usual. The process was very slow when the time became 11:20 a.m. within all the bickering coming from all women in different culture into the dungeon funk.

Chapter 17

The beautiful rain was coming down like an awesome high Title Wave just hitting the outskirts around Garden Walk area with a wind flowing through the atmosphere.

The rain was hitting the window as the home phone was ringing to death, when Rico finally woke up from his three-hour nap, as Sonora steps out for a few hours with an open mind freely. As Rico struggled getting up from Sonora comfortable bed, after the home phone was ringing about 15 times, back-to-back from the nightstand. After Rico came outta the bedroom to get back into Sonora's bed. The home phone was constantly ringing again, five more times around the surface. After the seventh ring was so mysterious in vain. Rico hesitated to pick up the house phone from an unusual fear that he was in, deeply. But wonder? Slowly he picks up the phone with his dry voice, that needs a glass of water immediately that's real cold. When Rico finally picked up the phone outta curiosity. It was Sonora's oldest sister Kimberly King, that was on the other end calling about Sonora's bad karma that happened. Rico asks. Who is this calling at this very moment? Hello, this is her sister Kimberly. Who am I speaking with right now? Kimberly asks. I'm sorry. My name is Rico DL. I'm Sonora's boyfriend.

Well... I'm here to inform you, Rico. "Sonora is locked up again." "That sister of mine, has caught another damn DUI last night." Damn!! Said Rico. This is her second DUI. Yes! She said. "Her second fuckin' DUI." "I hate this shit." I really do! When my sister caught the first DUI. "I had to bail her ass out immediately." And then: I had to put my house up to get her-stupid ass outta jail. "That's some bullshit!!" My sister isn't-shit!! "She's a loser!"

"And, Sonora can go straight to hell, for-all-I'd-care, and die." What do you need me to do, Ms. Kimberly? "I'm not doing a damn thing for her." "I really do mean that." We need to do something. Rico said. Well... That's on you Rico. Do-what-you-have-to-do. "I'm not bailing her ass out this time." Hell no!! Wow! Rico DL was so surprised at her vicious tone that he was receiving from Kimberly during this conversation. I'll tell you what. I can contribute towards getting my baby outta jail if you want? We both can go half on, getting your sister out right away. That sounds nice in-all, Rico. But. No thank-you. "I'm not bailing my sister out this time. No way!

After all the sorrows were outta her system, when she immediately hung up the phone on Rico. Rico's mind was blown away when Kimberly hung up in his face with disrespect outta nowhere. Time wasn't on Rico side, as he was sitting on the edge of the bed with both hands on his head, thinking of a master plan to get Sonora out of jail. First, he needs to figure out what area she's locked up in the district. While his thinking process was racing all over the place in his green and white boxing shorts, tripping over his white cocaine Timberlands boots. He was going around in circles about ten times, losing focus on what he was trying to do humbly. Rico DL had to dial * 69 the number Kimberly was calling from to get the information he needed to know Sonora's location to bond her out. Rico tried three attempts to call the number back to get a hold of Kimberly Myers. AKA Kimberly King directly. No feedback was coming back whatsoever on the house phone. So, after saying dammit so loud in a rugged high-pitch voice. The darkness was blinding Rico's vision inside the hollow bedroom while searching for something to wear inside his black luggage during the hard pressure, not having anything to drive significantly. Rico had to call a cab, after Kimberly called back with a clear thought of solving this mockery over Sonora.

Rico had all the information that he needed to go and get Sonora, his love, out of jail for good. Immediately he called a cab to get him from his location at Garden Walk. Rico wanted to take a Hollywood shower so bad, that. His body was feeling like he had cooties or something like radiation. But he didn't have time to do so, during his itchy uncomfortable body. As Rico DL was going inside his Victorinox luggage to grab his toothbrush to brush his teeth. A big black water bug came outta his luggage and ran for the border like the Roadrunner with velocity.

Chapter 18

A frustrated day begins to surface around Rico's fate, as he prepares himself for the long ride as the test awaits him to get his beloved love of, his life outta jail. Once the cab arrived inside the apartment complex into Garden Walk *Outworld*. The cab was honking his horn to let Rico know he was available for his service during the frustration. The whole outside and the atmosphere were making my skin feel so creepy from head to toe that I was walking into. Rico's mind felt like it was off balance throughout his whole energy when getting inside the white and blue cab thinking consciously with himself. After giving the cab driver, the direction towards the bond company across the street from City Hall precinct, while waiting inside the ABC Bail bonding company. Rico couldn't believe how many people were inside the bonding company to bail families and friends around noon time. As Rico DL stands and waits in line to conduct business, until his turn comes. Patiently be waits, as a young black woman rises hell through the ABC bonding company about her no-good boyfriend of hers that's locked up in vain. The white lady that was behind the desk, was being an asshole and a jerk right in front of the black woman face. The bonding lady was telling her. You don't have enough money to bail your boyfriend out mama. As the white woman uses the phrase, in poetic justice hood status. The conversation was getting so awful that. The bonding lady didn't have any patience for the young women's ignorance as they continued to baffle back and forth in front of other people waiting. The other people started to get real tense from the commotion that they were hearing from both ladies in line. Rico didn't mind waiting anyway, to get Sonora out for this occasion.

Just two hours passed as Rico was still in line, all cool-com and collect with two individuals in front of him almost ready for the finish line. That's when 2:00 o'clock arrived around the corner. Rico wrote a check for four thousand dollars inside his notebook nice and neat and proper.

After all that information and hundreds of questions needed to be answered. The bond lady finally finalized the release form to release Sonora Myers outta jail. Once Rico received release papers for Sonora slave freedom. Rico was seriously proud and excited to get the information about his forever love going out the door. It was so much of an exciting moment that. Rico ran out of the bonding company so fast, that. It felt like he won the cash three Lotto with both hands in the air running across the street like a wild deer that was blind with no conscious as a mad man. After rubbing his ankle from scrubbing the concrete, when he put pressure on the side of the curb after coming from the street almost fell into the green grass. One of the vehicles that was at the red light, with tilted windows was laughing at him when Rico DL slid into the grass like a Baseball player.

Once the light turns green and the person called Rico a stupid fool when he got up from the grass. Rico brushes himself with his bare hands like it was a bushy bloom in the mix. Mr. DL had to brush the foolishness out his mind and get his baby outta jail with the time 3:20 p.m. running. After going through the crazy procedure from the security guard by taking a few things off the body like a-damn-fool for security reason. Rico felt like a rape victim in slave mode, during this horribly mission, as he was in line to release his queen from jail for good. To protect his baby from the slum through supremacy from the dungeon.

Rico didn't want his girl to suffer any longer from a world that has bad diseases to make your mind bleed consciously into the system. The process took another two hours of waiting, just like the bonding company did across street with weird individual.

Rico's brain was getting very frustrated and weak around the moment during the information in line, while other people were talking and looking depressed for hours like zombies in the making. The process was so long, that. He had to grab something out of the venting machine and sit down and take a ten-minute nap for sake in peace. "It was damn-near 15 people ahead of him like a grocery store like Kroger. Rico DL went through a 45-minute transaction phase out the blue, with a bag of Doritos spilled all over him with his black Polo shirt, that was tight showing his muscle pics and chest. While waking up trying to get his mind in-order for the officer behind the counter typing on the computer screen. Rico looks at the time, that was 4:15 p.m. on his iPhone 6 traveling and strolling at the same time. Finally, when his turn came to give his information to the correctional officer that releases street violations and crimes. The black correctional officer was giving Rico a very hard time to release Sonora from jail, with the information that was given to her at the counter. Rico DL was trying to figure out why this stupid-ass-lady was giving him so much competition with the information that he had perceived in facts. During the mind thinking. *If I was a white man. I would've call her... a-straight-up black, stupid nigger with force. "That's how piss-off I was!!!!"* The situation gotten so deep, that. Rico kept saying to himself. "This is some bullshit." Three times in a row. Rico DL had to wait about 45 more minutes for everything was clarify, and prosperous through the waiting. Ten minutes later. The correctional officer told Rico everything was good and finalize for Mr. Sonora Myers release. The rejoice was healing. As he began to dance with joy inside his mind with a hell yeah without any movement or stiffness.

After hearing the good news from the correctional officer to Rico DL exciting moment. She told him. Sonora Myers will indefinitely be released in 30 minutes, after she finishes her meal before departing from the facility.

After that scandalous lie from the correctional officer, as-a-bastard that told Rico about 30 minutes ago. Sonora was finally released with honor, but no respect from the traditional system at all. As the moment was rising when Sonora came out the hell hold. She ran towards Rico with open arms like in the movie. *The Matrix Revolution,* when Trinity found Neo in the tunnel, lost in between three dimensions being jacked in temporarily. As love was united with hugs and kisses into the *Matrix system.*

Chapter 19

The beautiful sunset was looking, very dim from above with light-orange, and blue around the surface into the skies, when Rico and Sonora were kissing like two teenagers for the first time like a prom date from heaven. The matrix time became 5:45 p.m. sitting in the back of the cab in silence mode throughout the hold drive from beyond the distance. As Rico stares directly towards Sonora anatomy from the side view, from head to toe. He noticed a cut on the left side of her face that said *evil* in carving. Rico didn't know what to think in her moment of silence, as she stared into the city and lights through the smear window looking very fine. Sonora was feeling sad and blue with her legs crossed, mentally thinking with her arms as well in the back. Rico felt nervous and hesitated by feeling on his baby tights for comfort. You feeling okay over there my love? Rico couldn't get no answer from Sonora when he was saying something sweet to her once more. "Baby!" Are you alright over there? While he was holding her pretty- soft hand for support. Slowly she turned her head towards Rico handsome face with contact in her eyes. And begins to cry and lean her head over his shoulder for love and affection. The cab driver was coming down on Highway 85 up by the light next to Raceway headed towards Garden Walk inside the Garden

Wood Apartment. Immediately, Sonora exited the cab to go up into her cozy apartment, so she could dive into her queen size bed to kick back for the evening. Rico damn-near was in puzzled mode when Sonora left the cab and rushed into the wind like abracadabra through magic. After the cab had left from Garden Wood through the gate.

Rico couldn't believe how much money he had spent in his account to get Sonora free. It's a good thing he had money through the bad times, inside his account as a black man.

If not: Sonora would've been in deep madness, if-it-wasn't for Rico supporting the *Goddess*. She would've been trapped in the devil's demise forever. Especially in the Clayton County world. Rico was walking up the second level of the apartment thinking, what-the-fuck just happened today. The frustration was building up quickly as his mind was wide open, how money he had spent on his loveable girlfriend. While coming into the bedroom to check on Sonora. She took her black jeans and white blouse that went to her lower tights like a flowery dress to bed. Rico DL was looking at her beautiful curb booty from a distance when he was coming into the bedroom without a sound from his feet. His adrenaline was like a high blood pressure that has a lot of cholesterol that makes the body weak. At that very moment, in his sexual condition that he was feeling with his eyes directly towards the body. He wanted to grab her from the back with smoothness towards Sonora with one hand inside her red panties to stroke the Kitty cat for pleasure. Sonora was already in bed with a funky-black and white cover over her face like a dead person.

When the thought became a sexual moment in his mind as he feels the vibration of love, by wasting his train of thought through his appetite, when Sonora shoal no type of interests in sex during this awful second *DUI,* she just gotten hours ago. Rico felt the tension from his beloved woman when she gotten inside her bed like she has the flu or something through contact.After feeling the vibe from Sonora uncomfortable space that was very strange to him. Rico DL decided to leave Sonora alone for a minute, so she could get her mind, body, and soul intact while sitting back watching television for the rest of the day, through the night manifesting in pain.

Chapter 20

The beautiful dream that was in deep purple inside Stacy Myers mind, beginning to be a deadly coma so deeply, that. In between her sleep became a bed hangover. Stacy phone begins to ring like crazy when Sonora was trying to contact her around 11:17 p.m. tucked inside the covers like a new-born baby. She was trying to contact her sister Stacy so she could get a ride to work in the morning for Friday. Sonora didn't call her other sister Kimberly, because her mind was on some schizophrenia hallucinations while conversating with her. "This bitch couldn't-even-get me out of jail." *"That bitch!"* As her rage began to get hotter and hotter inside her consciousness world. She decided to give Stacy another call for one more hope for survival. While the phone was ringing on the other end. Another call was coming through, which was David when she clicked over for luck and joy for the moment. "What's up girl." What's up David! "Where you been at all day." Well... I have some disturbing news. She said. "Some disturbing!" Aw shit! "What's going on?" David said. You really want to know. Hell yeah! "I want to know." Naw, I'm not telling you! What!! Really Sonora! "You're going to do me like that girl?" Naw! "I'm just fuckin' with you boy." "But seriously." I just caught another DUI last night. "What!" "Oh, hell naw

Sonora!" Yep. How did you end up with another DUI? "Man... let me tell you." After I left my girl Dominic over some dude house that night. "I felt like bumpin' my shit before going home to my boring-ass boyfriend that I went out with earlier before all this-shit went down so fast." "Damn Sonora!" You were bumpin' like that in the street? "Hell, yeah nigga." I didn't give-a-fuck, when I was bumping. I felt like 2pac. "Fuck the police, with two fingers in the car, baby!" "That's why they locked your ass up, for doing dumb shit like that." David said.

"Fuck-you-nigga!" Said Sonora. David was in the background just laughing his ass off through the cell phone tremendously. What happened Sonora? "I got to hear this!" David asks. So. What happened was. Once the police heard my music up loud. He followed me from Main Street passing through the grave site to Bank of America, and that's when he pulled me over by the Bank. And that's when I ticked his ass, then. I burn rubber like the Black Night Rider on a high-speed chase, rollin'!!

So... "Wait a minute." When he pulled you over. You pulled off on the officer. Yep! Sonora said. I sure did!! Dammmmn... Sonora. "Why you do that?" I wasn't trying to get another DUI on my record, you know. "Hell." "By doing that dumb shit." You end up with another one, you-dumb-ass! David said. Go-head-on nigga. As her mind was mad about the whole incident in red visuals. David world was puzzled from the inside, until the word but came about from the mouth. And Sonora said. "Fuck that!" I do however I want to do in these street David. See, talking like that, got you in jail in the first place. Situation like that.

You deserve to be in jail. I wouldn't-non did that Sonora. "Whatever *negro*." As Sonora mind was in a different world. "You know damn well you would've done the same thing." So, stop it!! As she yells. Shitin' me! David said. I-wouldn't put my conscious through that, around my consequent energy. I'll be a good-little boy for the white officer like a *nigger.*

After Sonora heard that-bullshit from her *kiss-ass* road dog homey. She kept telling herself. He's a big pussy for real in her eyes. I'm kind of glad you called, because. I need a favor from you David. "What's up Sonora." I need a ride in the morning homeboy. You think your mother can let you borrow the car boo? I'll give her some gas money if you want me to. Naw! You are good Sonora. "You my road dog." Anything you need. I-got-you. Sonora Myers was pleased with the cool remark that David had said on the phone.

You just need to take care of that evil-ass DUI you just got. So, they got you for reckless driving and, a DUI. Plus, the high-speed chase that night. "Hell, yeah boo." "Damn Sonora!" "That's fuck-up girl." And then: this your second DUI too. Then. You have got to go through all those programs again, as well. Right! All that-bullshit again! Sonora said. The last time I went through all these trials and tribulation around my revelations. I went through hell trying to pay them people off with an honest living throughout this wick system that we brainwashed to. I feel you on that matter girl. But still. You need to take care of your business, homegirl. I know you hate to deal with a system like this. But. Please, take care of that DUI, a-sap. After saying dammit about five times constantly. Sonora was in a bad mood, by saying. Forget this whole DUI cap and program. I must go back to court next month anyway, on July 20th on a Tuesday. That means you must take another day off my girl. Yep. I sure do. I think, what-I'm-going to do is. Take that one week off for a vacation to get my mind right, mentally, and physically on some rest time. Sounds like a good deal Sonora. Probably the best thing for you girl. On the real. You need to slow your ass down with that reckless driving that you be doing. "Sometimes you be scaring the shit outta me, crazy girl." After laughing so loud on the phone with David. David had to end the joyful conversation with Sonora to end his night. Once David said his peace directly to Sonora Myers. Sonora begins to act weird and strange all-of-suddenly while getting out of the bed. By coming outta the dark from the bedroom. She noticed Rico was stretched out on the sofa with his black tank top, and black and red Basketball shorts sleeping good around 12:00 midnight. Sonora already gave him some powerful sleeping pills on the down low before he took a nap. Sonora approached Rico with his expensive gold clippers and begins to slave his pubic hair clean off like a smooth ball-headed monk. The psychological thoughts were kicking in. Sonora so viciously insane, during the carving on the flesh by his private part that spells. *Devil forever.*

Chapter 21

Midnight came to an end when the light-blue skies were rising around the Riverdale area in the middle of Southern Regional Hospital. The time was 7:50 a.m. when Draco rose from his bed during the heat high rise. Draco's mind was still tripping about what took place, between him and Dominic and the other woman, which was Sonora out the ordinary. Draco did his normal push-ups routine. About 10 sets of them back and forth in the living room.

The 31-year-old Draco had a nice chest plate on his firm body as a smart Leo. If Dominic had a chance to witness his whole physique around the chest. Her lips would've been watery around the surface of the mouth towards his pecs. Draco Dawn just finished his cold glass of orange juice that became delightful in his body after a smooth workout for an hour or so.

The time begins to hit 8:55 a.m. during the morning schedule, by coming out the cold shower feeling fresh and pure through the skin as he rubbed and caress his chest like a man. Channel 2 News just broke down another fatality, about a family just gotten gun down two days ago during a major burglary in Newnan County with three black teens in their black hoodies. Wow!! "These teenagers are off the chain right now." "What the hell is wrong with these mothafuckas in the world." These stupid ass kids don't have no type morsels with their selfies. The News was so graphical and disturbing, that. The TV went off immediately when enough was enough for Draco Dawn eyes.

Draco had to pick his fluffy Mohawk before walking up the road for a touch-up around the surface of his head. Mr. Draco had his Dickie suite nice and iron with a hard crease on the edges of his favorite color brown. While he was putting on his Dickie shirt over his white tank top. A bunch of gun fire was going off, up there by QT parking lot around people. Draco with his all-brown Dickie outfit looking fresh and clean outside the door. Carrie Pemberton just finished walking her precious little Yorkie Terrier around the cul-de-sac in the small neighborhood. Draco saw Ms. Pemberton and her black and gray mix with a little white around her legs and paw. As Draco caress Nookie on the head and body while Nookie was wagging her fluffy tail on the concrete. How are you doing this morning Mr. Pemberton? I'm doing just fine Draco. I had a hard time getting up this morning. I'm not young like I use to these days, young man. I have a birthday on his Saturday coming up. Oh, really! He said. "Congratulations Ms. Pemberton." How old will you be, Ms. Pemberton? Just guess, Draco! "I'm just kidding young man." After they both laughed at her corny joke. Carrie Pemberton told Draco she will be 69 this year in June. They said their goodbyes to one another as he walked away into the early morning sunlight as the day walker phenomenon. He pushed his self, up beyond the decipher street towards QT where they were shooting at earlier while he was getting dress for his journey directly towards the plaza in Riverdale. Draco begins to get very excited, as his walk felt good to him with strive on the sidewalk with his wooden dark brown staff. Draco felt so good, that. He wanted to dance like Sammy Davis Jr. the dance machine in his polish black boots with his style. As the walk was blending within Draco movement during the 10:05 high heat. A black, 21-year-old hood type dude with tattoos all over his arms wearing a dark green tank top, with holes in his gray jeans. Mr. Draco seen the dude from a distance with his white and gray Pit bull on the leash.

Draco noticed the thick Pit bull was jumping in circles with his trap music through his cell phone speaker. By crossing the path towards the black dude with the Pit. The Pit bull was so heavy, that. His leash came loose around his thigh neck from all the jumping up and down the Pit was doing with the music surfacing into his presents.

During the walk things became off balance, as the Pit bull came loose with no leash connected around the collar. The Pit came directly towards Draco immediately with a vicious look in his eyes from a distance, as he moved and dodged quickly into the grass. The Pit went in the opposite direction into the street, while cars were coming at the speed of light back-to-back. As soon as the Pit was about to make it on the sidewalk. The young, twenty-one-year-old voice was traveling all over the street for his beloved Pit. Just before the Pit can make a big U-turn back on the other side. An old beat-up white looking van just sideswiped the hell outta the Pit from behind real hard and seen him right back into the sidewalk with two broken legs and a cracked rib.

Draco stood up from the grass, and watched the young dude run across the street with his jeans hanging down from his butt, just showing his black underwear in public, trying to rescue his Pit bull. Draco felt sorry for the young man and his Pit bull just gotten hit severely. As bad as Draco wanted to walk across the street and show some love towards the young man and give him a tight hug for support and harmony. But the thing was. Draco had to press on during the situation like he normally does into the sunset with peace in his heart as the day walker.

Chapter 22

The skies went from light blue to gray on a frequently type chameleon faze, when Draco came out the Barbershop looking fresh too death with the side clean as a righteous man.

As Draco was in through of where he needed to go next while dwelling. Draco fingered he wanted some travel time as the day walker as usual. Dominic pulls up slowly like a window shopper type thug on cause, yelling out. "Hey man!" "What's up?" On the down low. "What's going on with you, Ms. Dominic?" Nothing much. Just doing a little grocery shopping for me and my kids. You have kids? He asks. Yes! And they are getting on my damn nerves. Especially boys. They are just hard-headed. "And they-just can't listen worth shit, when I try to tell them something." "I know they can't be that bad, are they?" Draco said. Hell yeah! "They some bad ass thugs to me." Damn!! It sounds like you have your work cut out, Ms. Lady. Right! As Dominic's mind was discombobulated during the conversation. Wait until you have kids yourself, Mr. Draco. Well... not to burst your bubble, Dominic. I have a 13-year-old son up in Chicago with his mother. So, yeah! We are both in the same boat, my lady. Okay. I hear you.

As she was speaking out loud. After changing the subject from Dominic Walker. She welcomed him with open arms to an imitation for a ride with her, on a lovely journey to get more personal and acquainted with him. During this strange vibe as he hesitated for a minute before getting inside the passenger seat for the big ride.

Dominic had a big smile on her face when Draco decided to ride along with her for this special occasion. As they were riding along Valley Hill Rd, going in the opposite direction towards his house for a quick stop.

Draco Dawn eyes begin to shift around smoothly and honest in the passenger seat, checking out Dominic's prospective how she carries herself as a woman. Where are you heading to Mr. Draco? I was heading towards South Lake Mall to look around and have some fun with myself. And. What else comes to mind. I see you like to stay to yourself a lot. Yes mama! "Don't mind at all." I been doing this routine for five and a half years straight. "Can I ask you something?" Sure! Said Draco. "What's up with all the brown you have on? It's-like. Brown is your favorite color or something. Yes, it is. My whole wardrobe in my closet is full of brown Dickie suits, that are nicely cleaned and cruise for the Outworld. "Are you serious!" As the woman in her yells. Hell naw Ms. Lady. "I know you just playin' right?" Dominic said. I am serious as a heart attack. Nothing but brown Dickies in my closet. Nineteen pairs of brown Dickies in the closet. Wow...! While the moment was surprising to her. Why so many brown Dickies? I can-see if you had 19 different colors of Dickies. "But damn!" I know it sounds crazy Dominic. But... I love my brown Dickies collection.

"I'm very proud." After having so much confidence in his weird and insane wardrobe. Dominic Walker had to erase all those crazy thoughts that Draco sync inside her mind that was so ridiculous and weird. The commitment was unusual when Dominic spoke of how Draco house was so cute when they touched base on the driveway talking. Dominic wanted to touch Draco's firm hand before he got out of the vehicle, wishing that she could touch and grab forever as lovers. Draco walks towards the side door so smoothly as a firm gentleman in her present.

The eyes seductively seduce her mind body and soul, as she watches Draco confidence as a man. Ms. Walker carefully steps out of the vehicle, as she follows Draco lead into his home again. Dominic came in and made herself comfortable on the couch with her legs crossed so beautifully, while Draco was in the bathroom feeling 10 pounds lighter and cleaning himself. Dominic was having a deep conversation with Sonora second DUI that she ended up with the other night. Sonora began to get deeper and deeper about what led up to this awful experience for the second round again. When Draco finally came out of the restroom feeling like a champ that was on the grind. It felt like déjà vu when I saw Dominic on the phone once more. Mr. Draco felt weird and off track when he was watching Dominic from the corner behind the white wall just investigating. Draco knew not to spy any longer around Dominic's present at this point in the game. So, Draco came directly towards her conversation and placed himself next to her with her shiny red fingernail, that he was surprising sitting on by mistake. By saying sorry and excuse me at the same time during the mix. Dominic knew what she was doing when she placed her pretty hand on the couch to touch Draco's booty on the slick side of things. Draco felt the present when he had saw her smooth shadow from the corner of his eyes. As the eyes recognize the hand that manifest on the sofa during the sitting from Draco's buttock that felt the wave and frequencies through gravity. The switching of the body posture that rotated the anatomy from the other side of Draco's firm chest, with the right leg crossed towards him so luscious. Her cute face, along with the girly conversation allowed her head to turn gently, as the same hand touches Draco's thigh, while Draco watches the tight vagina through the jeans like a Camel toe that looks tasty for the eyes. By rubbing on Draco's thigh like crazy, thinking it was her man for the moment.

Draco's penis begins to rise slowly, as she continued to rub constantly up towards the belt buckle to unfasten his Dickie pants of taunting him so severely. The feeling was genuine and appealing to Draco's spiritual youth of what he stands for as a profitable man.

Chapter 23

The massive heat was surrounding the knowledge of Draco Dawn weak spot with Dominic's soft hand between Draco's legs to decrease his man hood as the *G.O.D.* Draco kept telling her to stop her nonsense from all that loving and touching she was doing to him.

Dominic laughed and giggle at Mr. Draco's comments and language, as he was trying to avoid her sexual behavior with her gentle touch that was so wonderful. Draco was on shaky ground as she continued to rub and seduce his territory, that he was trying to resist.

While Dominic had the pressure on Draco during the talk with Sonora Myers. Her legs were wide open for Draco's love to engage inside her, as she kept rubbing him repeatedly over-and-over again into her sexual hormones begins to kick in between her and Draco's destiny that she was trying to conquer. The situation was beginning go in her favor, while Dominic increased the pressure after the phone slipped outta her hand, when she started feel the tickles into the mix of her vibration clitoris. Her vibration desire inevitably couldn't stop, how she felt about the lush over Draco on the couch that was so real. With all the touching that she was doing repeatedly all over him. Mr. Draco felt the gentle feeling that Dominic was still putting on him at that singular moment. His mind was amazed how Dominic was seducing him in vain and out of control within the gap. His lush wanted her more and more. As she continued to kiss and rub him at the same time, leaning on the edge of the couch so helplessly on hard. Draco kept telling Dominic to stop in a smooth and gentle low voice, that had him in a horny state of mind.

Draco couldn't take it any longer with his hormones being outta control, as he used the reverse psychology on Dominic's physical body and mind, when he was kissing her all over her face and neck repeatedly. The powerful impact of kissing her on her brown neck; made her grab her breast real insane, to make your head go in circles like a merry go round just pinning and making her feel good. Their chemistry of love making was absolutely, dynamite from the floor, and right back on the soft sofa again. The love making was so awesome, that. Dominic kept riding Draco until she reached her maximum overdrive, along with her grand finale. The climax! That makes Dominic sex goes so well with the flesh. As the humping ended up, around 2:30 *Thriller time* with Draco in between Dominic's legs feeling the splash from his tummy on down. Dominic just flipped the script on Draco to put more pressure on top of him, to make her go third gear all the way from heaven to hell and back. After giving him some slobber action on the brown flesh. Draco's mind begins to lush more of her mouth with the red lipstick that was going up and down from his juicy penis that she was slobbering on. "It was almost like." His dream has finally come true. But not really. He was telling himself. This shouldn't be happening in a low tone voice as the day walker with knowledge of self. The love was so good, that. He wanted more of the juicy vagina that was stroking on his brown flesh to make the pressure last forever when the rain erupted the passion of Draco's kingdom as the G.O.D. against the DEVIL.

Chapter 24

The afternoon smelled good and lovely without any funk in the mist into the atmosphere. The time was 5:26 p.m. when the crew was trying to decide what can they do for excitement this evening. What's the deal Sonora? "I don't know yet." Crazy boy! I'll finger something out for us. Her sister Stacy was doing all the driving and beyond. When she came and picked her sister up from work earlier. David was in the back seat chillin' with a Newport cigarette in his mouth, just puffing away. Let me get one of those cigarettes from you big D? Stacy said. "You want one Sonora?" Hell no! You know I don't smoke that junk, David. "You know you want one Sonora." You funny! She said. You ladies finger out where we hang out this evening? I'm still thinking. Sonora said. I have an idea. Let's check out the spot over there on Old National Highway. Don't they have about five clubs over there, something like that? Yep. They have a few of them around the way. Don't they have a club called The Ritz on Old National? Yeah, they do. Stacy said. But they closed that shit down two years ago. Stacy said. Really. As David spoke out loud towards Stacy. I had been to the Ritz about once or twice back in the day. How is it from the inside? Do-it be jumping off, up-in there Stacy? Yeah... But it has a lot of young niggas flowing in and out, while they act a fool and stupid. It's a lot of shooting going on inside that club. One of the dudes that I was talking to, while I was mingling with my girlfriend, that stays in the apartment called Biscayne. Right behind the Ritz club scene. Have y'all been to the bar called Grown Folks Café before? No. Never been in my life. Stacy said. What time do they open? They open around 8:00 o'clock. But it doesn't get real crunk until 10 p.m. into the night.

The time was 6:35 in the hot evening in June, coming from the Downtown city of Atlanta. Sonora and David, and Stacy were stuck in traffic around 6:50 p.m. just looking ridiculous, as Tunner Field Stadium was having a Baseball game with the Atlanta Braves winning 20-5 over the Red Sox. The temperature was 93% degrees at its high-surface level through the Downtown premiere. Stacy Myers wanted to turn on the AC to bring down the heat throughout the ride. Her gas hand was too low to turn on the cooling system from the front where David was sitting on his third Newport smoking. The two sisters were in their brown liquor game just rotating back and forth with one another laughing. Fifteen minutes later. The traffic had decreased by passing the Metropolitan College still on the expressway heading towards Old National Highway ready for the big fun tonight at Grown Folks. Everyone still had on their work clothes without going home to change and smell good for the crowd to be perfect. As time begins to creep into Old National Street way passing the green light down where KFC restaurant is. "Damn!" We should've stopped by Churches Chicken to get that 10-piece box half spicy with the dark meat mixed with lots of hot sauce in the bag. "No David."

"We're not doing that right now." I would rather have some hot wings, with blue cheese at the joint we are going to. "I know that's right sis." After giving each other some girly dap on the knuckles on some hell yeah tip.

The pretty 7:35 p.m. atmosphere was lurking around the dark blue skies in Old National busy street with thugs. There were only four cars in the parking lot when they pulled up to join the other people for company. By getting out of the vehicle for some good stretching when they release their selfies outta the car. Bones were just popping from every individual that jumped outta the car cramped up. David Dill's wanted one more smoke break before going inside with the ladies with some party all the time madness.

When everything was served at the booth table listening to some *Da Brat Funkdafied* throughout the club, while the Myer sisters were getting there mingle on. A crackhead chic approaches David Dill's on the smooth low into the parking lot for a cigarette and a blowjob for ten bucks around 8 p.m. through darkness. As the time became 8:16 p.m. getting a head job from a funky prick that was dark skin and ugly into her face. David couldn't believe it was 8:30 by looking at his cell phone when she got done having fun with his brown *flesh inside*. After saying shit about three times when the pressure was finished, after wiping her mouth with her stinky white shirt, with the big ole Scooby-Doo face in front smiling. He ran out from the back of the building into the parking lot, to join Stacy and Sonora inside the club to have more fun with the two sisters that were laughing and getting drunk as more people were coming in discombobulated from the outside radiation above.

Chapter 25

The sounds were sounding, tremendously insane when David finally came back from his interesting smoke break that he went through with the devil as a crackhead disciple. David was feeling like dance fever, while entering the Grown Folks funk dancing into the boogie, approaching Sonora and Stacy with his boogie spin in front of them like magic.

As David was coming along with his stupid dance in front of Stacy and Sonora during his bummy look, and afro just wild looking with the black pick in the middle of the head. "What the fuck was yelled out with voice." As Sonora ask the question? "What the hell you think you doing David?" "None of your-damn business, Ms. nosey!" After Sonora-done-told David to sit his ass down and stop dancing so much. David begins to act silly and stupid all-of-sudden. And that's when he gave Sonora a great big-ole kiss on her mouth just to be messing with her on the friendly tip. Even doe. He came close to hitting the kitty-cat from Sonora two years ago in her sex world. He was almost lucky back then. David sometimes reminisces in the back of his mind about that moment in time while riding with her occasionally on a club night. The time was 10:18 p.m. when other black culture was arriving with their nice outfits and jewelry like

GOD's. David was like. "Damn!" Look at those two fine ass females just walked in. "Did you see that shit!" He said. Yes! "We see those two bitches walking in." "They're not all that David." So, stop acting like that. It's not that serious with those hoes. "Oh, girl." "You so mean." Stacy said. "What!!" "I'm just being real Stacy." You know how I am sis. I'm just speaking my mind, whatever comes out of it. As the music played throughout the whole club while Sonora and her sister were talking a lot of trash and lies like they normally do as sisters.

There weren't many men walking around the club at this hour. You had, probably, about four to six men throughout the club scene. "Where the hell are the brothers at?" David said. "What 'cha mean where the brothers at?" Theirs two over there at the bar. And then. You have one in a white silk short sleeved shirt with loose pants, with white Stacey Adam's shoes on. Doing his Mack routine in front of the ladies. Last, but not least. You have two gentlemen at the table on the right. They look like gay guys on the down low. David didn't believe Sonora about the two guys was sitting at the table were gay on the other end of the club. As the gang continues to talk about. What they assume were gay men around the circle. It was three, different complexion of Lesbians was staring towards Sonora and Stacy at the bar with their fine ass shirts on, looking six-feet tall with some expensive hills with the toes hanging out looking nicely and polish. David leaned to the chair around the table, just watching the three Lesbians, while sipping on his Long Island Tea in the background. The brown skin looking woman was whispering something in one's ear, while she stares and smiles directly at Sonora and Stacy. But not David. As he was analyzing the situation too much into the tricky eye. As the staring continues with the brown skin and light skin, along with the Asian chic, that was fine as well to. All three had the same identical tight shirts on. But different colors out the three. David Dill's had his back against the seat just chillin' being quiet and sipping on his beverage. Mr. Dill's began to feel good and tipsy as he watches the redbone as she looks away like she's all that, like most light skinned women would do. When a non-good-looking man glances at them from a distance. The brown skinned chic with the long, short straight black hair, with the half dark blue color on the side looking delicious. That's when she stood up to show that petite body she had in the dark blue shirt, as she pulled it down slowly.

The Asian young woman just told the waitress to send this cocktail to that lovely lady over there with the dimples and the slick back ponytail looking like a Puerto Rican Princess. The waitress arrived with the cocktail with the Cherry on top and spoke. "Here you go mama." This is for you.

After the waitress sat the two cocktails on the table. Sonora and her sister were pleased with the pleasantry welcomed of the drinks. And... mama. This special drink is a compliment from the young Asian woman that's sitting over there with the other ladies and their companions. After the waitress, nicely drops off the drinks during the slow music. Stacy became very surprised to receive a drink from a beautiful Asian woman from the bar. The Asian woman and the redbone were waving at Stacy Myers. The situation was beginning to get interesting, of what was about to happen with Stacy and Sonora, the three beautiful and gorgeous ladies that was conversating and smiling. "Damn, ladies." Y'all got-it like that. As David became insecure within the man. We don't know what the hell you are talking about nigga. Stacy said. As Ms. Sonora started to laugh at David crazy stupidity as a joke in his eyes. Both sisters were laughing and giggling with a picture shot. "What've you think about this shit sis?" Stacy said. What do you mean Stacy? About our little admirer that sent us these drinks on deck. You know how I am sis. "I don't give a damn." Whoever bought these drinks for us. They can keep bringing them all night long, for all I care. Sonora said. "I'll drink to that." Stacy said. After toasting each other glasses for another victory as the drinks were up high. David continued to stare towards the brown skin woman with the dark blue dress as she was talking to her other girlfriends about Sonora and Stacy Myers beauty. David's mind begins to manifest upon the woman in the dark blue dress that he likes and keeps thinking about. "Damn that woman is fine." I should walk over there and socialize with this beauty I see for me and her.

He was licking his lips, and drinking his drink at the same time, as his eyes hypnotized through her body and soul. David wanted the brown skin to see him watch her when she turned and looks at David between his big brown eyes through communication at will. As she smiles and wonders with her pretty legs crossed for temptation into David's eyes, while she poked her tongue out for her ambition to use tricknology on him for eternity as the *demon devil in blue.*

Chapter 26

The night of the funk was resonating throughout the Grown Folks Plaza, from the parking lot and inside the club during the 11:25 p.m. night hour. The Grown Folks was full and off the chain with men and women just collaborating with each other in the mix of the music.

As the club went into a flow rhythm at 11:40 going and heading towards 12 midnight smelling like beautiful women in between. David couldn't wait on the cute waitress for another Long Island Tea for the second round again. David Dill's had to walk pass the beautiful ladies that was, gorgeous as hell in his crimson eyes. As soon as he walks passes the three ladies with an unusual smell around their comfort zone talking. He finally pays for his drink with his arms leaning on the counter, trying to act smooth and debonair. The Asian woman had to step out into the lady's restroom for a minute to prepare her exciting extravaganza for tonight. As Kiana walked pass David with an amazing stunning walk straight ahead behind him. Merial and Brandy smoothly left the bar to ease over towards Sonora and Stacy to have a group conversation with them on the down low, while David was gone. David had to rush and bounce towards the restroom to use number one and two at the same time. The pressure was really on when he had to run to the stall like a volcano ready to explode. His stomach was so full, that. He was blowing up like an atomic bomb with lots of dark smoke coming out. While David continued to take the pain away. Kiana, already done left the ladies restroom to join her other ladies with Sonora and Stacy at a better table. Which was, like the V.I.P at the booth to get more acquainted forever.

After the midnight hour had come around, during the music blasting throughout the club in and out, with such a crowd prancing around the bar with lots of women. All five women that was at the comfortable booth were jingling and moving at the same time. Just catching that stare down upon one another with their pretty eyes. The Grown Folks was mad pack with women versus men inside the place. The vibe felt like free drinks on Thursday for the lovely ladies around each table in the mix. By the club being so packed. David was wondering, where-the-hell are Sonora and Stacy asses at? He's been looking for the girls for about 15 minutes or so around the club scene. As his patients begin to level down, trying to find Stacy and Sonora. He told his mind. "It's time to give up on this shit." I'm tired of looking for their asses. When David told his self to fuck-it about three times in a row. He went back towards the bar and got him another Long Island Tea for his third round. David continued to sit and watch the beautiful ladies that were in his surroundings teasing the situation. Some of those women that David was watching were, walking the walk with the sexy wave in front of his eyes. On the other side of the club. The women were having so much fun inside the booth, that they were hugging each other and laughing, and dogging the shit-outta men in every galaxy. Kiana and Stacy were vibin' really-well as strangers when they were communicating and holding hands like best friends or something. When things got really-deeply and comfortable with Stacy and Kiana. Kiana face was feeling very exciting and vibrational as Stacy was telling hood stories and thug life reality, in her none-fiction world. A kiss wanted to be placed on Stacy's juicy lips immediately with an urge. The slow song from Silk made the conversation more compromising to one another, as the chills and goosebumps started to manifest frequently. As Stacy and Kiana started to blossom with a body touch. Sonora and Merial were getting very acquainted as well, along with Brandy being so touchy towards Merial's legs. Sonora was feeling so strange, that.

Her back begins to itch into an irritation sensation reaction. Sonora tried her best to scratch her back on an uncomfortable and unsatisfying feeling around Merial. Merial told Sonora. I got you boo on the slick tip, of rubbing and scratching her back gently and nice. After her itching fever was temporarily over with, from the love Merial gave on Sonora back. She wanted another itching rub from the back. Too feel that moment once more. Merial wanted to kiss Sonora with such an urge with her sweet lips. Even if Merial would have forced herself on Sonora with a big kiss on the lips. Sonora probably would-have enjoyed that amazing surprise from her. If David Dill's knew where the girls were. He wouldn't join the party as well. David didn't give-a-damn anyway. Because. He was enjoying himself with his Long Island Tea on the side like it was his wife forever. While David begins to groove with R. Kelly slow mix, of Step in the name of love type chemistry. The ladies on the other side were stepping as well with their drinks up high singing. The club DJ went into a R. Kelly marathon movement with slow jams back flowing like water. As the slow jams continue to hit around the five ladies that were at the booth. The Lesbians wanted to get really acquainted with Stacy and Sonora during the dark moment of the hour. Which was perfect for Merial, Brandy and Kiana. Kiana nice pretty feet, that were so smooth and warm was rubbing against Stacy's shinbone with her toe, just going up and down and slow into a tease to make her wiggle with ease. Brandy was massaging Sonora back, while Merial was saying some kind words towards her circle. Sonora was beginning to feel a little weird when Brandy was massaging her back with sexual appeal. But. At the same time. It was feeling very comfortable from a woman's touch versus a man's grip in-reality. Sonora Myers told Brandy, don't tease me like that with your soft hands over my back like that. Brandy knew that was Sonora's weak spot in the middle of her back and wrist. As Sonora turns her head in front of Merial pretty complexion.

Brandy was kissing on Sonora's shoulders and back so smoothly and slickly, while Merial touched and rubbed on both tights from knees, almost to vagina around her wasted for more to come.

Chapter 27

The midnight hour from the dark was beginning to look really, scary around the sidewalk street and behind the hollow closed buildings. Collage Park police had a DUI victim inside the Kristal parking lot up against his black Nova in the hood. The officer was traveling around the vehicle that looked like a 4x4 Jeep with big rims in four-dimensional image. The young man had his girlfriend in the passenger seat scared to death with eight open bottles of Jack Daniel's, and a strawberry Daiquiri in the back seat. The young black male knew he was going down for Marijuana, and procession of a pistol underneath the passenger seat, and no insurance for three weeks. While the young man was crying in the back of the police car with his pants hanging down to his knees. His girlfriend was really pissed-off with her immature stupid-ass boyfriend on the cell phone with her girlfriend cussing his ass out, while her friend laughs herself into heavy cramp. While she waits for her other girlfriends to arrive and pick her up, and head towards the Grown Folks club as scheduled. When the Tow truck finally came and hog the vehicle from outta nowhere into the wind. The young dude was looking stupid when the police officer jotted down all the information that he needed, as the police vehicle drifted off slowly with the look of sanity between him and her eyes for good. "I don't give a funk nigga, in her mind." Ten minutes later. Her wild and loud friends arrived, playing Young Jeezy with the windows down, and picked her up and rolled out immediately to the Grown Folks Plaza. As her cut-off boyfriend went the opposite direction into the midnight terror dome facility.

David kept looking at his phone repeatedly, continuously, but randomly. It was damn near 1:15 a.m. with the sounds still going on throughout the club. It was time to leave the club scene in the back of David's mind with five rounds in his system of Long Island Tea's. He wanted one more rounded to go, before he started looking for Sonora and Stacy his true home girls. When he jumped off his seat like a little kid, coming off the potty all-of-a-sudden. David tripped over the leg from the black chair, almost went face first onto the hard floor. Luckily, he caught himself directly with both hands into a pushup type position. No one really saw him because it was very dim in the middle of the club. By him being so cautious and catching himself with great reflex. It threw his bladder off track immediately. David Dill's mind was in a frustration mode, when searching for his friends all over the club. Twenty minutes later. They were nowhere to be found from the inside and out. "Where the fuck they at?" As he said, about three to four times out loud. Also, when he went outside to look again. David notices the car wasn't there like a magic tick outta thin air from the parking lot. "Where in hell is the damn car!" I know I'm not crazy. The car was just here, about a couple of hours ago. "What the fuck just happened." "I know these bitches didn't leave a nigga." Hell naw!! Maybe I'm just overreacting to the whole thing. Let me just chill a second. Once David took his frustration down a level and continued to look for his friends. Sonora and her sister left with the three gorgeous ladies, that was at the booth together to have more and private fiesta time as women in packs. David doesn't know they already dodge on out about 45 minutes ago, while he was fantasizing about Brandy and the other two fine ladies. As the tension begins to build high into a migraine pain reaction. He decided to take a chance for another round, to stop thinking about his friends' where-bouts inside the Grown Folks. David knew he didn't need another round, as his head was bangin' to death sitting with his back turned watching the crowd and some more ladies.

After the bartender slid him another Long Island Tea for the final round. He tried to call Sonora Myers to death about ten times, back-to-back like an emergency call, desperate in need for help.

Chapter 28

The time continued to creep around David Dill's watch, once it became 1:50 a.m. pushing time. He really didn't want to call his mother, because David didn't want to disturb his mother's beauty sleep at this time of the morning. At this point. David didn't know what to do for a ride to get home on the west side of Atlanta. It was already too late to catch Marta for this in-particular hour. David was still trying to figure out, what happen to Sonora and Stacy stupid asses. He had to finger out, that. They left his punk ass at the club like a dirty trashy dog. He kept telling himself, it was time for another drink. Which, the last round should-have been the final call for pour David. The way the situation was going. The moment felt like he had just gotten exiled from his friends for leaving him stranded at the club forever. It ended up around 1:30 going on 2:00 o'clock a.m. getting later by the minute into his sleeping time for work. David begins to look madly crazy and stupid at the same time, like his girlfriend just broken-up with him in person. It even gotten so bad, that. David was getting turned down by several women that was passing his way on the regular. He was hoping for that, one woman would feel sorry for him and showed him some real love for his behalf. David wanted to, severely plot on some of these beautiful women into a conversation so smoothly, where. That way he can charm his loving words into their weak hearts for an enjoyable ride home with the hours that he has left right now. The plan that was supposedly created wasn't brilliant at all, in his drunken eyes. It was a total failure.

David's pockets started to get very low on cash for a cab to go home to on his empty budget of money. David Dill's only had five dollars left inside his beat-up old wallet. With that much money left he has. That wasn't enough for no cab, or no Long Island Tea, or anything. David just lucked out from both ends. The game was beginning to get interesting, as he tried to figure out how in-the-hell he was getting home from here. While David was drinking away the pain so vaguely. The time was 2:06 a.m. morning sharp at will. Damn!! "I'd can't believe this shit." It's 2:10 in the morning. It was just 2:06 about four minutes ago. "Wow." He said. As his thought mysteriously travel against the grain about walking the walk home at this occasion. The walk from Old National Highway to Atlanta on Martin Luther King Jr. Dr., on the hollow ground, where the hood guys lay and rest like dirty rats. Little did David didn't know. The club was going to be shutting down around 3:30 and some changes. Might-even go into a little overtime if David is lucky. His beverage in his glass was beginning to get very low towards the end. Which he didn't like at all. Most of the woman was leaving the club scene on a Friday morning, for the ones that were off today. At this point. David was losing a lot of sleep time, by lingering around the club like he's doing at the bar. The predicament that David was in made him wanna find the crackhead girl, and get his rocks knocked off again for the second round, one more time. When David finally finished his drink and headed towards the front. David didn't have any more encouragement to socialize with the other ladies that were standing around the table, and on the dance floor currently. As the moment continues to drift away from his consciousness, as he walks outside the parking lot with a peace sign into a deuce goodbye. He found a black snakeskin wallet owned by someone car and picked it up and saw $200 hundred dollars inside and ran for the border towards the hotel sweet by the freeway, passing the bridge by Kilroy's Package Store area.

Chapter 29

The pressure became very intense after the amazing rendezvous Sonora and her sister had last night into the morning hour. Sonora Myers' hangover became a major exhaustion, as she was on her way to work feeling powerless. After coming from Conyers and rushing to take her sister to work. Sonora didn't have time to stop by a convent store to grab her a cold Red Bull for energy. But, deep in her mind. Her body felt demolished and ran over while going to work rushing. While driving in the rush with the time 8:50 a.m. specifically. Merial decided to give Sonora a quick call while she was on her way to work immediately. How are you doing baby? Merial said. I'm doing fine Merial. Sonora was very surprised she called her on this road rage adventure that Sonora was in before going to work. I'm surprised you call me at a time like this. I'm 30 minutes late. Wow! Said Merial. You know when I left your house. I had to drop my sister off first before I went to work. I'm just using my sister's car, until I get mine out of the impound. It's been in the impound for two in-a-half days already Merial. I remember you were telling me about that last night when we were getting better acquainted. I know you were telling me about your second DUI you just got a few days ago. You might have to slow down just a little bit, because. You might in up with another

DUI on your record baby. After that slick remark Merial had given at the end of the sentence. Sonora laughed in the back of her mind just a little. But. At the same time. Sonora loved it, anyway, coming from her. Well... let me let you go, so you can get to work for today. Said Merial. Before I hand up. What are your plans for this evening, Ms. Sonora Myers? I'd don't know yet Merial. I'd have to see.

I think my so-called boyfriend is mad with me. He's been calling and texting me all last night to death. So. Let me go home and make it up to him for an hour or so, when I get off from work, okay. Please, do Ms. Sonora Myers. I want to see you tonight. I might let Brandy come over tonight and join us as well. That sounds cool. Sonora said. Once the sweet conversation ended up with a phone kiss. Sonora was beginning to have tripping spell, of what's about to happen within her mind body and soul type method. Sonora Myers couldn't believe she went through a sexual experience with another woman last night. Come to think of it: I made out with two women. "I be damn!" In that shocking moment. Sonora almost lost it, when she was about to swerve off the expressway into the bushes and trees. That's how bad her flashback was when it finally kicked in. Sonora decided to take another route, travelling 285 Bankhead Bolton Rd. on 70 to 41 towards Target store. Sonora couldn't wait any longer to put a-Red Bull energy inside her system. She told herself. *FUCK-It* about three times, heading towards forty-one straight shots. As Sonora was coming inside the Target parking lot, right in front. Where it said no parking. The store wasn't even open yet, as she continued to read the store hour on the window. Ten o'clock begins the time for Target to open-up, as Sonora was on rush mode on the run looking crazy and confused. The time became 9:09 a.m. on her schedule time. So, Sonora decided to travel farther on 41 to Walmart Supermarket store. Then, Sonora had to find another way to gravitate on some type of energy for her hangover delay, that was hovering over her head constantly.

As Sonora kept on 41 heading towards Walmart Supermarket. And then, she began to think about her baby Rico DL in her brain from last night until she got up this morning. She knows Rico is very upset with her so seriously in vain at her curb. Now. When she goes home today.

Sonora needs to endure in some makeup sex with her beloved man, soon to be her husband in the future. Sonora had to put some pep in her step, while running inside the Walmart store to get a Red Bull. The two black ladies that were standing on the floor by the entrance way. We're laughing at her, as she runs through the drink aisle and back at nine-fifteen. After the long line was over with a long with 11 people deep around 9:25 a.m. pushing time running out the entrance tripping over the silver track, while the door opens automatically, as you go into the draft that feels like a mirage of a ghost. Sonora left the parking lot burning rub like the *Ghost Rider* with high-itch frames coming out. Sonora became a high-speed demon on 41 rolling like, I don't know what-it-is about this Red Bull in her right hand? After she flew from 41 into 70 going towards the freeway heading to UPS. As Sonora was proceeding on with a fast and crazy route. She was beginning to text Rico on some love-feel-bad-shit. Before Sonora could type one letter on the touch screen. A state patrol was posted on the side of

70 drinking some hot coffee during the mix of sitting. By Sonora going about 75 per hour on the road. She in up panicking and dropping her phone on the gas pedal when she seen the state patrol with a suspended License on file. Immediately she reduces the speed down about 45 that was safe, so she doesn't get pulled over again. Sonora Myers almost had a major heart attack when she seen the state patrol sitting on the side examining. After that crazy panic attack, that makes the body shake from hand to toe like a retarded human being. It ended up being 9:50 a.m. when Sonora entered the building by heading towards the office to get some recovery time for the mind.

Chapter 30

During the love conversation with Rico DL and Sonora Myers, on some falling out romantic fussy mess. Sonora had to walk the floor for her daily rounds around the dock, and the assembly lines and trailers as well. She had to tell Rico I have to call you back later. There's an important emergency I need to tend to right away. Rico quickly hangs up with conviction and, in a jerkish way at Sonora Myers. Sonora didn't catch or comprehend how Rico just hung up the phone on her busy unconscious self. When Sonora put her cell phone in the back pocket, while walking towards the assembly line to help-out for a little while. That's when Sonora was separating the boxes and other weird items on the assembly line as well. She noticed in trailer five. The light was-just flashing like crazy inside with one man working. Sonora stormed into the trailer, like. Where is David Josh? I don't know Ms. Myers. I guess he didn't show up today. What! "What do you mean he didn't show up today." This is his trailer. As Sonora holds her breath and spit, during her composer at the same time mad. She just shook her head and left to call David immediately to see what happen with his ass. Sonora ran back into her office with rage and aggression as the phone rang about 11 times in her ear. "Why isn't this fool not answering his damn phone." He never missed a day in the two years since he's been here. As her two elbows were leaning on the desk, texting about 100 miles per hour with her back arched forward in pain and pressure. With the frustration going on inside her hangover mind. She was waiting on some feed-back from David, as Sonora sits back and procrastinate and wonder if David Dill's will return her phone call or text with urgency.

Sonora continues to wait about 10 more minutes in the back of her seat, with her hands and fingers collaborating-together like the *Godfather*. Her impatience became provoked quickly when she rose. Sonora decided to rush into the break room to buy her a Powerade out of the vending machine, for the dehydration effects that she was going through. By killing half of the blue distinctive flavor drink. Sonora rushed back to trailer 5 to help Josh out for 30 minutes to unclog the boxes from silver line.

Chapter 31

Rico DL just woke up from a two-hour nap that he had needed from his stress he was in daring with Sonora. At this point. Rico was trying to figure out what had happened that Thursday night with Sonora on his behalf. Rico DL went into a migraine state of mind about Sonora behavior and took him a big shot of good Whiskey to wake his self-up from that quick nap. The time went into 1:30 p.m. when he had checked his cell phone, if Sonora made any unnecessary stupid calls. Today was a good early Friday for Rico DL to get into something with a lovely sunny day outside with him and other people as well. Rico wanted to hang and lounge out there in the atmosphere sunlight into his cool self like he normally does, when he's in California doing him. Rico decided to chill out, and watch some television, while he waits for his pretty beloved to get home from work. Even-doe, he's still pissed-off with Sonora's action about last night. Rico knows he has one more day left, before he flies back to California to go home for six more mouths to see Sonora Myers again. Rico DL has a flight that leaves around 9:00 to 9:30 p.m. on schedule for Sunday. After Rico DL got off the phone with his dad about life and reality. Rico was in the mood for some Martin on BET around 2:00 o'clock on the dot head on. Rico couldn't find Martin on BET whatsoever during the period between 2:05 and 2:11 with the Comcast remote control. Rico took another Whiskey shot to the head while Sonora gave him a sweet text saying. I love you so much, pretty boy. I'll be home around 2:30 lover boy. After reading the text about three times in a row. He continued to watch more BET.

Rico DL decided not to text Sonora back in his TV time, during his convicting ways between him and her that night on Thursday. Rico begins thinking to himself, that. What kind of exercise is she going to come up with next when she gets home. The way Rico was feeling. He feels like he's married to the woman from some sort. He really doesn't want to say anything towards her when she walks in. "Not a damn word!" That's how well Rico wants to keep it, throughout this dark mystery he's going through. But. We all know. It's not going down like that in his behalf during his personality. It was already 3:01 p.m. in the afternoon, with the heat steadily rising in the nineties. Rico's heart begins to pump harder and harder, as his blood pressure was flowing through his chest to the cranium while manifesting in the seat recliner. Once Rico started to have a personal conversation within his conscious and self. He took the whole bottle of fifth and put it on the side of on the glass table and had a quick shot for redemption. Rico DL just chased down 3 more shots into his small throat as he continued watching BET on channel three twenty-nine in mad mode forever.

Chapter 32

The feeling felt like Black Friday after a Thanksgiving mega festival, at a dinner table when Sonora came from Churches Chicken on Riverdale Rd. during the cruise on her way home to Rico DL which she was very nerves with the three-piece box on her lap, feeling like a warm oven in between.

While Sonora continues to eat a piece of chicken while driving mode. Her mind just clicked suddenly before turning on Garden Walk Street. She just remembers she had to pick her sister up from work at 4:00 o'clock on her schedule. After she finished eating her crispy fried chicken, and text Stacy to let her know she is arriving soon. Sonora hesitated by texting Rico, that. She is on her way home to make up for lost time for Thursday night. But she didn't. So. Sonora just said. "The hell with it." And made an amongst U-turn in the middle of Riverdale Rd in front of the car dealership like a crazy fool. Luckily, Riverdale police didn't see her make that major U-turn in the middle of the street with lots of traffic. But-time Sonora gets home later-on tonight. Rico will be too heated-up like a flaming red devil from a hot lava pit. Sonora Myers knew she was in shit creek when she turned around and headed towards Downtown Peachtree to pick up her sister Stacy. She felt bad, but. Sonora just said, fuck-it!

And flew the coop passing the Elementary School towards QT gas station. The time became 3:25 p.m. on schedule on her pretty white iPhone sitting on the passenger seat like a human doll. Quickly, Sonora made an automatic phone call to Stacy, to see if she would be ready when she gets there at four. And tonight, as well. As the she-say she say was going on with Sonora and Stacy on the phone.

The traffic from Riverdale Rd; and, into the usedness, when it was jammed pack like hell, going 285-South passing Hapeville exit towards Jonesboro under bridge, where Rich-way Department store use to be back in the days in the 80s, that became a ghost town of lost spirits and lovable memories, when kids and families use to shop at back when.

Chapter 33

As the beautiful mild sunset and the evening continued to drizzle down slowly into the invisible skies. Sonora finally arrived at her destination at 4:03 p.m. school district like a cab driver with the windows down. After getting inside the vehicle and giving Sonora some knuckle dap like two hood homies from the street. They took off like Batman and Robin, into a new adventure for some bad kick-ass out there in the dark streets. After the what-ups and girly greetings from two sisters. Sonora begins to text Merial. Is-it on for today and night sister girl? As Sonora waits for Merial to reply-back on the humble note. Stacy smoothly asked Sonora, are we going into *chapter 2* tonight like Thursday as a group? Yes mama! Sonora said. As the conversation starts to get real fun and juicy like Thelma & Louise, in their independent journey as woman. Merial finally called back to Sonora's text about 20 minutes later, as Sonora and Stacy were laughing and having fun together through the ride of destiny. "What's up girl." Said Sonora. I'm glad you call me baby. What took you so long to call? I've been thinking about you all day in bed Sonora. Especially, that Thursday night, when me and my other girlfriends got with-you-all that lovable night. What's going on with you, Ms. Myers? Don't call me that, okay. You make it sound like you are trying to seduce me again. Like you did in the club. And, inside your lovable comfortable ride. Where are you now baby? Me and Stacy are riding hard in these streets right now. Before we drive down to Conyers. Sonora said. Stacy was hearing all the good conversation that Merial and her sister were marinating about, with a Colt 45 in her hand, in the passenger seat. Once things gotten prepare for this evening and tonight special occasion.

Sonora and Stacy didn't have to bring anything for the night special arrangement for the girls. I'm surprised you didn't bring your own stash sis. As Sonora reaches in the back to grab her favorite Brandy of Crown Royal, of fort get me not into Stacy face. "I know you sis." You always keep a stash on deck. Stacy said. Hell yeah! You know how I do. I'd have to have something to drink when I'd get off from work sis. "That's the way I roll." That sounds all cool and stuff, but. You might want to be careful sis. You already have a third DUI right now. "I don't want my shit to be impounded like yours." "You know what I'm saying." Said Stacy. Girl please! I'm not trying to get your raggedy piece-of-shit impounded. Trust me: you are good! That's what I'm afraid of Sonora. "That cap you just said. That's what I'm talking about! After Sonora said whatever towards her sister quickly with ambition and took-off fast into smoke. The two-blooded sister began to head towards Conyers into the south to hang out with her new friends Merial and Brandy. You are sure we don't have to bring anything for this night? No. We good sis. But. If you want to. We can stop by the store and grab something, as a back-up plan. Well... let's get off on Stockbridge at the local convenient store on the left. When they were getting off on Stockbridge, flowing through the green light, turning like Starsky & Hutch with a deep turn. They glide smoothly into the convenient store without shaking from both sides while in motion.

While Sonora was waiting for Stacy to come out quickly. It was a major wreck during the wait into her love making, directly to her Crown Royal so effectively. Police were everywhere on the scene of the accident very profusely insane. Sonora started saying damn about five times in a row, by looking at the crazy line inside the facility store. "Oh, hell raw!" "What the fuck is going on in there?" "Is-there getting rob or something." As she continued to look through the window with concern in her eyes.

The street disciple was really getting incessant and strange, through the previous accident that happened two weeks ago on Stockbridge. Sonora continues to look back and forth, in between Stacy and the accident that was in progress for ten minutes along the way at 5:03 p.m. on schedule. Or, hell naw! "The line still long," Sonora didn't want to get out the car at all in this crazy situation. It was messing with her drinking time in this dehydration moment. After slamming the door on the gray 4 door Volvo, running in. The convenient store went into a robbery crisis, as Sonora began to enter the store so harshly with an attitude. Before she knew it suddenly. A stick-up was in motion outta the blue randomly. Everyone had to face down, with their chest and stomach on the hard-dusty floor immediately. The white skinny man with the smelly black ski mask had the whole store on lock down, from back to front, the whole nine yard. While he had the pistol on a vertical level perfectly. The funk from his dirty black overalls was spreading love throughout the facility store eating some Lays original chips and a big 2-liter Sprite into the mix of the scene. Sonora had the glass door, barely crack and suspicious when she tried to go in on the rush trip. Lucky, the balmy white male didn't see Sonora with the crack door wide open without no visual contact while drinking the free Sprite. Stacy Myers was beginning to get very frightened upon the mystery that was mystic around the robbery that was going on. The skinny white man had to be carefully and cautious, during the parade of the officers that was conducting the accident across the street.

While the white man had everybody hostages into the store looking crazy and confused. One of the hostages, which was a dark skin Jamaican chic, started to get loud on the skinny white man, as he stares through the window for precaution. Louder and louder as her voice begins to rise travel like she about to sing.

The victim quickly turns around with the pistol and told her to shut the fuck up. "Before I blow your brains out." Ms. Jamaican. After she told the victim. "Why are you doing this." About five times in a row, outta control.

The white man said. "Look here lady!" "If you don't pipe down with your bullshit." I'll end you right now, *OKAY!* After ten minutes of going back and forth with one another. Three shots went off as progress in discretion.

Chapter 34

The sky ends up changing from blue to gray in the climate around the cemetery, as the rain begins to fall. Kimberly Myers was paying respect towards her beloved mother. Ms. Jacqueline A. Myers. As Kimberly watches her mother tombstone by standing so remorseful with tears dripping down her cheek slowly and tight while she holds her umbrella over her head, while the gray skies surfacing and hovered around her head. As Kimberly stands tall with her black leather riding boots, with the 6-inch hills looking like a large Russian Amazon stallion at the Ellenwood cemetery. Kimberly always kept herself very stylish and phenomena with the stamina physique. The ground was soaking and wet, as both knees marinated in between the grass and the squashy water, along with her dark gray outfit with the black and white scarf around her pretty neck. Kimberly was really missing her mother dearly in sorrow, as she rubbed on the front of the tombstone graffiti symbol, from born till death in her forever. Kimberly carefully placed the beautiful flowers in front of the love and memory of Jacqueline A. Myers family tree. Kimberly was telling her mother in spirit, that. I don't know what to do with my two sisters at this point. "I really don't." While Kimberly was rubbing the hard tombstone with her fragile hands and pretty nails in red. Mommy, I don't know what to do with that damn Sonora of a sister that I hate so much, mommy. "What do I need to do mommy?" "Give me a sign, or something mother." Please!!! Kimberly was tremendously begging for *God* grace to help her sister Sonora out this hell of a place in torment and sodomy. After so much grieving took place around her sorrow with her mother inside the cemetery. Kimberly had to retreat immediately from the falling rain that was making her blind around the angels of the gravesite.

Quickly, she gets a call from her husband, that was urgent for their family sake of theirs. "What's going on Chad?" We have some disturbing news about Kimmy J. "What do you mean?" Kimberly said. Kimmy J. ended up hurting her foot at school today. What! Don't worry baby. She's just doing fine. We're at the doctor's offices right now. What is the doctor saying Chad? Well... he just examined her foot thoroughly under investigation with his knowledge theoretical. Since this is her first experience of being hurt. The doctor says. She just has a bad sprained ankle ligament going on right now. But, right now, it's being stabilized in his medical room at this moment. "Really Chad!" "That's all the doctors had to say." It's being stabilized in his office. Yes honey. He said. "Why-you-just-now calling me Chad." "It's going on 7:00 o'clock right now." "Well Kimberly." Once I received an emergency phone call from her school. I'd, immediately – what the hell Chad! You supposed to call me when you gotten that call from her teacher Chad. Not assumed. Just before Chad could say anything else. Kimberly calmly hung up the phone in pure darkness out of nowhere in disrespect.

Chapter 35

As the dark night occurred into the King's family when Chad and his daughter Kimmy J. arrived around 8 p.m. at the King's residence as unusual. The Cobb County area looked as pretty and normal as it supports to be in this civilized county. When Chad was pulling in the driveway with his daughter Kimmy J. Kimberly was in the living room reading her Terry McMillan novel. How Stella got her groove back, chapter 10 on the page with her legs crossed. As Chad and his daughter were walking in the hallway into the living room. Kimberly conscious went into a major attitude towards her husband Chad, and that stupid doctor named Jeff. By interning the living room so calm and collected. Chad felt his wife's unpleasant vibe, when he began to approach her with a decent kiss on her cheek like he normally does when coming home from work. His wife wasn't having no kiss from Chad, what's-so-ever. That's how bad Kimberly attitude became upon her husband Chad's handsome personality. Chad tried his one more time kiss on sweet Kimberly cheek. She smoothly moved her head back gently. But. No sign of being a jerk at the time, as she normally does mentality. Hey honey, how are you doing? Trying another kiss for the fourth time again. After Kimmy gave her mother a big hug while limping towards her beloved mom. How does your foot feel honey? Said Kimberly. It feels okay mom; but. The doctor said I need to say off my foot for three days next week. On Monday, Tuesday, and Wednesday. And, come back on Thursday. Why some many days off? You already have the weekend off. Good grayish!! Kimberly said. "Why you have to say it like that Kimberly." "What I'd told you about calling me by my first name, smart girl." Mom. "You know I'm just fucking with you right." "I know you are." Said Kimberly.

"You need to watch your language young lady." You're not glow yet Kimmy J. You are only 16 years old. Even if you become my age in the future. In between the mother and daughter conversation. Chad wanted some cold V8 vegetable juice for his thirsty body in a glass and relax for the NBA game tonight. The V8 juice tasted like a cold Budweiser down his throat so quickly and fast. Kimberly didn't budge or move from her comfortable pink reading couch, for two more hours. While the daughter and wife were occupied in different areas in the house. His best buddy Alex from the job, decided to give him a call on some funny shit before the game. "What's up my dog?" Said Alex. What's up with you Alex? Nothing much big homie. You ready for the big game at 9 my dude? Said Alex. "Hell, yeah dog. Is the bet still on you made two weeks ago dog? "You damn right, big homie!" It is on and poppin'! Ay boy! I'm surprised you gave me those ten points in the first quarter of the game. Alex said. "You better be lucky you're my homeboy from around the way. "I wouldn't-non given you shit player." As Alex laughed in the background so harshly towards Chad. Alex took his 40 ounces of Mickey's and drank away the laughter, as the substance began to cool down his lungs for more liquid for beer. What 'cha going to do about tomorrow night's game big homie? Alex said. I don't know homie. What-you trying to put up homie? Said Chad. Well... how about $50 dollars on the game with the Hawks vs the Celtics. That's going to be a good-ass game tomorrow night big homie. I agree with you on that homie. Chad said. I know you are drinking good over there, big homie. I have some cold Corona's in the freezer ready to drink for this exciting game. "I tell you what." Want we switch up the bet just a little bit, for tomorrow's game Alex. "What 'cha-mean big homie?" How about, instead of using the money to bet on, for one another. Let's bet for beer for beer, you, and me homie. What 'cha-think? Said Chad. I don't know big homie. That sounds cool, but. That's not the way I bet big homie. "Why not?! "That sounds like a great idea Alex."

I think so big homie, 12 pack vs 12 pack, tomorrow night Alex. What's up! Man come on! I need that money-bet coming from you, big homie. "That's how I roll." Alex said. Damn!! That's how you are doing this situation homie. *(Wow!)* Chad said. You can grant me this wish for the very first time Alex. You know you want to honor this wish, big homie. But. This is a very good bet that I'm often to you bro. Just do it one time for me, big homie. Said Chad. "Oh, hell naw Chad!" I can't comprehend on that bet my friend. As Alex completely said-it about three times on the phone with madness in his eyes. Chad made another offer that he couldn't refuse on his behalf. How about. If I lose. I'll buy you two cases of Mickey's in your best entrance to cool out with. (Well...) As Alex was, really thinking hard in between his mind with the deal that Chad had presented with a perfect layout. Made it three cases, and we have a complete deal. "Damn-it-man." You want three cases. That's right big homie. I need mines! Alex said. Okay. That sounds like a good deal. "Let's go for three cases then." If you win. You get three cases from me. And... If I win. I got three cases as well big homie. Chad said out loudly. "Alright now." I'm only doing this-shit for you Chad. Chad King was proudly glad that his best buddy made the unusual bet that made perfectly for his homie Alex the man.

Chapter 36

The hot July was almost flawless around the surface around Riverdale premiere, at the level of 99 degrees with a high temperature during the heat wave. The day walker Draco Dawn was coming back from Best Buy on Mount Zion area, across the street from AMC movie theater at the hour of 7:25 p.m. time. Draco was telling himself. I can't believe I'd had sex with Dominic Walker at my house on the count. That didn't support to happen with the knowledge and ability as a man. I let *Devil* intervene my creativity down to my soul and my man hood with this black woman. The circumference of my boundary was tamped with inside my spirit as the day walker, that walked around the whole city in Riverdale. During the walk the walk home, crossing the street on the railroad tracks with lots of traffic involved. Sometimes the heavy traffic can be very hectic for a person that's trying to cross during the movement at velocity as vehicles are coming with speed and madness in the eyes. The law enforcement says. Theirs shouldn't be no Jay walking in pursue for a man or woman in high risk like moment like these. Once Draco Finally crossed the busy street in the South Lake Mall area. Mr. Dawn felt relief from the pressure that he had witnessed from cars and trucks, and other vehicles, for this unparticular occasion. Draco had on his black Dickie outfit for the very first time since he been walking around the whole Riverdale area for ten years straight. With the knowledge that Dominic knows about Draco's walking abilities that he shared with her. She thinks he's outta his damn mind for doing stunts like that, with a clean Mohawk just gotten polish earlier from the Barbershop. Draco wanted to cross over, in between Olive Garden, and an empty Ghost Town area that's really carp up on the concrete with old black oil, that been sitting for ages over the years.

While walking through the cracks on the concrete parking lot towards South Lake Mall. A security vehicle slowly rolled behind him like a suspicious nigga that was exposure all-of-a-sudden without Draco's knowledge at all on the blind side. His knowledge kept him aware of his surrounding as a powerful black man forever. But, in his mind and body. He couldn't keep his sexual desires intact. But, to him. The sex was good for 45 minutes in his territory from his house. While his thinking process was manifesting so globally when he walked inside the mall. Eight o'clock was the ring tone for him to exit the facility to dodge his way out as a timer within. Draco left his wooden stuff in between the brushes where the interest that you go in smoothly. Macy's became very packed with black and white woman in all department of the whole store. There were three nosey white women staring at Draco real heavily with their sneaky eyes like demons. It was like. They never seen a black knowledgeable man come inside Macy's department store with, such smooth and strive before. Draco had the walk as a gentleman coming inside Macy's through the other department store with other people shopping around. There were a lot of people walking around the mall with their kids, and husbands and wives holding hands in peace. As Draco walks cool with his hands inside his pocket, loving life with passion. Normally, when Draco prowls around each department store, while window shopping so smoothly. A crazy unpleasant premonition comes to mind, while walking. The mysterious difficult verb was hunting his soul outta nowhere, as traffic was nerve breaking through people by bumping arms. After the frustrating annoyance was over through his mind. He walks into the music shop with a glance of a breeze through the CD collection, of that good-ole feeling from the CD case that was slick and smooth at the same time. Draco loves going through the CD collecting of good music while his mind races through time and reality. After going through the jazz section with his cool hand during the finger work like legs.

Hip-Hop had his curiosity, as he goes through the rap collection with an appetite in good lyrical ability. The feeling was beginning to be neutral at the place that he switched himself around random people, as the force began to gravitate on his behalf. As the time was catching up with Draco at 8:15 p.m. as it was detected, into the ten seconds. Draco had forgotten what time the mall was supposed to close that quickly. By shaking his head to snap outta this zone, like having Old Timers into the brain. Draco's laughter was silent inside his body, during the walk to the next destination in the other department. Draco was extremely happy to purchase two Boogie Down Productions CDs in his white bag with a smooth light swing between his right finger of his joints. After going inside his favorite bookstore to glance through some pages for some good reading from a novel, that was so intelligent. An old white man with glasses down to the bridge of his noise was looking at Draco with a funny ignorant look behind the tall desk in position. The short stocky guy decided to leave his wooden desk to be sneaky and noisy behind Draco's back while he was reading a few pages like a deacon from the city of Mecca.

Chapter 37

The night was beginning to feel like Friday the 13th on a psychological conscious faith when Draco came out the front entrance through Macy's around 8:55 p.m. on the needle. Draco quickly grabbed his favorite staff in between the bushes to keep pushing up the road. Mr. Draco had a wonderful time strolling through the mall for the day. His mind was already made up for his next mission to travel too, as he kept walking up the hill. Draco always has the same schedule every time he leaves South Lake Mall to hike his self-up to Jr. Cricket restaurant bar to have a few drinks before he goes home for tonight. Draco Dawn was beginning to feel a little hesitant by going up there towards the Jr. Cricket restaurant, in Dominic's presented is aware around the bar. If she is. He doesn't want to be bothered by the night occasion when he gets there to have a casual drink as normal. His thinking process was gradually beginning to knock on his cranium, of what's going to happen next on his journey. Draco didn't want the frustration to build up in his mind for a blood clot reaction rapidly. It was five minutes till nine, as he was close towards the plaza where Jr. Cricket is in the area. His heart was pumping like a Greyhound on a track, almost at the finish line with aggression. A little rain starts to drizzle from the dark skies, like evil about to fall outta nowhere. As he finally entered the restaurant during a slow drought on this unusual night. Welcome back Mr. Dawn. Bob Stewart said. What's going on Bob? Nothing much Draco. You can see, it's kind of slow tonight, Draco. I see. Draco said. Maybe, it will pick up later tonight, Bob. Well... it's already 9:30 right now Mr. Dawn. So, I don't think so my friend. Once Bob brought Draco, another pitcher of Miller Lite to the counter with two cups filled up with cold brew in the mix.

They both toasted to each other with love, by bumping cups in the air of what a day they had as men. While Draco took his middle size cup and drink it with trust during his rejoice being a black man. The conversation was beginning to get so interesting, between bob and Draco. Channel 2 News was showing a short clip of a murder case that took place about three weeks ago at the 6043 Booking bar facility. The FBI and the police force were surrounded, nothing but police cars all over the building, and from the back of the place so deeply. The police and three more FBI agents swarmed around the dead body of George the dancer, inside the public restroom on the hard, crusty floor smelling awful like a dead animal. If people knew how George was so nice, and funny he was. His fan base would be sad and crying at the same time, throughout the whole city of Riverdale. The whole murder scene was so harsh, that. They had to go into a quick commercial break in a flash. Draco and Bob were moved by the situation that just happened on channel 2 News, just a while ago with George. "Damn." "That's fucked up." Draco said. I know, right. Said Bob. After they took another drink for sorrow towards George in R.I.P. Once the breaking News was finally over on the television. They continued with another conversation to get off that heartbreaking murder scene immediately. How was your exciting day in the world been, my friend? Said Bob. I had a good day today, Bob. You remember that woman that was here last time we were talking. Yeah! The one that was in all white. Yeah, I'd remember. Bob said. How did that go between you and her that night Draco? I see when you left. She left right behind you in a heartbeat to chase you down. Yeah. I know. Said Draco. When she caught me before I crossed the street into that horrible traffic. Immediately, Ms. Dominic gave me a ride to my house up the street. Once we arrived too my house to have a little mingle time. An unusual woman showed up at my house unexpected outta nowhere. Oh, really. As Bob begins to act suspicious about Draco's story towards the random woman that he speaks of.

You didn't get a good look at the woman Mr. Draco? No, I didn't Bob. It was too dark to describe her description in my mailbox through the window.

Our light on the pole went out about three years ago. Never been fixed since then. And then. We have a small cul-de-sac around our area Bob. It isn't much. But it is a little something better than nothing. Said Bob. So... what are you going to do about this woman you dealing with at this point? I don't know Bob. I really don't. I even had the audacity to have sex with the damn woman, early this morning. "Damn, Mr. Draco." You don't waste any time, now do you. That didn't support to happen Bob. Not like that my friend. You know how our hormones gets when we close to a woman. Yeah. I used to be like that when I was young in my days as a teen. Bob said. You were all over the place, ah? I guess you can say my friend. I was a helluva-teen, when it came down to good sex with different woman in the pass.

Chapter 38

As the Conye fragrance here was cruising through smoothly like ice with skates, throughout the subdivision around Merial sweet home, with the music coming straight out the sensational fragrant of strawberries, flowing from the inside and out, in such love as the party kept going for the ladies. It was more women than normally from last night, then it was into the masquerade, when the women gotten together the last time. As the casual lady's night continues with five more women involving with the get together. Sonora and Merial drift off into a more suitable place to smooch off on during the moment, just a while for five minutes in her bedroom bathroom with lots of kisses for foreplay. "It is a lot of women downstairs." Damn!! Sonora said. I know, right. As Merial was trying to be courteous towards Sonora Myers. Don't worry baby. I will-not let the other women get to you while we downstairs having fun. After saying thank you baby from Sonora with a big kiss on the cheek. They hurried, immediately downstairs holding hands, and broke away as soon as they reached the bottom steps like nothing happened. As the other women were jamming and dancing at the same time.

Sonora and Merial decided to join the movement of slow dancing with one another like a prom date in heaven for the very first time in a year I'm glad you are coming again to Sonora.

After Merial kissed Sonora on the lips like a thank you loving wife. The other woman was toasting their drinks up like it wasn't not tomorrow. As the other ladies were toasting too many glasses into the mist air. Sonora and Merial were blocking themselves from the dripping of the alcohol like rain coming from everywhere in the atmosphere living room. "Damn!" "What the fuck!!" Said Sonora. Don't worry about that baby. It's just a little wine drip, that's all Sonora.

I thought you love being wet with my exciting little piggy. "Whatever Merial." "Not no damn alcohol coming down like a fucken volcano on my face. The enthusiasm was coming upon Sonora Myers action during her attitude behavior about the falling substance of the wine coming into her eyes so severe. "Girl, what is wrong with you?" "You are so silly." Merial said. "You need to stop your mess sister girl." After rubbing Sonora face so gently with her soft pretty hands on both cheeks to smooth her down for the count to make her feel nice and secure with a fix. With 30 minutes into the game of dancing and laughing, and all the women just conversating together while standing and sitting with lies, drinking themselves too death in Merial's kingdom. At ten-forth-five p.m. into 15 minutes until 11:00 o'clock around the hollow nights during the party. Most of the intoxicated women were dancing like vampires from Folklore in the European, like they had blood in their glasses with a habitat from a blood bath. As Sonora was inside the bathroom handling her business like a grown ass man spitting out, large amount in turds from her behind like a New Year in January the 1st into a new resolution for release. Sonora cell phone was ringing so crazy on Merial's white cloth love seat, about 11 times like an emergency car accident in vain. Slowly, Merial peeked behind her shoulders for Sonora's black shallow from the marble white floors with her face stuck into the mirror with tears of wine drops sticking on her mean face that Merial loves so much, when she was so close of loving her, when the madness makes Merial so seductive in rage. While Sonora was inside the bathroom, still bullshitting with herself playing the make-up queen into the mirror, during the count of 1,2,3, Candyman, Candyman, Candyman in the movie scene. Merial was strolling through Sonora's phone to see who was buzzing the noisy cell like a hot-pussy-call that's not prohibited in parental advisory in content.

She noticed the name Rico kept popping up severely back-to-back. "Where the fuck is you Sonora." This is the second time you haven't been home in two days, girl. "What the fuck are you up to woman?" "This is some bullshit coming from you right now!"

As Merial continued to read deeply into the long text so seriously in good manner, as her legs were crossed with her back leaned comfortably in her white couch. She wanted to go even further into the sorrow text. But. Merial heard the smooth flushing from the toilet when Sonora began to slightly crack the door open. So, it was enough for Merial to put down Sonora's phone immediately. After tossing her cell phone so quickly on the right. Sonora Myers came out of the bathroom ten pounds lighter with a slow limp in her walking condition from her constipated experience. The music was turned down just a tab when Sonora took a drive over Merial's legs as a scared tactic outta nowhere, as Sonora's valve system started to decrease intensity when she felt love right next to her friend Merial for the second episode together during this night.

While the music was flowing rapidly with Pandora Streaming Music, that was expanding throughout the whole night having fun everywhere.

Sonora was being occupied with her friend Merial during the locking of the arms, that was connected into one another in bonding. Stacy gave her sister a hand signal for communication to come here immediately; as Stacy's frown increases more into anger with Sonora's procrastination in front of her sister like a form of disrespect in the face. Her sister Stacy gave Sonora the finger about four times in a row so viciously and deliberately in her eyes. When Sonora finally got up from Stacy's signal. Sonora physically rose with an attitude to see what-the-hell her sister wanted with her from the outside deck. I'll be right back Merial. "I'd have to see, what the fuck my sister wants with me, okay."

After giving Merial a shadow kiss into the air from Sonora's two fingers. Merial went and mingled with the other ladies in the dining room, while Sonora conversate with her sister Stacy in the dark. "What the hell do you want Stacy?!" "What's up sis?" Let me holler at you for a minute Sonora. What about your so-called boyfriend, that you have been talking about for the past two months in my ears. You haven't been home in a day in half Sonora. I know how you are Sonora when it comes down to certain men in your life.

You have one at your crib, right now worrying about your ass from last night sis. Stacy said. I'm surprised he hasn't called you yet. Since we been over here chilling.

Chapter 39

The time was 11:35 p.m. heading towards the midnight hour around the spiritual warfare into the wide street life around the dark hour, that separates the sounds from heaven and hell. The confrontation between Sonora and Stacy Myers was limited, when it came down to pour Rico that was born in rise in Los Angeles California, around the West Coast in the Pacific area.

Sonora wasn't feeling the conversation from her sister Stacy to a certain degree about, how she's doing to Rico while he's on his vacation to spend some quality time with the woman he loves so much in his heart for Sonora, his loving queen. "Girl." "You are funny as hell." You know I'm right about leaving that man at your place like that, all alone. Said Stacy. That man, probably at your apartment jacking his penis off, dreaming about your stupid ass. Pour Rico!

As Stacy was shaking her head with a glass of Patron in her hand. Fuck-you!! You-stupid! Sonora said. As they both laugh together with a smooth knuckle dap to each other as black sisters. You know, you are wrong-right. For saying that stupid shit to me. Said Sonora. "I'm-just-saying sis, with both arms in the air. Like how they were back in the street days, when they were club hopping around the major city of Atlanta. Playing that game with different men in the world.

"If you wanna play the game." "Play the damn game sis." "I'm not stopping you." "Do you little sis." "You're a grown ass woman Sonora." "Whatever you got going on, with this nigga name Rico. "So, be it." But.

The main thing you need to worry about is. The fuckin' law on your ass, right-about-now. You have a second DUI on your record at this point. "Take care that shit girl!" Before it takes care of you Sonora!

Sonora was looking very confused when Stacy began to drop that unusual knowledge into her sister's face with concern. Sonora was like. "BITCH PLEASE!" "I'm not listening to that bullshit coming from you sis." As her mind was wondering during her imagination extremely. Her line was like. "I hear you sis." "But." Your ass is crazy and ridiculous coming from your little mind. But. "I feel you girl, about me and Rico situation that's off balance. While they were hugging each other with sister hood in bond. Sonora was saying to herself. She knows I can't do that type of shit from her. Her silence kept her soul quiet in between the sweet hugs and kisses during the connection on the lovely deck, as the soft jams were playing through the house.

The two sisters were coming inside jamming together, after making peace with one another in the living room singing out loud. Merial gave Sonora her cell phone; to let her know she received a pleasant miss call from someone out the ordinary for some reason. Someone was trying to call you while you were talking to your sister on the back deck. Quickly Sonora took her phone away from Merial hand, as quick as possible to reach out, who-ever it was trying to call. Merial already knew Rico was texting and calling her at the same time when she presented Sonora the Apple phone. "Hey baby." "How you-been doing since I'd been gone my love?" "Not good!" He said. "Where the hell, have you been at last night and right now?" Well... A great emergency has- "You haven't come home at all last night when I was waiting on you so bad and romantically. "I know Rico baby, I know!" I will make it up to you when I get home later tonight. "Really Sonora." "You want me to believe that story coming from you."

"Listen to me Rico." I'm trying to tell you my emergency, why I'd haven't been home last night and right this moment. My mother is very sick at this serious time right now.

Rico DL was silence for a moment in his mind, as he felt sorrow and bad for Sonora his love, that was gone from last night, that supposed to be made up from Sonora's behalf of making him feel better as her woman towards the black man. That's all I was trying to tell you baby. Don't be mad with me Rico. I should've told you from the beginning when I got off that Thursday evening. "I am, so sorry baby for not coming home last night.

As Sonora was spilling her heart out towards Rico her darling. While the gullible was agreeing and coming out of Rico's pure heart, of-what Sonora was expecting from him at this very instinct. Rico was taking the bate like a damn fool, while Sonora was lying and laughing at the same time. With a smile that was embedded inside Rico DL humbleness. Stacy overheard the bullshit that was coming outta her sister mouth, that began with a lot of filth and ridiculous from Sonora. Stacy knew Sonora was lying like crazy in her evil spirit of a woman. After Stacy Myers got through shaking her head on her pathetic low-down sister. Sonora kept manipulating Rico's mind into a bad influence, of believing in her knowledge of trusting in me and my honesty and compassion for your woman. Her psychological was getting the best outta Rico DL mentality in his character through her intelligence. Once Rico submitted into his sorrow, by getting through his conscious. Rico wanted to know when she would be home during his taunting grace, by needing her love in his deepest existence. Sonora didn't want to come home, the way her mind was telling her. She really didn't. So, she had to tell him in her accommodating lie to keep him wishing with her seductive words. I'll be home around 1:00 o'clock a.m. baby. Is that alright with you, my love? "One o'clock." He said. But. He had to keep his humble composer within his love of his life, Sonora Myers. "Okay baby." I will see you soon, my future wife.

Chapter 40

Rico went too far within the language that he said with his unfaithful girlfriend that he so denial about what's she's doing to him, with this fake love she's creating. After the fake conversation was over on the phone. Rico DL fell in love again like he normally does when Sonora ticks him into her on word play for two years. Sonora was laughing her ass off, so severely just to entertain her conscious. "Why in the hell would you lie too that man like that?" As Stacy slaps Sonora on the lower arm towards the wrist that stings like a Bumblebee so hard. "Why did you do that?" "You almost knocked my phone off my damn hand heifer." Go-head-on-Sonora. "You know you were worried for that." "Whatever!" Sonora said. As they both laugh like they normally do on some unnecessary appropriate girly shit. The minds of Stacy and Sonora were beginning to be like Batman & Robin, as far as sticking together as blood sisters forever and on. Even doe. Stacy agrees with her older sister Kimberly about Sonora's attitude and getting caught-up in the system and the laws of nature and pain. Stacy begins to feel like, she's not being appreciated of what she's done to help her blood sister to keep herself out of the law for the second time for a stupid DUI she made again in her devilish ways as the evil force continue manifesting into the horrible ways of the (D.E.V.I.L.)

When the midnight hour was finally gone, like a smelly unpleasant grave site at 1:20 a.m. around the county of Conyers. Half of the disco fever ladies were already gone from Merial's home, about 30 minutes ago from the women that gotten together in the early time. While Stacy was entertaining Brandy and Kiana on the lovely deck. Sonora and Merial were beginning to marinate on some spicy and moisture love in the large bedroom.

But instead, they decided to have a serious deep conversation about the current DUI she has pinning now. So, with this DUI you have right now, you just gotten. What are your plans towards this mess you created? Said Merial. Well... You know, I'm already working with a company with UPS services. So, I'm bringing in some good income for myself as a lead manager for three in-a-half years right now.

As Sonora was breaking down her situation to Merial. The loud voice said. I have a good friend that I have been kickin' with, for two years, off and on you-know. "Really!" Merial said. Yes! That was the one that called me about an hour ago, when you gave me my phone. Oh... As Merial was getting curious and jealous at the same time. But, while Merial was in a delusional mental state of mind with Stoney. Merial knew that was Rico trying to contact Sonora about two hours ago, along with a serious text, into Sonora's where-a-bouts from last night calling. My friend Rico. "That's his name baby." It was pretty, repulsive how Sonora was disowning, and not acknowledging Rico is her boyfriend for two years, instead of a friend as she speaks of in front of Merial. So, this, so call friend of your name Rico. What's he like in your eyes? Well, he's a charming and pleasant man. "But, gullible as hell." "Why you make-it seen like he's stupid, or something." Sonora Myers had to laugh out loud at that comment that Merial said. "Why was that so funny?" Said Merial. "Girl..." "You are a fool and-a-trip, you know that." Merial was looking for puzzle in her frowned-up face when she pulled back quickly. "Why was that so funny?" Merial said. "I don't, but." "You are a fool baby!" As Sonora laugher begins to hype up even more insane during her giggling repeatedly. The only thing that Merial could do was. Whatever the situation in front of Sonora's cute face, that she truly loves so well with a big smile. Once things started to get down to business between Stoney and Merial with all the laughing coming from Sonora Myers. "Now."

Let's talk about this DUI case you got going on right now. I already told you about my financial status with my UPS job as a lead manager at this point. I make good money as a manager. I bring home eight-hundred dollars a week after taxes with a decent check with my salary I bring home. It's pretty good money towards my fine that's coming for me soon. I hate this situation I put myself into, but. It needs to be done after my court date on July 10th on a Tuesday morning around eight o'clock sharp. Are you ready for this court date, that's coming up in two months? Merial ask. "Hell naw!" "I hate courtrooms, and those high intelligent lawyers, and the whole facility of the law." The whole subject was making Merial nervous, but anxious to love and care for Sonora more than the way she dislikes the court system so hostility towards laws and Amendment of the United States of America. "Why you're looking at me like that?" Sonora said.

I just love watching you with such inspiration when you talk with aggression around people. Even doe, Merial was honestly humoring Stoney in her ghetto matter the way she talks with, such stupidity in her behavior. I have enough money to pay my way into society, as far as the law goes with my situation. But. I will accomplish this second DUI again Merial. "I promise you this." That sounds like a good deal Sonora. But. I have- "But check this out baby." I'm not going to use my cash to pay my fine, that's in progress right now. "What!" As Merial was very shell-shocked about Sonora's statement she made about paying her fine in a sneaky way with somebody else to pay the financial payment for Stoney's court cost. Well, I have a better idea for your situation, Sonora. "What ideal." She said. Just come-down Sonora. I will tell you. Whatever it is. My friend Rico will cover for me on my fine. You really do trust this Rico fella, don't you? Something like that. Sonora said. Merial knew that was Sonora, so called boyfriend down low by reading her text messages on Sonora Myers phone earlier that night manifesting.

Since I like you so much, Ms. Sonora Myers. Me, myself is going to pay your full fine when you go to court on the 10th of July. I will do that for you baby. Because I love you, Ms. Sonora Myers. I want you to be my friend and lover for the rest of my life, as your new girlfriend from now until infinity. Merial continues to hold her hand and face with two separate joins on two different body parts towards

Sonora love. While their hands join-together like they were praying to God forgiveness. I know you mean well Merial, but. Your generosity is good enough baby. As Sonora squeeze Merial hands so gently and tight with pressure into each other eyes. I got this baby. "You don't have to worry about me girl." This is going to be taking care of. Trust me! "I know you do." But! "I got this one." I have enough money to pay three fines in one lifetime in this beautiful world. "Damn!" "You make-it since like you're a millionaire or something." "Not yet." But getting close honey. Maybe in ten years. "I'll be a rich damn woman, along with Brandy and Kiana as well. "Wow." As Sonora appalled was getting the best outta her consciousness from the information that she received. Sonora was like: "Damn!" "Yeah, some rich bitches around this camp." "Sonora." Sometimes you can be ignorant when you speak without thinking. "Not to make you feel bad, honey." But. "Crazy as hell when words come out your mouth automatically. With both ladies laughing towards the comment that they made to one other during their girly dap like strong men playing. I have loved my occupation as a model for many years in the business. Let's just put our jokes to the side, right-about now and listen to what I have to say. As Merial holds Sonora hand so gently for some important information to secure her probation fine forever, by kissing her forehead as a curse for unity. The time became 3 a.m. so quickly with four woman that was left inside Merial's home. Brandy, Kiana, and Stacy were down on the third level of the basement watching an action movie of their favor from Merial's collection of DVD's and Blu-ray's in the large cabinet.

During the movie, Lords of the Rings was playing with the door shut tightly. The long negotiable compromise that Merial gave Sonora to stand by on her fine that's not forever in Ms. Myers case. Once Sonora took the offer so sweet and honest, with a check for five-grand in the prom of her hand. What Merial did not smartly realize by giving her that amount of money into a check, was. Merial was getting manipulated and taken advantage of at the same time, while dealing with a devilish woman like Sonora Myers. What Merial did not realize about her loving friend was that she cared for so much. Sonora is a low down, evil son-of-a-bitch type of individual that Merial is dealing with in this present crazy of a mind. Merial has no clue, or ideal of what she conducted and done about giving Sonora that type of money up front. No one will never give some one that much money in their lifetime; If-it's-a worthy type thing, as a good truly friend towards an emergency call, during a life-or-death situation. The time of the morning was beginning catch-up with the ladies in Merial's comfortable home around 10 minutes until 4 in the froggy morning. Sonora wanted to leave immediately, because of the check she received from Merial Miller for five-grand in Stoney possession. The money had Sonora mind wide open and very excited like a high blood pressure on dope. With that check folded in Sonora's pocket. She wanted to snatch Stacy and herself outta dodge like a bat with rockets coming from the back. So. "Sonora had to come-up with an ideal to play it off, like she wasn't too excited and pretend she still sorrow within her appearance." After hugging and giving Merial a thank you-big kiss on the cheek. She was telling Merial, it was time for her and Stacy to go home now and prepare for work in a couple of hours from now. Look at the time baby. "It's almost 5:00 o'clock, And." Me and Stacy needs to get going immediately. Before Sonora could walk away towards the front door. Merial grabbed Sonora's gentle hand and pulled her slowly to her and said.

"Don't go about four times into her eyes, so Merial could persuade Sonora's mind, body and soul, along with her consciousness within. "Don't leave Ms. Myers. Stay with me for the rest of the morning and the new day that's going to arrive." Said Merial. Before Stoney could say one word. Stacy was coming up the steps to tell her sister, we need to be going now. "I don't know about you sis." But. "I need to be leaving, so I can prepare for work at 8 a.m. sharp." "I'll be waiting inside the car sis." After seeing Stacy leaving out the front door of good riddance in Merial's dark mind. Merial didn't-to-much care about Stacy as much. Or, that stupid ass Rico Sonora, so-call a friend. "Which, Merial thinks it bullshit coming from Sonora's mouth that's suspect into her eyes as an older woman." If Merial wants this relationship to go into play in her favor.

She needs to take Sonora into her on wings as a loving wife to conquer in two weeks, as soon as possible with no patient around her circle. "And that's the type of woman Merial is with her personal relationships." This will be the 6th relationship she has been in in three years. The other five she has been on, was a waste of time and painful in the past. But, for some straight reason. Merial thinks Sonora is the one of the other five she has painfully been with. But the way the situation is going is from Sonora's world. Merial is up for a rule of wakening with Sonora Myers craziness that she is. Merial's blindness and weakness, dealing with Sonora's behalf, will get the best outta Merial's lush for Sonora with the curse and love she has. "You have two levels of possessed women that comes in different dimensional worlds in love, that's going to crash in vain and heartbreak. "Whatever happens in both lovers, during the course of the matter." "It's going to be a hellified collision for Merial behalf on her end. After Merial persuades Sonora to stay and spend the rest of the new day with Merial and miss a day of work, with Saturday and Sunday coming up for both couples. While Sonora was outside with her sister Stacy Myers.

Merial Kiana and Brandy was having a ritual, so-what type conversation as grown women during a solemn meeting with each other in a religious matter. The two blood sisters were having a verbal cat fight with one another, while the rain was coming down on Sonora, as she continues to stand and argue with her favorite sister to death like hood women in the deep south in the land of ATL.

As the rain was coming down so severely into the driveway with Sonora and Stacy in it. Merial and her two apprentices were watching the two preys go back and forth against each other in a pandemic way. "As Merial was loving that hood girly method shit from two personal blood rats." The three ladies were laughing their asses off like awesome professional women that gives great inspirational towards their spiritual colt. During the position, where they were standing with the window wide open, while the skits was spread open with blinds nearly crack for one eye to barely see for Merial and her friends. As the white blood sisters were in a copy-cat, white evolvement for Merial, Brandy and Kiana to join their women's colt as black women that needs to be trained under the high system for a light skinned woman with power over the chocolate black woman. After Stacy pulled off with such rage in her eyes like Carrie towards Sonora, her blood sister by burning rubber from the driveway still raining. Sonora came back inside the house all wet and frustrated with her sister Stacy. "Is everything okay with you and Stacy, Sonora?" "Like Merial gives-a-damn, or concern with Sonora's outburst towards her sister Stacy. "She doesn't even like her sister Stacy anyway." "Little does Sonora knows in Merial's mind."

"It's almost like." Merial and Sonora has the same mind frame exact approximately."

When Merial told Brandy to grab a dry towel for Sonora to dry off with. Merial had her arm around Sonora's shoulder for comfort, on a physical note. Merial right arm was getting wet. "Which, she didn't care anyway in the wet process." Once Kiana brought the towel that was achieved from Brandy with a fake concern. All the ladies were in a group hug, during the snuggle peaceful type, that was very commotional of love in the warm living room with serenity.

Chapter 41

After the rain desecrated around 7:15 a.m. with sleepy heads still resting during that time, as the sun begins to come out so brightly on the driveway, and sidewalk, that has a little crack in between the surface on the concrete ground that's down beneath the core.

When the sunshine hit inside the open window that was halfway crack with the black silky curtains on a Wayfair elegant type style. The sun bean was-just hitting Sonora on the four head so randomly in vain, when the time came around 12 noon on Merial's stove, after crooking Stoney some breakfasts in the kitchen. Sonora was feeling good in between the thick white covers, after popping her bones and toes at the same time during a major cramp in her symptom. By grabbing her thigh with both hands so tightly into a heavy grip. Merial came with a cheese omelet with French toast on a white dish for breakfast, to keep it sexy and romantic for her and Stoney. During this wonderful time of rejoicing on a good breakfast meal to start off into the morning. Merial seen the painful situation that Sonora was going through with her cramp, while coming outta the covers jumping around like a wide rabble. Merial had to stop Sonora from balancing all over the bedroom like a crazy bull, ready to hit anything. "Sonora, just com-down." "What's wrong baby?" "My leg is killing me baby." "I'd just caught a major cramp in my thigh that hurt like shit right now." After the pain went away intensively when she hit the floor. Quickly, Merial picked Sonora up slowly with both of her hands, underneath her armpits like a paramedic that's comfortable in her white silky panties, as she helps Sonora up from the floor.

Merial decided to pick Sonora up like a new wedded wife, just gotten married after the ceremony into the honeymoon, after seeing Sonora with no panties on. But the bra still on, just after being throwed on the bed half nude with Merial's strength like a man. Sonora Myers' leg and body were beginning to feel better after the terrible cramp she just went through about 10 minutes ago struggling. While Sonora had one hand on her sweaty four head, and her legs moving like a rhythm octopus all in the bed with her hairy vagina shining in Merial's eyes during the help, Sonora needs while Merial feeds her beloved. During the feeding, as her face looks at Stoney's tasty hot spot so clearly and nice with the cheese omelet between her lips with the fork. During the feeding process for some unparticular reason. Merial Miller placed the tray over Sonora's lap with white clovers, to cover Sonora's legs. So, no food drips wouldn't fall on Merial's pretty sheets and clovers for the feast she needs for energy and strength in today's adventure. The time was 12:30 noon, just flowing around the house like a dancing ghost letting Merial know, it's time to begin her day with Sonora and herself out there in the open world.

Merial was cutting a juicy grapefruit in half to put something in her belly to keep the carbs down for her nice shape as a modal. While stuffing her face with good grapefruit juice all over her lips, just eating wide and crazy on her white marble counter that she loves so eagerly in vain. Sonora was enjoying the tasty omelet inside her mouth, along with a piece of toast in the mix. As her nerves were beginning to build up inside Sonora's heart. Sonora mind was wondering if Rico mine've text or call for some strange reason. Her nerves started to pump up like a lite balloon inside while she grabbed her phone for some notification from Rico. When Sonora swipes her cell phone twice, to see if Rico text, or anything.

It was no word from Rico DL, like he never existed. Or no release information for Sonora, that Rico didn't respond at this moment during the disappointment from Sonora.

At this point. Sonora Myers is on a whole new level of moving on from Rico DL to Merial Miller for the upcoming new relationship towards the next chapter. She loves Rico DL dearly, for a man that can provide her needs and wants at the same time for Sonora's sake.

Finally, when Sonora finished her lovely breakfast that Merial prepared for her baby. Merial slightly came from behind, while Sonora had her back turned and scooped down in a stretching type of technique without getting the food tray off the bed. The scar from Merial's gentle smooth touch, with her arms around Sonora's waist. While her tongue tingling on Sonora's right ear for some more play time and inflation. "Woman." "What 'cha think you doing?" Sonora said in a soft loving voice After holding and caressing Sonora from behind. And saying into her ears. How should we start our day today, Ms. Sonora Myers? As Merial's sweet words were getting to Sonora's inside like butterflies, just gotten injected with a love position. We are going to start off with a fresh clean shower, just the two of us. And then. We are going to put on something very extraordinary for you and me. This is what I want you to wear, Ms. Sonora. As Merial laid down the outfit for Sonora to wear for the outside world. Ms. Sonora was flabbergasted in her eyes about the outfit that Merial presented in Sonora's presents on the unmade-up bed in her smiley face. Sonora was really pleased about the outfit that Merial laid out for her on the bed looking very cute for her size as a slim, 24-year-old. While vibing on the outfit. Merial was running a nice warm shower for her and Sonora big day out together. "Sonora couldn't believe how nice her short black boots, with the silver long tips were hanging on the leather with nice hills at the bottom."

As the white jeans catches Sonora's eyes in a daze, with the long black blouse that comes over the buttocks for the world to see as a stunning queen that lasts forever and ever in this loving quest.

Chapter 42

Throughout the hot shower that was beginning to levitate more and more, as the brown and redbone caress with one another in the see-through glass shower, as you walk towards the white marble, and the beige hard walls of love making. After 30 minutes of soap caressing towards each other during the warm shower-me-down clean water. Merial had the look of a beautiful kitten, while her wet tongue goes round her lips like a Marry-go-round at Sonora's behind and legs, while the wet water runs down her anker to feet into Merial eyes through the smear-glass door as her queen. As the time became 1:15 for both black queens, that was pulling out the garage in a turbo 2010 black Porsche with penny power included. Merial was always a fast in the furious type of fiend on the road as a stun driver. Once everything was in motion from leaving the residence in their fine convertible black Porsche in the wind heading towards the freeway in high gear. Sonora and Merial were dressed the same, but in different color outfits. Merial had on the white long blueish with tight blue jeans, along with her white boots just like her queen Sonora as well. During the song, the creep by TLC expanding through the atmosphere inside the convertible Porsche into a sound wave effect. Merial was shifting the six-speed gears in the black Porsche. You had four low-class hood brothers inside a cruising four-door brown Cadillac, low at the back going up and down in slow motion during a smooth sell right beside Merial on the expressway. As the two arrogant black dudes that had they head and one arm out the window with a 40 oz in their hand acting stupid and whistling.

"Look at those two hoodlums over their baby." Merial said. Yeah, I see them niggas over there. Said Sonora. Merial looks at Sonora from the right side with a smart remark. Those are your type of people, ha. As Merial laughed into a cute smile directly towards Sonora's face with her dark shades on looking fabulous. After Sonora gave Merial the middle finger, of saying, fuck-you! The other pair of shades are on the top flap where the mirror is. How does this look baby? Sonora said. "Looking like a true queen."

After Merial planted Sonora a fascinating kiss on the lips of being her sweet queen. The hoodlums were still trying to get Merial and Sonora attention regarding the speed Merial was in on purpose side. They were side by side next to each other going the same speed around 50 mile-per-hour neck to neck from the music blasting. Merial and Sonora began to participate in the kissing game towards the hoodlums inside the 79 Cadillac, with the hand signal at the woman on smooth control, playing the song. Pimp in my own rhyme, with the 40 oz in their hand just hanging out the window like fools. "That's what us hood niggas do in a high drunk pace." With all the unnecessary translations going on, during the sound language on the expressway. During this course of the high-speed escapade, that was driving this excitement for both drivers into the wind. Merial was playing mind games with her driving skulls at the four hoodlums that was driving the old beat-up Cadillac, that became a slight smokey from the pipes in the back of the car as an issue. As the side-by-side action continues to go into overtime for both Cadillac and the six-speed Porsche, that can process more speed than the old Cadillac automobile. "Her patience had enough of the bullshit from the smokey Cadillac next to her horse-power stick." Once all the horse playing was over with. Merial put the Porsche in high gear, along with the six speed real fast, and took-off like Merial had Nitrous coming from the back.

When they finally left the hoodlums from the back, by looking through the rearview mirror still smoking in the background like crazy. After laughing so hard with the ladies in the black Porsche. The four hoodlum guys end up getting pulled over by a state patrol for drinking and driving on the expressway passing South Lake Mall, and Morrow City as well. Merial wanted to get off on the South Lake exit before passing it like a speed racer. Especially, dealing with those hoodlums playing and stunt driving all over the freeway so foolishly. "Merial was damning herself three times during her mode of making a u turn on the freeway in her six speed Porsche in gear once more."

Chapter 43

As the climax was risen around the area of Tara Boulevard, with high paste traffic from everywhere, coming in or out. They were coming from the expressway from a high intolerance for speed. Merial Miller made a major right turn by the bridge towards Tara Boulevard, heading left by the traffic light. As Merial proceeded with caution through Dixon Dr. into Forest Park City to pick up Sonora's car from the impound. They finally approach the Forest Park impound from a nerve rush in Sonora's mind for a drink to celebrate getting her precious Lexus out the impound for two days so far. Before Sonora could realize the outside vision from the sun light. Sonora missed Draco's walk around the city life, passing the Insiute Lodge towards the car lot next to Burger King restaurant, heading to Forest Park Farmer Market, up by the bridge into Highway 85 in Riverdale. That's where Draco was heading as a peaceful walker from the last city of the angels. While processing on foot, coming from Forest Park City where all the cops hide like mice in between the cut and cracks of the building as they laugh. We are here my love. Merial said. After kissing each other and getting outta the car to handle their business to rescue Sonora's vehicle from the impound. The white lady that was behind the glass, became an issue with Sonora not having no license in her procession during the moment with all the badgering that was small, but not outta control. Stoney was trying to tell the lady. The court system took her license over a high-speed case, with a DUI as well.

It was hard to explain to the lady in perfect intelligent words, that make sense from a black woman's view to repeat herself five times over again.

When the situation started to get so deep between Sonora and the white lady. Merial wanted to but-in immediately and clash in on her behalf. But Sonora did not awl Merial to do so at this very minute from Ms. Myers. It was like! The hood almost came outta Sonora with vicious rage inside the impound. Merial was trying to get Sonora to be on a more professional level when it comes down to conducting business with facility people in cities. Sonora had to calm down just a little bit if she wants her precious ride back today. Merial gives Sonora some knowledge, how to be very perfect and direct with her words towards professional people of the way they mind works as human beings in the new era. It sucks how the world can make you think sometimes around the universe. Once the diva herself, Merial convince the white lady to release the Lexus in Sonora's possession with the keys. The white guy with the old beat-up red cap bought out the clean Lexus for Sonora and Merial with great surprise. The check for three-hundred dollars was nicely exchange when the white lady gave Sonora the receipt and the keys, on having a nice life.

"Heyyyyyyyy." As Sonora was waving the keys into Merial's face for fun and laughter. "Girl, give-me those damn keys." After horse playing and dancing around the Lexus like little girls at the playground. They both took off, burning rubber from the impound like drag racers from the parking lot. While Merial was behind Sonora, going past the Bank of America. Sonora had a little flashback of déjà vu in between the street, as she was slowing down passing the green light. Forest Park police were sitting on the side of the grave site, waiting for a bonus profit for a suspect speed demon to come by. During the drive.

Merial made an immediate call to Sonora to park the car somewhere, so they could ride out into the sunset to have a nice lunch together as girls, wilding out towards the world. During the course you are going through Main Street. Sonora wanted to stop by the convenience store on the right side, passing the old Volkswagen car shop with the music turned up parking in front of the store. Merial, was-like. "What the fuck." "What the hell is she doing?" Sonora rushed inside the liquor store to grab a pint of Crown Royal in the mix of driving to her apartment.

"Merial couldn't believe Sonora kept the car running, along with the rap music playing, so the whole area can feel the flow." There were only two cars in the parking lot.

Quickly Merial goes inside Sonora's Lexus to turn down the volume, because it was too loud, while disturbing the city of Forest Park. Sonora came towards the vehicle with both arms slinging like a fast windmill, ready to do the snake by entering the low sounds from the rhythm with a kiss. The tone was turned wide open. As the smelly breath came with a voice of disappointment in Merial's eyes in confrontation, by laughing at her girlfriend, saying you are stupid with the head shake. By grabbing the arm so hard, but elegant like a lady should be, and feel on the skin.

"They both was trippin' off the bullshit just happen with the liquor and loud music that was going into the situation, where Merial said." "What the hell were you doing?" But. I love you so much, with a kiss on the lips so gently. The hugging was over and done in a clean feel around Main Street, with all the loud music being turned down respectively. Merial had forgotten that Sonora had the pint of Crown Royal in her procession inside the Lexus with the music turned up again. As the tinted windows were looking sharp, but dirty from the inside or out.

Sonora Myers decided to make a call to Merial that instinct to go towards a carwash as soon as possible, for a good wash up on the Lexus. When Sonora and Merial were on Hwy 85 discussing if not, it-is a good ideal to wash her car right now on this enjoyable day together as boyfriend and girlfriend. Merial convicts Sonora to wash the car another time on her on schedule.

Draco Dawn was beginning to approach the green light, just before it turned red when Sonora came up-on the white walk line like a race driver, as Sonora and Draco look at one another with deep eye contact in the springtime.

Chapter 44

During the smooth and swift wind that was coasting between Sonora and Draco, with the temperature at 79 degrees, where Raceway gas station located at. The familiar look that Sonora saw from Draco's face and unform passing through Super-H Market. "What the hell!" I have seen that guy before. As Sonora mind started to reminisce back in time for the memory of Draco Dawn.

She passed her turn on Garden Walk, while thinking about the familiar of Mr. Draco. Sonora immediately had to text Merial while making a right turn so quickly at a red light. Merial text back, saying. "What the fuck Sonora!" "Where are you going?" "The loud music got you going, for some reason?" After that pissed-off text from Merial Miller. Sonora slowly turned down the volume inside her vehicle, to avoid any confrontation from the police for a loud audience in the area. After that last text from Merial about Sonora's loud sound from the background. Sonora became mad and anger with Merial's languages through the long text back and forth and the whole nine. Ms. Myers decided to brush her shoulders off with Merial's lecture about herself and the music. Sonora continued with speed and stupidity, as she hit the accelerator just a little bit with the window down as the left arm hangs out into the wind and atmosphere while laughing towards people that's walking or struggling to find a way for transportation.

The cruises through the right turning line, next to the Aldi store where Sonora made that deep turn on Garden Walk on the right so quickly. The gate, for some reason, was already open from both sides in or out for access to a random driver. Merial was telling herself on the mental tip. "These are some nice apartments." I'll-be-damn! "She has good toast, for a low budget classy woman." Not bad at all. Said Merial. Sonora and Merial had to park in the first section of the Garden Wood apartment for safe mature, away from Rico DLs appears. I had to park right here for my safety, away from Rico. I stay on the second section of the apartment on the other side. (OKAY!) "I like these." I wish I could go in with you for a few minutes baby. As Sonora leans on Merial so closely with each other arms in a loveable way against the Porsche, just watching the whole apartment complex like the blue ocean scene. A thought came across. We might want to leave right now Merial; because. Rico probably walking around the complex looking for me. "That's stupid." "Why-would-he do that?" Said Merial. "If he wants you so bad." "He'll put out a lost and found report on you." "Is-it that serious Sonora?" "Before we leave." You might want to leave that liquor bottle in your car for safe reason. A sack on the booty made Stoney butt string just a tringle for a cute move outta nowhere. After they drove away from the Garden Wood complex in high gear, going towards the left side on Riverdale Rd. to the right, heading and cruising on their destination to Cobb County in the Marietta area at 75 miles per-hour. Passing the Mc Donald's still on Riverdale, getting on the freeway straight shot towards Downtown Atlanta. They knew the ride was going to be adventures and outgoing with the conversable wide open like Outrun from Sega Genesis, as the hair and clothes blow into the smooth wind like a flowing kite. The coasting was going nicely as well into the diff from the feeling of spring under bridge as the Marta train sells to the next stop.

Merial driving stunt was beginning to look like a video game, passing all vehicles from side to side in sixth gear adrenaline in full suicide untempt. She was just switching gears to show off in front of Sonora her love in the black Porsche. Merial didn't see no state portal on site in her review mirror with dark shaves on her face, playing give it up by T.L.C. Sonora Myers was grooving as well with the clear sounds from the iPod that was connected to the stereo system.

The traffic around 3:10 in the early afternoon wasn't that busy at all, during the increase speed of 90 miles per-hour, just looking at the Varsity on the right. And the Aquarium on the left as well. Oooh... "Look at the Aquarium baby." Maybe we can go there one day.

"What you think?" As Sonora was talking through the music. Thinking that Merial wasn't listening at all with a smile, as her head turned to the left delivering Sonora a shadow kiss. Saying, I love you. After the invisible kiss was over with. The sunshine was still out for the out-going people that like traveling with their families and friends, or any culture around the world. Lenox mall was the destination they were heading for a romantic lunch together inside the restaurant. The time just hit 3:30 p.m. on the dot, as the parking lot was full of vehicles in the front by the side in the back, where the movie theater is located. Merial was going around the parking lot several times like she drives around in a cul-de-sac doing ticks. Merial does these stunts every time she comes to Lenox. "Damn bitch!" "How many times you're going to go-around this mothafucka?" After throwing the middle finger up towards Sonora's face as a joke. Her and Sonora bolt laughed at the same damn time, still going around circle like Mario Kat on Nintendo 64 racing. "Oh, shit." "That was fun." Merial had to laugh to herself, before getting out of the car. "Are you done having fun yet miss thing?" "Yes, I'm done for right now." I always do that when I arrive here at the mall for pedicure. "You are crazy Merial, you know that." "Yeah, I-know."

Merial had her arm around Sonora's shoulder, during the fast-paced walk with lots of stupid laughter everywhere, with the familiar that looks like Cara from the background, when Merial came in. It felt like a spotlight city, as the ladies were walking in with shive in everybody eyes, by coming in the building. "At this point." Merial was ready to shop for her and Sonora with the girly prissy moment. Sonora didn't have any problem with that method outta Merial's mouth inside Macy's department store. After spending an hour in a half in Macy's having fun. They decided to shop for some shoes in another department, while mingle in Macy's looking around talking girly mess and lies.

Chapter 45

As the wonderful traffic of people were coming in and out through Lenox mall like vehicles, that's outta control during Merial and Sonora's eyes. They were heading towards the food gallery on the bottom level in the middle, with such a crowd. Sonora and Merial decided to leave for a few minutes to put their bags inside the car, and rush back in line. The line was still full around 4:44 in the afternoon, waiting patiently. "Damn, it's a lot of motherfuckers around this line." "Damn!!" "Girl, you stupid! Merial said. "I'm-just-saying!" Sonora said. "What-the-fuck!" "Sonora, just com-down." Everything is going to be fine. "Just chill out, with the attitude girl. Which, Sonora had so quickly in her head turned right like a little piss-off girl. After having two more little girl attitude within the conscious. Sonora's psychological thinking became vicious, and emotional around Merial's circumference zone, while heading towards the eating table. The eating table around Sonora and Merial was making Sonora more angry and powerful like the Phoenix from the X-men. The whole surrounding was jammed pack down from the bottom level in the mall. If you were on the top level inside Lenox. The view was looking like a Braves Baseball Stadium from everybody's site. While feasting on the dish with the black, long chopsticks holding with finesse. The women crimson eyes were complex for 10 seconds, as the eyes was in a state of shock playing two dimensional roles, during the conversation that the beloved Merial and Sonora had from their vision that was combine once more. But a voice came across Sonora's complex so dark, but smoothly without the madness intervening the brown skin mind in her. Once the dimensional magical was zipped outta Sonora's mind from the voice and the food.

The reality came back into Sonora's eyes in 5 seconds when Merial kissed Sonora on the brown cheek by surprise. By snapping back into reality that instinct. It since like the pattern was familiar around Sonora's face and eyes, while she and Merial had a wonderful time elaborating about life. What do you think about the shopping spree experience we just did, my baby? Merial said. That was very sweet of you, Merial. "You didn't have to do that." As Sonora holds one hand on Merial's left hand for love. The mind from Sonora Myers thoughts was using Merial's shopping sprees towards her moment. By lying at the same time, once Sonora became hypnotized towards the five grand Merial had given her so quickly, with no strings attached. Sonora was ready to kick Merial to the curb, and window immediately without no boundaries as a no-good friend as a woman. Sonora was ready to go, during her exciting vibe that she was going through in her itching soul; as her symptom is to kill, psychotically when Merial decided to drift off into the restroom for some girly time while she remains on the cell phone with Brandy about New York's big event. That they need to tend on Wednesday for their next big extravaganza amazing tour. As Sonora was traveling back to her area of

Riverdale to see her baby Rico DL, that she truly misses, or hasn't seen in a couple of days. Sonora was rushing with a purpose on the expressway in the Range Rover at the speed of 95 miles per hour, passing the Dealt Airport to get off on Riverdale exit around 3:25 in the evening. No music was played during this weird moment that's going on. That's how bad she was trying to get home to Rico her love. The delusion was getting the best outta Sonora, along with her hangover she was experiencing with. During the journey. Her appetite was building up very rapidly. Mind body and soul type anger. She wanted to stop by the wing shack in the plaza, while she was waiting time at the red light, on the right side of Auto Zone Advance. Her thoughts on Rico DL, was heavily in love with him, as she was getting close to Garden Wood Apartments.

Little did Sonora knew. Rico DL was no longer there, no more. As Sonora mind forgotten that his flight was last night. A long with Merial as well. That's how denial Sonora's mind was at, during her hangover coming through the gate. As she was getting out the Range Rover with all-four windows down, running upstairs. Her neighbor male friend was trying to speak and wave towards Sonora, as she was rushing outta the vehicle. As the old G wonders what's going on with her. When Sonora finally gotten inside the apartment with shaky hands, after breaking the key with purpose, as the other half still suck inside the nob. Her voice was-just sounding off like crazy in the kitchen and the living room. And the bedroom that wasn't kept up nice. After realizing Rico was gone, and his appearance wasn't seen. She needed a cold one from the refrigerator. Nothing was inside the cool box for her dry soul. The only thing that was inside the refrigerator was three swigs of orange juice that she took and sat down on the couch and started thinking in an imbalance conscious. "As soon as she about to leave to get into some dumb shit." Stoney recognizes a one-page letter on the living room table, in front of her to read Rico DL's disappointment from Sonora Myers lies and deceit. As a low-light sonofabitch of a woman. As the situation is about to get real deeply before reading.

Sonora needed a drink badly for this occasion she was about to endure in the next dimension that's finned to happen soon. Her knowledge came to be realized. She didn't have any beer in the refrigerator during this chillin' time, that made Sonora go insane, so quickly in her mind. The only thing she had to do was. Kill the crave from her system. She decided to drink the unpurified water from the faucet inside an old Wendy's cup for the body. After Sonora sat back down to read. Sonora fever begin to rise quickly once her eyes hit the first draft during the reading.

The second draft had Sonora paralyzed from head to foot, as she gotten into the rhythm in deep Portree into the third draft of the letter. Her heart was happy, but sad in the mystery.

Rico DL:

Dear Sonora:

"I love you so much in my heart." I really do! I was hopping one day. We would've gotten married in the future. For you and me. That was the plan, Sonora my love. "It really was." I finger! once we gotten married in the love of paradise forever. We would've had kids in the mixed form in our love as husband

and wife, between our connection that I thought was true. I thought you were my true love Sonora Myers. We had been going back and front for two years with this madness of love, that wasn't real. "You never love me from the get-go with your ungratefulness' as a black woman. You have let me down for the 4th time, since I came down to see you from California to Georgia. I thought you and I were going to spend some great quality time with each other, while I was here in the land of ATL for one week. We spent some time, only three days. And we went out that day when I arrived at the airport, as you came and got me with that fake love you presented. Wednesday was the final time I saw you face to face that weird night. So... When I finally woke up from that weird moment last night, that was unbalance towards my situation. I felt like something happened between you and me. "Didn't understand it." But, weird. I got up around 1:31 p.m. that noon. And I noticed a curb cut was on my left side. That said. The Devil. And., I said to myself. "What the hell is going on here?" What-the-fuck! You were in the second quarter on your job site. I didn't bother you about the indict. But, had some concerns about the cut on my wise. So. When you didn't come home that Thursday night. My mind was panicking throughout my whole body, that night into the early morning rise.

I was waiting for you to come home, Sonora my love. To talk about this curb indented last night. When I finally conversed with you, while you were working. The situation was crazy and weird for me. When you gave me that promise from your voice to make-it up to me that Friday at noon. "I was done with you Sonora." So... This is the end of me, to you Sonora. I didn't text or call you for nothing. I was tired of all the excuses

from you. I didn't see you through the whole weekend at all.
"That's a damn same from you." You knew I was going back on
Sunday to California. As my flight left as scheduled at 10:00
p.m. on the double. So... This is forever indebted, your lover
boy. Rico DL. Your King.

After reading the letter with sorrow in her heart from
Rico DL, her future husband. Sonora stood up softly. And
ripped up the two-page letter, as the rips were coming down
on the table like snow fakes from the sky. Sonora was kind of
disappointed. But not really. By coming out the apartment
with a joke smile in disguise during her face expression
towards the Range Rover. Her next-door neighbor was
trying to get her attention, by yelling towards her from a
distance with concern. Sonora mind was at a depression
state. But not the pure body in mind. Sonora Myers was
sitting inside the Range Rover for 10 minutes. Just
reminiscing on some fake love shit, while playing with her
fingers so slowly. The crazy made her start to rise quickly, as
her mind begins to go back to the source of things. When
she left the complex to get load-it once more like last night.
Sonora decided to head towards her old spot, where George
was murdered that night in 6043 booking club on Hwy 85
frailty. Her mind was ready to get shuttered, once again like
last night, that became bad mayhem with the biker boy's
interruption. During the motion, by passing each apartment
on both sides going through Garden Walk towards the traffic
light. The hangover was decreasing thoroughly in her brain
wave as she basted that right on Hwy 85 passing the Raceway
heading to the club.

Sonora was, so outta her mind, that. She ended up crossing the grass to get to BP gas station for a cold beer for some revelation, as she drinks, which Sonora didn't give-a-damn about the illegal crossing through the grass on Hwy 85 in front of Holiday Inns. Throughout the sitting in the parking lot of 6043 behind the building. A strong smell was coming out of the black can from the 211. However, the time Sonora walked inside the joint with flames into her eyes when she seen Bob the 52 old bar-guy. Her happiness was glad to see him for some old catching-up, like always. Well-well-well! "Look what the devil dragged in." "Sonora said, right?" That's me! Sonora said. Have a seat, Ms. Sonora. "You look like shit!" I haven't seen you in a while. How-you-been? As he gave Sonora a cold one for a nice great welcome. When Sonora grabbed the cold Budweiser. After releasing her breather so smooth and com with pressure. She felt a little relief, as her body relaxed on the seat during the circumference of the buttocks. Before the conversation began to get interesting from Bod and Sonora. A flashback began to crawl around her head, as she leaned back against the seat, while taking a slip for dehydration. As Bod had his arms folded up on the counter, glued to Sonora's eyes. His mind started to wonder about the death of George, the 27-year-old? I need to tell you this, Ms. Lady. The last time you were here was that night. I found George in the restroom dead on the floor. Inside the stall, with his throat split wide open. And the weirdest thing I have ever seen. He had the word Devil cared on his forehead, as he lay in peace. As Sonora said, wow..., with her head down at the same time. She was feeling bad. But rejoice about the murder she conducted that night, but a victory in her behalf. What happens between you too, as yeah conversate, But. Not your type as a low-light man for some strange reason? "I'd don't know." Sonora said. He just wasn't the one for me. "I'm sorry he's dead." "That's awful for him." That's a shame! At this point. "Sonora didn't give a damn about his murder, or death in her mind."

She really didn't. As the night went on about George death, and question of what happen? The scene was drifting away by the minute like a mercy, that's leaving life during the moment in history. The music was playing beautifully in the background from Frank Sinatra's greatest hits around the club about 6:45 in the afternoon. As the street, cars, and people just everywhere in the area, along with Draco Dawn walking home to his craving for the rest of the night and beyond his loving days.

Sonora's New

Era

Of

Life

A New Beginning

Chapter 46

During this beautiful era of 2014 in January the 2nd flowing through the cold mouth for a new year. As the New Year party went down last night for the new wedding couple of Mr. and Mrs. DL Franklin family. As well as friends and co-workers all together like family tradition.

The New Year Eva party was spectacular that Rico and Sonora put together on December 31st that early night, as things began to get real cozy for the new married couple, that gotten married last year of May 2013 the wicked symbol of the year during the mathematics med Christ in human race. That was the year Sonora wanted to get married on. The wicked number in man kindled. Rico DL wanted to be on the date of May the 9th during the springtime of pure love. But Sonora wasn't having it on her calculation into numbers. They arguably went back and forth so viciously and cold herded about the schedule of the wedding date. As far as, who oversaw the verbal battle in the wedding date last year. The winner goes too. Mrs. Sonora Myers for the remarkable victory over Rico DL Franklin. Sonora didn't want to change her maiden name to Franklin, prior to the situation in hand, from the famous Rico DL Franklin. The third generation of his man hood, and the next four fathers in history. That's the reason why Sonora didn't want the last name from Rico DL. Because it's a horrible man to have in her behalf as a new wife. (No way!) She told her husband to be, that. My last name will remain Myers for life, until I die. "Where is my supper?" Sonora said. While Rico was still laying in the bed fully naked in between the covers with a happy face. With the second outrage from Sonora Myers about the damn supper towards Rico. He didn't hear a word Stoney had said while he was in *la-la land.* The love potion had Rico ruin mentally and crazy at the same time during the plot. "Where is my fuckin' supper at Negro, that I ask for. As her voice pounded his ears once more, that made him jump like a scared little boy outta the bed. He ran into the bathroom like a skinny-punk-girl towards Sonora's question to solve the answer about the liquor and supper once again. "What the hell was you doing, when I was calling you from the shower about five minutes ago?" "I was still struggling to get up baby." "That's bullshit Rico." "You heard me from the shower, goddammit!" "Next time I tell you to do something." "You better do-it, you punk." After saying yes mam, if-it-was his sweat mother from the soul still nude. Rico felt stupid and embarrass in front of his new wife with no balls as a man. After her disrespect towards her new husband Rico DL like a slave black man. Sonora walked pass Rico DL like he wasn't nothing, while she was naked and wet going into the bedroom to chill with her friend from today that was magnetic connection within one. The five minutes became undone of being in a trans from Sonora's devilish voice to make him feel a certain way during the vibe that was conducted. Rico decided to come out of the bathroom, after his wife left the bedroom in a powerful rush for today's enjoyment, as she levitated her mind into the outworld. Rico DL felt good about his week off from his job, while he was putting on his white tank-top with the gray Nike shorts, along with the long black strikes, and white dots inside the middle. Before he could feel good upon himself in conscious. That crazy voice attacks him again into his ear box once more. Sonora said. "When do you go back to work Mr.?" I need some time for myself in this nice new house you bought me last year. Rico heard that awful and unpleasant comment from his wife Sonora to make him sit like a baby puppy standing still. While peeking from the pretty hallway, to see if his wife was gone. Sonora was marinating in the kitchen drinking a nice cold Corona in memory of Merial matter, while pouring good beer on the wooden floor to remember the times.

Sonora was looking very pleasant, coming into the garage in her red long bouse with dark black jeans. A long with her flavor red stilettos as well. As the automatic garage came up slowly and smoothly. Here comes her 2013 Lexus pulling out so nicely into the sunshine around 2:00 o'clock p.m. ready to ride out for the world to see. When Sonora left her advantage being happy. Rico was glad. But, wondering what the hell she is planning this evening. Especially, the outfit she had on when his wife zoomed her ass up-outta here. After watching her leave, by closing the curtains, with a look of. "My wife just left!" "What the fuck is going on today?" "Do I have a sign on my forehead, that says. Disrespect Rico today. And make him feel like a puck of a man as his conscious was speaking on both sides of his ears like a ghost as a message.

Chapter 47

The evening was beginning to turn into night in four hours at about 8 p.m. during the flow of the atmosphere. The mall was about to close in 45 minutes, when Sonora came out the South Lake facility, at the same time when Draco came out behind Stoney in 15 seconds. Sonora didn't know the man she seen at the light three years ago, was the day-walker, Draco Dawn was behind her. Going the opposite direction towards the Olive Garden heading to Tara Boulevard, as he heads home for good. Before Sonora got herself inside the vehicle. She releases a text message from Antonia, around 8:38 p.m. on her new iPhone, that her husband brought last year in December. Immediately, Sonora called him back right away after the text relieved that instinct. What's going on baby? As he said-it in a smooth-tone deep voice like Barry white, the greatest of all times. Nothing much, baby. Sonora said. Just did a little bit of shopping for me and myself. Guess what. What... As he listens closely in the mist. I brought you a nice Nike outfit for your fine ass, baby. "You are going to love it, boo." "Oh, yeah." Antonia said. "What color?" "It's black boo." "Your flavor one." While she was being sweat towards her dark skin man from the future. Not only, I got you one. I brought me one as well, baby. "What color did you get Sonora?" "I'm not telling you nigga." You're going to be like that Sonora? Yes, I, am, Negro. "Okay, okay." He said. That's messed up, you had to do me that way girl. But. It's cool. I will, wait on that ass... girl. You don't have to tell me. Antonia said. As Sonora was apiol, so quietly. The question was like. What are you doing right now? Sonora baby? "I'm not doing shit..." What about your new husband, Mrs. Sonora Myers? What up...?

As his voice got deeper and deeper. What about my husband? You were at the wedding, last year on May the 13th on Friday. "Did it seen like I love him?" Sonora said. I don't want to answer Sonora. I know the answer to that. I was in the front aisle when you did your vows towards that stupid fool, Rico DL, of a sonofabitch dude. He's, a pussy to me. "He really is!" "As Antonia was going off on the young punk as he is." "Enough about that mothafucka." "What's up?" What about me and you tonight, Sonora? "How about-it?" I'm cool with that, boo. Sonora said. But right now. I'm at the parking lot at South Lake Mall, right now, baby. So... Let me get my thoughts together in my pretty shit! "You, sexy, chocolate-ass, nigga you." I will be right over. "You dark skin, mothafucka." I will be waiting for Sonora. After hearing that smooth baritone from the phone. She left the parking lot. Like-it-wasn't nothing in the world, but. Her on the planet she sees. During the hang-up time, while she was rolling to Collage Park area at 9:03 P.M. A lovely call from Rico DL. Her husband. Decided to give Sonora a buzz, from the man she truly doesn't love from her existence, at the very first time she met him in the beginning. Didn't like his energy from the get-go, as a strong man and a woman like a hermaphrodite with both sexes combined in the morality.

"Hey, baby." "What's up?" Sonora said. I'm just checking on your baby cakes. That's all! Rico said. What time are you coming home tonight baby? I will be home around 10:30, if it's okay with you, my good husband. After they got off the phone with each other. The lies and the deceit started again, once more on Sonora's end. The distance that Sonora was going. Wasn't that far from Union City. Where she and Rico are located now. A brand-new house, and everything. With the three-level high structure from the new couple. Collage Park was the destination Sonora was heading to see Antonia, her lover boy that she loves in the Old National area on Flat Shoals Rd. passing I-Hop restaurant. During the cruising through old National Hwy in her 2014 Lexus with the AC blowing so smoothly.

The night was dawning around 10:20 p.m., as Sonora was bursting a right by BP gas station, passing I-Hop to get to Antonia house around the block on Flat Shoals Rd. Sonora told her husband a lie from the rip, when Rico called her when she was in the parking lot at the mall. Sonora told her husband; she was going to be home around 10:30 tonight. But that wasn't the case in her mind. At about time Sonora arrived at Antonia's home. It was four old school vehicles on the hill of the driveway. Sonora had to park on the street by the mailbox. Because it wasn't room on the driveway for her. In the back of Sonora's mind. She was saying to herself. "This is some bullshit!" "I'm in the middle of the hood right now." As the bus, 189 flew by Stoney like the Final Destination scene with deep impact. A strange dude outta nowhere scared the living shit outta Stoney by the curb, and the mailbox in a state of fear. The strange dude that got off the Marta bus, gotten off too late in the hood around the dark area, where they will rob you if you-are a suspect from the dark straight. Sonora became scared towards the random dude that made a U-turn back to Old National Hwy to Kroger. After texting Antonia about 10 minute earlier, before the Marta bus scared Sonora half to death. The spooky word, boo that came like the heat wave in the back of Sonora's neck like a dragon. She was mad with Antonia for making that stupid mess in vain. "I'm sorry for doing that baby." As Antonia holds his baby from the back with love. After all that sample love-mess was over with into the darkness from the hood. They walked together holding hands and meeting the rest of the family as he introduced, while his mom, and his three brothers were playing spades on the table drinking Colt 45 in cans, and other things as well. Sonora was feeling some type of way about his living arrangements. Which, she thought it was his place for some strange reason. Antonia's mother owns the house. But, not on Antonia's behalf. The whole night was wick-it, and crazy around the family tree.

The whole night wasn't perfect for Sonora occasion on a bad night around 11 p.m. in the black neighborhood. Before the hour hits midnight around Old National black nation. As the lovers in the world started to acknowledge the frequencies that were penetrating their minds and body. Along with the data trying to finger out the equation of life from a black man, and black woman's DNA to find the path.

Chapter 48

The new day was beautiful when Draco Dawn just finish walking Ms. Pemberton Poodle, name Nookie around the cul-de-sac area. The time was 10:10 a.m. when Draco came back in from his exercise method for right now. After his 30 minutes of studying for the day. It was time for his journey walk for today as unusual, then any other day he walks. Draco decided to go into his garage to crank up his 69 Camaro for a few minutes to hear it warm up in his ears for good interest, every seven days, and so what. That's why he cranks his Camaro every time, to hear that great quality-sound that he likes in peace and serenity. If you look at it. It seems like it's crazy and weird in some people eyes in witnessing. When the Camaro drove Draco spirituality inside the clean hot rod. It was like everything was going so well. Until the hot rod lowed him into a big adventure on the road for five hours max. And. It felt wonderful throughout the moment of time. His mind was made up for the next journey for him and the Camaro during this adventure date as husband and wife. As the time became 11:30 a.m., when he came out the house to ride. Draco was suited up in his brown short-sheeve shirt, with the brown Dickie shorts and black high-tech boots. Along with his black socks to the shinbone. As he pulls away from inside the hot rod Camaro with smoke. Ms. Pemberton gave Draco a nice wave for his journey of good luck, for today's adventure. After waving back to Carrie Pemberton as he burns rubber from the driveway. Dominic flew pass Draco without knowing that he was inside the light brown Camaro by a blind spot. Once Draco was gone in his Camaro, heading-straight-through Tara Boulevard into Forest Park dead zone reality. Ms. Pemberton was looking at the strange woman.

Which was Dominic getting out of the car to see if Draco Dawn was home for now. As soon as Dominic turned around to see if someone was watching.

Ms. Pemberton was already inside her little home so peacefully and safe. Dominic was doing a ten time knock on the door for his love as a woman in need. She was sitting on his three-step concrete for five more minutes, if he was coming back before she leaves for today. Dominic didn't know Draco wasn't coming back now time soon with his Camaro. And, at this point. Draco was gone in his famous hot rod forever, until he came by for good. His appearance wanted to be seen until 12 midnight during rest of the day as process. After 12:07 noon came quick-then the eye for Dominic Walker. She left the scene with worry in her eyes, as Dominic made a major right like Draco Dawn did before Dominic came in. And... Ms. Walker went back home to her bad ass siblings that she's use to in her own small home that she rents for in the past ten years in vain and sorrow.

Chapter 49

As the evening turn pretty and magnificent around the skies of the heavens in McDonough Georgia from the beautiful winds, coming through Draco's hot rod in the leather seat of a peaceful man. The ride kelp him com and cool, away from the negative energy between the man woman and child; during the wicked ways from the (*DEVIL himself.*) "Draco was rolling like an insane phoenix on the expressway heading to Walmart shopping center straight on, and beyond. Draco loves traveling through cities and stores. No matter if-it's feet or wheels through psychological warfare, into his brain circuit chemistry. Stores was his thing that he indoor without the outside people in the world that's walking on earth as flesh human beings. The cruise continued into his hot rod experience, while the boot hits the accelerator with more speed and stamina on the road. The time was 1:30 p.m. during the daytime going towards McDonough Georgia and heading through many cities, and everything else he loves from the moment on. For some strange reason. The traffic became hideous around this time of the hour in the cold weather. It took 45 minutes for the traffic to die down in this cold season at 22 degrees. Crazy it might seem from Draco Dawn. He had bolt windows down inside of his Camaro. Feeling the freedom from life, which most people don't do in February that's cold. It was two couple inside a stunning ride, was living a prefect life that can't be tamed from a black male, and female that don't understand life with one other, if you go back into the beginning from the source. After the traffic decrease from the cold below temperature. Everything was rejoiced.

As the traffic was separated at 1:50 in the afternoon, things were selling down when Draco reached the exit to get off on 103 approximately. Draco was very happy to indoor the activity and adventure that he was about to witness right now. During the sitting and waiting. He wanted to get his personality together for the people inside Walmart facility, as the vibe pump like a heartbeat within. If he was an alcoholic rick, while sitting in his hot rod marinating. He'll be drinking like a fool in the mix of his Camaro leather as loves. Draco vibe was like the (G.O.D) of the universe, as he walks around the store with his beat-it cart; along with the bullshit-ass, twisted black wheels that was causing frustration in his thoughts and rhythm to avoid the bad Cancer from stress from the evil. With knowledge of self-looking at different characters in each person eyes as he pushes and walks to except the reality of the numerously income. Draco Dawn was in the store to look, and to shop if he wanted to, as his own boss. An old lady in an electrical smooth cart approaches Draco with questions and information around his circumference, as he stays focused of what he needs to do. The old black lady was confused about what she needed, as she delivered the question for Draco, to remind her during her old-times disease she has mentality, at the age of 62 years old, just powerless. "How are you doing mama?" "What seems to be the problem mama?" Um... "I'm trying to find the medicine section young man." Can you help me with this sir? Sure, mama. You go back to the front. Like, how you came in Ms. "Don't go out." Just go by the front where the McDonalds is located. You will notice all white capture in three aisles. After getting the needs and wants out the way from Walmart. A situation had broken out at the front entrance of the walkway doors. McDonald police assisted a seven-teenage old teen out the automatic doors to take him to jail for stealing food from Walmart and other things as well. When Draco seen the incident from his own eyes, as a black man. He said to himself. Without knowledge of self.

You are lost and unbalanced for life. After that the mess was over with. Draco was coming out of the store with two white bags in his hand around 3:02 p.m. in the cold. During his drive away inside his Camaro. Draco was looking for a place to think around the McDonald area for the rest of the day. So, he decided to go back to the South towards Clayton County area, to Union City for a lake to chill. Draco was rolling like Smokey the Brandan in his hot rod Camaro, just cruising smoothly in the wind. The speed was feeling so good to Draco hands and feet at this moment towards 138 to the lake. Mr. Draco had to slow down just a little bit. Before traffic starts to catch up with him on his bumper. It was already one vehicle in front of him, as he was getting out with the Walmart bag. He had his peanuts, and two Powerade of green flavor in his precession like a cold one. Draco was touring and going through bushes like a lost deer to look for some food to eat for the babies in the wild.

Once the struggle was over with into the woods. Draco seen paradise in front of him with the lake looking pretty, but ugly. It was a white guy with his son fishing together. While Draco was finding a spot to marinate his mind traveled through the fresh air during the feeling. Draco forgot to bring his book of knowledge on this prefect occasion to accumulate the mind body and life as Draco.

As the white man continues to look at Draco so strangely at a distance, wondering why he's not fishing as well? Draco knew he was being watch from the man faraway with the eyes like his son at the other end. Draco acknowledged the situation and kept doing like he always does when he's at peace in his zone. While meditating for 30 minutes and releasing some energy into the air of life. Draco persisted on being the *G.O.D* in conscious within the good of a superhero, vs the bad villain to any devilish acts in the universe that's trying to conquer the power in good men that's real.

Chapter 50

The power of knowledge was spreading around the un-pure lake of fifth, as Draco finally opened his eyes to continue his view of the black lake. The white man and his son decided to leave and drift off for today's fishing from the lake. Draco felt some type of bad energy from the white gentleman's eyes and body connection. And it wasn't good on his behalf. Draco Dawn was glad his appearance was gone from his site. He felt like the government was watching his moment like a clone, that the lab had created to spy on him like a drone from the lake. If that was the case with them. "So, be-it." "I don't give a damn." The conscious mind was totally free from his energy circle as the peaceful man within. After the spiritual site was done and finished, of what he had experienced.

Draco was feeling good about the nature of life. As he sits and wonders what's next in his reality check for himself? He was wondering, that. Life isn't a game, while thinking the moment is so cool for 30 minutes in your mind. "That's, bullshit in today's digital society." Draco was learning the knowledge of a lot of things in his circumference by watching the water go through rhythm, and smooth movement from his own eyes in the lake. Life before time had his mind going for two hours so deeply. That. He overstayed his welcome, by being spaced out, how reality works through creation. When it was time to drift off back into his Camaro for another adventure. It was time for some more revelation around the atmosphere of life through cities and people and different situations.

As Draco drifted off with a U-turn that was so dangerous, while the traffic was at high speed. The junk that was in the middle of the road was spitting like Ninja blades into the cold. Hitting random cars outta nowhere on 138 Rd. conjuration. You can say. The impact was cool from the wind and the surface. As the destination was looking so shell coming from 138 into Old National Hwy with no police in site. Traveling continued for Draco through Old National, heading across the bridge at the traffic light, where the Waffle House is located on the right. After the light change green immediately. Draco proceed with percussion straight ahead, up-around the loop. Making a quick right at the traffic light again. Once he started rolling again, after the light turned green five minutes ago. The cruise was cool passing through College Park station heading towards East Point area going 40 miles per-hour. Before his mind was clear. East Point police were behind Draco on the sneaky tip; just checking his information on his tag to see if he's perfect or negative with the red bream craning. The police officer wanted to stay on Draco's ass, as long as he can, before Draco reaches the West End district. Krispy Kreme donuts smelled tasty in the cold air, as Draco made a nice left turn by the West End mall. The police officer wasn't located in the review mirror, as Draco looks thoroughly twice with his vision. The light Camaro was looking very hot coming through the parking lot of the West End looking ready. While riding around in circles in the whole parking lot. Six older black brothers were staring at him and his hot rod with evil intention to steal his ride if necessary. By passing the six Negro with his clear eyes; and his arm out the window. Draco decided to change his rotation immediately. As the six men continued to stare in vain, as he went around one more time before he leaves out the parking lot. Mr. Dawn wasn't having that stare down, eye contact at all. Hell no!! The prophet of the black brother was wise, and observant about, what he-has seen from the niggas. His consciousness was telling himself.

He needs to change his thinking and come up with a different way of parking. But his mind was strong and wise to get that walking out his system to bounce his self for today. Once his mind was made up to get his walking in. His scene was amazing from a distance, as he turned deep on the left where club 559 used to be at back in the days in the nineties.

Draco was coming out of the Camaro like Shaft, ready for action from the West End station, walking away from the parking lot to walk the walk around the West End blocks. As his walk was coming across the street in front of Krispy Kreme to get four donuts for a snack or two. It was three-old-school cats between the age of 60- to 69-year-old, were dropping jewels and knowledge to the game on the sidewalk. Draco was alert from one of the old gees, that was dropping that science from head to toe. After a smile and grabbing a flesh gaze at the donut. He gave all three of the old gees some hard-rock dap for that good-clean knowledge he heard, before entering Krispy Kreme. The job was well done. After Draco walked around the whole block from the mall for an hour and a half, just before he went in to cool off for many seconds. He had to sit down for a breather and minutes to rest his strong legs that he has as a powerful walker as Draco. When the clouds begin to turn dark gray suddenly in the mist. Draco quickly went inside to enjoy some of that good AC as a chill mode session. That's when he accidentally bumps into Sonora Myers and Antonio, the smooth dark brother, as a side piece lover.

Chapter 51

The beautiful evening became very cold when Sonora and Antonio were making out in the back seat. One thing about having good sex into the back of the leather inside the car. Funk is very pleasant. And Sonora loves every moment of it. After that good loving from the back seat. Antonia felt like Rick Ross the Don, as he was driving Sonora's Lexus like a king.

The king in Antonio was making his way into the spot life into Sonora's evil world as the queen. Even doe. He was staying with his mother, and three brothers at a trashy home with many roaches. Which was totally disrespectful in Sonora's ware being as a woman. The time was 6:35 in the evening, when the lovers left the mall from the West End. Heading straight, underneath the bridge from the Marta train station, passing the Blue Flame at the traffic light, by turning on red where Stewart Avenue connects with a straight shot to Metropolitan where the Collage is located on the left. But, if you continue feather meeting Cleveland Avenue, towards the expressway, by traveling more to Old National Hwy where Antonio is from and the whole zone in ATL. The ride was flowing through the expressway so smoothly, passing the Delt Airport. As the thinking process begins in Sonora's mind. While reminiscing about Rico and

Merial's flight that Sunday night around ten or ten-thirty
from the ex-lovers three years ago in her mind. Her whole
body was folded up like a little girl, just been raped from
a man she loves from a bullshit club, like the Glown Forks
scenery. As my legs and arms were cross like a tight hug
looking out the window with bolt eyes, seeing trees passing
by every three seconds, as the vehicle goes faster each time.
Revelation was catching up to Stoney's evil ways inside her
soul, as she continued to hurt people in her next move.

She knew Rico and Antonio were next on her death
wish, as her vagina begins to vibrate so hard. Sonora had
that itch to kill right about now towards Antonia, as he
turns the sternwheel to make the suicide untempt to cash
into the sidewalk and the bushes on Flat Shoals Rd. where
houses are located from. "Girl, I thought you were sleep over
there in the passenger seat." "You thought wrong Negro." I
was just enjoying the ride, and the pretty trees I witnessed.
The zone had me going for a minute. It's amazing how your
mind wonders inside when self-draft separates sometimes.
Antonio was trying to figure out what the hell Sonora was
talking about outta the blue, from the air she breathes.
Before he could finger out the whole method she said. They
were already there at Antonio's house before he could figure
out what she was thinking about. Baby, do you want to come
in for a few minutes, to play around? He spoke. No! I need to
head back home right now. You know how my husband can
get sometimes. A nagging woman outta the blue! Because.
In a little while. Rico is going to be texting me like crazy.
"Which is stupid to me." I feel like. I shouldn't listen to him
at all. "I don't give a fuck, if he my husband or not." "I'm in

control of this bitch." I wish all woman was on my page in this world. Control all men from pass or present. "Because I love this controlling shit as a black woman." I'm going to be like this forever Antonio." A controlling bitch!! After that lecture from Sonora Myers. Antonio was like. I heard you baby. I really do. Antonia said. You need to do the research on a Taurus yourself. We are the most crazies mothafuckers of all times, like a vampire through a pedigree bloodline. And we are not going to stop until we rule the world. That's why most woman kill their husband outta random. Because they open their fucking-mouth too much. "And us woman, hate that shit." Most men would've consumed that. And got the hell on completely. "With a woman so crazy, in her on demise ways eternity." That's what most men would've said about Stoney's mental condition. But Antonia wasn't trying to hear that.

Matter fact: All Antonia wanted was the sexual desire from Sonora's body temporarily and throw her away at the end like trash. He knew connection wasn't there in his behalf, no matter if she was crazy or not. Like he gave-a-damn about love or Stoney. Witch, he really didn't! After they kissed each other, it was like nothing didn't matter. So, Sonora just drove off with a purpose in her on mission to get home and cuss her husband out in rage. As Rico just texted her a while ago with murder on her mind as Sonora Myers.

Chapter 52

As the rain was coming down to wash all the filth away from the dangerous streets of not understanding how life works through the mind. The time was 7:40 p.m. when Sonora got off on Union City exit to stop by the Shell station to grab her a cold 211for the brain. As she wonders and thinks, while she slips on the drink for some mind-blowing laughter. Eight-thirty was the time Sonora was halfway done with the cold beverage she had. Sonora told herself. As soon as she got home. She was going to start a verbal fight with Rico, just to begin with first. As the plot thickens to make night interesting. She knows, Rico is very gullible of being mutilated into his mind as a trapped man through generations. And, far as the second plot is to psychologically hit him on purpose to calls more friction between me and him, when I land home for tonight. They living argument was far away through the county, passing US Food facility with no bus route along the destination that's hollow. The way Sonora was traveling through the forest. It seems like a scary movie about the dark road around 9:03 p.m. approximate. As her crazy mind was wondering about another premonition killing streak. She wishes bolt, Rico and Antonio was inside the vehicle through the motion at this speed Sonora was in for the kill. So that way, she can throw bolt bodies out the wind, as cowardly men for bate for the wild. Her madness was starting to get outta control with the rage she already was building up for years to come. The demon in Stoney was ready to come out, as necessary as possible when the time was right. Sonora was so raged up that. She was coming through the dark road, going 98 miles per hour like her ex-lover Merial.

As she kept repeating herself, over-and-over-again inside her mind, to kill another black man that loves her; and take their physical form from their power through earth resistance for good. And that's what she wants from here on out. (*No more men!*) Sonora pulls inside the garage for good, making it safely from the home for tonight. Sonora was ready to physical fight with Rico that very instinct like an ignorant-stupid nigger in thick chain. And that's how she was going to threat the weak Rico DL as a black man. When the garage finally went down for tonight. A strange vehicle had been sitting on the curb for four hours, since 5:30 p.m. that evening. If you were outside by the cute yellow mailbox in the dark moment. "You would be like." Wow... "What the hell is going on over there?" The soundwave was off the chain inside the living room during the peaceful home of the residents of Sonora, and Rico DL present. The scene was like a HD moment from inside the house, to make you say damn in a heartbeat out loud significantly. As Sonora was throwing dishes at Rico like frisbees, as her right pinky was dripping in blood on the kitchen floor like Kool-Aid in between Rico's red eyes, like he's the devil himself for revenge. Sonora continues her control with her voice and hands. As she was cutting Rico's arm through thick flesh, just carving the word *Devil* on his manly arm, that was masculine at the age of 25 through a Scorpio that's deadly as a zodiac sign. So, Sonora fingered his tail that needed to be cut insanely and fast. After Sonora made some Posta Sause with his blood into the pot with smooth loving. She added some blood, as well from her DNA to add more flavor into the pot. As she laughs forever and more. After drugging her husband with pain and laying him to rest inside the bed with blood all over him, into the yellow tight covers of being seduced. Stoney was decorating the kitchen table for a romantic dinner for herself tonight, as a bloody feast with red wine. By fixing herself up in a yellow skirt with red hills, with no shower, that wasn't required. Blood was on the floor.

As she made a nice Lasagna dish on the wooden table for her bloody excitement at midnight. In the mist of sitting down so properly with a drip of blood dripping from her pinky finger on to the table. The ghostliness from the atmosphere was screaming to death, as Sonora continue to lick her pinky finger, before eating in piece. Rico was already out for the count before 10:00 o'clock, when she drugs him earlier during the day. After the bloody feast was done around eleven. Sonora decided to have a pleasant conversation with Antonio when she came home; and broke down everything what had happened to her and Rico. The situation was so cold-blooded, that. She invited Antonio to come and spend some more time once more.

Chapter 53

The rain was coming down heavenly when Sonora pulled up towards the Ellenwood cemetery in black. As she watches her older sister Kimberly stares deeply towards their mother's tombstone in the rain. The lighting was flashing like crazy from the background, as Sonora continued to sit inside her warm car honestly. Kimberly been standing in the rain for an hour with her black trench coat, and black umbrella over her head just missing mother to death. Sonora hasn't visited her mother's grave site since she passed away 20 years ago. It was a bad sorrow during that era when the death came for Jacqueline A. Myers for her evil discretion. It was 12:22 noon, as Kimberly continued to watch her mother's grave site. As Sonora said damn slowly and drove away peacefully in vain. Kimberly knew Sonora was staring from a distance, when she left slowly with Kimberly's wondering eyes, just watching her leave up the road like a coward. And Kimberly hates her for that. As Sonora was heading back towards Bouldercrest to Gresham Rd. and on. Rico mysteriously gave Sonora a call, while she was inside Bouldercrest Package Store to grab a fix for her drive quest back. "What's up Rico?" "What do you want?" As Rico became misunderstood why Sonora was talking to him like this with smart, hurtful words to kill any man spirit.

The question was. "Why is her voice tone being-so vicious towards me?" *Why?!* "It shouldn't-have-to be this way." Rico said. Stoney repeated herself again to Rico. "What the hell do you want Rico?" "I'm very busy." I just want to hear your voice baby, that's all. Rico said. "Make it quick." I'm just calling you, because. I want to know. "What happen last night?" When I woke up this morning.

I was feeling very sluggish and drained, by getting outta the bed. "Where were you this morning, Sonora?" I don't see you or know. If you were coming back home or what? "What's going on with you?" He asks. And then: I have another crab on my other arm. Which is weird to me. Well... Can we discuss this later Rico? Because I have some important business, I need to take care of it. As Sonora begins to hype up. Just before Rico could say anything else. A white Trans Am almost sideswipe Sonora on the expressway, going towards Candler Rd. exit. Sonora couldn't see the invisible driver, because the tinted windows were black like hollow night after Sonora shook the paranoia away. The Trans Am became impeccable flowing straight through Wesley Chapel exit and beyond the scene. After the pulse. Rico was calling Sonora's name in screaming rage, with his high-pitch tone on the phone. To make any woman wonder. His high pitch, womanly voice called Sonora's name about nine times. If the situation of Sonora became demolished in the background for good. But instead, she heard the horrible scream and giggled just a little bit in between. Rico kept calling his wife repeatedly. But no answer from her voice. While heading towards Wesley Chapel exit to get off and grab another drink. A second round was need-it throughout the pressure Sonora was going through with her beating chest that was going so fast from the white Trans Am. Sonora decided to pull over into the Shell Station parking lot, to go in and out the store. The situation took about seven minutes for her to come out during this weird delay of an unknown-attractive guy Sonora was talking to.

During the moment with the black gentlemen's number program in Sonora's iPhone. Sonora knew she wasn't-going to call him no time soon in the future as a premonition woman like her. As she drinks, and laughs at the gentlemen, that she'd played inside the store. The 40 oz of Bud Ice was tingling inside her throat in a cool sailing way down her beer gut tummy. The unknown gentlemen finally pulled away in his vehicle for good.

That's when Sonora stood back up from not being seen during this recovery. So, the black gentlemen wouldn't see Sonora in her Lexus just chillin' inside. While Sonora had the back seat lean back just a little bit thinking about last night. Rico gave his wife a, are you okay text out the blue. And Sonora didn't apply what-so-ever with her husband Rico. She finally forgotten about the sideswipe incident earlier on the expressway 45 minutes ago. As more texting information was coming across the screen. Antonio was calling in between the mix of the texting in perfect timing. "What's going on baby?" As he asks. How-you-doing! Sonora said. "I'm good girl." "Where's your husband at?" Is he around baby?" "Hell, naw boo!" I'm all-the-way in Wesley Chapel, slipping on a cold one. "Damn Sonora." I'm thinking, you at home doing you. But you way-over in Wesley Chapel. "What 'cha doing way-over there for,

woman?" "Just, mind your on-damn-business-Negro."
Sonora said. I'm-just-saying! If, our-your husband. "I'll put
your ass in check." After that outrage comment of a message
that clapped Sonora outta nowhere. Sonora smoothly stayed
com and change the subject like the ratchet woman that she
is with her voice, with everything else. "Hell!" "Since you
way over there, not doing shit." Let me meet you over there
on that side of town Stoney. "How about that." "That sounds
good baby." But... "I'd really can't." So, don't think I don't
want to see you, anything like that. I-just need to spend some
time with my punk ass husband for today. He doesn't go
back to work until next Monday. "And the day just Tuesday
too." "I be damn." Sonora said. "Let me just meet you right
quick." So, you can spend some time with your husband
tomorrow. "That would be best for me, to you. Antonio said.
"You really trying to persuade me, aren't you?" After Sonora
finally made her mind up, of going straight home to her
husband. Antonio felt some type of way during the pulse on
the phone. Before I let you go baby. I had a very good time
at your place last night. "I'd couldn't believe you let me come
to your house like that Sonora."

"I thought you was bullshitting with me or something."
"I will say baby." "That is a bad ass house you have Sonora."
The only problem I had getting over there was. The darkness
was getting the best outta me when I was trying to find your
house. The road was so complicated and dark. I started to
turn back and go home on your ass. "I was that close Sonora."
"But I didn't." I just kept on trying for that good love from
you baby. I'm glad you decided to recruit yourself to come
see me, Antonia. You didn't have to worry about anything,

while we were making out in the living room floor. Like I told you before, when you arrived over here last night. My husband was halfway dead on the queen size bed. Sounded to sleep for good.

Chapter 54

As the bruises and scars were over with, at last night there was a vicious scandal in Sonora's dangerous mind. Sonora Myers finally came home around 6:21 in the late afternoon. Rico was delighted to see his wife this evening occasion, for him and her on Tuesday. Their home was so beautiful inside and out, like her old friend Merial back in the day. Sonora complicated the ideal of Merial's vision since they brought the home last year. During the time they got married that same year in December. Everything was just totally white inside the three-level home from Sonora and Rico DL. Home is a gorgeous piece of work. When the construction workers were working on it for a while. The whole house is built with white smooth wood throughout the outside of the house. Even the automatic garage doors were white as well. Sonora wanted a three-door garage built in, instead of two during the creation. And, until this day. She's still mad with Rico DL. Since then. In her mind. She is going to continue to stay mad with Rico until the day he dies and beyond the next life. Rico was trying to tell his wife last year. They couldn't afford three garages. But Sonora wasn't trying to hear that from her husband back then. How did your day go honey bun? Rico said. It was alright, with the dragging voice from Sonora Myers. Did you visit your mother and sister this morning at the grave site? Yes, I was there this morning Rico. And guess who was there when I arrived. Who? He said. "My damn sister, Kimberly." What...! Rico was amazing that Kimberly was there on site. What did she say to you Sonora? "Nothing Rico." Because, when I finally pulled up to the cemetery. It begins to rain like crazy. Like hell and frog at the same time from a distance, as I relax in the A/C. "A/C."

Rico said. "Why you had the A/C on for?" "It's too cold for that, isn't-it." "Why you worry if I had the A/C on or not?" "That's my damn car." You know I like the A/C in the wintertime during January in this season. "I'm like Sub-Zero in this bitch." Like the character frozen from the MK in history. "Like I said." Until you stupidly interrupted the story line with me and my sister at the grave site. In the memory of Jacqueline A. Myers. And my blood sister Stacy Myers in these condolences of resting in peace. So, after the condolences were over with the mother and daughter passing forever. The R.I.P. was done with between Rico and Sonora's discretion that happen in today's confusion between Sonora and Kimberly at the land of the dead that's decade forever. What are we going to do for the rest of the night honey bun? "I don't know Negro." "Have some bloody Lasagna for our remedy dinner for tonight, Rico. "Is that what you want from me, you stupid so-of-a-bitch of a man, Rico DL.?" "Ha!!" "Is, this what you want Rico!!" "You tell me now Rico!" "As she slaps the silly outta his face for being a bitch ass. As the man that he, when Sonora's slap became demonize outta hell from her living soul as a black woman. She totally slaps the crazies towards her husband by grabbing his throat with her soft one hand outta nowhere on the sofa by the lamp. The ground was shaking with impact, as the bodies hit the floor like hard bricks when Sonora was scratching the mess outta Rico's chest with her fingernails that were sharp like a Hyena tooth through Rico's skin. Rico was fighting back with ambition in his heart like a scary little man with strength in his hands, to hold Sonora off from avoiding more scratches on his prefect chest as a good husband. But. Sonora kept coming at Rico with more vicious attacks, with a broken glass in her hand. Nothing but blood drips coming from her middle hand, that was sharp like a chef knife with rough edges from the groove. Blood was everywhere through the white carpet from Rico flesh in the rain.

She was so mad, that. Sonora was cutting Rico, for assuming he was looking at another woman in Little Caesars Pizza two years ago. That's how mad she was cutting. "The fight was so bad, that. They were totally nude, up-in-this-bitch from the living room, and the man cave to continue the catastrophe that's normal. They were flipping over tables and chairs in the dining room, that was peaceful and quiet. The rage in her was so incredible, that. The spitting became vicious and bad outta her mouth, when she was cussing Rico ass out, in face-to-face combat in her nakedness with blood. As the scene got worse. She was looking like, bloody Mary that's insane with blood coming from her eyes that can kill forever and ever. Once the incredible battle was finally over with Sonora and Rico throughout the whole house. They ended up looking like. Mr. and Mrs. Smith at the end of the devastating massacre.

The ambition of Sonora was very vague inside her evil soul, that was unbidden within unity that she loves. The table that became so sweet with decoration on the bloody wood with two plates at each end like king and queen. That's branded for life. As Sonora continues to drag Rico once more into the bedroom. She eases herself downstairs in the kitchen to pour some red wine to open her mind to serve two Lasagna dishes for her and herself with candles in the middle of the table, to enjoy the moment. She finishes one dish in 20 minutes at one end. And finish the other end in thirty. The ghost kiss she gave at the other end was crazy. But. Pleasing to Sonora's emotion. As she carries the glass candle walking with a decent smile in the air. Sonora left the table and went back upstairs to tuck Rico inside the bed with broken-up glass inside. Once she read Rico a vicious bedtime story from Stephen King's novel Carrie. Her thoughts were scary. But fulfill in her dark woman hood tales. As a movie came to mind around 9:09 p.m. in the woman's cave. The channel 2 News was broadcasting through the airwaves about David Dill's death, about three years ago at the 6840 club on Hwy 85 in Riverdale. The police and the FBI were alert.

As well, as the two detectives on the rampage at lodge. After one detective was serious about finding the suspect that did this horrific fatality in the men's restroom. Sonora turned the channel with an evil smile of, come and get me you-sonofabitch law enforcement, with two middle fingers in the air. By saying. "Fuck all cops, and FBI agent. "And that stupid ass mothafucka detective, who was talking on the News, with his white ass." As Sonora was thinking about her dead sister Stacy Myers with a tear and a smile with a celebration in her eyes. She decided to make a visit to the cemetery to show her bad condolences to her mother and blood sister with love. She put on her black Adidas jump suit with the Stand Smith in black as well with a six pack of Corona's in an ice red cooler. The clouds were looking like October on Halloween night. As Sonora pulls up on the windy tip of destruction. As she changes her Adidas into her black rubber boots for safe keeping. If the atmosphere decided to rain with vengeances in the sky. The retribution had Sonora ready for the deserved that her mother and sister needed for this walk occasion marathon. As she was walking like the undertaker, with her long black trench coat, with two candles, and a black umbrella that's collapsible around the hour. Sonora was sitting Indian style, with the hoodie over her head, praying to the devil in peace, love, and prosperity with two hands together in harmony. She took two beers from the cooler, and placed them in each tombstone of Jacqueline A. Myers, and Stacy Myers in front of the stone. Just, chilling and celebrating life for her loving family. After praying for all the dead souls in the cemetery with a cold Corona in the air. She felt like the bottle was a beautiful urn of preserving the dead into life in her moment of laughter. As Sonora poor's the substances over the tombstone with her love in vain one at a time for history rates in her mind. The rain smoothly moves in with small dips into the atmosphere, that was very eerie in the dark. By rubbing the tombstone of Jacqueline and Stacy one at a time with cool rubs.

The smooth pace from the clean rain was making all souls feel rejoice from the heavens above during the climax.

Once two candles were lit, from each tombstone in front of them. There were two black vehicles behind one another in the back of Sonora's car in a sequel precipitation. The dark side from Kimberly view, was raging inside her body to walk where Sonora was. While praying to the dead, and interrupt with a slap on the face. The other immortal person, that was a mystery in the random bunch was watching Sonora with their eyes too. As the random person steps out the vehicle in their rain gear with no umbrella. The person stares deeply behind the black car with their binoculars, just watching Sonora like crazy. As the heavy rain continues to fall with nice crease in the skies of blackness. The scene was too much to bear in Kimberly eyes. As the vehicle behind her started to make the situation nerve-racking on Kimberly's behalf, as she drives away into the puddy of water with a U-turn.

Chapter 55

As the continue of the rain deceased when Sonora gathered her belongings and stuffed them inside her truck of her car. The A/C from the temperature was making her body feel like a corpse into a cold box like a freezer. The shivers made Sonora turn to the right, by watching a random person outta nowhere in surprise with an umbrella in use. Wondering, who in the hell is out there at this time of night? The question remains, as Sonora drives off slowly, heading back to Union City territory in the East. When Sonora approaches the bridge on Bouldercrest Rd. at the red light. The vehicle that was at the cemetery was behind Sonora's bumper by an incense with their high beans on like a flashlight in disrespect in the background. Sonora was asking herself, that. "Who in the hell this car think they are having they're bright lights on me like that." As the frustration was getting the best outta Sonora's conscious at the red light for two minutes. So, she decided to pull off intensity at the red light without hesitation, heading towards 285 South on the expressway passing Moreland exit to Jonesboro. While rolling on the freeway with high-speed-intensity, playing her Hip-Hop rhythm inside. The same vehicle that was right behind her from Bouldercrest was on her freakin' tail like the police was chasing her without Sonora knowledge at all around 11:31 before midnight. Sonora was pissed-off, because. There wasn't any beer in her comfort zone in the passenger seat driving. Sonora didn't know the random driver was right behind her like that. "She really didn't." She wanted to stop immediately, on the side of the road, off from the expressway next to Hapeville exit. So, Sonora Myers decided in her mind to keep on the freeway, towards the Riverdale loop on the left half circle mile. Going straight on Hwy 85 to 6840 club. Sonora didn't feel like going home just yet.

The night was still young at the time of 11:50 p.m. with the lights still shining towards the red light. From Sonora's peripheral from a distance into the rearview mirror. The club looked like it was close from her eye site, when she made that quick U-turn on red as cars was coming straight at her with pressure. When she finally approaches the scene at the 6840 facilities. The club was shut down for personal crime reasons. For-least, six months straight. Until remodeling the whole building with no memory of the murder scene as scheduler. They had a picture of George Walls in front of the glass door. As well as the farewell words that were printed on the yellow sheet in small letters in black. Sonora was mad at the shut down for six months. As she rips down the picture of George Walls, along with the farewell letter as well. Before Sonora can head towards her vehicle for safe surrounding in the dark. A smooth swift detective came outta nowhere in front of Sonora with her hoodie on top of her head. "How are you doing sir."

"What brings you out this type of the night?" As the ball headed detective assumed it was a man in the dark gear, as a hood rat. "Hey!" "I'm talking to you Mr." Sonora kept walking towards her vehicle during the panic. Five Riverdale offices pulled in front of Sonora's vehicle with no hesitation with all bright lights in demand quickly. Sonora was like: what the hell is going on here?! "I'd didn't do shit." As she said. "Mama." "Step out of the vehicle, for me please." While Sonora was occupied with the police and detective Pete in the mix. The random suspect was watching from a distance in the parking lot of Super-H Market with binoculars, once more in black. When the suspect left the parking lot in high gear, passing the green light, and slowing down for a quick peek in the middle of the road for three seconds. And pull off, without the police knowing the black vehicle was there. The vehicle was gone like a ghost into the wind by the hotel next to the freeway to continue the mission. During the conversation with detective Pete in Sonora's vehicle, between him and her accuracy.

Pete left her with a question in mind, before leaving the parking lot for good. Are you sure you're telling me the truth about George Walls murder that night? I know you and him were having fun, with more drinks coming during the good conversation that had between you and Mr. Walls, and the bar tinter Bob Stewart. After being an-asshole from detective Pete about her two DUIs on record, by telling her have a nice night. Detective Pete told one of the officers to follow Mrs. Myers until his district was ended in his location for this morning early rise. Along the journey to Union City area. Sonora was mad as hell about the situation that came down from the closing of the club with the detective and the police. Once the district was over and done for the Riverdale police on 138 Jonesboro Rd. for Sonora Myers, during the midnight hour with detective Pete. "Sonora was glad the evil mad man was off her tail from Riverdale behind her in that 15 second time."

The coast was clear for Sonora Myers, as she pulled into the Raceway gas station in the Union City area. She parked right next to the air machine to check inside the truck for something to drink for the deep pressure she had been through on information that the detective wanted from Sonora Myers. Just her luck: she had two more Corona's inside the cool cooler, that was still cold from the temperature from the truck. Once Sonora opened the cold beverage in her procession too kill that instinct. Sonora had to kick back immediately, like she was at home with her toes out for air. And, had a wonderful time texting back and forth with her new lover-boy Antonio the man.

Chapter 56

When the new day arrived so beautifully, with the temperature at 22 degrees into a grayish atmosphere, with very cold dormant of life. That's when Kimberly gets up before Chad do in the morning. But, for some straight reason. Kimberly was still sleeping and snoring inside the comfortable bed as the queen to be. Kimberly decided to take two days off, Thursday and Friday, to else the mind and, other things. Chad was downstairs preparing breakfast for him and her, during this morning occasion. Chad took a one-day vacation for today. So, he can have three days off for this weekend with his wife. Kimmy J. was already in school before 9 a.m. on the dot. Chad became very happy it-was-just the two of them in the house all alone on a good Friday around 11:21 before noon. The king of the castle was working on breakfast for him and his wife for a good eating moment. Until Kimberly was reminiscing about last night's rendezvous from the grave site with her sister intervening at the cemetery like the gatekeeper from doom. Kimberly wasn't please about Sonora's visit from last night as blood sisters that, really hates one another to death that killed the family tree forever girls. The flashback came back once more; wishing she was in that moment in time during the rain falling while approaching her evil sister face to face. Just slapping the taste outta Sonora for all sins from Kimberly.

The car behind Kimberly prevented her from doing so, during the motion towards her feelings. Once Kimberly scrapped outta her daydream that she was going through that morning. Chad the man begins to call his wife Kimberly for the second time from the bedroom, while Kimberly, slowly gets out her comfortable bed with her night gear still on.

By coming down the steps so slowly, like she's experiencing a hangover with the girls from a club. His words came. "Hey, honey." How're you doing this morning? After he gives his wife a kiss on the lips. His voice said. "Sit down baby." And enjoy this breakfast that I made for us. The breakfast was lovely that Chad had made for Kimberly presented at the time she wasn't hungry during the moment. She didn't want to hurt her husband's feelings at this lovable memory that's happening in this degree of Kimberly. Are you okay over their honey? As he rubs her shoulders from top to elbow. All the way down towards her pretty hands to the grip muscle. She yelled out: "I'm fine Chad." "I'm-just pissed off with my, so-call sister of mine." I thought, you and your sister had patch things up between-you-to. Chad said. "Hell, no." "We're never going to patch things up, between me and this bitch!" KIMBERLY!!! "Why-would you say that towards your sister like that?" After Chad tied to com his wife down about her sister. Kimberly gave Chad a crazy look from hell, with a devilish expression, if she was her sister Sonora in an evil demeanor. Chad wasn't surprised by the face she was giving him, as he falls back, thinking about the next question that could be safe in his behalf in front of Kimberly. So, at this unparticular point of mind thinking. Chad had to use wisdom during this logic around his cleaver while eating. Let me ask you something. Chad said. What happened when you went to go see your mother and sister's grave site yesterday morning? As Chad holds his wife hand with a gentle touch. As he continues to say. And then! You left again last night, without saying anything to me. Or, where you were going. "Not saying you were cheating, or anything in that nature. But, just wondering? "I-haven't said nothing." "I was just waiting, if you were going to say anything to me Kimberly." Like today, of cause. I'm not mad with you. But... It was-just off bounce, that's all. As Chad continues to hold her hand once more, waiting for her to respond on Kimberly's terms. "You know why I'm so angry with my sister Chad." (*Why!*) He said. Because. "She didn't-even-wanna come to her on mother's funeral before our mother pass away into heaven or hell. The more she explains to her husband with tears coming from her eyes. The more the story begins to get deeper around the amazing tale, that Kimberly was telling to make Chad realize, Sonora is a sick person since we were little girls growing up.

Chapter 57

The situation became weird around the Cobb County area when Kimberly left again. After Chad wanted to continue this conversation with his wife about her and Sonora. Chad told Kimberly to hold on for a minute; so, she can com-down and take a good breather within the comber mines. Chad cell phone was ringing through the interruption, that him and his wife was having together as a cancers section. When he screamed out, by saying, hold on baby! Kimberly grabbed her beige trench coat from the hook and slipped on some tasty wine for the frustration for the matter. Bout time Chad was off the phone with his mother. Kimberly had already gone from the house. "Dammit he said out loud at the front door with his white tank-top and red poker dot pajamas with black on." After that scene was done between Kimberly by leaving. Chad was mad. But he knew, it was time for a big glass of cold Lemonade, along with his breakfast, that he made for him, and his wife Kimberly. Chad didn't want the food to get cold, or waste in his behalf. So, he decided to take her plate and combined it with he's in one big position altogether. After two minutes of warming up the bacon and eggs with cheese in grise into the mix. As channel 5 News begins to come on, for a recap from 12:00 o'clock noon an hour ago.

One-fifteen became the time to wonder and surface. When the News became the discussion about the murder of George Wallace three years back. Detective Pete was discussing about, reopening the investigation for 2014 this year. And. Detective Pete went on about sopping this massive murder case. No matter how long it will take to find this murder suspect. "I am on the case for the rest of the year and beyond.

That's when Chad turns off the TV from the wall, and call Kimberly to check on her. Hello, she said. "When are you honey?" "Are you okay out there Kimberly?" "Tell me something." Chad said. Don't worry Chad. I'm fine. I will be home in an hour before Kimmy J. comes home from school, Okay! Kimberly said. But. "Where are you?"

After repeating the question about four times through her ears. Kimberly heard the question. But pulse for ten minutes, on her way back to the cemetery, where she started from in the source. Well... If you must know. I'm going back to the cemetery to confront her. If she's out there in this mad rain. "Honey, I think you should turn back around and come home and finish our conversation we had before you left. "How'll about that honey." Chad said. "I'll be home in a little bit baby." "Just come down, okay." You know, I wanted to spend a quarter of the time with you earlier, on this good Friday we had off. Just before Chad could say anything else.

Kimberly immediately hung up the phone. As soon as she arrived on the scene at the grave site, watching Sonora from inside the car. The cold flow started to hit the surface around 2 p.m., as Kimberly steps outta her warm car to walk straight, where Sonora is standing directly in front of her sister, and mother's tombstone, right next to one another.

Two Corona's was enough for this rainy occasion for one more blood sister in the family tree. While Sonora gave her final farewell to her precious loving mother and sister.

Kimberly finally stepped up to the reaper of a sister, after five years since they saw each other back then. As the background was looking like the revolution of life, with heling winds, during the flashes of thunder, that was the color of thick yellow in orbit. Kimberly and Sonora had to overthrow each other's life, to bounce the moment, so one can go forward in the future; whatever it took as sisters from the blood. Hello Sonora.

As Kimberly walks up smoothly by her hateful of a sister. They bolts had strong umbrellas, that were black and very wide for rain. Would you like a cold beer sis? Said Sonora. Sure, sis. As Kimberly replies at her as well. I didn't bring a bottle opener with me. I might have one in the car. Let-me-see. As Sonora continued to look straight in between the wind and the rain. Kimberly knew Sonora was full of shit, within her soul. So, she opened the beer on the edge of Stacy's tombstone like Sonora did. They both were looking disturb, as strong sisters in a military stand, talking like grown women in the windy rain. Ask me this Sonora?! Why didn't-you come to your sister funeral two years ago, before the quarantine found the missing body in Conyers, in-between the bushes stabbed and raped? "I don't know Kimberly." Maybe, she was beginning to become you. When she realizes all the trouble, that I was getting into with my second DUI back then. And no one helped me back then. "That's bullshit, and you know-it." Kimberly said. Kimberly kept her straight face very well, and intact, as they continue talking straight-up and real. "Stacy did help you in your horrible, MESS..." She may not have the money to help you. But. She helped you Sonora. "And so did I" But. "It wasn't enough Kimberly." I needed more from my sister at that time. "I really did." So, she failed me. When Kimberly heard that worthless excuse outta Sonora's mouth, she turned her head slowly to the left. Kimberly wanted to slap the living taste outta her mouth. But she didn't. She just held her composer like the strong woman that she is. And, kept focus. You said no one helped you. Isn't that what you said. As Kimberly was speaking the truth towards Sonora's face with tone and facts. "I helped you Sonora." Because you were my blood sister. And, you said you were going to pay me back. Once I found you a job at UPS. And that was the deal. I took care of your first DUI with love and blood sweat. Especially, your fines, and everything else you did. Once I find you a job, that will be handed to you, automatically.

"You had forgotten about me, Sonora." You didn't keep your promise, like you-said-you would. You fail me! When I got into trouble with the law again. I call for your help Kimberly. You didn't return my calls, or-anything. I left you with all kinds of texts and voicemails on your phone. "You didn't want to help me at all. It was like! You erase me from existence as a good Kimberly, and-a-good-girl that was white. "That's not fair Sonora." It's not. So... If that's how you really feel. "So, be-it." "I love you Sonora." But. "Enough is enough." You're a selfish bitch!! "You know that!" "So, stop making excuses for yourself." You-really-do. You just use people. And mutilate for the good and bad to please the *devil*. And... I'm sick of it!! "And you need to stop Sonora."

While Sonora was holding all that aggressiveness, and information inside her devilish body with a smile. Sonora wanted more from her big sister, that was worth wild with vocabulary in words towards her, when they were kids as a smart ass. The verbal abuse kept flowing between Kimberly and Sonora in the dark mist of time, and beyond. You would think the massive ejaculation could've stopped between the two in round three at 3 p.m. through the light rain in vain. Like I told you Sonora. You don't give-a-damn about anything. You just think about yourself at this point in your life. That's the reason why I didn't help you with your second DUI. Because you didn't deliver it like you should, Sonora. "I wonder baby sis?" Who really belled you out from this one, Sonora? Or... did you rot in jail, like the rat that you are. Kimberly said. Sonora took the major hit from her sister, that came with a slap in the face into a visible-ghost-blow outta nowhere, after Sonora popped her stiff neck in humbleness. Well... If you must know, big sis. My husband belled me outta jail. And my friend. That I haven't seen in two years. Put up the five grand, to finish out my case for good. Um... I'm not surprised. My, unparticular little sister. Always find a way to get your ass outta trouble. "I'm impressed." I guess we bolt smart bitches! What 'cha you think? Kimberly said. "You know what Kimberly."

As Sonora and Kimberly look dead at one another, with vicious eye contact. "I hate you, Kimberly." "I really do." As far as mother goes. "I hate her too." "She always been your flavor daughter, over me bitch." But... That's okay. I can deal with that, big sis. That's the reason why, I'd didn't tin to our mother's funeral. She loves you more. "And she hated me." Mother looked out for your best instress, in your education through life. "She really has." "Isn't that something Kimberly." Last. But not least. My flavor blood sister, Stacy. She is just like me Kimberly. "Isn't worth shit." So. I'm glad she's gone. How about that for a reality check. Big sis. Since you put-it that way Sonora. I'll drink to that. Kimberly said. After it was all said and done. Kimberly slipped on the warm beer, and pure some love for her beloved mother and sister, of. I will see you soon, between heaven or hell. And hug and kisses her sister Sonora on the forehead for good riddance as a big sister during her final resting place into the rain, while Kimberly walks pass each tombstone, by touching it ready for the next life through the dark and the gatekeeper's arms forever.

Chapter 58

The hot July was rising some stream around the mist of the new summertime era, as happy people were playing in the middle of the park in Peachtree area. Where the Ambassador department is located at, from the Five Point station by the underground sound festivities. Draco Dawn was chilling and sitting cool with his new Dickie gear. That was all white from head to toe for a good look at the summertime weather. Draco was lean back on the beach with his old Walkman back in the days. That is played out in the 2000 era of new technology. DJ Jazzy Jeff and the Flesh Prince were inside Draco's Walkman. As the album, Homebase was-just kick-it through his eardrums, with the song. Summertime flows through his blood stream to make you dance outta control into the mix. Draco was drinking on a cool-smooth Bud Weiser during his zone, and relaxion, as the tone drifts into his ears. An older cat that was walking around in the park. Had an old school boom-box from the 80's, just jammin', as he made his way back around, where Draco was sitting cool with his drink living life. The boom-box was sounding so good, that. Mr. Draco in-up taking his headphones from his ears to get a better-quality sound from the radio. Which he didn't mine anyway to save his battery. So. When he takes the train, and the bus back home. That way, he'll have some music to listen to on the journey back to Riverdale, on Hwy 85 site. Draco was feeling the rhythm coming through the boom-box of Maze classic album. As one of the community services workers, was glad his last day became final towards the end that he been through. If you look at it: It was a long journey for the young black brother, that was caught up in the judicial system as black man. The older cat, that had worked for the Ambassador corporation wasn't making shit for a living, especially the whole team.

The poor brother said. While Draco overheard the young brother was getting diss from the older cat, and the dark skin chic, that was terrible looking like charcoal-stone working there as a slave cattle. She laughs, as the older cat told him. "He'll be back." Along with the frustration in his mind, that. Your own brothers and sisters, hate to see me come outta this legal system as a free man in the government plantation. The black young brother was furious with the Ambassador slave workers, that was in the same predicament as me. "You stupid mothafuckas!" Draco heard the young lad, from his spiritual useful reality. That's been misunderstood for years. I hear you, my brother. Draco said. Stay strong young blood. Everything is going to be alright. Stay away from those, miss led angry people that doesn't care about you, in this caught new world order. *My Brother!* You need to learn, knowledge of self. If you want to bounce the equation from the system. Stay wise my brother. Said Draco. So, don't worry about those worthless clowns, that's trying to put you down for the final last days that's coming. The reason why the older gentleman told you, you-will back. Because...

He knows, the more community service prophets there are. The lesser the prohibited pressure the workers have-to encounter into the hard labor for themselves to watch you make a fool outta yourself horribly. So, they can laugh all together in a happy slave-master demeanor. As the intervene between Draco and the young brother combine their vibe with strength and random for some straight reason. The combination was mint to happen in their collaboration with one another as wise men. As the wisdom continued to flow more with each other about the frustration just took place. The young brother wanted to go more in depth with Draco Dawn's philosophy method, during this deep game for sure. But he couldn't. Because the older cat needed his help for sure right away, through this assistant from the lost brother. Draco knew the older dude was feeling, and seeing the knowledge was being spread into the young brother's mind. So. At that point.

Draco was done with the whole situation, and the Ambassador mess. Draco left the outworld, from-such-of-a park without any understanding, why our culture acts so dumb, and miss led about the simple things in life. Some people are cruel and manipulative to one another, to get by to come up through deception. He was walking pass the Ambassador building very slowly with conviction in his eyes. As he heads towards the UNDERGROUND to walk around the scene like a tourist for the very first time in his life. The black brother like Draco became aware into the walk, underneath the UNDERGROUND, with exquisite eyes everywhere in detail. Draco eyes was amazed about the whole scene, that he hadn't seen in years, when he was in the Army fighting a war during the ten-year period. The more he was amazed. The more his eyes got bigger, as Draco kelp walking around the UNDERGROUND in motion. During the enjoyment from his site seeing. Draco ran into the younger brother once again, for the second time today. "What's going on, my young brother? We meet again, I see. "What's going on, Draco man?" As the young brother shook Mr. Draco hand so firmly. Before the conversation begins to get deeper once more. Draco turned around by addict. And, bumped into a dude with his wife. Which was Rico DL, and Sonora Myers out the ordinary on the shoulder. After saying, I'm sorry from Rico DL out the blue.

Draco said. It's okay my brother. Before Rico and Sonora can walk off for good. Rico realizes the young black brother, by his face expression, that was foramina back in the days in Los Angeles as dope boys in Lax. "Quincy." "Is that you dude?" Quincy took a pulse for a few seconds to process the memory of passing time. "What the fuck!" "What's up Rico." As they bolt bump shoulders like cool young boys back in the street. How have you been Quincy? I haven't seen you in years dude. What-have you been up to man? Man... As Quincy was trying to get his thoughts together for Rico.

Sonora was shocked by the collaboration that she was witnessing with Rico, and this random individual. Sonora wanted to interrupt the nonsense as she sees, to move on through the underground moment. But she held her madness within the surroundings of other people that was nosey and looking. While Rico and Quincy were catching up for old times' sake. Sonora began to look at Draco strongly in his eyes during the recognize. I know you from somewhere in time. As she wonders? The connection was tints between Sonora and Draco distance for one another. Before Sonora spoke to say hey towards Draco. Her tantrum was raging up so bearably. As she watches Rico from the side of her left eye, looking at her husband, and Quincy as they converse like family in the circle. My name is Draco. How are you? With a perlite welcome towards Sonora. "I'm doing good." What's your name? You call me Sonora. After they shook each other hand with an almost firm grip like two men. Sonora had her arms crossed, waiting for Rico to finish his conversation with Quincy. Another question popped up for Draco Dawn to answer Sonora Myers. I remembered seeing you three years ago, on Hwy 85 walking towards Raceway on foot with a mohawk. You had on, all brown Dickies on that hot day. Did you have some type of long wooden stick in your hand? Yes, I-surer did. How did you know that? Sonora is the name, right? Yes, it is. As she embraces her name with love. If he remembers her name or not, back then. I was the one with the silver Lexus, that had the music up loud with the windows down. Umm... I'm trying to think. Draco said. I don't know, Ms. Sonora. You said, about three years ago? Yes sir! "Damn." He said quicky. Three years ago, is a long time to remember. "I-know-right." Said Sonora. As they bolt laugh at the same time, during this Ackworth moment. If, I do remember. How can I reach you in the next dimension, of some sort, Sonora? As Draco was trying to be funny with Sonora as a joke. Well, here's my number. If you decide to remember out of the blue.

While Draco was smiling towards the situation. Sonora was trippin' for a moment at Draco. "Why you laugh?" Sonora said. "Sorry." "I didn't mean to laugh Sonora." But the whole thing was funny to me. "Don't mind me baby." "I'm just out here having fun. That's all. Who is your husband? No! "That's, just my dumb-ass brother." "He's no body!" She said. While Rico had his back turned, still talking to Quincy during the mix. Draco and Sonora, quicky exchanges numbers without Rico, even knowing what-was going on through the invisible transport, from phone to phone into the UNDERGROUND with digital flowing everywhere.

Chapter 59

As the Marta train was smoothly coursing through, different destination. Leaving from Oakland Station. Draco continued listening to Jazzy Jeff and the Fresh Prince, during his mentation mode throughout the ride. At 9:55 p.m. sharp. Sonora gave Draco a cool text, about the nice conversation they had with life and reality, and so-on. The text kind of hit home just a little bit in Draco's mind. As he pulses the Walkman when the train touch base at East Point Station, as some people were getting off, Draco removes his headset immediately, with no detraction while he texts Sonora back with his appreciation. With the knowledge Draco had as a black man. He wasn't big on cell phone as an old program for the present. Texting wasn't his thing at all. When Sonora texted back. The words were like. When can we meet again, like we did today? Draco was like wow! With a big surprise look on his face. His reply text became complex through the fingers, by saying. I don't know. What about Monday at eight p.m. sharp? Does that sound good to you Sonora? As he sent the flowing text back to Sonora Myers, when the train landed at College Park Station for his end of the stop. After saying okay to Draco's request from Sonora. The dark night had Draco paranoid from the dangerous street of evil as a strong man. The misted street had Draco driving again. When he got robbed that night on Flat Shoals, between Chase Dr. heading towards North Clayton High School to Riverdale Rd. and on. He remembered that actual day so cleanly, as Draco reminisced inside his hot rod Camaro. He still visions that moment, when the three young ignorant niggas came from behind, and snuff him outta nowhere in their black hoodies.

As Draco pushed down on the accelerator with more pressure, when he thinks back to how they came outta nowhere on him, at the time around 11:32 close to midnight robbing time. When Draco approaches Old National in the turning line on the left, on Flat Shoals Dr. where the magic happens that night. He put a sign into the deep ground that worded. Welcome to the Old National terror dome, in creepy writing into a graffiti format to make you turn back. By crossing the creepy sign that he had created in February the 14th on a Saturday night, during this same source in the beginning. He made a quick right on a dark street that led to the hollow grounds of the black villain. After putting on his black hoodie and black Dickie pants with his High-Tech boots, that's skinny to the black Negro's that robbed him. It was an adversary night for Draco with his Samurai Sword to slice anyone that stands in his way tonight. The sword was very sharp to decapitate for this deadly hour. As Draco sit Indian style with the sharp sword on his lap like a small baby with his eyes close marinating. The house behind him was burned on hollow grounds, as he sits on the gray and black ashes from hell during his smile into recovery. When Draco finally took off, by passing the Flat Shoals Park heading home. He felt sorrow about cutting the throw of Dominic

Walker friendship from his behalf by setting him up for the robbery on February 13th during that Friday night around 11:45 p.m. on black villain. After fingering out Dominic was the master mind behind all this mockery, with her side-kick Antonio. That's now in a wheelchair for life, through a shootout with a dude named little C from the Grown Forks club that midnight. It was one more suspect left, that was executed in the master mind alliance with Dominic. Draco mind was like Shaft, with the soundtrack in bedded through his thoughts of prowling into the city of Riverdale. Draco had to look from his rearview mirror for the police. To make sure he wasn't being followed back from an hour ago on Flat Shoals Rd. When he was meditating on the burned grounds from Old National terror dome.

Draco Dawn reached the street said Valley Hill, straight down to South Regional Hospital. That's when he receives a short text from Sonora Myers that said. I can't wait to see you on Monday night at 8 p.m. Draco. And she quoted. Your knowledge is my knowledge from the black sister of power.

Chapter 60

With the night is gone into the new Sunday morning blues between 6:00 to 6:30 in the a.m., while the birds are chirping and flies around the clean atmosphere skies of life; from cities, through trees and the whole land market that's free during the risen of the sun and the universal God energy. Sonora was already up, sitting on the deck drinking on a cold Corona-like hot coffee looking at green trees and nature. Sonora begins the process by texting Draco this time of the morning, with no patience around 6:45 A.M. Which was crazy on her end. Draco was still sheep when her texting started to get outta hand, in a sincere form from Ms. Sonora and Draco's gathering, that begins tomorrow night, around 8:00 o'clock sharp together. It was like she couldn't wait for this exciting day to happen with Draco and her on a strange Monday for a date. Which was weird. But, interesting in Sonora's mind, as well as Draco too. Around this time during 7:10 a.m. with the damping and dry moisture in the month of July. It was too warm for the robe Sonora had, that was so thick and light blue with the camouflage head scarf wrapped around her head like a skinny pirate for war. Her comfortable fluffy slippers were dirty, but still white as Sonora slid back into the cool A/C during the touring inside the home. Sonora was feeling pleased and comfortable, while sitting thinking about Draco on the court. Sonora didn't want to bother Draco once more. But... Her sadness and craziness didn't stop her from continuing her mission of texting Draco. Draco was Sonora's new chapter in the back of Sonora's mind to emasculate the knowledge more than ever from Draco. And can't wait to visit his kingdom for delicious knowledge from, Mr. Draco Dawn.

As Rico DL. was coming down the stairs, after an uncomfortable sleep in the bed. Rico noticed Sonora was lying on the couch with her sky-blue robe on, resting on her right side. Rico tiptoes towards Sonora's face to see her eye to eye real close like she's a lab experience as a dead corpse. While staring in between Sonora's eyes with stare repeatedly in vain, wondering what I'm dealing with as a husband? The way he continues watching Sonora from face up.

His mind wanted to choke the living daylight outta his wife for being the woman that she is. But still. His heart didn't allow him to do so. As he stares around the living room, at her with the half of Corona on the floor by the couch, as Sonora sleeps and lays. Rico went into the kitchen to grab him a cold one as well from the refrigerator. Once Rico eyes were glued through the kitchen window. His eyes started to travel, by looking at the trees, and everything that was moving from the ground down and up. Rico wishes things would get better between him and his wife, from the pass or present as he stands in the pretty window. When Sonora finally woke up from her sleep and dream. She quickly rose up thinking Rico was still standing in the kitchen with a Corona in his hand. As her mind begins to play tricks during the run upstairs to see if Rico is still in bed; and his body was. The movement sedated Sonora's mind just a bit, while clapping and laughing at will. In the mist of Rico still sleeping around 1:16 p.m. with his awful form from last night. Sonora decided to jump into the shower for a few minutes to feel clean and fresh.

When Quincy the kid was calling to see what-was up with Rico DL. Immediately. Sonora's wicket ways hung up on purpose. "And she didn't give a damn." But... She had another strange idea of manipulating once more. The kid, Quincy left a short text for Rico. *And said. Text me. Or just call me back homie.* And so. When Sonora read the text. She replied, like she was Rico on the touch screen. Sonora sent a text, saying. You think we can hang out for old times' sake? "What's up!" Sonora said. When Sonora got the okay from Quincy the kid.

The excitement was joyful around the table, as Sonora stood up to get ready for her date for this evening. While Sonora was upstairs taking a good shower and singing. Antonia once again gave Sonora a call for the fourth time all this week. Along with a short text as well in his heart. As Sonora gets out the shower around 2:18 p.m. staring at Rico to see if he was still sleeping into the covers at two-thirty. Once Sonora came down the steps with her dark-blue blouse, and tight blue jeans, along with her dark-blue Stilettos coming through the kitchen like a fly girl. Sonora looked through Rico phone again, to see if Quincy delivered a text once more. And the text said. That's cool and homey. Can you pick me up from East Point Station Rico? And Sonora replied. I got you kid. The way she texts that. Made it seem like he was a little boy or something. Even doe, in the back of her mind. Quincy really is.

Once everything was finalized with the time of 4:30 p.m. for the evening date. Quincy the kid was very pleased, and ready towards the end of the bargain. Little did Sonora knew. Quincy lives right behind the City Hall of East Point. Where the house is located from the back. His Grandmother stays two blocks down the street as a roommate for only temporary in Quincy case. The time was 3:20 around the evening time. As Sonora Myers flows through the house, writing stuff down that needs to be clean in each room. After Rico finally got up from his beauty sleep in dreams. The list was laid down smoothly, as Sonora drinks her Corona on the cool deck thinking through abysmal. The time was 3:30 on schedule when Sonora hauled her ass up the street frantically. Rico body was still tried around 4:15 p.m. from his overtime sleep looking crazy on the side of the bed. Rico DL. had to brush off the cobweb from his skinny body, as he stood up slowly. Rico kept wondering why he keeps getting up so late, so randomly? "What the hell is going on with me?" "And then, I still have the same cloths on from last night too." After he took off his black slacks and beige long sleeve shirt off at the time and jumped into shower.

Physically Rico DL. stands in between the warm water thinking if his wife is making him something wonderful to eat downstairs in the kitchen. Rico came down with his black tower around his wrist to see his loving wife, of, what are you cooking baby? But. That was only a visional dream in the back of his mind constipated.

Chapter 61

It was a pretty inspiration today around 4:40 in the afternoon waiting on Quincy the kid, and the color that stands out in red. Sonora was in a reverse preposition waiting on that red shirt to pop up any moment around her instinct. Quincy had to walk all the way up towards the train station on the other side, to make it seem like he was coming from inside the train station to meet Rico DL. When Sonora saw Quincy walking down just halfway on the sidewalk going in circles like he's confused, or something. Sonora had to come up with a plan to make it seem like she's a different species in Quincy's eyes for safe purposes on her behalf. Once Sonora fixed herself up in her gold long wig, and more makeup on her face. She had to move quickly to cross the street, while Quincy the kid was looking down at his phone attached, without seeing the dark blue image from Sonora's beige as she sat down quietly. Quincy didn't know Rico wife was watching him on the left-hand side by his shoulder during the laugher, while other people were walking in front of Sonora and Quincy during the text. His thoughts begin to wonder in his text. Are you coming my dude? Quincy said in his text. As Sonora replies like Rico on his cell phone, by hitting send. Quincy kept looking at the woman with the dark blue on, from the corner of his left eye. After receiving the okay from Rico's text. The false individual said. I'll be there in a minute. Everything was cool. Until Quincy kept looking at the woman with the long gold hair into the nice dark sleeves on her skin. As Quincy was waiting for Rico to arrive. Sonora walked past Quincy like it-wasn't nothing in the world to throw him off in his man image. And other many men that was watching as well.

Sonora chameleon had to back just a little bit during the six feet before she turned around to ask Quincy a question, as the games began in her soul and cranium. Sonora is the mind controller for all men that she controls, by tricking them, and thinking that they-are-right from bolt species formality, when it's not bounce from man and woman. "Hey?" "What's your name pretty boy?" Sonora said. But. It was only a vision in Quincy's mind at the time. As time rewind back for five seconds before he thought about when he seen Sonora leave from the bench earlier before she sat there. That's how his brainwave was working at the time, when Sonora started from the source as she walked past him for the first time, as he says hi. Is this East Point Station? As she voices it softly to him. Yeah... This is East Point Station, while trying to be cool, but sophisticated with no eye contact at her. Do you know a good restaurant around this area? She said. As Quincy thinks for four seconds of the question that was delivered in prefect form within the situation. No, not really. As the mind switches back into boy form. Not realizing the beauty had him tranquilize in his man state of mind. Before the body could drift off into the atmosphere. A voice marinated and said. "Hey?" "What's your name?" As his face expression makes him smile like a happy clown with the hood lean to the side like a Mime figure. As the question remains in the air. Sonora told Quincy, hold that thought. Merial just call me. As he said OKAY, with bolt hands combined with each other in complex form in a sweet 16 feeling. While the two random allies were having an incredible conversation with one another. A straight person, that was in front of the Trans Am was watching Sonora in their all-deep black outfit, in light shades on spying on the suspect with detail. This suspect has been watching Sonora since January in the beginning of the New Year during the wintertime warfare.

While the individual drives off slowly watching Sonora and some stupid kid in their rearview mirror in the evening sunset close to 1 P.M. Sonora and Quincy were talking for a long time on the sidewalk by the train station in the July heat.

Once Quincy knew Sonora name was Merial from a lie she told a while ago, when she first walked pass him in the beginning. Quincy announces. What shall we do now, girl? "My name is Merial." As she was being a jerk in front of Quincy's whole persona. Which, he didn't catch from the noble woman of Sonora Myers. Men are slow and weak sometimes during a complicated vibe that's intricate, when the pressure is high. That's what Sonora was saying through her deep thought inside. In Quincy's mind. He thought the situation was going well on his side of the fence. But. It really wasn't in Sonora's eyes. Quincy only had 40 dollars to last in his pocket to next Friday when he gets paid from his low budget job. Quincy mind was all over the place with no bounce around Sonora's anatomy from top to bottom. He had forgotten that Rico was supposed to pick him up around 4:30 before meeting Sonora. After checking his phone twice. Sonora asked Quincy. Is everything okay over there? "Not really." As he said. I have a longtime friend, that I ran into yesterday at the Underground with him, and his lovely wife. He's supposed to pick me up from this station around 4:30 today. But he's not here yet. I don't understand what's going on with Rico. "He should've been here about ten minutes ago." The name Rico stunted the mass outta her mind, to make her sweat immediately in vain. "Hold-on-for a few minutes." "Let me call him right quick." While Quincy was making the call Rico, to see what was going on with him. Vindictively, Sonora had Rico cell phone on vibrate for safe reason around Quincy boundary for strange reaction. Sonora was texting Quincy on Rico's phone to tell him he wasn't coming today. He's under the weather this afternoon. "I'm sorry buddy." I couldn't make it this evening my friend. We must catch up another time in the future. PIECE!! "He's not coming Merial." So... "What's the deal Merial?" "I don't know." She said. Well... If you want to do something. I'd only have 40 bucks inside my dark pockets for the next four days, until I get paid. When Sonora heard that outta Quincy mouth. Her eyes rolled in the back of her head so quickly, that. It was ridiculous. Sonora didn't need all that extra shit from him. *Never!* "I can't believe this nigga is broke!" "This mothafucka only have 40 dollars in his pocket." Hell no! "I'm trying to sabotage my husband too." "Not to jump into some more bullshit." But, not trying to do some extra stuff with a bomb of a man." Not me! During the process around Sonora's stubborn ways on the sidewalk of East Point.

Quincy suggested that. We can chill over to my grandmother's house for a little while. Until you are ready Merial. It's up to you. "I don't have enough to take you out miss lady." "I really don't." After saying hell naw twice inside her little mind from Ms. Myers. Sonora was ready for a nice cold beverage for the frustration she encountered with Quincy the kid at this point. Before Sonora could say anything else out the ordinary. The kid was like. "I don't know about you." But I need a cold one right now miss thing.

After arguing about the cold beverage from the thirstiness of Quincy the kid. They decided to walk towards the Shell Station in peace like they were holding hands into the halfway sunset afternoon, just imagining walking through the beach into the sand and water feeling the gray high rise around East Point.

Chapter 62

It was amazing how the 4th of July begins to pop-off into the night atmosphere, while entering towards the hollow between the green, red, and blue, and yellow, with a little purple and white mix-in together around the East Point parking lot. While conversating inside the vehicle and hanging out around the Kristal restaurant eating a stomach-hurting Kristal of ten, just laughing, and joking with one another. The question sizzled around Sonora. AKA, Merial, and Stoney Myers in a daydream form that's jacked in into a vertical name from a person doesn't exist through Sonora Myers. Why didn't you tell me you stay down the street through this area of East Point dead zone? "You right by the City Hall of police territorial." I saw you coming from inside the train station, through the turmoil grates with red on. "You saw that ha?" The kid said. "Yes, I did." Sonora, aka Merial said. That wasn't me, miss thang. That was someone else through the mix from the grate. I came around the other end of the station from the East Point area through the hood. When I came from the dead zone through the building from the City Hall. I see another black dude with the similar red shirt with the famous Redd Foxx face on his shirt. But, different from mine. That was the difference miss thang. As Sonora turned her head left and right slowly, feeling tipsy with her hills off, just popping those funky toes into the driver seat on the floor. They both were feeling awesome about their self-watching the wonderful fireworks, just going all over the place into the skies of the night. The whole night became acclimatize with Sonora, aka Merial and Quincy the kid. Quincy was feeling so good, that. He wanted to kiss Sonora on her lips immediately with a drive. But his conscious didn't allow him to do so as a low budget man. You have a nice vehicle miss thang.

You really do! Thank you. She said. Why do you keep calling me miss thang for? "Like I'm-a hooch of some sort." I didn't mean to pry you of your woman hood Ms. Merial. But. It-just sounds catchy to me, to say that to you as a man. After saying, yeah right, and whatever so quickly towards Quincy. He did a little giggle within himself around Sonora's saying of what she said. The time became 10:40 p.m. around the time the fireworks were over from this practically night. They killed four 24 Zos of Hurricane in cans. And, working on the third one from Quincy and Sonora with fun in the air. Sonora was feeling like a superwoman at the time. But really: she needed a little more element into the game for this occasion during the laugher. Sonora shouted out. "Let's get some more drinks." As she shouted out again. That sounds cool miss thang. But. I have something even better for you and me. I have that bunt at the house miss thang. Knowing, she didn't like that hoochified saying from him. What's-up! He said. "Hell naw!" "Let's go and get that shit nigga!" "You didn't say nothing but a word, miss thang." Let's-get-this-shit poppin' Merial!" As they coast down the road, passing the City Hall going towards his grandmother's brick home. Sonora, aka Merial couldn't get a full view of the home from the dark moment in her drunk mode. As the brick home kindle stood out from the vision Sonora was looking at the driver side. Did you want to come in for a little while miss thang? Sonora was getting used to Quincy saying miss thang towards her repeatedly, over-and-over-again when he went into the house. While Sonora was waiting on Quincy the kid. A strange vehicle pulls up on Sonora's bumper, at a two feet range with bright lights on the situation. The strange person that gotten out the car, with the color that bent into the black dark, that matches the hollow magic they had on during the blackness. "What the fuck!" Sonora said. "Why, is this stupid person having their bright lights shining on me like that for? *WHY!!* As Sonora turns right to see who this person is from the dark distance.

That's when Quincy finally came out with his special treat inside his old, black jeans, feeling good about himself. Until he bumps into a random person that scared the living-darkness outta Quincy's spiritual form, while stepping outdoors in the black. "Oh, shit." "You scared the shit-outta me! "May I help you?" Quincy said. "Yes..." I didn't mean to scare you sir. But... I'm looking for a missing person I know. "You think you can help me?" As the random person asks. "I don't know." I just moved over here two weeks ago. Said Quincy. Quincy said in his confused conscious. "Why is this strange woman asking me, all kind of question, about a missing woman for?' Why?!!"

Once Quincy mind started to piss-off the unusual stranger, in a madness faze. "He was like." "What is the missing person name?" The person's name is Sonora Myers. AKA, Stoney Myers. If you see her. Just give me a call. Here's-my-number. Just before Quincy could raise his head slowly. The person was gone in an instinct into the dark shadows. Quincy was puzzled, before getting inside the passenger side from tripping. As the strange vehicle took off fast and made a major U-turn right in front of Sonora's ride like flash with superpowers, as the bright lights blinds Quincy, and Sonora with the same fate in danger. "Who was that mothafucka?!" "God..." "Damn!" Sonora said out loud. "That was fucked up!" "Hell..." Naw!!! Quincy said. As the dark vehicle went straight pass the City Hall, close by the train station. Sonora did her crazy U-turn as well, when Sonora and Quincy laughed at the cool shit together with the fat bunt that Quincy gotten earlier for the mix. After they forgotten about the strange vehicle that did the dumb masseuse thing with the bright lights. Sonora kicked the vehicle in high gear facing the road. Feeling good, and drunk within the moment, going 65 miles per-hour feeling free as a rebel with Quincy the kid forever.

Chapter 63

The night was going so beautifully, when Sonora came out of the Shell Station store with five more Hurricanes cans, into the black air laughing so drunk, and tumbling towards the car. "Miss thang." You-are-right! "I see you tripping over shit." After rolling a bunt from the kid, as they roll out from Shell Station with the music continuing going around circles. The time became 11:22 p.m. for Quincy and Sonora, on this fast-paced ride from Sonora Myers, with the half of can of Hurricane in her hand driving hot going 70 per-hour. As the music was going on, while in motion with one more slip from Sonora. Sonora was like: what was the deal, back there with that person you were talking to? Sonora asks. While thinking about the kid from his red eyes like a dragon. At first. I couldn't tell, if-it was a man, or a woman in the dark when I came out the front ready to go. "The he-she, or whatever it was, scared the hood outta me." The way I was looking at the strange person. I think it was a woman, I think. I-don't-know! As I continued to look deeply at the shape so closely. You would think it was a woman, you say? Sonora said. "Yes, I think so." Quincy said. And then, she said. She was looking for a woman name Sonora Myers. "Who-ever that person is?" When Sonora heard that name from Quincy mouth, as he was puffing and smoke from the passenger side. Sonora became astonish and looking crazy like the Scream Ghostface mask from the motion picture movie. Just, looking disfigured from the whole face. While Sonora was stuttering from saying. "Why would the name Sonora come out her mouth like that, out the blue from a strange dark woman that's searching? During the thinking from Sonora that was frustrated from the name that was formally known in her evil ways.

The frustration was getting the best outta Sonora's mind, as she popped another can of Hurricane in the mix of driving back to East Point area with loud music. Sonora and Quincy were smoking the hell outta that long bunt he rolled up for the bolt of them to ride to into motion of life and beyond. Too Short was playing through the mix into the CD system of Life is Too Short from the album Too Short. The best album of all time that year when it was condoned by the artists. Life became lovely through the ride from the West End, back to East Point area in the city of the dead of humankind. Sonora was feeling good about herself with Quincy the kid, as they flew past the East Point Station going 85 miles per-hour with the window down singing. Quincy was so high, and drunk, that. He ended up pulling out his 9 mm from his right side and started shooting in the air like he was crazy out his mind. After the gun fire came out so randomly. Sonora screamed and went into a panic attracted by Taco Bell. As the moment came. "What the fuck are you doing nigga?!" "You scared the shit outta me!" "I'd didn't know you had a gun on you like that." "You should've wanted me, or something when you did that shit." Sonora was so shaken, that. The frustration made her hold her chest with the left hand so tightly like Sonora about to have a heart attack. After recovering from that shocking experience with the gun Quincy just fired. Sonora came up with a cold-blooded ideal of setting her husband up with his on phone to confuse his mind, like he's cheating on his evil wife. "You, good over there miss thang?" "I had you scared, ha?" *"Damn right Negro!"* But. "I'm fine." "Let me see that *9 mm* you're holding." Sonora said. "I didn't know miss thang." "This is a powerful peace girl." "It-isn't nothing too plays with, while holding a 9. Boy!! "Let me see that damn gun!" Give-me-that-pistol! After snatching the gun from Quincy's hand. "He was like." Damn miss thang!! "Okay..." With his hands leaning back in a frozen position. "It's your turn to drive now." "Move over." "What!" Quincy said.

"I'm on probation with a suspended license miss thang." So... that wouldn't be a good ideal. "I drive crazy miss thang." "So, what." Sonora said. I had two DUIs in the pass, during my probation deal, while driving without a license Quincy. SO, DRIVE BOY! "You didn't say nothing but a word miss-thang." Once they switched positions from Taco Bell and went past East Point Station again. The time became 12 midnight, when Sonora was making shots into the atmosphere three times with the Hurricane on the other hand hanging halfway out the window. Quincy liked the idea of driving Sonora's Lexus in high gear going 80 miles per-hour to the West End area. As Quincy the kid was feeling good and great. He went through the West End Mall parking lot like a flying fool, just outta his mind with Sonora laughing along during the ride. When Quincy approaches the red light, facing straight by the West End Station, on the left-hand side, going right back to East Point Station for the third sequel tonight. "How many bullets left inside the chamber miss thang?" "What." She said. As Sonora was looking crazy from the outside of her face. Wondering what Quincy is about to do next? "Let me see that shit for a minute, miss thang." While looking through the chamber for one more bullet. Sonora asks one more question? "What the hell you about to do *boy*?" Just be cool miss thang. It's one more bullet left inside the gun. "It's time for some bad stunt driving miss thang." Are you ready? Not really! Sonora said. When the light turns green. "I want you to fire." I'll take off like. Gone in Sixth Seconds, the kick-ass movie. As the engine was roaring from the inside of the hood. They took their Hurricane brew straight to the head before drafting off through the roads of hell. As the gunfire went off on green from the impact. Sonora ended up wasting her drink on herself, immediately on that pretty blouse that was deeply in blue on the material. The Lexus became flawless during the moment of the speed passing Kristal, and an East Point police officer, while sitting in the dark watching.

When the police car took off. East Point was heavenly behind Quincy and Sonora in madness mode. The officer was dispatching three more officers during the high-speed chase, once again for Ms. Sonora. *AKA Stoney Myers, for an upcoming DUI.* "After saying, oh shit twice out loud from Sonora Myers. Quincy was loading up more rounds inside his 9 mm that was tucked in between his legs. Once the bullets were loaded into the nine. Quincy the kid started shooting like crazy at the officer, that was dodging all three bullets, as he shafts back and forth so the police vehicle want-get hit. And Sonora loved every minute of the action. The action became impactable in her eyes like 3D. Quincy was running outta bullets inside the chamber, as he shot the last bullet in the gun. "Miss thang." I'm walking up to my grandmother's house, to grab more bullets for my nine.

While Quincy the kid was in the house getting more rounds for his pistol. Three cops pulled up on Sonora vehicle, like the swipe team and FBI with bright lights all on her hard. The only thing you heard was. (Freeze!) On Sonora Myers with lots of guns. As they quickly pulled Sonora out her car. Quincy came out shooting with bolt 9 mm towards the police so gangster with eight rounds going everywhere in hollow. Quincy wasn't going back to jail in this unforgiving moment in his life. As Quincy the kid had his nine shooting perfect rounds. "After saying, fuck all enforcements forever." When-all eight cops were everywhere in front of Quincy's grandmother's house. Quincy continued shooting in vain at all police until he hit one towards the head for a casual impact. The bullets were coming so fast, that. It was a great hit towards the white cop that was chasing them earlier through the chase on wheels. When the white police officer died instantly from the silver bullet, if Quincy just killed a werewolf that was insane with rage. Quincy begins to laugh with joy and passion, as if he was a free slave under the law enforcement as a kid.

It was cruel when the other officers called Quincy a stupid nigger for killing the officer from long range, as Quincy continues to shoot in midair towards the cops. Quincy had landed on the ground hard. As he kept shooting directly at the cops with anger and pain. One cop gotten so mad, that. He pulled Sonora out from the back seat and push her against the police car and called her a dumb nigger as well like Quincy. While Quincy was shot down and killed on the muddy ground. Sonora became weak standing in front of the police vehicle looking sad and pitiful. While the paramedics came and remove the body with the white sheet over Quincy and put him inside the ambulances to haul the fleshly dead remains to the Gary hospital, along with three more bodies that was killed at the hands of Quincy the kid.

Chapter 64

After the killing fields were over and done, with four fatalities escalated two hours ago in the dark neighborhood of East Point area. Channel 5 News had their reports intact for the whole Atlanta broadcast to stay tune for the next few days to marinate and gravitate for more information for the people. After the male reporter demonstrated the four deaths, that was gun down from a hideous shootout with the cops, in the hands of a young black male, by the name of Quincy Matthew. And his female companion Sonora Myers during the high-speed chase last night.

A few hours later. Detective Pete Anderson had Sonora Myers in custody for questing about the high-speed chase, and the major shot out with the three dead cops from the black shooter. It was 2:18 a.m. when Sonora was inside the East Point jail isolated for questing about the murder of three-good-officers from the hands by Quincy the kid.

Sonora became helpless, by handcuffed to the steel stair looking shameless into the eyes of death. Detective Pete walks in with a smirk on his face during the dropping of the beige folder. His eyes were deep into her eyes as the situation became intense for the second time around. Ms. Sonora Myers. We meet again. This is the second time we ran across, with another face to face, Ms. Sonora Myers. As detective Pete Anderson started to get sarcastic, in a way making Sonora feel bad about herself through insanity. But that wasn't happening in Sonora's soul at all. Not on her watch anyway. Do you know. "This will be your third DUI, Ms. Sonora." "Do you know that?!" When Sonora heard that reminder, over and over about the DUI-crap, that was eerie. She was in the faze from the DUI, to be misunderstood of what happen, or.

Just gotten hit with the element of surprise, that was tenacious towards the dark detox. The incredible look from Sonora became very evil. As they bolt stared eye to eye with one another into a rivalry confrontation that's happing. The questions were raw and deeply firm with detective Pete lawless of laying down the law on Sonora Myers behalf. Sonora kept saying to detective Pete. Where is my phone call? And, kept saying it, about three times back-to-back towards the detective. I'd just have a DUI, that's all. "Why are you asking me these foolish question for?" What's going on? She asks. What's going on! Pete said. "You have a bigger problem, more just a DUI you have. "This one here, is going to blow your mind Ms. Myers." You have a murder change, at this point. "What!" Sonora said. "What murder changer?!" Well, Ms. Myers. Your fingerprints were on the gun, that the officer was killed with during the gun fire that went down. The gentlemen that you were involved with through the high-speed chase. His name is Quincy Matthew. "You-too were carrying this gun right here." As he threw the pistol down on the table, that was inside the clean plastic bag in front of Sonora. "You see this Ms. Myers." "Fingerprints all over this weapon Sonora." This is the *9 mm* that you and Quincy used last night through the chase.

I have some more bad news for you, Ms. Myers. Your friend Quincy just died about 30 minutes ago. "Sorry for your lost." Pete said. Which. Detective Pete didn't give-a-shit anyway. As he cares less, with a big smile on the side of the detective. And Quincy said before he died. He thought your name was Merial, when y'all first met before all this went down. After knowing your name was Sonora Myers; and, married to his hood buddy Rico DL, and his street homie back in the days. That's what took detective over the top with his death. Sabotage was the shocking truth, of who you really are, Ms. Sonora Myers. By the way? Who is Merial?

That name has been lingering throughout the whole mayhem from last night. So... Tell me this, Ms. Myers. "Who is Merial Sonora?" Can you tell me that? Or you can't compute on that level? Which one is-it?! Pete said. Sonora wanted to say, fuck-you in the detective face like a clap, if detective call her a bitch of being an ignorant man from a wicket force. "Don't look at me like that Ms. Myers." It makes me think your mind is up to something. So. Tell me who is this Merial chic for the second time. She, just an old friend of mine that I met three years ago. "She doesn't mean anything to me anymore detective." So... That's it! But this murder changes you're pinning on me. Is very deceiving coming from you. "That's not right." Sonora said. I was so appalled in the back seat of the police car with handcuffs real tight, just uncomfortable inside my hands dilled in between the cold black, as a *Negro girl* into the weather that makes the white cops feel like mighty *GODS*. I didn't kill those cops with that 9 pistol you calm I'd use detective. Quincy is the one that killed those cops with the gun. Not me!! "I wouldn't do know shit like that." "I guess." Since I'm a *nigger.* You would pin that-type-of-shit on me, ha? "Just, stop the act Ms. Myers." This is not a race thing Sonora. "And you know that." The fingerprints, that's on the gun. Is yours Ms. Myers. So. "Stop fucking with me!" Just stop it!! In the back of Pete's mind. He wanted to call her a stupid *monkey* straight-up.

As the redness was showing through his whole entire body like the *Ghost rider in flames.* "Let me tell you something Ms. Myers." "Quincy the kid is dead Sonora." So. The system of law is going to pin this massive murder on you Sonora. So, you can look crazy all you want too. "It doesn't mean a damn thing to me." "This is all on you Sonora." At this point, Sonora's factor in consciousness. "She was done mentality insane from this murder charge investigation. Sonora knew she was being set up, in some sort by the system, as the detective kept daunting the pressure on Sonora about the murder charge that Pete was trying to put on her.

"It was like." The murder charge has been sealed with detective Pete, and the justice law system, from here and beyond. Until Sonora meets her maker in the grave with her mother and sisters in the ground forever.

Chapter 65

The break of dawn became the coming of the movement, as the radiation through the air sinks around time into the mist of the atmosphere. To make you wake up in the morning, as the body is not ready to get up with activation of life. Sonora was able to wake up from the cold air, from the hard steel around the old walls of evil structures. Sonora struggles sitting up through shiver from the body and pressure to make the mind go wild, as trouble still exists.

The message that detective Pete gave her. Dawn on the mental, as she wipes the crust from her eyes during the complex function Sonora was dealing around 7:30, to 8:10 A.M. The only thing Sonora could think about was. She had 24 hours to bond out before the State Federal, gets a hold of her through the gates into eternity in prison for good.

As Sonora became weak and thinking powerless in front of the pay phone wondering what's next? Detective Pete was taking a long stroll to Union City to fish for more information that he needed from the cold streets of disciples. After traveling so wonderfully into the beautiful nature of winds, that was coming through the air form from the sun's energy as waves. The detective was really amazed with the homes he pulled up on, as the environment made him sweat within the chemistry he felt. As the knucks pound on the brown wooden door three times through confidence at random. Rico quickly opens the door with lateness in his eyes, trying to get himself together for work at nine-thirty A.M. "Hi." Sorry to disturb you. My name is detective Pete Rico. How are you doing this morning?

As his right-firm-hand extended for Rico to shake in respect as a man bonding in greeting. Rico became confused from the welcome that was going on at his front door, with this detective guy. "May I help you detective?" "I'm late for work."

"Excuse me rudeness detective." "I am seriously late for work." Rico said. "What can I do for you detective?" I'm sorry for your convenience this morning sir. But I have some serious questions that I need to ask you Mr. DL. Hold up! "How you know my name sir?" Or detective. "Whatever you want me to call you." "Detective would be fine." Pete said. Do you know Sonora Myers, Mr. DL? Yes! "That's my wife." "She didn't come home last night." "I don't know what's going on with her?" "Sonora been acting so weird these days." "I don't understanded!"

As Rico was getting complex at this stage. Well... I have some good news, and some bad news. Which news do want to hear first? Detective said. What!! As Rico shouted out. "I'd don't have time for your word games. Right-about-now detective. "I have to go to work." "I don't have time for this." Well... Let me get down to it. Said Pete. Your wife is in jail, Mr. DL. And she was charged with murder last night. What!!! Rico said. "What the hell are you talking about detective?" "What murder charge?!" As Rico mind was overwhelm of what the detective was trying to tell Rico face to face about his wife killing somebody. The misunderstanding was coming outta Rico's pours for more questioning towards detective Pete about Sonora Myers situation. "What the hell is going on here?" "My wife is being charged with murder!" Or, hell naw! The way Rico was looking from the outside. His mind wasn't ready for work this morning. It's like detective Pete ruins that for Rico DL, as they continue to converse with the door wide open. This is not true, whatever you are telling me detective. "Can't be!" As Rico continues to be surprised. Pete was like. Well. Believe it or not, Mr. DL. "Oh." I almost forgot. Here is your phone, Mr. DL. You might want to keep up with this sir. Everybody else in the world is.

You need to do the same Mr. DL. These targets are very important these days. Truth me! The future is coming with AI, and new phones. "What do you mean?" Rico said. As the detective adored the question and kept talking. How did you know where I live, and locate me detective? How?" Well... If you must know. Your wife had your phone all yesterday, and last night. What!! "How the hell she ends up with my phone detective? "I was looking everywhere for that damn phone." I was so mad! I almost rip through the whole house looking for this device.

I see. Detective said. Yes. The phone was in her procession, all yesterday, and. Including last night Mr. DL. Do you know a guy named Quincy Matthew Mr. DL.? As Rico wonders and thinks about the familiar during the five seconds while sitting down. "But anyway." Said Pete. This guy Quincy was with your wife all yesterday, and throughout the night from this high-speed chase, and the shootout with the cops. Detective Pete said. "You said." This guy you are talking about, was with my wife yesterday? Yes, Mr. DL. She was! WHAT-THE-FUCK!! "So..." You're saying my wife was fooling around with this guy. "Who-you-say his name was?" What...? Said Rico. His name is Quincy Matthew. And. As far as messing around on your wife. "I don't know about that Mr. DL. Don't have a clue about that information. "But I do know this doe." Your wife has another DUI on her record right now Mr. DL. You might want to bail your wife out as soon as the problem is before midnight. Or. Sonora Myers would be going down the road for a very long time, Mr. DL. I have another weird question for you. Listen to this. I noticed on your cell phone, around 2:15 p.m. yesterday. You text Quincy as you got up yesterday from your beauty sleep in between texting him. "And continuing on texting him, during different times." "What the hell are you talking about detective?" "I'd don't remember that." For some strange reason. My mind hasn't been remembering much lately detective. I don't know what's been going on with me. I have been getting up late all last week, around two something.

Well, Mr. DL. You need to start remembering, because. It's some weird stuff happening Mr. DL. You must remember something about these texts you have been sending.

As Rico stood up quickly to think what's going on, while walking in a small circle four times during this moment of remembering. Until the name Quincy knocked on his thoughts, with a flash back when he ran into him at the Underground from downtown Atlanta a day ago.

Chapter 66

The mind became like the pecking-order. As detective Pete continued drilling questions and answering through the head of Mr. DL. When Rico discovered who Quincy was. As the kid popped up immediately. Yeah, detective. I remember now. I knew Quincy back in the day. We grew up together in California in the projects. Rico had to stop-it right there, because he didn't want to go deeper in dep through memory lane as drug dealers in L.A. I remember the time, detective. I used to call him Quincy, the kid in a certain situation that we went through. "Like what?" Detective said. "It was on some kiddy shit detective." "Nothing major." The text was saying. Let's hangout and catch-up for old time's sake Quincy. That's where the text came from, Mr. DL. So... You two planned this that day Rico? No! Said Rico. "Yeah, we're-going to catch-up, sometime in the near future." But not that soon detective. And then. After 4:30 P.M. You text him, saying. I will not make it today buddy. Something came up. Catch you next time. That was the last text you finally sent him during that time, Mr. DL. As Rico was thinking and looking crazy through his mind, while he trolls through his iPhone searching for the text. Detective Pete was throwing more deadly information towards Rico DL consciously, as his mind started to open even wider for more pounding. And. By-the-way! The kid, or. "Whatever you call him back in the days. He in up dying last night through a major shootout with the police. And it was fatal Mr. DL. And your wife. Ms. Myers. She was part of the shootout as well. It seems like to me. Your boy, Quincy the kid, was on a date with your wife, Ms. Sonora Myers. Their escapade became extra on their sweet high-speed chase, playing bang-bang with a nine-millimeter that night. Once Rico knew the text, that detective Pete was talking about.

Rico was dumbfounded and astonished, as he trolls through the texts, that he was exposed and uncovered by. In the back of his confused mind. He knew deep down inside. He didn't text those messages yesterday. The only thing that Rico could come up with, that. His wife sabotages the whole plot to make it seem like Rico did the texting from his phone behind his back. While hypnotize on the blind side, and space out staring towards his phone. Detective Pete was calling Rico name about six times in a row repeatedly. During the questioning and more information, directly at his present. The hypnotizes was so vain, that. Detectives wanted to give Mr. DL a quick slack on the jaw to wake up to. Before that could happen. Rico stood up Quickly and gave detective the reality moment that Pete was looking for. You were right detective. I typed the text on my phone to my buddy Quincy. But not really. "What does that mean?" Said Detective. "You didn't, or you did?" "Which one is it?" "My wife did this bullshit to me." "How could this horrible monster do me like this!" "And, I had the audacity too married this woman." Wow!! The surprise of betrayal was getting to Rico DL mentality, and physicality. To make him laugh, but weird and crazy from the outside of things. "No." Not confuse detective. But. "Piss the fuck off with my ex-wife of mine!" "Your ex-wife?" Detective Pete said. I thought you were married to Mr. DL. I am a detective. But, not anymore, at this point. After throwing his iPhone against the white wall.

The detective felt sorry for Rico DL situation with his wife Sonora Myers. "That's enough questions for today detective." No more! You can see your way out. I don't mean to be ruled, but. I just need some time for myself detective. Detective Pete understood what Rico was going through consciously in hate. Here's my card with my number on it. If you need me. Or, if anything comes up you need to share. "Just call me." You have 24 hours to bail your wife out on bond, Mr. DL. Just, be aware of that in mind. Pete said.

"I'm not bailing that *Bitch* outta jail detective. "She can rot in jail, for all I care." Fuck-her!!! *Me and Sonora are done!!*When the message was loud and clear from Rico DL. Detective Pete became very pleased and happy with this case he has on Sonora Myers behalf. "Oh yeah Mr. DL." Don't get married anymore. Just stay safe, and observer your women next time in the future. That's why I'm not married to this day. "Don't have time for the crazy bullshit!" After Rico smile, what detective said about his crazy circle stands, that's miss led. Detective Pete told Rico face to face to have a nice day, as detective comes out with the swag of Matt Daman all the way in a sulky form. As seconds went on. An all-black Changer been manifesting around Rico's house since the detective been questioning the whole time and place. The time became 12:20 noon, when detective was jotting down information that Rico said about his ex-wife. As the black Changer slowly passes by detective Pete vehicle with eyes. The black Changer vanishes forever, until the next time in life.

Chapter 67

After the horrible noon hour was over with, that became 1:31 p.m. through the cool jail cell. Sonora's appetite became unbearable for a tasty meal for her tummy that was growing for some wings and fries from the wing shack on Riverdale, across the street where West Elementary school is located, in between the dead plaza where Sonora is thinking from.

While Sonora became impatient, by being incarcerated behind bars with a third DUI, and a misunderstanding about the murder changed. The moment Sonora started to feel lazy and angry towards the detective, that's trying to frame her with the fingerprints on the gun. The woman deputy that was white, but sulky. Made Sonora's day by being bonded out immediately. The amount of *10 grand* that was delivered from an unknown person about an hour ago, with a written check for the East Point City Hall jail. Sonora couldn't believe she was bound out from jail just like that, with no phone call on her own attempt. Sonora danced her way into the release area to sign out right away. With the question in the wind from the back of her mind? As she wonders who released her out the blue through madness? After the deputy gave Sonora the release forms and the court date information to sign in print, and on the sheet in black and white. Sonora asks the question? Can you tell me who bailed me out mama? Why?! The deputy said. "You're free." Get outta here!! I just want to know the deputy. That's all. "Wasn't my husband mama?" "This person wasn't no guy Ms. Myers." It was a woman. "That's all I can tell you." So. If I were you. "You need to leave and get you a good lawyer Ms. Myers." You gonna need it for your court trial coming up on October 31st on Halloween. "Isn't that something." Deputy said. What!!

Sonora was surprised at the court date, and wondering who bailed her out? "I can't believe this shit." Well... Believe it Ms. Myers. You have two months to get yourself attorney mama. Now go!! "Before I put you back into the cell."

Sonora was reading the information about her court date on the 31st of October outside the entrance to East Point facility. As the check was released in her name, made her grabbed her chest instantly with a pause. As the 10 grand had Sonora in a daze for a drink immediately.

While walking. Sonora went inside her purse to grab bolt phones, which it was only hers, when she pulled out mad. "What the fuck was the word, that came outta her mouth instantly in shame." Ten minutes later. My heart was still hurt, by coming outta the Shell station with three cans of Hurricanes at the vol. of 8% alcohol in the mix. Her thrust crushing was ready for one once Sonora reached a destination to chill and drink. The steps of concrete she found were suitable for her buttocks to sit down and slip for a little while looking at the world. About time Sonora finish one can for the road. Traffic became ridiculous, as people were coming back and forth through the high steps with interruption that made Sonora leave quickly. Especially, when the vibe gotten creepy during fast pace of people that breaks the surrounding from the craven. Once the traveling of people was broken up and done. Sonora's little moment of privates was killed indeed. The walk was taking to be satisfying for something fine to eat on this sad happy day as a false murderer. Sonora was lucky to have her credal card in her possession for some tasty Krystal for the little tummy. During the walk to Krystal. She was still piss-off about her iPhone being dead in her present. Her expression can't believe those fuckers kept Sonora's other phone, like it was theirs. While arriving towards Kristal on foot and tired. Sonora was saying to herself.

This Krystal kinder looked close from her distance, as she got closer to the entrance to eat inside and marinate. When Sonora approached the counter to place her order for ten Krystal's at this hungry moment she was facing.

After the cashier place Sonora order and ready to cash out. Her card was declined at an embarrassing moment from the card and the cashier confrontationally four times. The fourth debit card that she uses during the final attempt. The cashier told Sonora. "All your cards have been declined mama." "Try another card." Sonora couldn't believe all her credal cards were decline from the card service about eleven times straight, as the frustration hits the blood flow of the body. "I can't believe this shit." "What the hell is going on today?" *What-the-fuck!!* "What's wrong with my credal card?" *Fuck!* After being decline about 50 times. Sonora heartbeat was beating so fast with rhythm, that. Her chest plate seemed like it was about to come out, automatically in the restaurant. As she was walking fast like a mean Army soldier. During the walk with so much angry. As the purse bag was nicely trucked in between her funky armpits in Geometric deep blue. The fast black Changer, that was loudly absurd. But stunted Sonora's nerve vibration instantly. The suspect quickly rolled down the window and spoke. "Hurry, get in!" Now!!! Sonora heard the voice. But, said. "What the fuck out loud." After saying. "Hell, naw towards the suspect during the complete of yelling." The dark person said. "Get the fuck in Sonora!"

After Sonora, aka Stoney Myers heard the name, and almost fainted into consciousness while confuse around the nerves in random. Sonora gotten her ass up and dove herself into the Changer for the ride of her lifetime, without thinking what's next?

Chapter 68

The drive and distance were quiet during the journey into the exit on Riverdale Rd. at the red light horizontal on Phoenix. When Sonora woke up from her ten-minute nap. Sonora was hit with the déjà vu through a blur vision dreaming, if Draco was walking past the apartment, going towards the QT for energy. The drive was weird, as Sonora stares at the unparticular suspect, when Sonora thinks she's been kidnap like a little girl. If you don't mind. Can you stop at the wing shot at the plaza? Whoever you are? Sonora said. The black Changer came through like a mean monstrous in front of the wing shack with victorious intention. As the voice extended said. "Here!" "Take this, and order." By snatching the 50 dollars from the strange person hand with black gloves on that was tight. The order was placed with a 50 piece on the way in ten minutes or less. The stranger was glad Sonora remained outside, while waiting for the food to release some beathing air outta the lungs. When the black do-rag was pulled back around the nose. Sonora comes back with two Styrofoam Hot wings in a white bag, that's warmly ready to feast down in the car. Sonora leaned back comfortably eating a Hot wing vain. And, asking the-all-black individual would you like one? While Sonora was smacking on a second Hot wing with laughter on the face. "No Sonora!" "Wait until we get home." "No eating in the car." What!! Sonora said with surprise in her eyes, while clogging down the third wing with sauce around her lips. Sonora asked the person for the second time. "How do you know my name?" As the mystery person hit the gas intentionally, and deliberately in reverse to avoid the question.

As the eatable 50 piece was in bagging squish in between the legs of Sonora on the fool during the fast pace in reverse from the Changer, that scared the living daylight outta Sonora. The ride was quick. But, hit with reality in Sonora eyes as a flash-back. "What the fuck is we doing here?!" As the stranger looks at Sonora like. "I know what you did last summer type vibe." The individual parked in the first section in reverse, like back in the days when love was in the air like lovers did from the source.

While Sonora became crazy. But, misunderstood about her pass into the Garden Wood apartment four years ago with Merial and Rico. The stranger had the food while walking and dapping the old school gentlemen that was black but, mature like Sonora used to in the days was so sweet. Sonora had to snap outta her memory lane fazes so frequently to catch up with the unknown suspect that Sonora was witnessing in the eye. The heat was creeping into a rhythm, as Sonora ran up the second level of stairs, while her old apartment door was wide open. Her eyes continue to travel through the hollow entrance, while remembering the times from her single days as a diva and so forth. Sonora slides the door lightly, while the wind glides and pushes for support as a friend through the scenery. Sonora walks slowly around the living room, which was gray and dark like the Chainsaw Mascaras scene from the mid-sixty's era. As Sonora looks around through the kitchen and living room area. She was invited into a scary scene outta nowhere. As Sonora eyes took her back into the source, where Sonora carb the word *Devil* on her husband lower arm when he was sleep deeply.

As soon as Sonora turned around from her scary moment through her old apartment of the pass life. The mystery person scared Sonora once more from behind again. And said.

Well, well, now, Sonora. It's been a long time, hasn't it? The eyes of shock. Almost take Sonora into a heart attack dissertated faze, looking thing from Sonora. "After saying, what the fuck from Sonora Myers voice."

A kick came into the scene on Sonora's chest, with Merial's shape hill from her black leather boot with good impact, from a mean woman that has a grudge on her old lover. After Sonora said. "Why did you do that to my neck?" Merial stood down on Sonora level with her pistol holding it tightly towards Sonora's head and ask. "You still don't recognize me Sonora?" "What is your problem *bitch*." "Look at me Sonora." As the eyes of Sonora connected with her old lover in the face. The expression was unbelievable in Sonora's eyes of. "Or my God!" "Is that you Merial?" As Sonora was sliding back slowly like a little girl towards the wooden table. Merial was walking slowly with her nine, straight directly at Sonora's perfect face for target practice as an assassin. The Invictus look in Merial's face was very evil and over the edge of killing Sonora at this deadly second. As she shares deeply into Sonora's eyes of shooting the devil in the head of betrayal, of doing so. Sonora was mad during the moment of truth, that Merial was coming towards her, but. Heartbroken of what she did to Merial Miller three years ago. After telling Sonora to stand the fuck-up like a drill sergeant. Merial and Sonora were face to face with sorrow and hate upon one other for the future. After saying what happened to your face and personality? A smack from the gun was very devastating from the iron impact from Merial, after hugging Sonora with pain and anger in the soul. "How, eat your food!" As Merial walked away fast like a diva. Sonora gotten herself up slowly from the pistol slap with blood dripping coming down from her mouth. Sonora stormed herself out the front door with a cracked tooth down the steps, holding her mouth with blood flowing through her hands, by running towards the black Changer in rage. While recovering from a crack tooth from Merial nine smack inside the apartment running in pain.

Blood kept running outta Sonora mouth continuously through hell from the complex parking lot. Then she grabbed her brown paper bag from the floor in the black Changer. Immediately Sonora took a swig from the Hurricane like mouth wash while gargling and sitting on the sidewalk to walk off the angry from Garden Walk perimeter. Her voice penetrated through the airwaves cussing loud, by saying. "Screw you Merial with fuck-you behind her back." She continued sitting on the side where the grass in dead at. Still cussing the fresh air out, along with Merial as well. As she turns around slowly. A kind smooth gentleman politely asks Sonora. "Are you okay mama, with a touch?" I'm fine, sir. "I'm okay." But thank you. The flowing from her blood into the sleeve. Became unbearable in Draco's eyes. As Sonora was embarrassed in front of him as a shock all-of-sudden. Draco face was like. Do I know you from somewhere? Not really. Sonora said with pain in her mouth. When her memory came back at that exact second, like they first met that Sunday evening at the Underground. "Now I remember you now." Your name is Draco, isn't? Yes, it is. Draco said. And your name is. Umm... Let me think. Is it Sonora? As she looks very puzzled within. "Wait-a-minute, don't tell me." While Draco was thinking of the right name. Sonora had to spit again before telling Draco her name to help him verbally. Draco began to get very happy. After giving her his handkerchief to wrap off her mouth with blood leaking between the left side of her lip that's dripping. During an unaccommodating walk back to Garden Walk Rd. around 5:45 P.M. Merial just completed a mission at the 6043 club with an assassination that was terminated. During the good conversation that Draco and Sonora had like a date. The question was asked. Do you have a girlfriend, Mr. Draco? No Sonora. But. I dated twice in my lifetime. The relationship didn't go so well with me. "The first one cheated on me." "But wasn't no biggie! But... "The second one." "She really fucked me over." Damn... Sorry for that baby. As Sonora became concerned and sorrow towards Draco situation. What was her name? If you don't mind me asking. Well... Sonora. "If you most know." Her name was Dominic Walker. I met her through a random situation at a bar.

The name, Dominic had Sonora in a state of shock during her choking and spitting more blood on the ground. "Are you, okay?" As Draco guilds Sonora with support into a gently touch. While Sonora was wrapping her mouth with the brown handkerchief. Reality was setting in for Sonora like crazy, as they bolt kept walking and looking straight towards the beautiful Hwy 85 traffic around Riverdale.

Chapter 69

The heat high rise was beginning to cool down. But not really. As the temperature slightly drops down to 90% warm level. The sweat moment, between Draco and Sonora at the Raceway was truly a hot blaze for one another at 6:50 P.M.

When can I see you again, Mr. Draco? Knowing. This isn't an official date that we planned. Yes, I know Ms. Stoney. You can call me Sonora baby. I like that name better. Sonora, aka Stoney said. Okay, Sonora. That's a pretty name you have. I like that! Draco said. We will continue this date, some other time Sonora. "We don't have to wait baby." Said Sonora. Do we want to continue this tomorrow night Draco? As the mind was thinking from Draco Dawn form outta space. It's too soon for you and me to condone this right now. Said Draco Dawn. But. I'll take-it a pond my schedule to pursue this interesting date for tomorrow. When the continuation was finally sealed. Sonora wanted to kiss Draco on his cheek to change his mind about tomorrow night's date. Merial seen Sonora, and swiftly turned into a stunt like an angry rider in front of Sonora and Draco's interruption. Sonora knew Merial had a purpose from the sounds of the mean Changer that was coming. And then, all black leather outfit Merial was wearing at the Raceway in her black boots. Let's go!! The whole voice control, that took over Sonora's body that's been controlled through the mind mainframe for decades over the years. Which was a problem for humankind in the era of all nations, that Merial hates since being born into this brain washing A.I. Merial blames her mother for calling her *a bitch of a little girl.* Knowing that type up bring, while teaching her own daughter that evil knowledge of power.

"The word, stupid *bitch* was inside her mind." As Merial sees the vision inside her imagination. Her mother didn't teach Merial anything about the way of the knowledge as a black mother to Merial as a little girl in her brain, back in the days of weird life.

When Merial's mind slapped back into reality. Her voice lashed out twice like the Hulk, in a green rage of pain. "Get your ass in this car, Bitch!" During the soundwave it pitched like poisonous radiation towards Sonora Myers. Draco received a call that came through in his headphones, as he stepped back a little bit from the impact. After Sonora, and Merial were done with their debacle as women in front of Draco Dawn. Sonora said her fell-wells for right now towards Draco's physical being with a tight hug. Bye was pleasant. When Sonora said. See you tomorrow, Mr. Draco. Draco was quiet with one index finger in the air because his mind and conversation was occupied with another individual on his phone. When the peace sign was secure into the wind-wave towards Sonora, with a smile of wonder? Sonora watches Draco vanish up the hill in his white muscle shirt, along with brown Dickie shorts, and long black socks wearing black high-tech boots as well as the day walker. The

U-turn was dangerous, but illegal somehow in the pavement destination where people and traffic are zooid in mind control. The ride through Garden Walk was flowing hard for the next mission on Merial's mind as she looks at Sonora weirdly. "This is some bullshit." "Where the hell are we going, now?" After screaming out loud from Sonora. "Can you take me home now?" "Since we're riding around in circles." My husband is at home waiting for me. I know, he's wondering why I'd haven't been home last night. He's worried sick about my whereabouts as his wife. Throughout all the miscellaneous various talking, that Sonora was doing from the passenger seat about her stupid husband she doesn't love. Merial hit the accelerator going through Riverdale and proceeded on 285 West to Union City in Sonora's territory for no place like home.

Sonora couldn't understand by looking at Merial. "What happen?" Or what has changed over the years. Sonora was glad Merial didn't wear that purge-skeleton, black mouthpiece around her face. That was kind of shallow in the mist of darkness, for hitting her earlier with the *9 MM*. "You didn't have to do me like that Merial." We could've talked about our problems like glow women. The look on Merial's face, was the eyes of a mechanical Terminator ready to kill and eliminate you any seconds. "Listen to me baby." "I know you are mad, of what I'd had did to you three years ago. As the purse of sadness in Sonora's eyes was painful. That when the moment of making up, was only daydream, as Sonora sits long side, wishing Merial would forgive her for all sins and immortality as a *Devilish widow yet to come*. The thinking of Merial wanted to kill Sonora Myers for all the killing she committed as a physical war path in a woman, visioning Sonora is a male *nigger, that needs to be hanged, if Merial was a white man through immortality for blood.* During the sorrow and pleasing towards Merial heart of forgiveness from the pass. Around 7:15 p.m. Merial parked deeply in Sonora's residents, that had many trees for Merial's hide out that she was prepare for in her intuition. "Why you parked way down here Merial?" "What's going on?" "Just, shut-up and go to your house!" "This what you wanted right." "Now, go!" The serious look made Sonora jump out of the Changer, so she can see her sweet husband she misses. The walk was seen far on foot, while Sonora was nerve like a little girl with her hands in her pocket. Two Union City police officers flew pass Sonora, as her heartbeat went up, when the draft from the wind startled her. Merial became-startled herself, as the eyes seen the police as well. Merial put the Changer in reverse real fast, and gotten out the car, and went into her trunk in between the trees. During the slowness of Sonora coming inside the dark haunted house, tiptoeing with the TV on. Sonora headed towards the flat screen to shut it down. Until Rico scared Sonora, if she were the Boogie Man herself.

"Oh, shit Rico." "You scared me." As he laughs, with no sound, or anything from his mouth with no sorrow through the voice. After turning on the dim lamp while standing up. A fake welcome of love, came with open arms when Sonora to her husband chest plate of missing him, as they kiss for six seconds, and walk towards the dark kitchen. Sonora was glad Rico didn't ask her where she had been last night. Because he already knew his wife betrayed him, from what detective

Pete told him, what his devilish wife did with Quincy at East Point that night. After the hugs and kisses were over with. His mind, body and soul were glad her disgusting flush was off his flush like cancer, that grew with growth over the years. "Why was it so dark in here when I walked in here Rico? "You know better than that Rico." As Sonora was talking to Rico like a little boy, in a slick mommy way in his mind. With the sarcastic voice that came outta Sonora mouth like it normally does, that he hates. His mind became raged, and killable at the nature of death on her behalf. "How dare this EVIL DEVIL of mine, comes into my home with her hood ways of fucking up last night with Quincy. While the mind was still thinking of punishing his no-good wife forever. Sonora looks for a nice cold Corona inside the refrigerator, as she pops her neck side to side, as woman time catches up with her through old age yet to come. Right at that very, great moment. Rico wanted to flip the wooden table over his wife's back, with his red eyes. As he huffs and puff, over his wife back like a fiend for death in vain. More police officers were arriving in furious without signal, or sound in the residents. Merial's acoustics ways was ready, as more cops were showing up in her eye site to destroy, in between the bushes with nines for warfare to kill all cops that work for the government, and others as well. *PS. In Merial's mind. YOU ARE... ALL DEAD!!!!*

Chapter 70

After the break of dawn from the surface was over and done with the time of 8:10 p.m., during the mix. Rico DL left his phone on purpose. So, Sonora could grab it from the table, while he was upstairs, hearing, and watching the whole thing with his eyes. As Sonora took the block off, when she grabbed her husband phone like a foolish woman, like she did in the pass. Sonora was happy in between strolling through the phone, as Rico creeps 'down step by step slowly, by watches his dumb wife go through the phone once more like a woman naturally do against the grain. "Look at this stupid *DEVIL*." As Rico laughs to himself during this setup with him and detective Pete arrangement. After one last stroll with Sonora's finger into the mix of enjoying the phone. An electrical explosion had occurred in her face just a little. Which, it was very derived in this case. The sparker, and small flash of power hit Sonora's whole flesh, as she drops the phone immediately, when dropping on bolt kneels seriously. Rico rushed down with a laugh, as her body was turned to the side. To where, she couldn't see him laughing at her. But I am concerned about what will happen to Rico. "Baby, are you okay?" "What happened honey?" As Rico rubs her back with finesse with his hands. But glad the situation went down. After holding his laugher for so long like a Blowfish with big cheeks. The pressure made Rico burst out, and Sonora, turned around and clap her husband in the face, as his body turned so deeply into a dance, like the drunken master of kung-fu. "You did this-shit on purpose mothafucka!" "What the fuck is you talking about Sonora!" "I haven't done shit!" After checking to see if he had any blood coming from his mouth with his index finger.

"Look at my face nigga!" "It has a burn mark, right under my right eye, you bastard." And. "You have the nerve to laugh at me." Before Sonora could walk away towards the restroom to look at her face. Rico, her husband, made a disrespectful statement, and spoke. *"Maybe you deserved that shit bitch!"* Out loud and powerful. As she quietly heard that-shit outta his dirty mouth. Her mind snapped. "What did you say Rico?" As they bolt were eye to eye, ready to fright. "I didn't say anything Sonora."

You are trippin'

I'm not trippin'

"You said, I'd deserved that shit." "I heard you!" As his back was turned. And walk towards his phone. Sonora came and pushed him from the back with anger and moved the kitchen table during the movement. The kitchen floor because like the bed. When Sonora started punching Rico in the chest, if she was a gorilla with power. The anger progressed, as Rico pushed Sonora off him, and kicked her in the breast with his left 92 white Air Jordans. The beast really came outta Sonora, as she screamed loudly and dived on Rico with bolt bodies on the wooden table. More back-ups were coming when detective Pete dispatched his team of cops for the drop. There were 15 officers on deck in front of Rico and Sonora's residents, as they continued fighting inside. Rico had Sonora on her back for questions and answers for his wife? "Did you murder your sister Kimberly Sonora?" "Did you!" With pressure on her neck real hard. "So, what-if I did mothafucka!" As viciousness came outta Sonora's flaming voice. The rage was so bad, that. The confession became reality, and truthful in Sonora eyes, as a clap in the face. So... It is true Sonora. You did kill your sister. The flashback made him realize; she did do it. Wow, Sonora.

The News and the reporters were talking about this case for two years since we had been together. "I be damn!" The shock removes his hands around his wife's throat slowly. His mind was in a denial state mode. As he asks her again. I know you didn't do that Sonora. I did mothafucka! "And it's nothing you can do about-it nigga!" "I'm glad that bitch dead!"

When detective Pete heard all that from Sonora. But the wrong murder case with George Walton. It was time to bust Ms. Sonora Myers for the murder of Kimberly Myers in 2010, during that year. At about time Rico could marinate about Quincy, and Sonora night out together during that moment. Detective Pete and ten other officers were marching towards the front door with their guns and flashlights. Out of nowhere. Three more officers were assassin by a smooth sniper from a distance outta desiccation. As Merial became invisible, by coming from the backyard. With more cops were coming from the front, and to the back, to find the random shooter that killed three officers in the dark hidden place. Merial with her silent sniper eliminated all four officers that were rushing from the back aggressively. Blue and red lights were flashing everywhere in front, as the nosy neighbors' watches in their front pouch. Detective Pete made his recovery on the right side of the house to find the suspect that's randomly shooting his men from the dark area. When more police arrived on the scene during the shootout. Detective Pete rush back to the front, to wanted other cops to be aware of a dangerous killing sniper outta the ordinary. The power was cut smoothly by Merial, as she inters quietly from the lower level through inside the house. Rico had to light up a match quickly, so Sonora wouldn't try anything funny or crazy in her mind on the table. The conversation started to get real-deep from the hated, or love-it couples, that's in a hectic predicament of disgust. Rico grabbed Sonora by the shirt real hard for more answers as a threat to get-it outta her.

Merial came from behind and knocked Rico DL in the back of his neck real smooth, until he was knocked unconscious. While Merial was trying to pick up Rico DL.

Sonora became shocked outta nowhere, as she remains sitting on the table looking pitiful and discombobulated worth nothing. Come on!! "Don't just sit there!" "We need to move fast." "More cops are on the way Sonora." "So, we need to tie him up before we leave this shit hold." It was 9:30 at night when they tied Rico to the chair real tightly with blood on the back of his head and face sitting there, looking like a nuclear time bomb. Sonora looked directly into Rico's face with the slightest touch in pieces. But. *Carved the word Devil on the side of his face instead.* More damage was in mind, while Merial was looking through the living room window, seeing plenty more cops arriving at the front door with their guns. "Sonora." "We can't stay here much longer." "There are coming." "I'd can hold them down, much's I can." "Hurry-up and do what you need to do with him." During the punishment that Sonora was giving her husband. Merial ran upstairs with her sniper for comb-back on some Call-of-Duty in the hollow of target practice. Silently, Merial put a small hold into the window for a long time. Before the cops raged into confrontation with their massive weapon in hand.

Detective Pete was yelling in vain, for Sonora to give it up at this point. As the voice pattern became cold like airwaves through the house. But instead, was annoying around the whole procedure of all ear's frequency. Detective Pete gave the hand signal towards three officers to seek in smoothly on the bust to gun down Sonora for death, as the mark of the breast for all sins through eternity and beyond. As one cop was coming from the hidden hollow. He silently was gunned down through the thick neck, as the blood spread out into the grass around the house that was pitch black as midnight. As more cops were available invading the front door, as the eyes spotted with a clean shot into the dome between heaven and hell.

After so many fatalities, 20 cops laid down on the ground laughing, that's deserved. Merial rounds were empty as she was coming down the steps rushing. "Sonora, we have to go now!" "I'm outta rounds." Sonora didn't hear anything from Merial Miller when she approaches the kitchen and headed straight to the door for cover. "What the fuck is you doing?" "Let's go!" Sonora wanted to punish Rico more, but Merial was already gone. When the raw enforcement was busting through with vengeance. Sonora's mind was overwhelmed by the collision of massive gun fire, that was hyperactive. That made her fidget, when Sonora remembered the phone incident, that busted into flames automatically an hour ago. The impact of the door, that the cops were trying to conquer inside. Had Sonora's mind in a state of shell shock through an emergency, to keep up with Merial's pace between the trees and darkness. The black Changer became a breast in reverse, with clear smoke, just watching Sonora run her ass off in the back of the review mirror, as she laughs with the music turn up.

Merial wanted to leave Sonora during the confirmation with the cops, and detective Pete for her murder outcome in the pass. Merial, The Cyborg, which was Miller, when she and Sonora, once dated back in the loving days of passion. Merial wanted to proceed with precaution on her speed, by going back to Riverdale, to her home base cave for tonight. But meanwhile. Merial had to stop Sonora for becoming a whining characteristic kiss-ass of a woman, that was Manish with, so such power of evil. That. Merial, slowly increase the vehicle for her bad, no-good ways of a woman that she is, once was forever. After putting the Changer in reverse with the windows down. Merial told Sonora. "Get your ass in this damn car." And move-it! Sonora dived into the window, bumping her left knee on top of the door metal real hard. Without no- patience, or carefulness of trying to be perfect during the cost. As they drift off into the dark side as wanted women for the next mission to kil

Chapter 71

The shadows of death started to feel like heaven or hell for Merial and Sonora short fate on this earth. The dripping in and out came quick inside the Swift convenience store with two 12 packs in each hand cuffed tight like heavy luggage's into the black street. As soon as Sonora was about to open the last Hurricane, that she had in the bag earlier before the throw-down. "Merial took the disgusting bullshit away from Sonora's hand and threw it out the window on Garden Walk Road like paper." "Sonora was like." "What the fuck man!" "That was my last Hurricane." Merial was like. whatever *Bitch!* In her mind. She wanted to clap Ms. Myers and pass her a clean beer. With the tone. Drink this and be quiet! And went through the apartment complex for tonight. The time was 11:40 p.m. when the relax mode was decreasing through the night after the aftermath took place. The hatred from Merial started to increase, as the Corona slinked through the DNA bloodstream of, feeling so good right-about now to Sonora. "But don't get-it-twisted home girl." I will clap you with this pistol again, for the second time, missy poo. Ms. aka, Stoney Myers. "Which, is some bullshit coming from you!" Merial said. As the spouse was thinking, when Sonora kept talking through Merial's thinking, how Sonora persuaded her to fit into a life as lovers that wasn't true in the beginning, that was betrayed by an evil person of her kind. The vibe was so strong... From bolt women. It was beginning to build from the kitchen table with Merial, and Sonora evil ways of not understanding why the bond was broke apart from two women that did the mating, by processing with the system to divide the man and woman from populating the earth, when the year 2070 hits. "What happen to you Merial?" "You're not the same." As Sonora wonders?

While Merial flips Sonora the middle finger in the air. "See! "That's what I'm talking about Merial." You have no ambition in me- "I was brain wash into this-shit, with most black culture that was implanted with much data, in this biomechatronic system that became the *New World Order* against the ignorant *niggas* that's a part of the new life, as Merial's mind sees it through psychological theory. "You are a stupid bitch!!!" "You know that!" "That's why I hate some-of-you black women today." "I really do!" Y'all, go along with everything in these cosmic paradox's form that's lad out for us blacks. When I was in New York doing my modeling gig with my sisters. Looking inappropriate in a Joker smile. "Other bitches in their exotic fashion." Was feeling some type of way about my body. So... I decided to use my body as a serious weapon for mankind on earth. "Not a dancing machine for the business. Not me! "I am an assassin bitch for this black culture." And. That's that!! "I'm making away for the new women, in this new era today, and beyond the next millennium so on. "That's how you feel Merial?" "To unify as an assassin, by annihilating humankind Merial." "Is that what you want?" Sonora said.

"Merial had enough of Sonora's bullshit, by pulling out her 9 mm into her face of evil that's been control for years and years." Everything was pleasant. As the nine was place towards Sonora's head to respect her as the woman of the house. That made Sonora run and jump onto the court. As she folded like a disfigure lost moment, that made the immune system shut down for the rest of the 30 seconds. Merial came back in sorrow with her *9 mm*, in Sonora's face, as tears were running down her eyes. "Why you have to do me like that Sonora?" Why?!! As Merial lowed herself on the side of the court, with the pistol right in the face of her smooth forehead, to end the great Merial Miller legacy forever. Merial was crying herself to death into abyss on the floor. Just holding the pistol with no dignity and honor. When Sonora rose to the occasion during the crying into sorrow in Merial's madness in sister hood.

Sonora was scared and frightened to touch and hold Merial with care in her heart for eternity. In the mind of Sonora Myers, that was very confused and cloudy, as the situation gets deeper and deeper with the two. Sonora took the chance, by holding Merial from behind her cry and emotional. But instead, she did a get-off-me rejection type renewal, as Sonora kept showing love and affection towards the source she loves.

As she tries to hug Merial again. Merial couldn't resist any long from Sonora's comfort for love at this dangerous time, that went down tonight. The crying was so deep, that. She finally gave into Sonora's arms like an infant child that's heavenly born and made love hones again in the rest of the night, until the sunrise reaches the surface once more in sister hood.

Chapter 72

Every time a new month occurs around the equation of new form, into the surface with mind body and soul through energy and physical life, that's eerie into the fall of October the 1st so windy. As time goes back. The time was 9:38 a. m. into the morning light. When Sonora put on one of Merial's jogging suits, that was all black from the inside closet. Sonora couldn't believe it. All Merial's jogging suits were leather down to the T in her dress code so manly. As she strolled through her wardrobe with curiosity that was all the same. Sonora took a very good glimpse at herself in the bathroom mirror, once Sonora saw the aggressive change that was in her sad reality through self. The horrible burn mark that was bad. But. Kind of unique at the same time in her woman hood. A few tears came down on the burn mark flowing from her left cheek and wrapping the drips off quickly. It was time for some good air through the atmosphere during the bright sunlight. Her gut wanted to grab the keys and take the Changer for a nice spin. But her mind couldn't engage in the moment of fear. Merial was sleeping peacefully with a lot of animosity, that. Sonora left the apartment. Running down the black steps with lots of energy. Sonora came across her old school homie, that was cool as a neighbor where she used to live three years ago, back in the days. After reuniting, and glad to see each other once more with a loving dap for peace. Through the black power of inspiration in each other's eyes. Sonora Myers begins to feel like the day walker herself like Draco Dawn. Her visual was thinking about him, heading towards the Swift convenient store for a cold Red Bull. Her moment was beginning to be bright again, as time started to rewind, back and forth into the store 100 times.

If she was Dorothy from the Wizard of Oz. Like, there's no place like home. As Sonora continued to be happy throughout the store for her earlier morning substance.

She bumped into a mysterious black gentleman by mistake. Which was Draco Dawn again for the third time. After she said excuse me and walked away. Draco slightly said. Sonora! "I-mean, Sonora." Is that you? Sonora slowly turned around with her hoodie on, with a pulse. "Oh my God." Draco! "What's up." "What've you doing here?" As they embrace the hug with love. Well... Just doing my regular routine girl. And, getting one of these cold drinks. I see you like Red Bull, yourself boo. Sonora said. What've-you doing-up-so earlier? Well. I decided to do some walking this morning. I had a rough night last night. I see Ms. Myers. As Draco looks at Sonora's body with an appetite around her thick leather. The conversation started to get real- deep in line with four people ahead of them. That disappeared so quickly in three minutes. As soon as Sonora had her 5-dollar bill to pay for her drink too kill. Immediately, Draco told her. I got you! "This on me." After paying for the drinks with his cedar card for the next chapter. Sonora, softly mention. Are you following me, Mr. Draco? This will be the third time we have bumped into each other. I find that strange, Mr. As they bolt smile at each other like couples. You want me to follow you, Ms. Sonora Myers? I would be glad to do so. After they bolted, came out of the convenient store together by smelling the wet air from Draco. The rain already receded smoothly, as they walked through Garden Walk again like last time. Does it feel like déjà vu again? Or. Am I'm dreaming once more? He told Sonora. You're not dreaming, Ms. Myers. This is real for us. So... Let's keep walking and talking until we can't walk anymore. And, Sonora said. That sounds great to me. I'm just following your lead, Mr. Draco. What are you listening to? If you don't mind me asking? As Sonora's mind wonder? I'm listening to Pandora Box, before I ran into you. So.

"What 'cha trying to say, Mr. Draco? While his eyes got bigger during her statement in laughter. "I'm just kitting." "Don't mind me." I like messing with people I met, for the very first time, that's all. "Don't take-it personal. As she grabbed his hand for comfort like a friend. But, in her mind. Sonora wanted more than just that, as his hand felt so good to hers. She wanted to ask him something, as she watched him deeply throughout their pleasant vibe. When a call came through for Draco Dawn's convenient in the mix with Sonora Myers.

The caller on the other end, told Draco. I will meet you at your house an hour from now. About time they reach Raceway again, like last time. I'd guess... This is our finally stop huh. No Sonora. I decided we can walk farther than last time. "What 'cha-think?" Or do you have something else to do instead? No. I'm good at Draco. My friend picked me up last night "Was trippin' bad." She didn't get enough sleep yesterday evening. Wow. "She much work late too huh." Y'all must have the same gig as well. Draco asks. No. She just stays up late. That's all. Sonora was beginning to get worried about what happened last night with Rico, that was deserved. And detective Pete, and his alliance of cops. Sonora knows, she's wanted for murder for her sister death. That detective Pete heard through the confrontation in the house. If Draco knew Sonora was a murderer on site. Which in her eyes, is a beautiful thing in Sonora's view? But, for Draco. He probably would've disowned Sonora for good and forever. And give her the thumbs down for the murder. The walk was very intriguing, as they reached Hwy 85 going to Valley Hill Rd. on, upper Riverdale Dr. "Where are you taking me this time sir?" As they are continuing holding hands with love and pride into the walk. The enjoyable journey became a disaster in Sonora's fate, when Merial pulled up again to score Sonora once more. Shit...! Was the word Sonora said in front of Draco? After saying it as well, under her tongue, while piss-off again. Merial gave Sonora that silent look like last night.

"To get your butt inside this car as a hent. "I'm sorry Draco." I- Lets go Sonora!! Before Sonora could complete her sorrows. Draco was already gone with thumbs up. "It's all good baby." In a conscious mind sign. She stares and watches him walk away in the fog of the morning as the day goes on again. Once Merial and Sonora took off into another mission as victims. Merial became vindictive towards Sonora's journey this morning with foolishness, and stupidity in public. "What the fuck are you doing Sonora?!"

"The law enforcement is looking for us, at this very moment."

"Especially, your ass." "They're, really looking for you!!" "I'd thought you was still sleep Merial." "Shut up Sonora and listen to me right now!" "This is some real information you need to hear. As Sonora's heartbeat begins to increase in her chest in the passenger seat. Merial broke down the fax and information she needed to hear immediately. "For one Sonora." I bugged your phone yesterday evening when you got outta jail. What?!! Sonora said. "How did you know I was locked up?" I saw your mug shot on the News that morning. Which. "It was a terrible picture of you." I just wanted to tell you that in person Sonora. It was horrible! "Very funny." As Sonora looks at Merial with a crazy look in her eyes. "I'm the one that bailed your ass out for the second time. "Any that something Sonora." "You-just-keep getting into deep shit, every time we are together." "I wonder why?" While Merial went into a flash back within herself during the look of. "Why-is-am fucking with you Sonora?" Sonora eyes begin to get bigger and bigger, as Merial started to get-deeper into the tales she was expressing. So... "If-it wasn't for my ass for bailing you out." You would still be in jail until Halloween. That's 30 days from now. And. "I know you don't want that, do you?" As Merial kept being precise so deeply into Sonora's eyes. While sitting back listening like a little child in space. So... In this case, Sonora. "When I paid your bail, to set you free."

That was a plot to lower you into my world, of finding you. And killing you for doing me wrong. "By giving you money to help a greedy witch, outta a situation that was struggling that suited Sonora to get by." "So..." "At this point, Sonora." "Your ass would be dead and decrepit inside my apartment stinking." "If-it wasn't for me." As destruction comes and craves death for your soul in the living days, while walking humble and peace on earth, while breathing.

"That's how bad I wanted you dead Sonora." In a Malcolm X assassination way. After hearing that from Merial's voice. Sonora was petrified and scared in her seat like a terrifying movie from hell. As she continues to speak in vain. And, that stunt thing that you did with that young dude, name Quincy. That was a weak, and pussy move you did as a woman. "That, really was pitiful, coming from you." You are supposed to be aware, Sonora around your surrounding as the black Goddess. That's how, mad and discussing that I was with you. "I really was." "That's how I felt about you, Sonora at the time, as I wanted to kill-you." "No-offence." "But, let me tell you who started this whole stitching crap." Your white bartender friend. Bob Stewart. That, I assassinated with joy. That made my pussy tingle with sensation, too were. I want to disintegrate and kill all bad flash of men until the rest of my deadly days as a black *GODDESS*.

Chapter 73

The woman in Merial became acceptable towards Sonora's heart, as she stays tune with Merial's truth about Sonora's murder that came out as a woman killer, that's repeated through history as a deva. "Oh." "Hell, naw bitch!" "You killed the bartender at the bar." Sonora asks. "Yes, I did!" Merial said. Bob needed to be assassinated immediately by Sonora. "Just, come down Sonora." "I-didn't do an inside job. "Is that-what 'cha you worried about." Just chill out! "We have more things to worry about than Bob dead ass." "So, he needed to be taken-in out with my 9 pieces.

I was watching the News when you were killing your dead friend, during y'all bullshit observation. That whole night you were going through that experience. I was two houses deep down in front of the whole thing, when they were putting you inside the police vehicle. Now... The whole murder thing about murdering the cops on your behalf, was a plot to manipulate your mind as a Jedi trick, as the News sees it with law enforcement, and detective Pete. "That's the ass hole wanted me incarcerated for good Merial." "Tell me about-it." Merial said. "That's the same bitch had me for questioning at the East Point facility that morning." "He was a mothafucka jerk when him, and the other cops put the pressure on me through custody. This is not the first time he questioned me either! It was one night, when I came up at the 6043 club for something. Yeah! "I just remember." The place was close temporary for six months, of the death of George Willison. I remember that night. Merial said. I was the one in the dark shade on watching the whole scene Sonora. So.

You were watching me that whole time, as I was being questioned by that selfish devil as a detective. Yes, I was: "I wanted to annihilate and obliterate his ass. "And, I had a clean shot too." "Wow, Merial." You have really changed over the years. "I wonder why?" After that common Sonora made. Everything was silence for 20 seconds during the ride to McDonough Georgia for another mission. That's when Sonora asked the question? What happened to you Merial? What change? Merial didn't want to answer, as Merial dash into the bushes with the Changer like a pissed-off ram from hell. "What the fuck Merial!" "What are you doing woman?" Throughout the confusion from Sonora's mind. A bunch Deer's ran like hell as Merial swerve in the middle of the field for target practice as normal. Amazingly, tire tracks were all around like a big circle in the field, as the Changer parked in front in first gear, halfway into the bushes. "What's going on Merial?" "Why are we out here?" Grab the Coronas. As Merial said to Sonora. "I know you want one." As Merial was grabbing the weapons and her black bullet proof vest that was very comfortable in good taste. "When you get through with your cold beer." You can join me if you want to. Once Merial left Sonora with a complicated situation, by throwing an extra vest on the pretty green grass, that made you wanna snuggle. The eyes of Sonora watches

Merial walk away into the field in confusion. Sonora continued drinking, wondering what the hell Merial is up to with these weapons she is about to do? Four shots came back-to-back into Sonora ears, that made her jump back into reality of what's going on. Slowly Sonora drinks with no dignity, or passion to smash like she normally does when there's cold beers in the house. Continually, Sonora watches her ex-lover repeatedly, as her body structure formulates termination with the smooth sniper, that's hitting the target nicely and prefect. Sonora was amazed at how well Merial looks at things to question her on faith of who's going to live or die in this law of a democracy.

Sonora sees the future of her death, from many murders that she had committed over the decade. The shooting from Merial, reminded Sonora of who she is as an assassinator of many deaths down the years. Sonora finishes her beer and grabs the black bullet proof vest. And ask Merial will you train me, of what's about to come in the mouth of October, during the days about to happen. As death begins to come through the eyes of the devil with Sonora Myers revelation. The eye of the demon was recognizing the master passion of rejuvenating the apprentice for the next mission to come. As Sonora begins to have trouble with her shooting towards the target with Merial's assistant. With the shooting that went on and on through the atmosphere on fire from Sonora, that needs more practice. The voices in Sonora head, that was coming from Merial's visions tone of more punishment that needs retribution. The integrity became vicious inside Sonora's heart for more killing and so on, while the Intensity of Sonora kept shooting to death with good intentions to kill detective Pete for the upcoming. As the confusion wanted to escape from Sonora's soul, to tell Merial about her evil deeds. That's when Merial said. "Your gun aim is-getting pretty good, crazy woman." Keep it up! While smiling from Merial, as she walks like Sarah Connor with style, heading towards the cooler for a cold one from two hours of practice. After 45 minutes of good drinking, as the New Blood Hounds. The new revelations started to begin for the two assassins as the new Black Panther of black power. Sonora's confession, ask Merial? Do you want to hear my confession? While the vibe needed to build up for 10 seconds. I killed that dude inside the 6043 club before I met you. Merial heard the voice. But, continued drinking like-it-wasn't no surprise in her vibe, while the cool Corona flow through her warmly body of laugher within. More arrived from Sonora's confession towards Merial's ears as things started to get very interesting for more.

As Sonora's cruelty of communing with Merial made her releases more confession towards the death of her own sister Kimberly, with rage and envy and, revenge from her *DEVILISH WAYS* in Sonora Myers. "Well, well now." You're the one that killed your own sister three years ago. I heard about that when I was on tour in New York. "It was a horrible tragedy." But, clever, and cold-blood-it from an *EVIL WITCH,* coming you. How do you feel being a murderer for so many years Sonora? As Merial continued slipping on the flavor beverage she loved. After going back and forth with sharing, how many victims she killed in the pass, with lots of laugher in the air. Things started to get deeper with another confession from Sonora Myers towards

Merial, her conscious friend as Blood Hounds for life. By keeping the bond tight forever as new revelational women towards the law enforcement during this era. Sonora stated. Once at a point and time, when I was a little girl with my sisters. We had so much love as little girls together when we played all day long as blood sisters. The world that we lived in back then was so free as children until you reached the age of eighteen. And that's when life changes for me, and my sisters. My sister Stacy left home at the age of 17 when she found a job to manage herself without our mother's support. Our mother loved Kimberly more than me and Stacy back then. Mother always supposed Kimberly's life with money and love through her childhood as things gotten good for my deceased sister Kimberly that my mother loved more than others. So... Over the years of growing up as sisters under our mother's power. I started becoming hatred, and envy towards Kimberly up-bring under mother's love. During the time of envy. Stacy was already gone with her life. I remained at the house to make a difference, to prove to my mother I'm better than my smart sister Kimberly in the mix. "But that didn't work." My mother still showed more love towards Kimberly possibility than me. So, I began to hate my mother from that point on.

The envy really came outta me through darkness in my heart and soul. So, I hated bolt of them at the same time. Then, it got to a point, that. Kimberly started to blossom and-being bossy around me in front of mother and Stacy. "I hated that shit!" And it continued. Until. That very night on her birthday. "That's when the magic begins. I in up putting some clean bleach into my mother's milk, when the was still vicious that Friday night towards me. That early morning, around 7:15 A.M. She passed away. And. "I was happy too, when she died." I felt rejoices in heaven like Jesus. That's how peaceful I was when she heavenly die in her own fate. That's why I had to take them out Merial. When Merial heard that touching story. She wasn't impressed with the murder thing. Not at all! Merial felt like it was a normal thing to do in a demonic world. Merial opened the trunk and loaded everything out of the Changer. And headed through the pathway in the bushes that was a clear passageway to her Cabin as an underground living. "Where are we going?" As Sonora started yelling all over the outside field like an ignorant Negro.

After the trumpet sound that was register from Sonora's voice. Merial wasn't hearing Sonora's loudness from the flow through the trees and atmosphere, during the silent walk around the nature of life. And then. Another thing Sonora how to do was. Stay humble and quiet and follow Merial's lead in an economic way so common that the vibe itself wouldn't hear you within the anatomy.

Chapter 74

The night became to be creepy, but. Very scary into the dark side of reality around the black moment. Merial had the fireplace going like the hot wilderness throughout the living room cabin, feeling real cozy as Sonora was coming in from the outside, wondering what the hell is going on here? "Wow, Merial." "This place is dope." It's not as luxury as the other place. But. This can work! While Sonora was investigating the whole scene inside the cabin. Merial was chopping up some deer meat with her sharp Bucher knife in a samurai way and style. The whole scenery became amazing in Sonora's eyes, from up and down bolt level of the home. The cabin was becoming chilly in a ghostly type of vibe. As Sonora walks towards the fireplace slowly when the heat continues to build up. Merial had the kitchen smelling meaty and tuff with great joy when a woman brings good love into the kitchen. Two hours just went by. And it was time to eat by the fireplace, like Merial does best in a warm environment during dinner time. The position was very awkward the way she had the two single couches from left to right. With the table in the middle, in between the two comfortable seats that were settled around the fireplace. After the feast, and a good conversation around the wooden living room. As the two deadliest women was manifesting into the couch with a shot of Brandy talking about the messy world in front of the warm fireplace bear footed. While drinking their Brandy like warm tea, just as quiet as they wanna be, if it was a library of reading or thinking for humans that's present on earth and reality. Can I ask you a question, Ms. Sonora Myers? Sure Merial!

"What's up, with you in-these multiple relationships you gotten yourself into since you been married to your so-called husband for so many years as a *devilish thang*. Why haven't kids been populated since y'all been together unfaithfully? "Why is that?" "I don't understand." Merial said. "Let me tell you why I'd became a lesbian the first place." As Merial's mind begins to get deeper in the mist. I didn't want to indulge the pain and shuffling through my torment as a queen. "Why, struggle with that shit!" "You just doing it, just to get a pay day." Not love! "If you look at it." It's a sad reality for men and women put together. That's why I'd don't date men at all, on this planet we try to stive for. My mother told me before she passed away. Never engage with a man. No matter what color they are. (NEVER!) What happened to your father? Sonora said. Well... Hate, to tell you this. She murdered him in a plot she planned when they first met in the late 70's. My mother told my father straight-up in a grocery store. I'm not having no relationship with a man. She politely, told him over-and-over again, about ten times in his face. *NO!!* "It's not happening." But he kept persisting in vain. Like men normally do when they want something through their man hood. So... My mother went along with the situation for a decade. Until she was pregnant with me. Which she'd hated and hated him forever causes of that.

Their relationship was terrible for 13 years in the making. So., she told herself. After the 13th year of being together. Which is her favorite number of all time. So, that's when my mother decided to have me. And take good care of me and show me so much love, more than my father.

Everything just stopped with my mother and father during that era. After she had me. The sex was completely stop forever as well. And my father was pissed-off for years – because of that! Sonora said. "My mother didn't give a damn." Even if he wanted to cheat on my mother. "She'd didn't give a flying-fuck at that point." "She just had enough with his ass." "Just done with him."

"So." "You-mean to tell me." "Your mother quit having sex with your father?" Yes! Merial said. Oh, hell naw!! As Sonora was tripping about the celibacy from Merial's mother. So, at that point in their relationship. My mother was fed-up with his mad dog ways and took him out. She didn't get into the details of how she finished him, but. "It was a rap!" My mother hated sex. To her. It was a disgusting chemistry, in her mind, body and soul situation. How did she get her mind to adapt to that? And how? Sonora said out loud. My mother had the willpower to do it. And she just did it. The only thing that Sonora could say was. Wow! About four times straight with voice. That's why I'd can't date men because of that. "I'd don't have time for that pregnancy shit." "That shit, isn't fun to me as a strong black soldier."

Once the dap became committed with knuckle power from the blood hounds. Sonora told Merial. "I feel you on that shit sister girl." And gave Merial another strong dap. "What about you, crazy Myers?" As Sonora laughed a little bit slipping on her Brandy. It's nothing to tell. "I'm just a crazy mothafucka!" "That's all!" Merial was just laughing her ass off when she heard that funny moment from Sonora's mouth. "You stupid!" As Merial laughed again. I'm 'ma stop calling you Sonora; or-is-it Stoney, which-one? After Sonora gave Merial the middle finger with a laugh. Merial said to Sonora. Your new name will be. *Crazy Myers*. That-fit-you! With a finger pointed to recognize the character of Ms. Sonora Myers. *AKA, Stoney Myers.*

As Sonora begins to get deep into her character with Merial. Merial was starting to feel peace and rejoice within her soul as a black woman with Sonora Myers once more. I can't see how you do it Sonora; with these men you be screwing around with. "I can't see myself doing that shit." Never! "I don't want no parts of dick into-me like that. Hell no!! "Girl..." You don't know what 'cha you are missing. "You need to try that shit." It might loosen-you-up a bit. While Sonora was fucking-with Merial about her sexually self. Merial was like!

"I'm not doing that shit!" "You-can-forget-about-that." Said Merial. Sonora just went on and on about her sexually adventure with different men in her life as the laugher continued with Merial throughout the whole night. Sonora was glad to see Merial laughing again, since the crazy escapade went down between her and Merial, and detective Pete from this confusing mayhem that's circulating.

Chapter 75

A new day has arrived, with the temperature being 62 degrees on October 16th into the cool atmosphere around the surface. Merial has been training Sonora for the past two weeks, on the open ground, turning into a massive assassinator with fire power. The time was hitting around 8:45 a.m. when Sonora prepared herself on the field with her own sniper. Just tearing the living daylight outta the target zone. Sonora was training massively hard on the field with blood in her eyes. Her strength became impactable for a blood hound of destruction, as she rolls six times into the grass so smoothly and com. The embrace from the nine-millimeter was sharp and sweet, with the technique that Sonora delivered over the weeks. Merial was impressed with the skills that she taught Sonora as a sniper from a distance on the wooden deck. While Merial stands like a soldier with her arms in the back in all black wearing her bullet proof vest looking tuff. Crazy Myers. As Merial sees it. Walked back into the cabin to watch some early morning News like always at this time. Before Merial, turn on the television. She wanted to hear that 4th of July sound one more time from Sonora's 9 mm a few sounds more like music. Pop-pop-pop, as the sound goes towards the target of death in polarizing. Pop-pop-pop once more while Merial stands firmly in a general position with beautiful impact. Finally, Merial turned on the TV, while running up the stairs with no rail on the steps with no support, coming up or down. Merial had a one-bedroom cabin just for her, that was rather unique in her condition. She grabbed one of her snipers from off the wall that was all black for some decent cleaning as she watches the News to relax.

After she left, watching all her precious snipers that were on the wall mounded like manuals, if-their-were animal heads. Sonora's name was streaming through the TV screen repeatedly, as the male reported reveal new information about the murder of Kimberly Myers, by her sister Sonora Myers. Merial rushed down the stairs to hear more. When the reporter was speaking about a random sniper that was taking out many officers that night, when cops were about to burst Sonora. Channel 2 News was showing a terrible picture of Sonora Myers face on the screen. Along with an unknown black picture beside Sonora's. And then. The reporter said. The two suspects are seriously dangerous and wanted in the state of Georgia. The only thing Merial could say was. "I be damn!" As she holds the sniper so tightly. McDonough police cars were everywhere in the front area. But, scattered at different doors of questioning. Merial left the scene from the window, by saying. "Oh shit, too wanted Sonora of what's going on." Merial tried to wanted Sonora, by screaming from a distance to stop shooting immediately. But Sonora didn't hear Merial at all. As Sonora continued shooting with pride, during the shooting. Merial running her ass off to stop Sonora in her militia, as her back was turned. And bum-rush Sonora like a vicious hard spear outta nowhere from her.

The impact made Sonora say. "What the fuck man!" "Why did you do that?!" Shut up! "Just listen to me." As Merial's raging voice became powerful outside. "We need to leave, now!" "Cops are everywhere in the front." "In the minute." They will be knocking on the door in 60 seconds. Everything was rushing hour through the mind, as they were cleaning up the evidence of all the weapons. "Where is the Changer Merial?" "Don't worry about that." "We need to leave!" When Merial came out the garage with the 2012 Range Rover, like she did three years ago, at the time Sonora took her to the airport back then. Sonora was amazed and shocked Merial still had the Range Rover in her possession.

After telling Sonora to get in, she shut down the cabin for safe keeping. Sonora had the snipers broken down quickly into the stern suitcase nicely in the back. Sonora was waiting for Merial to come back. But, 30 minutes later. They burned rubber through the field to exit out into the freeway. But they couldn't. Because of the blockage from the wired fence that was towards the expressway to be free. The white stone wall, in the middle of the freeway, was the other lane they needed to head back South towards Clayton County in Riverdale. The danger of fast pace really had Sonora in a dilemma for the passenger, as they went through some bushes through the field to get on a random road to their destination. Cops and State Patrol were flying on the expressway, heading towards the field where they had just come from in Merial's rearview mirror. "That shit was intense outta nowhere." "God..." "Damn!" "I see why you stopped me." "I'd almost gotten us busted." Shit!! "I'm sorry, girl." "Don't be sorry Sonora." You must be careful around your surroundings. "We are wanted right now." Well... Least you are, at this point. "I hate to say this to you like this. But. Welcome to the real world. "Crazy Myers." As Sonora laughs quietly to herself. Try not to get too comfortable over there.

"We are in a dangerous position, right about now." So, you can't be slippin' like that back there. I've been doing this for two years now. That's why I'd stay sharp, and on point as a sniper. My mission must stay perfect, for all surrounding Sonora. And. That's reality. So. You believe in being perfect Merial? Yes! "Do all women do." Yeah... "You do have a point."

Sonora said. Me and Rico used to argue about that all the time. Sometimes, for months. I remember when we first moved in into our house. Wait! You don't have to listen if you don't want to Merial. I know you didn't like Rico back then when we were dating. "I still hate his ass." "But." Keep going." Said Merial. "I need to hear this." Merial remained listening while one hand was on the steering wheel, and the other resting like a baby.

The perfect of being a woman, became deep. But, interesting through the smooth ride to Riverdale around 1:20 p.m. in the early daylight. So... Are you going to tell me what made you who you are? Or. I must force it outta you? While Sonora was smiling at Merial. By getting off on Riverdale exit. Proceeding straight passing Checkers where the West Elementary School lactated at. "You, got to tell me Merial, what happen to you." Later, Merial said. "Their-go-your-boy." Look! "Oh shit!" With surprise in

Sonora's eyes. "That's Draco." "Let's give him a ride Merial."
Hell no! "I don't know him like that." "What's wrong with
you bitch!" "You are a wanted person Sonora." "You can't
trust know one right now." Hell! "You-wanted-too." "Please
don't do me like that Merial!" You wanted too! Yeah! "But
least my picture isn't shown like yours." "They got your
picture all over the News." So. "I think, we shouldn't give no
one a ride, right about now. Especially, him.

"We don't know him like that." "That reminds me." This
is the third time I have seen him. The other two: I'd rolled
up on you guys. "What's going on with-you-two?" "If you
want to fuck him." Be my guess! "But you need to be careful
Sonora." "You're a grown ass woman." Do-what 'cha-do
Sonora. "That's all I'm saying." As Merial threw her hands
back to release some pressure away from Sonora's vibe.
Sonora quietness watches Draco walk like he normally does,
every time she sees him in a moment like this for the 10th
time. Riverdale police were everywhere during the scene of
finding Ms. Sonora Myers as a wanted murderer. "Oh shit,
was the word that came outta Merial's mouth." As Sonora
had the 9 Glock ready to kill a cop when they approach
the Garden wood Apartments on deck. "Put that shit away."
We don't want to cause a scene Sonora. "Just, chillout." Let
me head over here at the ALDI right quick, so I can get
my thoughts intact. "Is that cool?" Sonora said. "This some
bullshit, right about now!" "Everything is going to be fine
Sonora." "Just come down!" "Grab a Corona, or something."
While the blood hounds were enjoying their cool Corona's.
Merial notice, Draco was conversating with one of the
officers for five minutes with a smile. "Look at this shit

Sonora." "Check-out-your-boy." As Sonora looks with concern, in her eyes. But not really. They just asked him a few questions, that's all. No-biggie! I don't know, crazy Myers. "Something looks fishy about that." What are you going to do about this Rico situation? It's nothing to be done Merial. The marriage is over. It's no going back now. Even if I went back. He would kill me. And that's the fact. Even if you wanted to work it out. "He will still kill you?" Yes. Rico would still kill me. Said Sonora. "Damn!" "That's fucked-up Crazy Myers."

Hell, even you wanted to kill me for what, I had done to you. Yeah. As Merial agreed with Sonora. After four hours went by talking about life and relationships towards one another through the pain. The cops were retreating from the resident at 5:39 p.m. during the Riverdale traffic to check in for the day. Merial had to park at the very front, where you come through the grate on the left side of the parking lot, by the bushes on the side where the burgundy tinted Changer, that was similar-to Merial's black Changer back at the cabin.

"Damn, that's a bad-ass Changer." "Look Merial." Merial was engaged as well with the same taste. "Whoever Changer that is." "That's-bad-ass-hell." It almost looks like yours. It is mine Sonora. "Bad machine, isn't-it." Wow! Sonora said. "There you go with those surprises again." "It never fails with you." "What's next Merial?" I'm glad you said that. "I'd must leave you now." What!! "Where the hell are you going now?" Off into another mission Sonora. "Be back." Wait-a-minute. "I can't ride?" I thought, maybe we can test out the machine right now. Another time Sonora. I must go back to the cabin to rethink a new plan. Here's the keys. And don't think about taking my car, either. "Whatever you do." Stay in the apartment. After that. Merial was gone for a whole week and beyond.

Chapter 76

The wind was blowing cool air on that Saturday night, as the 22nd of October flows around with eight more days to go, until Halloween arrives with trick-or-treaters just waiting. Sonora and Draco just left the wing shack walking back to the apartment to finish watching a movie on Blu-ray, that was on phase for one hour. If Merial knew Sonora had Draco throughout the apartment in five days. She would be furious with her blood hound sister, that lost site when Merial left Sonora by herself unguarded while Sonora was eating her share of the 60-piece hot wings watching Resident Evil. Draco was talking on his cell phone inside the bathroom, about business on Halloween day. The person wanted the situation to go down tonight, in full alert and throttle with the deal. After Draco told the mystery person. Give me eight more days, and it will be over. Draco came out the bathroom cordial and happy, during that moment with a kiss on Sonora cheek for missing her for 15 minutes. Is everything okay in the back baby? You took so long. I thought I'd have to go back there to see you. You could've. "I don't have no problem with that." As Draco grabs Sonora on the side with aggression in a manly and kiss her if they were a new couple. Draco and Sonora were full off the wings and a movie at 11:30 p.m. close to midnight. Sex was on the brain from bolt different worlds as the TV was off temporary when it was time for Draco to walk back home for the night. While holding hands, by looking at each other in close range towards the door, nose touching with the third moment for the night. Draco Dawn left as the night walker, that suited him well than the day walker back then. The cold midnight was feeling good for Draco as he walked back home, as he picked up speed into jogging back to Hwy 85 running. About time he made it towards the Raceway.

He released a special text from Sonora Myers. And it said. I'm here. Draco was like. You here! What!! Before he knew it. The bright lights from the Changer almost blind him immediately from the Changer. The panic from Draco, almost made him call for back-up as he pulled his 9 mm. "Draco, it's me, Sonora." I didn't mean to scare you. You can put your Glock down. "Damn, Sonora!" "I could have shot you woman!" "You scared the living night outta me." "I'm sorry baby." Just get in please. Slowly Draco put his 9 mm back into his host and watched Sonora for 11 seconds eye to eye. "Please baby, get in." It's chilly out there. "Please Draco." After his mind slap back into Draco made. They were good rolling out together to Valley Hill, on Upper Riverdale Rd. The ride was cool and com. When she finally pulls up to Draco's house for the very first time since they met. "This is quite nice Draco." I like it: do you want to come in for a little bit of Sonora? "You are welcome." Just before Sonora could say any sweat words. Merial was calling. "And it scared the shit outta Sonora's vibe." "It really did." So, she took the call quietly, and the conversation began. And. What was so funny, in between Sonora talk with Merial. A call that came through Draco's phone was important as well. The situation was spooky, but weird at the same moment. Draco had to step out of the car for a second to handle this business. Sonora was cool when Draco gave the thumbs up on his behalf to take this call. She was glad he stepped out to camouflage the sound as a human being for her safety. What Sonora didn't know. Detective Pete was watching the whole scene, from the inside of his vehicle laughing. Merial was asking Sonora, what's been going on at the apartment since I been gone?

You been staying outta trouble, *Crazy Myers?* Dominic stepped into the scene behind Draco's phone call outta nowhere from the back. That made him say. "Oh, shit." "What are you doing here woman?" In the back of his mind. Draco had to cut his situation short from the phone with the detective quickly. "Sonora." "I'm sorry."

"I had to take care of this old business with this woman, that's old news to me. Sonora had to hang up right away, so Merial wouldn't hear the voice in the background that's going on what she sees. "Fuckin'-A!" "I finally got your number bitch!" The Taurus was really coming outta Sonora soul when she seen her former friend, Dominic in a long time since 2012, the good old days. It became 12:40 a.m. at the QT, as Sonora phone continue to ring back-to-back from Merial. Sonora came out the QT fully hoodie-up over her head. So, people wouldn't recognize her as a wanted killer around the scene. Detective Pete was in a position-very-well in the cut by the dumpster at QT watching Sonora. As she was coming out heading back to her vehicle. Her friend Dominic pulls up by the gas pump for a full up for next week work schedule. Sonora looks at Dominic from pump eight with a plan to plot her downfall. The voice scared Dominic with Sonora's loud county ways through one ear, to another. Dominic turned around, and Sonora was right there touching noise with Dominic Walker. "Oh my God!"

"Sonora." "Is that you?" Yes. It's me. With a quiet tone. "Girl." "Do you have to be so loud." After telling Dominic in hush verbal. The weirdness from Dominic face begin to wonder about Sonora tone at her. When you get back from paying for your gas. We need to ride out somewhere and talk. After Dominic gave Sonora the okay, as she walked in. Sonora jumped in the back seat of her car and lay low like a grocery bag in the dark. Dominic became suspicious as she was looking for Sonora, after pumping gas for five minutes. She waited for five more minutes. And she left heading towards Upper Riverdale Rd. to Walmart shopping center. Detective Pete couldn't believe Sonora wasn't on site. After he pulled it off as well. Dominic had the same 86 old-school Lincoln two years, when Sonora and Ms. Walker were cool back then. Just before Dominic reaches the red light on Valley Hill Rd.

A shot went off immediately into Dominic's skull from termination. After the massive kill. The blood hound Sonora drives away feeling so good with deserving music in the dark atmosphere cold.

Chapter 77

The month of October the 25th was getting colder by the minute, through the night. When Sonora stayed low for two days on a peaceful route. The Tuesday News was on.

Sonora received a call from her bloodhound sister Merial. Through the 8th day separation from Merial and Sonora that was changing through the mayhem experience as wanted women. "What's going on sis?" Nothing much Merial. "What's the deal with you?" "You act like, you can't come home-in-shit." Don't worry Sonora. I'll be back tomorrow night. I promise!! We had to separate, and lay low for a couple of days, until the heat went down. But. Little did Merial know. A lot of unnecessary drama was going on since she been gone in eight days. "Hey." Did you hear about, what happen to that black woman on Saturday night; that was shot in the head? Yeah. I'm watching the News right now. "That's a sad tragedy. Even doe, Sonora didn't give-a-damn what happen to the woman. You been keeping my apartment safe, Crazy Myers? Of cause! Sonora said. Don't forget, this used to be my apartment back in the days. Yeah, I remember. I was trying to come inside, too. But that's when you had that Rico dude I hated. "I know you hated him back then.

Sonora said. As they bolt laugh. Just before Merial about to say something else. Blue and red lights were flashing in front of the complex, five cars deep. Looking for Sonora. "Damn!" "What's wrong?" "Why are you damning?" "I'm, okay." It-just five police cars looking for my ass. That's all. Well. "Don't take your ass out there, then." I wouldn't mind doing it, at this moment. "I have my Glock ready too." "Don't be stupid Sonora." "I know you been train for this." But. "Just, cool out."

Sonora had the nerve to be outdoors, with her black Cargo pants on, and black tank-top with the bulletproof vest ready, in black socks holding the 9 Glock in her hand. The word boo, scared Sonora half to death. As the 9 mm was pointed directly at Draco's chest.

"Dammit Draco." "I'd almost shot you." "What the fuck!" Did I scare you? Draco said. "Hell, yeah you did." After he hugged and kissed her and said, "I'm sorry. The question was like." "What are doing with that Glock girl?" I didn't know you carried a 9 Glock like that. "Let me see that thing." As he was holding and waving the 9 with her back turned looking at the cops. Sonora doped her phone, while Merial was still on it on the bottom level. As she slumps low on the balcony rail watching her phone on speaker. Draco had the bust in the prom of his hand, pointed at Sonora's back for the kill. Sonora turned around slowly, so he wouldn't be recognized by his action with his penis being so hard in the murderers' eyes. What've you doing here Draco? I just came to see you Sonora, that's all. After a kiss on the lips. He asks her to take a ride with him. For a nice stroll in the street. She asks. Where-we-going? It's a surprise baby. As they walk slowly towards the living room. Telling Draco to sit tight while she put her boots on in the bedroom. Draco took six pills of Tylenol extra p.m. and crushed them with his gun handle for an easy smash. Quickly, he poured the powder into the Corona for smooth doping. "Damn, girl." "Where are you going with that carrying case in your hand? I need to visit my niece and brother-in-law while we are out Draco. Can you do that for me baby? As she rubs his face softly. The deal was complete with an okay in Draco's eyes of, let's ride. Sonora headed towards the burgundy Changer for another ride in it, for the last time. "Hey, Sonora." "Where are you going?" We'll riding in this car." "Let's go." What the hell! "When did-you get this?" I have been doing this for years Sonora. I just don't drive as much these days. "Why didn't you tell me you had a ride, all this time?" I see you walking all these years when I see you.

I thought you were a bum or something. Said Sonora. "Why would you think that." Everybody that walks. Isn't always what it seems Sonora. Remember that. That's how I'd bounce life. Don't do too much around your rim as a person. You should've, please told me you had a ride. "Why." Draco said. "You must make people think you don't have shit." Never let anyone know your next move in life. "Don't do that." I learned that in the military for 20 years, as a combat fighter. "Damn." Was the word Sonora said towards Draco's lifestyle? I'm-just-getting hit with all kinds of surprises. Wow! "Sonora was feeling all fucked up, right about now." Well, Sonora. Don't feel too bad about the whole situation. It could've been worse for me. Those 20 years in the military made me a strong man. "I'm just glad I survive, that's all."

So, you know about combat fighting? Yes! I was specially trained for years Sonora. You didn't get married when you got outta the military? No! "I'd didn't have time for the activation and bullshit from the wicket fresh." My buddy, that was in the military with me. Went through that horrible situation with his wife for 22 years. He was a good man. A powerful man, and a good dude as well. He's one of my heroes until this day, and forever. Do you still talk to him? No, I can't. Because Bill committed suicide when we bolt retired from the military. Wow! That's a terrible way to go out. "Damn, Draco." I'm sorry to hear that. So. What happened? Why did he kill himself? So, when he finally came home for good. Bill caught his wife with another man in his bed nude. Then, after that. I haven't heard from him in two years. And, when I receive the feedback from the missing report of Bill. He shot himself three times in the woods. Wow, that's awful. Sonora said to Draco. That's why I'd didn't deal with any women, while I was in the military. The first thing they would say. I cheated on him because he's been gone too long. Or. It's not my fault you wanted to join the military. Well... She might've had her reason for doing that. Sonora said. "Fuck that Sonora." "Don't believe that brain washing bull clap."

It isn't, nothing but lies towards an ignorant man in this wicket system. So. After my buddy die. I put out a hit on her. So, she wouldn't get his beneficiary and will. Or nothing. I hired a sniper to terminate her from this world. Wow...! "Are you serious!" Wow!! "That's how that works." After hearing that from Draco. Sonora was quiet and done.

Chapter 78

The night and the hour around 10:40 in the Cobb County area was slowing down when they reached the resident of the King's family on the side by the red wooden mailbox. Kimberly lovely home still, remain looking stunning with life after death. Is this the right house Sonora? As Sonora stares at the house from the moment of fear. Yes, this is the right house, Draco. I'll be right back, okay. Cool, he said. Sonora got closer to heaven or hell towards the red front door. The knock three times made her vibe feel, not wanted from the ghost of Kimberly behind Sonora's back as a wanting. After three more knocks. The wind went away temporary, as Chad opens the door with madness in his eyes. Hey Chad, became the welcome from Sonora voice to him and her, if the hug was impossible to Chad. "What are you doing her Sonora? "You shouldn't be here." As the voice wanted to choke Sonora to death with disrespect. You know I want to kill you, right. So. You might want to leave before I'd call the cops. You didn't have to do that. The cops were already looking for me, anyway. So, don't worry Chad about me. I'm turning myself in. You already know I'm wanted for murder. It's all over the airwave. "Good." Now, you can leave. Okay. Before I'd leave. Can I'd speak to Kimmy J. for a moment? If you don't mind? No!! "You can't Sonora."

"Please Chad." I know you are mad with me right now. But. I just want to speak with her for a minute, or two. It's my last chance. "After this." You will not see me again. I promise. Chad face was angry with Sonora outcome, of what she did to his wife Kimberly. But the sacrifice was mutual on his behalf from Sonora. "Alright." I'm only doing it for Kimmy J. Not you. You have 30 minutes. And that's it. "After that." You must go. See you around Sonora. I hope God spare your soul.

After Chad gave Sonora the evil eye, of not returning forever. Kimmy J. slowly comes down the steps in all black with depression in her heart from reality. Daddy told Kimmy she had 30 minutes with Sonora in an eerie voice, to make her look at her father with evil intention. How are you doing Kimmy? I've just found Sonora. You are just like your mother. Just feisty like her. Sonora couldn't believe how grown Kimmy J. had gotten over the years. I see you like black too. It looks good on you. I'd like it! As Kimmy J. looks straight at the world with her arms cross, in a complex state of mind. By looking at her niece with great concern in her eyes. Sonora knew this situation wasn't going to be easy for her during this conversation. Sonora had to be patient and relax. But. Don't show no type of emotion towards the 19-year-old Kimmy J., that, one day will be a full-grown woman. Sit down. Let's talk for a moment. Because. I'd like to ask you something. Do you hate me Kimmy J.? Because if you do. I can understand. Whatever you are feeling. I truly understand. Even-if you want to hate me forever. I will-still love you to the day I die Kimmy J. I don't hate you Sonora. I just being doing some thinking about this whole mess.

It's almost like, I just had a revelation about what was the real purpose behind my mother, and grandmother's death. It was like. My reality needed to be rebooted through my pedigree of brainwashing that became the pressure into my mother through me, to make me submit to this education system through hypnosis as a program for the future. I feel so sad from the inside, that. I don't feel human anymore. I'm beginning to sound like a Google soundtrack through my mother's lectures of achieving to be the best, when I was a child with deadly purposes of being perfect for her. It's sad she died. Just like my grandmother. But she was wrong for syncing me into this system that the white society has created for their technology, when the year 2099 hit for digital mankind. I hated school Sonora! "I really do." I hated all types of subjects through history to this point, and on. You know why, I'm so smart Sonora.

As Kimmy J. continued to look up into the moon and stars like Armageddon were coming. Tell me baby: as the cycle of life continues to get deep for Sonora to have a seat, for more knowledge from Kimmy. Every subject that I get wrong. My privilege was taken away from me. And it progressed on and on, until I age through time to be perfect for my, mother!!! Tears were running down her cheek from pain and suffering, as Sonora watched her niece go through life and reality. I hated my mother for doing me like that. But. You know what Sonora. That made me a strong little girl. Over the years of being tortured by the subject of Ms. Kimberly. Which-is-my deceitful mother. I train myself, not to do TV, video games, movies, and outside activities with kids. "Which, it was fucken boring to me." "I hated toys, when Christmas came, and my birthday as well. "I'd didn't want shit from my presents." But books. Because that was the key to life for me as a girl. You know, why I'd hate math so much. Why! Sonora said. It's a cinematic symbiotic symbol, that was initiated into AI to measure life on the moon. Through gravity and other planets for their theory calculation into space. That's why they have built schools for children, for many decades. That was the reason why they brainwash presents through their kids with education. "That is an hellified purpose, isn't-it." That's when I knew I'd become a product of my own mother's creation when she made me. She taught me how to master words and numbers as a program through a digital phase like the Matrix. With all the A's and B's that I have accomplished for my mother and father. Doesn't mean a thing when technology hits the fan for human race. The system uses money to create schools and education to trick people into-believing that, human race is going to last forever from the flesh. I love my daddy. But. I hate my daddy with much love in my heart. "I hate him some much." He sat there and let his wife brain wash me with that bull clap as a father. "I feel like a slave Sonora." Fuck school. "My daddy is a brainwash fool, like my mother was.

All that education she has accomplish in her life, didn't mean a damn-thing." Look at her now." "Dead as a doorknob." But. "Guess what Sonora." I'm going to finish school, and get my diploma, to prove to my father, and my dead mother, I'm not a drop out. And show him my diploma in his face and burn it. So, that way. When I moved out from my dad. I will be free forever. And that's my next mission. Kimmy said. Don't you feel-it Sonora. As gravity from the sun is getting closer to the earth. "I feel-it." I know you do. I felt it when I'd was a little girl. Now, I'd come to realize. Why education is very important to parents. To use our minds and sync it into a mainframe component as data. So. To answer your question. Do I hate you for killing my mother? No. I don't Sonora. You did me a flavor. I was going to do that anyway. Once I became your age. I love you Sonora. And forever. After those future words from Kimmy J. She hugged and kissed her aunt Sonora on the cheek and left. Until Sonora told Kimmy to come here to give her something to use for life. You take this black carrying case and go to your room. So, when you open it. You can apply this towards your life when you become a strong black woman in you. Another hug became unbreakable, between her and Kimmy J., once more as the rain was coming down smoothly. The moment made Sonora cry, as she stood and saw her niece close the door slowly, when the chapter came to an end for the Myers family. So, Kimmy can carry on with her life for peace.

Chapter 79

The massive rain continued to increase through the sadness of Sonora and Kimmy's lost love for one another in ten years. The rain begins to make Sonora recognize, is life supposed to be like this for humankind with scient? By looking at Sonora from the corner of his eyes. Draco felt the depression through Sonora's poor dying flesh, the way she was watching the rain flow on the windows. At midnight, around 12:10, on Old National Hwy at the red light by BP.

Sonora Myers was sound to sleep in a deep coma, as they cruelly got into Flat Shouts, where he got robbed on that same street a couple years ago. As he stopped for 25 seconds, by Camp Ave to relive the moment of his robbery. He touches Sonora from the cheek bone. And moved it slowly to see will she wake up immediately. Draco called detective Pete about the good news, that he has Sonora Myers in his custody. "Mr. Draco." We have sòme, exciting news who killed Dominic Walker. Talk-to-me detective. "You wouldn't believe this." That pestilent, Sonora committed that murder on Saturday around 12:30 a.m. that morning on Valley Hill Rd. I have the evidence in my hand, right here. The bullet came from a *9 mm Glock*. That's missing. "Hold, on detective." I have it right here. I'd just pulled it out from her back side. Good! Bring her in when you get to your side of the town. "Not just yet, detective." I'd have more evidence about the random sniper through Sonora Myers, that you were looking for. (REALLY!) Detective Pete said. "That's excellent!" So. "I tell you what." Drop Sonora off by your house. And go-grab – what's the suspect's name? The name Merial Miller is the hidden sniper we have been looking for. "That's lovely!" So, go grab Merial, with your back up team – hold-up detective. She hasn't been found yet. Merial still on the loose. Dammit!!

As detective get more outrageous with more-shit. "Don't worry detective." I have a plan in mine. Don't worry about Merial right now sir. We will catch her in time. "What about Sonora? "We can take her in now, while you have her. "No, not yet detective." "Give me six more days." Said Draco. And she's all yours. "Why!" "You-have her in your custody." "We can book her in now." And go after Merial with extra force with the unit. "Listen to me detective!" That sounds good. And – I'm ready! Said Pete. But. "I have Sonora dose-up right now." As the detective was thinking, what Draco said. Alright! I'll give you six more days of this. "I'm ready for this to be over with Draco." "If-this don't work." "I'm blaming you." "Trust me detective." "This will work." I promise you! She is still my false girlfriend, for right now. So, at this moment. She's drugged up. And she-would-be continuedly drugged. About time Sonora wakes up. "She want-know what hit her detective." That's clever, Mr. Draco. "Guess what Pete." Happy Halloween. As detective Pete was wondering and thinking? "Wait minute Draco." That isn't until six days. Oh... I got 'cha! Pete said. I'd know, was the last word from

Draco's voice. During the hang-up from detective Pete. Somebody from the background was getting robbed viciously in the hollow dark, by three dudes in black hoodies with nothing to do. One dude that was getting robbed, had him upside down like a rag-dog, just wiggling until he had a headache with money coming out.

The pounding made Draco reminisce of when he gotten rob three years ago. Draco said to himself. "That looks like the same mothafuckas that rob me, back then." Hold-up! Draco put the Camaro in reverse and charged backwards with no lights. At one of the robbers, that was going through the young dude's bag, and hit'em into the bushes, where the house on the left was located with green and white colors. And shot his pistol in midair. The young dude laid there for 15 seconds and got up. And start saying. Fuck-y'all niggas!! "Hey man?" "Are you alright?" Slowly, he said yeah to Draco.

And helped him with his groceries, that he got from Walmart and fled outta dodge. Draco finally arrives at his castle through the garage for shut down time for morning. With Sonora in his arms. And tied her up. Just lying there like a little baby at 1:00 A.M.

Chapter 80

The day has come when the rise and fall shall praise forever from the *God Son Draco Dawn.* Draco was daunting that message about those times, every day. For the past five days Sonora was drug up from the Tylenol p.m. that Draco had given her. Sonora's iPhone had a good change, when she was out cold like sleeping beauty on the couch with her on Glock to her head by Draco Dawn, just aiming towards the face. Sonora's phone was ringing three times straight, until he looked at it. With the name Merial on the screen. Got 'cha! Said Draco. Draco waited five more minutes, until she called back, before he answered. The phone rang four more times, this time.

Then he answers. Hello, as he was curious, and polite with Merial. "Who is this!" Why are you on Sonora phone. "Where is Sonora?" As Merial voice begin to wonder. Just, calm down Merial. Everything is all right. "Oh." I'm sorry! I forgot to introduce myself. My name is Draco. I'm Sonora new boyfriend. She talks a great deal about your Merial. "Let me talk to Sonora right now." Well... she couldn't come to the phone, at this moment. Apparently, she ended up being sick, so she went over to her sister's house for a nice dinner. That they prepared for us. What!!! Was the voice that said to Draco in his ears. "What, the hell is going on!" I've been trying to call Sonora for the past five days. She didn't answer, or anything. "And, you say." "Y'all was over there at her sister house." "That's not true!" Do you know, her sister died three years ago? Oh! I didn't know that Merial. Wait-minute! Must have my fax mixed up. "Sorry again." You know-what. It was her niece Kimmy J. I'd just remember." But. Like I said. She told me to tell you. If Merial calls. Tell her, I'm sick. And. I will call her back later. "Wait a minute."

What!! When Draco heard that. He had enough of the bickering from Merial's mouth and hung up. He looked at the phone and paused. And told himself. "You are going down Merial." And, put the phone on vibrate. Detective Pete called 10 minutes later. Is everything going to plan, Mr. Draco? Yes, it is, Mr. detective. Just remember. After this big bust. You will have your money. Detective Pete said. Where is Sonora? She's right here, laying on the couch sir. Good! Said Pete. "Oh yeah Pete." Just got off the phone with Merial. Really! As Pete was happy. She's at the apartment right-now sir. "That's good news Draco. "Good job!" "I'm on my way, with my team to bust the witch!" Copy-that Pete. The plan was official, for Sonora and Merial to be busted at the same time. Draco was ready for the big bust, with his tight white T-shirt, and the bullet proof vest. Along with his blue jeans and favorite High-tech boots for war. As the great day walker. It was 4:12 in the afternoon, when Sonora woke up from her beauty sleep. Sonora was tired, and exhausted, as she stood around surrounded during this wreak moment. Welcome back, sleepy head. "Oh shit, Draco." "Where you come from?" Wait-minute! "Where I'm I?" You're at my house baby. Just sit down. I'll be right back. Sonora was complex right now. Don't know, what's going on with her head feeling weird.

Draco came back with two cold Corona's for the evening occasion. Thank you, baby. As she rubbed her forehead gently. What happened last night Draco? I shouldn't be here. I know baby. Draco said. After we left your deceased sister, with your niece. We headed back to this side of town. Oh, yeah. That's right, as Sonora slips on her Corona slowly. I tried to show you where I'd gotten rob at. But. You were knocked out of sleep. You didn't have to show me that Draco. "But I did." Draco said. "Where's my phone. Have no ideal Sonora. It might be in the car. Let me go check. I'll be back. Hold up! What day is it? Sonora asks. "Didn't-you-know." It's October the 31st baby. "What." Said Sonora.

The day is Halloween Sonora. "Tricker-Treat." Sonora eyes got bigger and killed the Corona she had. Where is your bathroom? I must go home, before Merial kills me. It's behind you in the hallway, to your left. After she said thank you. Draco went outside and used the phone.

Carrie Pemberton was outside waving at Draco, as she was walking Mookie around the cud-cu-sue. When the detective picked up. It was a lot of gunfire going on in the background. Detective! Sonora just woke up. "Where are you?" "What-is-all that noise, I hear in the background sir?" "We have a major problem right now." "We're trying to make the bust towards the target with swift team." But-three were gunned down in combat. And 10 officers have been assassinated. "And the bitch is really piss-off right about now." You said, Sonora is up right now? Yes! Draco said.

Stall her. So, I can bring back-up over there, until I arrive. "That's-in-order. Roger-that Pete. While detective Pete was busy with the sniper Merial. Sonora was reading the Holy-Kara in Draco's bathroom with curious from a knowledgeable man she doesn't know about. Her mind started to come back into reality. When Draco makes his way back into the house to burst Sonora reality. Sonora came out of the bathroom feeling normal again. Before Sonora could go into the kitchen, to check his format living. Sonora seen her phone on the floor by the couch where she was sleeping at. Merial was calling. And Sonora picked up. "Sonora." "Listen to me!" "Get outta that house immediately." "It's a trap!" "There are on to us." "Your boy Draco, is a fuckin' cop." "He's been on to you, since you met him." "I told you it was something weird about his ass." "I told you!!" As Merial was in danger. "You need to leave, now Sonora!!" I can't!" "Cops are everywhere Merial." When Merial said shit into the background. Things started to get real in Sonora Myers. Sonora! Find away over here, as soon as possible. Remember, you had said, you wanted to kill some cops.

"Now, it's your chance. So. Scrap up!! "I love you." "See you soon! Sonora was sad." But devastated, in a furious way towards Draco. During the madness, while walking into the bedroom with rage with wondering eyes. Sonora seen four 9 Glocks in Draco's messy room. And two snipers that were fully loaded as well. Cops were everywhere in the front, 15 deep. Sonora threw the two snipers out the bathroom window for this bad bloody war. Sonora was ducking in position like an invisible ghost, ready to kill any moment.

She crawls from the bathroom into the living room floor behind the crouch. As Draco peaks through the cracks from his visual with that one eye watching. Everybody that lives around the small cul-de-sac was outside looking and taking pictures at the big show that's going down. Draco finally came in, like he didn't know what was going on. Or. Why were the cops outside surrounded. Sonora! "Where are you!" "Do you know." "There are cops out here." Sonora remains on the floor, with her back against the couch with a confession to make with Draco. "I must tell you something baby." What is it. Draco said. I killed my sister Kimberly. About three years ago. What!! "What are you saying, Sonora." "Stop saying that." "You don't know what you're talking about woman." You sound delusional. Finally. Sonora rose from the couch with her arms wide open, with another confession in mind. While Sonora pretend Draco was surprise about her killing her sister Kimberly, and George Wilson. That's when, another voice reached out once more towards Draco's distance in the house. And it went. Hey baby. I have another confession to make again. Why! Said Draco. "No more confession Sonora, from this day forward." I'd do understand baby. I really do: Sonora had to make it since like, she needed help from Draco at this serious moment. "Look baby." I have your flavor color. Your brown Dickie shirt. Draco didn't take the bait so well. So, he went ahead and shot her four times in the chest immediately. And Sonora fail on the wooden floor hard.

Chapter 81

Before Draco looked over towards the couch. He was looking through the building to see if detective Pete had arrived soon. No sign from Pete at all. Draco gave the sign to the other officers to inter in. And grab Sonora, as soon as, two cops inter for the kill. Crazy Sonora fire towards Draco five times in his chest. As he slid into the kitchen. The cops fired back at Sonora as she ducks and rolls so smoothly. And hit one in the ankle and leg. And shot him in the face. "After saying, fuck-yeah to herself."

Draco slid towards the window in the kitchen. To alert the other officers to come in with his hand single. As five more cops were coming in. The one cop, that was in the house. Sonora immediately tripped him by the leg and kicked him in the face real hard and shot him dead. That's when Sonora ran to the window and laid low for ten seconds. Until one peeked in and shot him in the jawbone twice with impact. More was rushing in for Sonora, as she burst back with two 9 Glocks in her hand. Killing, left and right in blood. Ms. Pemberton had to rush back into the house with all the shooting going on. Until Nookie gotten loose from Pemberton hands, in between the cops' cars with the run of her life, as two bullets intervene into the side that took her down instantly in vain. The emotional was hard on Draco's mind to release gun power on Sonora's soul, as he continued shooting at her. Bolt guns became impeccable in his hand with rage. As Sonora ran straight towards the window with a dive, using her body as a rock coming out the zone on the ground. "Fuck this shit with gun power." Sonora said. After she landed on the ground for recovery and picked up the two snipers. She went around the side and slang the other sniper weapon around her back for back up.

Her mind was glad she remembered to grab the car keys from the table for her escape to leave. Draco yelled out. "Where you at Sonora!" "I need to take you in baby." Her mind said. Fuck you!! "I'm not going anywhere, you bastard!!" "You have to kill me first, before I go back to jail, Draco." Enough was said, as the sniper sprayed with love through the windows, when the bullets went hard at Draco's chest leg, and shoulders with digital visual. Draco was hit hard by the impact of Sonora's sniper. By, hitting four more officers on the side of the house. Sonora was almost near the Camaro of freedom and victory, as the swap team was coming. Sonora had to think fast to avoid the team of destruction. One of the swap team members threw a gas grenade at Sonora to blind her vision. But. End up putting on her shades and dude rag, that was black. And drove into the ground for recovery. As she punishes more cops on duty with the sniper. As the swap team threw more gas grenades at hand. Sonora was already inside the Camaro going through the grass that was bumpy into the tree and sidewalk, to cause fatal impact around the accessor from the wheel. The coast was clear when she hit the Main Street on the right. Going pass QT, and Valley Hill Rd. to HWY 85 into Riverdale.

While Sonora was rolling through the plaza by Food Deport coming through hard. A dude named CL with no legs, just got hit by Sonora Camaro. That made his electrical wheelchair fly through the Well Fargo ATM machine, with his free goodie that made him sick. After the hit. Sonora said. "That's what you get bitch, for missing around with my girl, from the first-place you bastard." And threw his 2-Pac, and Biggie CD out the window. The police and the Swipe Team were right behind her on HWY 85 rolling. Trying to shoot her tries from the Camaro when she turns by the Chevron with a left turn to keep straight at the red light, without stopping. And turn right again, with a clear shot to Garden Wood apartment to Merial. As the bullets were coming into the back window, while she was ducking and driving, playing Shaft, the anticlimactic track, flowing on the road.

One of the tries was blown immediately, from a shot made by one of the Swipe Team units coming fast. The impact made Sonora cash into the parking lot of ALDI store inside. Blood was seeping out quickly, from inside her body, while getting out the up-side-down Camaro with cuts and scars on its flesh. The Swipe Team machine came through, like the Hurricane of Katrina into the parking lot. When they came hard with power and authority. Sonora was hurt, just a little bit. As people were coming out hurt, and bleeding with broken bones in the mix. Some people die instantly through the crash from the Camaro of destruction. Sonora was in the dark aisle where the wine and beer was spilled massively everywhere in vain. As she pulls a piece of glass outta her stomach that was big through the right kidney while sitting on the floor. She begins drinking a big bottle of wine, calling Merial for support. The sound of breathing hard, was getting to Sonora of missing you. Merial!! Hello! Hello! "Can you hear me!" Merial!!! "I, hear you Sonora." You were breaking up. "What's wrong?" Sonora said. I am alright. I just got shot in the shoulder, that's all. But I'm good. "Where are you Sonora?" Inside the ALDI store Merial. Trying to build up some momentum, with a bottle of wine, I'm drinking. That's good Sonora. I should have listened to you Merial. I'm sorry. Don't worry about it, Sonora. I'm glad you made it. Merial said. I had a little bit of trouble getting here from Draco's house. "Did you kill that mothafucker Sonora?" Not quite. Sonora said. But I, clobber his lying ass, for being a traitor. That's good. As Merial was tried. What's all that commotion in the background? Well... Throughout the shooting, through the apartment complex. People came out everywhere in fear. It gotten so bad, that. The police officers were trying to get the people back inside their apartment. But. Some are cheering for the causes that we had committed, as a justice right-type hero's, Sonora. "Wow..." Sonora said. "That's some shit Merial." When Sonora felt that historic moment from the people in the street.

That gave her, and Merial hope to keep fighting until death. "It's time Merial." To show the people who we really are as the new blood hounds forever. So. "We need to get our asses up." And kill these mothafuckers, much as we can Merial. "Are you down, or what." And Merial said, at the end of the phone. Fuck yeah!! "Let's kill these bitches!" Especially, that bastard-detective Pete. "I'm down with that."

Sonora said. "Let's do this shit." As they loudly said-it together. Riverdale police had the whole Garden Walk block. From one end to the other. All people, that lived in all the apartments in Garden Walk was cheering like crazy. Sonora had the strength to get her ass up immediately, when she finishes her big bottle of wine from ALDI with energy. The Swipe Team told the people to stand back, as far as they can. So, they can't get hit during the mist around the parking lot. As the gas bombs were coming like crazy inside the destroy building of ALDI.

The bombs were coming tremendously like grenades. When Sonora pulled up her black dude rag over her mouth, with the white skull on it. Sonora loaded-up. Ready for combat with the bullet proof vest on. Sonora went out the emergency door, that was lucky crack in her flavor to exit through. The Swipe Team was coming in heavenly strong inside. While Sonora ran into the woods, preparing her sniper in position for many men to come. Two Swipe guys, from both sides of the building were coming in fast. As the aim was clear for gun point to kill immediately. The two Swipe guys got annihilated fast by Sonora Myers. While more were coming with full impact. They were killed instantly as well. Sonora ran fast. And, jumped over the iron fence that was pointy up top. The whole scene from Sonora was truly amazing in her eyes. How people from everywhere were protesting with single. And telling the police to go to hell and eat a dick. Sonora was proud and happy, as she called Merial, I'm here at the apartment. During the conversation for another strategy in mind.

Merial told Sonora her black Changer was in the parking lot range to get inside for her and Merial to ride out. The keys are already inside the ignition for you to take off Sonora. When Sonora took off the brown Dickie shirt, to wrap around her waist, as a rag to whip off the blood for each cop she kills. Cops were coming in heavy in front of the bottom level to get Merial, while she was arriving down the steps. Three gotten shot quicky, as she moves closely on flat ground. Four more cops were hit with Merial's smooth sniper towards their head. Detective Pete eases his way in between cars and stays low so he wouldn't get hit. Sonora was already inside the black Changer. Telling Merial to get in. Until Pete saw Merial talking to someone and took a shot clean and hit Merial in the shoulder and went down quicky.

Chapter 82

The evening started to get eerie and hunting on Halloween evening, around 6:30 p.m. with screams in the background. Everybody throughout the whole street on Garden Walk had on different scary masks was throwing bricks and bottles at the police officers from Riverdale. The Swipe Team were like the Roman soldiers back in A.D. years ago in this digital war. The troops were-on both sides of the street to avoid more conflict towards the police officers. Detective Pete told Merial to get-up before I kill you as he was on top of one of the vehicles. Pete was determined with his white dress shirt, with the sleeve's half roll up. And black dress pants, along with the bullet proof vest. After Merial was gun down on the shoulder. Sonora hit the gas hard and sideswiped another car on the side. And, made detective Pete hit the concrete, by landing on his left ear hard, and shoulders first. The impact made his head significantly ring inside his brain and body to make him lay for 50 seconds. After the damage was fatal on detective Pete. Sonora hollered outside the grate. As the police was still shooting, as Merial was down, pretending to be dead. Five more cops were hit hard like Platoon when she got up and headed towards the car. During the shooting at Merial, when she stumps into the accelerator of the Changer and hit two cops in reverse and proceed with precaution through the grate. Sonora was already out of the car. When the impact from multiple bullets burst through all the wheels to make her cash into the sidewalk in front of ten Swipe Team that was shooting. Sonora got out the Changer and started shooting for her life. Merial came down, going 90 miles per hour. And jumped out of the car. As it kept going and hit 12 members of the Swipe Team for Sonora. Darkness was coming, when the rain became a heavy factor through the whole atmosphere with wind and rain.

Merial became unstoppable, after killing 15 Swipe Team of men in the street. Sonora herself kill about 18 Swipe men. Until one shot viciously hit the kneecap about three times, to make her drop to one knee.

When detective Pete ram the police vehicle in the back of Merial's back. Going 85 miles per hour. The body few by, hitting the concrete killing her with a broken neck. Sonora was devastated by the impact she had just seen. And try to run for her. Until the madness made her go insane with bolt 9mm in her hand shooting. She was shot 10 times by the Swipe Team that was angry, because she was wanted. When Sonora was on her back, slowly getting up in pain and anger. Detective walks towards Sonora with baby steps, as his gun rises. And, said. "It's over Sonora!" Get up! She stood up slowly, and, turned around on one knee. And, said. It's never over. And pulled her 9mm Glock right in Pete's face, as the massive bullet shot off her thumb to stay down on bolt knees from one of the Swipe Team. Sonora face landed on detective Pete's stomach for support. And, said. I hate you with blood coming outta her mouth. "Just stop

Sonora." "Please." Or. I will gun you down. As Sonora was pulling herself up on detective Pete chest. She removes her do rag and looks into Pete's eyes for 10 seconds. As the sharp blade from her knife jabs detective Pete in the middle of his Adam's apple and, said. (*Go to hell.*) With a shot in Sonora's head, from detective Pete's Glock. When Sonora fail backwards real hard on the street. The rain was finally over from the sky. The people that were yelling and protesting with black power towards Sonora and Merial. Became silence in harmony, by taking their masks off, in a moment of sorrow. After pulling the knife out-from-outta Pete's throat with a laugh of victory. The detective dropped on bolt knees and fell face first. And that's when everything was officially over on Halloween night. The time was 8:30 p.m. with lighters up on bolt sides of the street in the Garden Walk area.

The people rejoice with sadness and pain, as the helicopters swoop around into the air with more cops on the way. The cloud of people had candles in a small glass. Just putting it around the remains of Sonora Myers, and Merial Miller for rest in peace towards the blood Hound sister forever. On November the 27th, during Thanksgiving Day at 6 P.M. The barrel was sealed for Sonora and Merial Miller at the Ellenwood cemetery with hundreds of people, or more from Garden Walk in Riverdale. Once everybody pays their respect for Sonora and Merial, one by one. The rain was coming with umbrellas up and candles, as fists were up like the Planet of the Apes with their black do rags over their face. The funeral was finally over around 7:10 p.m., with dark blue skies in the atmosphere. The 20-year-old,

Kimmy J. wanted some alone time with her family's tombstone, while her daddy watches in the background with his umbrella over his head. Kimmy gave her grandmother a rose on her tombstone. And gave her mother, Kimberly Myers, an urn with ashes inside from her Diploma in front of the tombstone. But, last but least. Kimmy J. hugged and kissed Merial Miller tombstone with a shadow punch dap in front of it. And walked away with Sonora's black boots on, and black Swipe pants too. With the black trench coat, as well as the bullet proof vest for black power. And the new blood hound queen for revolution. As far as her Aunt Stacy Myers goes. The cremation had already been finalized three years ago, in a beautiful gold urn inside her room, sitting on her cabinet shining. After Kimmy J. read Sonora letter that was in the travel case, that Sonora gave her. She requested to be cremated as well like her blood sister Stacy Myers into an urn. In the letter. Sonora left her niece a check for 15 million dollars for her for the future, without the system's help. The black limo was waiting for Kimmy J., as she got in softly with Sonora's black urn with Merial's ashes in it too. As far as Kimmy J. and her father's bond. She moved out of her father's house. And stayed in the county, in a nice cabinet like Merial Miller did in the woods.

Sonora told Kimmy J. in the letter. To give Rico DL 5 million dollars to him, for miss treated him over the years, as his girl and wife, for not being a good woman. And. Tell Rico, I'm sorry for all the wrongdoing that I have done to him. And make sure you tell him... I love him so much. From Stoney. AKA Sonora Myers, and forever. After Rico DL reserved the message from Kimmy J. Rico DL sold the house and moved back to California where he was born from. He remained married to Sonora's disease, in spirituality of remembering the times they shared. Even if it was good or bad. The love remains the same in his heart, with bolt rings inside a silver and black jewel box on top of his dresser. About three years ago, in 2017 in the new era. Kimmy J. father was assassinated by a random sniper at his home. While grieving over his disease wife, Kimberly Myers in the living room sad. And, two years later. Draco Dawn was murdered, with his house burned down through an invasion that took place at midnight around 12:30 A.M. At the age of 48 when he died. Kimmy J. just finish target practice in her big field, own by her on will of freedom as a black woman in 2019 the new world. As she stands on her wooden deck as a new general of what's to come. The song vibe was playing from the background in the living room, that was requested by Sonora in the letter, when you get a moment of peace, prosperity, and love. Your life will be happy, forever until the last days when you perish between heaven or hell as dust.

Coming Soon
The Blue Mind Goddess

After sweet hugs and kisses, were all said and done with Mother Hill waving to her daughter. While Maria climbs out the window for recovery. As her eyes glazed, by watching her mother burn to death. Not-even thinking about her weak father from her mother's theory of men. Maria Hill stands there, in all black, with her black hoodie over her long black hair in a ponytail with a small black bow. As both hands were inside the pocket hoodie jacket, that was long to the thighs with wondering eyes, watching the house burn down to a simple crisp. Due to the thunder around the skies. While the rain comes down on Maria Hill. The new Goddess for the future. Ten years later. In 1988, when the Goddess was born. At the age of 28, brainwashing men in the year 2000, with a new decade has arrived. And everything was looking so clear, with a new man in her life. And pregnant with a baby boy that Maria despises, wishing it was a girl instead. And mad with her husband, because of it. The plot thickens when Maria decides to keep the baby for her husband Tom Cooper. The boy's name became Tommy Cooper through the mother and father. Which Maria hated. After giving birth to Tommy Cooper.

That's when Maria changed the last name on the birth certificate to Hill, without Tom consent at all. The last name was seal forever, without his knowledge as a man in 2003 as a perfect family together. Little Tommy just turned 3 years of age, at his birthday party, without his father. Tom Cooper, that was missing outta thin air for one full year. As a memory in Tommy, and Mother Love's eyes during a hateful loving quest for a family with pain and deception through black magic power, that was passed down to Maria.

Don't miss out!

Visit the website below and you can sign up to receive emails whenever Ted Williams publishes a new book. There's no charge and no obligation.

https://books2read.com/r/B-A-VTWGC-EEGZE

BOOKS 2 READ

Connecting independent readers to independent writers.

Also by Ted Williams

The Purple Mirage

9 798227 575180